CLAIM DENIED

G R JERRY

Printed in the United States of America

ISBN: Softcover   978-1-64376-948-6
         eBook   978-1-64376-947-9
Republished by: PageTurner Press and Media LLC
Publication Date: 03/08/2022

To order copies of this book, contact:
PageTurner Press and Media
Phone: 1-888-447-9651
info@pageturner.us
www.pageturner.us

TABLE OF CONTENTS

DEDICATION

To you, the men and women,

the backbone of the insurance industry so often wrongly ostracized as some evil entity.

Silently, your veins pump blood red; tears pour from the heart.

I know . . .

I'm one of you.

PROLOGUE

Another typical day at BestEver Insurance was not as typical in the way it began; but in the end, we were all here, soldiers stuck in a hole on the front line, shoulder to shoulder protecting the fort. And there, she struts once again. Sondra, the slave driver, just entered my field of vision facing the aisle between the two rows of side-by-side cubicles running the course along the fortifications of the third floor Claim Department. Cellblock is a more descriptive moniker for the dens in which these people burn their lives away. I wondered which hand was carrying Sondra's invisible whip today.

In my current focus of vision from my appointed lookout here in my trusty swivel chair, Sondra walked to my right in swift, short steps stiffly, as though all her backbones have been welded together.

"Good morning," she said, not bothering to look my way. Focused on the drills of the day, she strode sharply past in high heels with thin but shapely legs, a lean waist bearing little more than a spine and plastic wrap flesh, and modest pointers on her chest, probably enhanced by a steel bra. And resting atop this robotic frame was forty miles of bad road and a mop shielding the back of her Ichabod Crane–looking neck, but the fish stuck in *her* throat was a bit smaller.

She dressed that way with the purpose of keeping the eyeballs of any audience down below. Some would not touch her with a ten-foot pole. I would, but I wouldn't touch her with anything else. Maybe that was why she walked the way she did, that funny little strut step. I could see it now, the ten-foot pole. After passing through her craning neck, lean and mean torso, it was just a half inch away from busting through those tightly packed buns on the outer surface of her ass. Imagine that, a woman with a stick up her ass. *Hey, Sondra,* I silently spoke to her, *catch this half-deflated basketball, and see if you can balance it on the upper end of that pole.*

So that was why she walked with that funny, familiar strut. As I climbed off my chair for a backside view of the reeling ball, she twisted her head to engage her glare at the underlings chained to their computers, notepads, and telephones. She didn't look so regimental right now, but the basketball thing was a neat touch, bouncing away, keeping time with her sway, stride for stride. All I could hear when she first walked by and mumbled hello was "Woo, woo, woo." It must have been that pole down her throat masking the pitch of her vocal cords; the tone was too low for a canary woman with a stick up her ass.

My gaze drifted from the cattail swinger. Talk about hot—Trudy, Trudy, Trudy. Just as Cary Grant once spoke in a movie or something like that. She was so hot stoves lit up when her reflection passed over their shiny surfaces and oven windows. I was a fan of tanned and bronze skin, but I was in no way prejudiced against her fair, white complexion. It was so smooth and creamy that every time she parked in front of my eyes, I reached for my jar of Bosco Chocolate Syrup to go along with the milky allure of her unblemished flesh. I kept telling myself, *I want my Bosco.*

She was packed solid and didn't need to dress hot to look hot. Her glittering blue eyes garner as much attention as her moist lips and that heavenly goddess body below them. Her silky black hair ran smoothly across the nape of her neck and back. What was she doing in this madhouse? The twenty-seven-year-old beauty belonged on a magazine cover, or better yet, a 3-D Technicolor silver screen. My eyes would cry in pain whenever I forced them to move away from the cleavage she so innocently displayed every now and then. On special occasions, she would even grace me with a hug, of which I modestly restrained myself in resisting the full-body press I so desperately required at the moment. And the best part about my whole imaginary affair with her was that her mouth was blessed with a tongue just as bright, silvery, and disgusting as mine. She was my path away from reality.

In her duty block in bondage at the desk opposite Trudy sat Helen—not the beautiful version such as the actual lady from Troy. She was rather plain looking, would tip the scales a bit beyond Marvin Gardens, but she was the queen of a realm nevertheless. She toiled every day under Sondra's whip, the controller, until her wavy brown hair would curl with sweat. But, at night, she would retire to her three children, the diamonds and jewels of her poor life, and the wonderful man who gave her this wonderful life. That wonderful, loving person must be crazy, but she found the grass was actually greener on this side of the fence, and she achieved it all without Trudy's eyeball-gripping legs.

And then there was Tim; at least there was Tim. He was either a part-time slob, or he dressed daily for Halloween as a bum. And when you talked to him, you would think he was living Christmas Day with Tiny Tim every day of his life. He not only tipped the scales but also bent them backward. And his hairdresser must have been hard at work daily because his light-brown wings never seemed to land in the same spot twice. He also had blue dreamy eyes. And he did dream. You could see that when you looked at him face-to-face, straightaway.

He did not fantasize, as did some of us in the shop—yours truly with a bit more regularity. He dreamed. He genuinely loved being around kids, not for any perverted reason. He was still a kid at heart, and he wanted to teach. So he spent his nights laboring over books just as hard as he did during the day, and one fine day, not-so-tiny Tim walked his BestEver ass right on out of this boot camp. More than one eye cried in joy for the man, as from behind him, they watched that big beautiful old, loving behind of his waving goodbye to them. He found his balls, grabbed them, got his college degree, got up, got out, and followed his dream.

There was not so much luck for the rest of us stuck in this particular hole from hell. We'd picked our own poison, so we just plodded along from day to day following our BestEver Employee Manual, and we loved it accordingly. There were no perverts in BestEver-land. We were all good little boys and girls. We were not allowed to be perverted, but we sure as hell could fantasize. And that was where I came in because I could fantasize with the best of them. I was one BestEver fantasizing fool. Maybe that was what had kept my sanity intact here in my daily encounters with the BestEver public clientele. They all had trouble, and they all had problems. They all knew they could look to BestEver Insurance to magically make these problems vanish into the thick greasy, fat air.

I had trained myself to wave the magic wand and do my BestEver to make these dreams come true. I placed myself in their positions and dreamed their dreams, and I made them come true, at least as true as truth could be realized. So I fantasized, and sometimes it worked. The BestEver clients would walk away with a smile on their face. And then sometimes the clients would walk away with a smirk or even a scowl-laced tongue.

We at BestEver were not demons as the Lifeline News Network (LNN) would have the public believe. The adjusters were actually human beings. And they really did have blood running through their veins. Honestly, it was not cold either. Sometimes we might feel like we were in the Battle of the Bulge as robots responding to our generals and commanders. But we could all just pick up our behinds out of our seats any time, any day, and just give up and walk out. Beyond all the long hours, tedious documenting of every move we made; every conversation we had; and every analysis of case facts to comply with every rule, regulation, law, or management whim—mounds of documentation that could readily fill a thousand-gallon septic tank any sane person would haul away to a dump—we actually would get satisfaction from what we were doing. We would get a feeling of accomplishment that in some small ways, we actually helped people out of a jam, an ugly set of circumstances. At the end of the dragged-out process, we tried putting them back in a place a little bit better than where they were after that first frantic call they made to open the dam and let the water gush out in a flood of high-strung emotion. Sometimes more, sometimes less.

We didn't receive medals of honor, accolades from the audience, trophies, or lifetime achievement awards; but maybe, once in a while, a thank you, a pat on the back, or an attaboy should come our way. What we regularly achieved were endless streams of new claims, more assignments. Every new loss was a priority; each one in the minds of the client was our only priority. That insurance companies were out to screw everyone in their paths was the LNN fantasy—select soured stories put together by a conglomeration of mopes who had no clue about what was going on in the real world because they had no real world.

Ratings brought in the almighty buck through the power of advertising, sometimes the same damn hard-on drug ten consecutive times in a one-hour broadcast.

Personally, I chose to limit my screwing to a certain family member who wore a ring on her left hand, although lately, there hadn't been much of that either, aside from the receiving end. That went for the screwing and the ring-wearing. That was another story in my life. The rest of my screwing got done in my fantasy world. And maybe my gift of fantasy was what brought this thing to life. Sometimes I tend to overdo things.

You see, I saw it for the first time this morning. For the first time because I knew it would come back. Once born, something as horrible as this did not just fall into oblivion and disappear forevermore. I was dead certain this thing, this monster-looking thing, came out at will to pluck chosen people back into its own comfy four-flat suite smack dab in the middle of oblivion. With my own eyes, I saw the hideous thing following me, step by step, at least its eyes. And from the mirror, it spoke to me. It spoke in Frances F Murphy's voice.

You see, Frances F was one of our BestEver claimants, and we were compelled—I mean, we loved—to keep our BestEver client in our highest regard and subvert ourselves to her every whim through high wind, high water, and every ass-kissing challenge that currently, she could dream up at the time she was ridiculing us to death. Believe me, Frances had no middle name. The middle *F* was supplanted by yours truly—your one and only BestEver fantasizing, ass-kissing Benjamin F BestEver Johnson, or Benny for the short and long of it.

And again, I enjoy superimposing that good ol' *F* word. And my middle name is not Frankie, Freddie, or Fritz, for that matter either, but I enjoy pre- or post-naming a lot of things with the *F* word, maybe for emphasis or just maybe because I love the ol' *F* word. It is so melodic. *F you. F you too, Sherlock.* A little imagination, but I am in compliance with the BestEver Employee Manual, Section C, Communication—"Do not use vile, offensive, degrading, or improper language when conversing in person or when communicating in writing with the F'ing client." I couldn't resist. I just love the sound of the spoken variations of the *F* word. A verb—F you. A noun—You F! A gerund—I like F'ing with her mind. To me, I get just as much enjoyment hearing the sounds of the *F* word as I do picturing a couple of beautiful ponytailed young women wearing ball caps and tight bikinis holding hands to balance each other while rollerblading their way through a crowded boardwalk at a sunny beach. I guess I have a funny way of explaining things.

The thing that spoke to me from the mirror was horrible, but it did not reveal too much on its first introduction to my world. It didn't even bother to say hello. It wore a black cloak with a hood folded over, curling in and out in the front, concealing its face and head, which hid together back there in the dark shadows. It seemed to be swaying a bit side to side, almost in a pendulum motion, as if it was hovering and preying over something, somewhere down below the bottom edge of the mirror and the sink countertop where the balance of its ogre entity was hidden from view. The cloak draped down over its shoulders to the edge of the bathroom sink in the 5:30 a.m. dimly lit john.

What lingered below the figure, I cared not to guess. Two beams of deep red light broke out of the cloak and pushed themselves out of the mirror, almost poking me at the back or burning a hole in my butt. I thought I heard something ricochet off the wall to my left side, but it could have been the chatter of my teeth rebounding off one another. And then it happened. After passing beyond the mirror to make a sharp right turn to the urinals and stalls, I could swear on a stack of *Mad* magazines that Frances F Murphy spoke my name. But I was almost sure she omitted the *F* word, as best as I could recollect. You might imagine I was a bit distracted at that particular moment.

I was fortunate enough to reach the crapper and get my belt down below my knees before everything inside of me departed in one expansive blast. Ten minutes later, when the rattle of my bones subsided, I crawled out of the john on all fours, making certain my eyes were planted on the handle of the swinging door set in a frame on the wall opposite the mirror. At that juncture, I was in no mood for a second helping. No appetite whatsoever. Once I planted my belly on the hallway carpeting, I crawled into the ladies' john and took another dump before returning to my desk.

My stomach was still upside down, my nerves were shaking, and I couldn't rid myself of the awful glare from those dead burning eyes. I wished to the Almighty that I had been fantasizing. Frances F Murphy's vocal cords continued to rattle around inside that average-size, hardheaded skull of mine.

Now . . . what would come next?

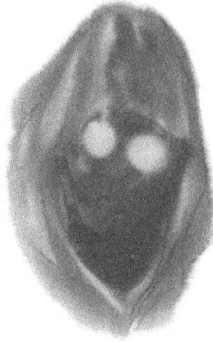

CHAPTER ONE

TRUDY

I caught a glimpse of Benny at the other end of the center aisle when I slipped through the side door situated halfway down our bank of cubicles about 6:30 a.m. or so. I wouldn't say he was as white as a ghost because for one thing, he was kind of dark skinned, like he was wearing a permanent tan. He said it was the American-Indian blood in him. Besides, I'd never really seen him scared of anything. He didn't seem like the kind of guy who would puke or anything like that if he saw a dead skunk or a splattered snake or something on the side of the road, but I was not sure how he would react if it was a dead person. He told me some tales about his days with the Coast Guard, when he was a Coastie so he said, so I doubted that a real dead body would scare him much either. But the look on his face told me he was . . . well . . . shaken. That would describe it.

So I decided to check on him and swayed my way up the aisle toward his cube. He was a specialist in boiler and machinery (B&M) claim coverage, so I guessed the big bucks I figured he got paid also rated the extra space. I struggled with over 120 files in a six-by-six coffin sandwiched between two other girls and facing another three adjusters sitting in their own skimpy foxholes, all of us with our matching five-foot-eight fabric cubicle dividers cluttered with photos of our favorite people and pastimes. Mine was filled with pics of my adorable niece and a variety of Tribe, Cavs, and Browns paraphernalia. In my book, they were all winners even if they didn't, but Alicia was numero uno.

Benny's trench sported a huge L-shaped desk with a couple of chairs set in the space between the desk and a waist-to-ceiling window view. Even though it overlooked a parking lot, he still had the water fountain in the middle of the turnaround and trees to remind him there was actually a world outside the chaos inside that began daily precisely at the strike of eight o'clock. I imagined, like usual, that Benny had already put in at least two hours or so trying to catch up on the paperwork from the sorties he encountered yesterday.

I plucked my daily chocolate ration from his chili pepper–decorated bowl at my left, as I leaned in toward him. Benny sat staring at me, leaning back in his chair with the computer quietly purring on his right. I waited a second and then broke the silence. "Earth to Benny," I began.

He replied as suddenly as he sat up, "Oh, hi, Trudy. I didn't see you."

"Wow," I answered in response, "I must have worn too many clothes today. Sorry I covered my legs with these pants."

I had my body parts fairly well shielded today—long black slacks with a matching black print sweater that didn't expose too much boob action. The long souvenir turquoise earrings he brought me back from Arizona jingled as Benny's brown eyes came back to life.

"Well, you can take some off and stuff them in that suitcase I have waiting to stow you away on vacation," he suggested. It sounded like the Benny I knew was coming back, but I wasn't too sure, so I decided to probe.

"You looked a little bit out of it when I walked in this morning," I started. "I was worried."

"It was something weird," Benny said. "I must not have had enough brews last night. I thought I saw something in the john this morning, but you know how dark this place is before six o'clock. I usually have to feel my way over to the stalls. I thought I saw something creepy, but it was probably nothing."

I got the feeling it was a little more than nothing. I pressed him on the subject, staring him down and stepping in a bit closer, just like I did when we were flirting with each other and he started getting nervous. He was a married guy—and as faithful as they came. I knew he would never really act on one of his flirtations, but he sure loved to play. He was quite a bit older than me, maybe not that much older. He was about forty-two I think, but he still had all his hair. He worked out a lot and was probably in better shape than most guys half his age. He not only looked good, but he was also good looking. And I'd bet he enjoyed his time in the sack too. He told me stories about the old days, as he put it, when he was single and how no rules applied. He said it like he was some kind of a machine.

I wouldn't mind going back in time someday to get a firsthand observation. I heard the stories about the old days, but lately, Benny had been mostly mum about his life at home. He once told me I was probably like, what, a four-year-old the first time he ever balled a chick, as he put it, which I guess means losing his virginity. He wondered if I looked anything like I did now when I was four. I just told him, "Yeah, but my tits were a little smaller back then." Also, I told him he was a cradle robber to the max! We'd kept the tease going ever since, but we needed to keep our voices low just in case Sondra was around. I wouldn't want to be accused of causing Benny any verbal sexual abuse. But I was sure he would love every minute of it and would beg for more.

Anyway, as I leaned in, Benny's eyes turned away toward his knees. I knew right away something was up, and it wasn't something down there between his legs. I figured something might be up at home, but there was something else. He still looked . . . shaken.

Then Benny's phone rang. "F," as he would put it. Maybe I could pry it out of him later. It was getting close to eight o'clock. The skirmish line was beginning to form, and the troops were about ready to lock and load.

"Hello," answered Benny. It was followed by an utterance of an *F* curse under his breath. "Uh, good morning. This is Benny Johnson, BestEver Insurance B&M Claims. How can I help you this morning?" He frequently alternated the "may and the can" approach.

"Well, if it isn't the conniving, well-wishing, backstabbing, lying little puke, Benny himself!" answered none other than Frances F Murphy.

"Mrs. Murphy," he replied. That familiar voice again stunned him out of the hypnotic trance he had holding him in a headlock since his early morning episode. This time, it was ringing in his eardrum rather than his head.

"It's miss to you, you damn stalker. You know I divorced that spineless little twerp of a husband. I told you that the last time I had a claim with you, bozos. Best ever, my ass," she continued on her rant.

"I apologize, Ms. Murphy," interjected Benny. "I do not understand why you are so upset so early this morning. Please explain, ma'am. What can I do?"

"Okay, quit beating around the bush and tell me where you hid the microphone," Frances demanded.

Benny imagined the heavyset curly red-haired sixtyish woman was currently displaying a matching shade of scarlet on her face. She was normally rude and bullish, mostly unwilling to cooperate when information was needed to complete a coverage investigation, but right at this moment, she was blowing off an inordinate amount of steam. She usually had cooled off after the first barrage of firestorms, and Benny thought they were well beyond that point in her loss adjustment by now. He simply rationalized that the woman had a way about her . . . domineering, brazen, and boorish.

"Microphone?" he asked. "I don't understand."

"Don't play stupid, stupid," she fired back. "The transmitter you people planted in the women's powder room in my restaurant. You know, wise guy, the recording you made with our demented little greeting. LNN had a nice special some time ago, and I heard about the tactics you underhanded people pull, but this one really bakes the cake. You get somebody over here right now and get that damn thing out of my establishment, or I'll have you tossed in jail so fast your spinning head won't be able to keep up with that skinny little ass of yours!"

"Ms. Murphy," he began. "Please try to be calm. I realize that you are very upset right now, but I can assure you I know nothing about any kind of microphone."

"Listen to the innocent little boy. Don't try being so coy, you little liar," she ran on.

Becoming a bit impatient, Benny was letting her get it out of her system, but now the personal attack was wearing him thin. "Ms. Murphy," he replied, raising his voice, "I think it's about time you tell me just precisely what the problem is that you are having. What microphone?"

"And how did you get that damn video in the mirror?" she asked. "Are you jerks thinking my claim will go away because you can intimidate me by trying to scare me off? That's another tactic I learned from LNN. Well, I don't scare so easy, my puny little puke-faced friend, you!"

Well, it's nice to know we're friends again, thought Benny. "You say you heard a voice and then saw a video in the ladies' room?"

"Like you were born five minutes ago. Puh-leeze do not insult me with your stupidity, jerko. It was your voice. I heard it as plain as day, 'Mrs. Frances F Murphy.' Where did the *F* come from, you conniving little squirt?"

"Holy sh—" Benny stopped short, with his chin dropping with the force of a trapdoor.

"Well?" she asked, breaking the silence.

"Mrs—uh, I mean, Ms. Murphy. Can you describe what the thing in the mirror looked like? Was its face covered over with some kind of a cloak?"

"You should know, wise guy. It was your video," she added sarcastically. "Nice outfit."

"Ms. Murphy, I think you need to settle down because I have some news for you. That was no video. It was real. I saw the same thing this morning. And it wasn't my voice I heard. It was yours. If something is stalking you, it sure as hell is not me." Benny was shaken for the second time this morning. He pondered momentarily on the use of the word *hell*. Did it violate company rules against the use of profanity? "You need to be careful."

"Listen to this line of bull. 'Be careful' like you give one toot on the hooter about my ass," she began again. "I'll show you careful. I'll find that damn microphone, speaker, and the camera or whatever else you jokers planted, and I'll get my butt down to your office and plant the garbage right up your ass!"

"Ms. Murphy, please calm down. And whatever you do, don't go back into that bathroom."

"We here at the restaurant call it a powder room, you jerk-off," she replied. "I'm going to get back in there and get the evidence. You people are always looking for evidence, right? To prove the claim, right? Or more likely deny the damn thing. Claim denied, right? That's what you BestEver people are really good at, lying and denying! Well, I'll get me some good hard evidence, and I'll see you pay, buster. You and all those suit-and-tie jokers up there in that little insurance ivory tower back east. You'll all pay. I'll get me enough evidence to plant it up all your damned asses."

"Ms. Murphy, are you alone?"

"Listen to you still trying to scare me. I don't have anybody coming in for at least another hour. Plenty of time to tear apart the bathroom, as you prefer. Nice try, kiddo."

"Ms. Murphy, don't—" he warned before being cut off by her hand slamming down the receiver with the End button on her cell phone.

F

Benny stared at the phone as he pulled away the headset. All kinds of thoughts were twirling around in his mind. Frances F Murphy was not on his top ten client list, and usually, when she did submit a claim, it was elevated to his desk. In the Major Loss Unit, he was normally assigned losses in which damages exceeded $100,000. Other assignments included those involving complex technical or coverage issues or when the urgency to reach an amicable settlement was elevated due to sensitive issues arising with the client, and it became necessary to get Benny on the front line. This generally occurred when the assigned adjuster could hear the clients banging their fists on a table through his telephone receiver.

Once Benny was assigned, sometimes after two or more other adjusters failed to reach an agreement, it was necessary for him to turn down the volume on his headset when he made the third first call to the specified, insured contact. He would be greeted with, "Jeez-us, I gotta go through this again? How many times do I have to repeat myself? Where the hell is my damn check, Denny?"

"Well, actually, ma'am, the name is Benny." Those were the first exchanges of words spoken on his first claim with the one and only Frances F Murphy. From there, the conversation went downhill.

"Benny, Lenny, Denny, Kenny, Jenny—who gives a fat fart? Where's my check already?"

On that first encounter, Benny was able to calm her down after a long engaging conversation, assuring her that she had only just made the income claim a day earlier. He had just received the claim file documentation and had reviewed the policy itself, along with all the electronic notes, the files contained on the communication exchanges between her and the previous adjusters, and documents submitted by her to BestEver to date, which was exactly none. Standard procedure. Be ready for the onslaught and be prepared to explain what information was missing from the file to wrap it up and provide her with reimbursement for the damages she was demanding and so richly deserved—such as the missing copies of invoices for the $18,500 she was claiming for an air-conditioning repair and missing copies of financial documents to verify her claim of $150,000 for her loss of the restaurant business income.

"I told those bozos I collect thirty thousand dollars a day, and it took five days to get the air-conditioning fixed. So do the math, Einstein" was her casual response.

Benny knew he was no Einstein, but he also knew he was no dummy either. And long ago, Benny had come to realize an elementary fact of nature. For every Einstein in this world, there is an equal and opposite asshole. Plain and simple, but he would put neither himself nor Ms. Murphy in either class. He figured the two of them floated back and forth somewhere far apart from both but well between, depending on the best or worst days of their lives. The Einsteins and the assholes of the world could deal with their own problems. He and Frances would deal with this one.

After learning the restaurant had never closed during the mechanical repairs and the outdoor temperature during her loss period ranged between sixty and seventy degrees, Benny was able to convince Frances to holster the pistola. He then calmly explained that he would need to verify the level of her business prior to, during and after the loss so he could verify her average daily income during those periods to figure how much the business had actually lost when the air conditioner blew a tire. Then he would deduct the cost of the drinks and the food she did not sell because she still had the same booze and fresh chicken marsala to sell to the next customer walking through the door.

"Oh, really? Where does it say that in the stinking BestEver Insurance policy?"

Then Benny explained exactly where she could find it, and he also put it in writing for her, just in case she needed some good nighttime reading, not to mention keeping BestEver in compliance with Best Practices and just as equally important, state law.

From that point, Benny was able to keep Ms. Murphy relatively calm except for the enlightenment period when she discovered her claim was inflated by about 250 percent. About eight months later, she filed another claim. And when doing so, she immediately demanded Benny be assigned. She had explained at least that asshole knew something. *Thank you very much for the confidence, Mrs. Murphy.*

But that was then, and this was now. More than a year had passed, and throughout all the moaning and complaining, Frances F Murphy kept her insurance with good old BestEver, even when her agent suggested she could try to place her coverage elsewhere. "No, I am happy," she replied. She was probably happy to punish the bastards every time she submitted a loss for review. Maybe everybody else had already learned their lesson. This time, things were a bit different. Well, she danced through her normal ranting about how devastating the loss of her heating boiler had been, how she could not afford to pay for the repair, and what in the world was she going to do to keep her restaurant open and keep all the pipes from freezing.

Benny charged to the rescue. After determining the boiler could not be repaired, Benny cut a check to pay for a new one and did not stop there. Because it could not be replaced right away, Benny, the asshole, made arrangements to get temporary heating in the building. All that was needed was to obtain the records of her sales and operating expenses to button up the claim, not to mention the verbal rants.

And now, with her business running smoothly again, Frances F called again this morning and opened up wider than Mount Vesuvius. Benny could not understand what was happening. Even for Frances F Murphy, the behavior seemed erratic. And, after his probing, Benny felt she had witnessed the same thing he had seen in the john, whether it had been a spirit, a ghost, a hallucination, or the damn devil itself. The only difference was the voice. In his case, it was her, but with Frances F, it was Benny.

But Benny knew nothing about what it had said to her other than her name; Ms. Murphy never elaborated what she had heard. She merely confirmed that it was Benny's voice, or as she put it, Benny in the raw flesh, if raw flesh could somehow be audible and if it could somehow be deposited in a mirror. Benny had heard her voice from the entity or maybe even beyond the mirror call out his name. Did she hear the same thing, just a name? Or did the demonic thing actually have a conversation with her? Knowing how big a bag of spite she carried around, Benny had no doubt she would probably have been ready, willing, and able to fully engage in quite a heated and hateful exchange in person with the devil himself, if devils even came in him or her categories. God forbid if it had spoken anything personal, or, heavens to Murgatroyd, even remotely sexual. He cringed at the thought of rounding a corner in a dimly lighted alleyway and suddenly confronting Frances F in her total and unabated nakedness.

"Ooh! Aah!" he exclaimed aloud.

"Whoa, you just run over a rabbit in the road, Benny?" That was

Joe, an inland marine adjuster located on the other side of the divider in front of Benny.

"No, no, I'm fine, Joe," he replied. "No blood, no bones. But it was really scary." However, not as scary as what came next.

F

Benny

Holy moly. I must have been sitting there stiffer than a scarecrow stuck in a dark and breezeless cornfield half the morning. Glancing at the computer clock display, it read 7:10 a.m. I had guessed that was right. Sondra, the stiff-legged commando, usually walked in about that time. I went into the john about 5:30 a.m., so I must have been out of it for over an hour before Trudy stopped by and then my favorite client called to dump on me.

I had wondered what would happen next. I didn't really think I wanted to go back into the john right away; maybe I could follow somebody when they took a break to see if I would start hallucinating again. The lights came on in there about 6:30 a.m. or so. I got the feeling that whatever it was, it probably liked the shady part of the place, so it wouldn't be around until it got dark again. At least that was what I was hoping.

But what would I do about Frances F? If she went back to the john at her restaurant to confront whatever the heck it was, she might just get the thing pissed off, thinking it was actually me playing some kind of stupid LNN game. Plus, at that point, I really wasn't sure whether or not light in the room would frighten it away or cause it to otherwise conceal itself. Then again, it just might be enough to help it bust out of the mirror and to burn a couple of holes in her ass. She could get in trouble.

Maybe I was dreaming, but I swear I could feel heat coming off those beams creeping out of the mirror. I needed to get over to her place before she did something crazy. She was a hard shell of a woman, but she was my client, so I decided to get my BestEver butt in action. *Wow, where does something like this show up in the BestEver Employee Manual?*

***

My voicemail was all set and ready to go, so I got to my feet and kicked the wheeled chair back. The phone rang again. I made the mistake of answering, without all the hullabaloo. The telephone digital display told me it was Harry, my boss, up in the Hartford home office Claim Department, the place that LNN tells us all the ivory towers are located. Killing helpless elephants is against company policy, so I doubt the towers contain genuine ivory. I'm not sure about the angry, helpless elephants you might find roaming around the neighborhood park. I know they are out there somewhere. But I'm sure their ivory is also off limits.

"Good morning, Har," I greeted, knowing I was in trouble. "What great tidings do you have in store for good ol' Benny?"

"Ha, ha," he chuckled, "you always read my mind, Ben. We got a hot loss for you. It got called in late last night. It's a big electrical fire down in Kentucky."

"Call the property carrier," I had replied. "We don't cover fire in B&M. Besides, I didn't think they had electricity in Kentucky yet. There are too many hills down there."

"Haha," once again. "Nice try. They called us. BestEver doesn't carry the fire coverage. This could get big, and it's moving really fast. It could go several million fairly quickly, and the income loss could get a lot higher. This is a large float, glass manufacturing plant, I think making mostly sixty or eighty-four-inch-wide plate glass. The main electrical power center is down. They figure they can get partial power back but will need a lot of generators to get the quarter mile float line moving again. So far, their installed emergency power has kept the furnace in operation. If that goes cold, they'll be down forever to rebuild it. They have a duplicate power supply in the main power center, but it's not isolated, so the backup got whacked with a lot of smoke damage, taking the whole plant down. Just what you would expect from an old plant like this one—good ol' Murphy's Law. Do your magic, Ben, and get this thing under control."

Murphy, I thought. "My wand is in the garage for repairs right now, Har," I replied. "Mind if I get an independent general adjuster? I'll hop on an electrical expert and see about getting some people out there right away."

"The crunch on expenses is coming down the pike," Harry had explained. "Some people would be you. You'll have to take this one on yourself. Plus, it looks like it could penetrate our reinsurance, which kicks in at five million, so there will be a lot of eyeballs all over this one. Go ahead with the electrical guy. Christine will email you all the info we have up to this point and get you a copy of the policy. The coverage is written in Cleveland so you can get in touch with the local underwriter. I checked and found we have a good engineering report in the database. Let me know how things go after you talk to the property insurance contact and the point person at the plant and make plans to get out there as soon as you can. All American Insurance advised the client wants the two carriers to make a joint investigation to simplify matters and sort out who gets to pay what. I imagine an advance payment will be warranted to get all the emergency power in place. I believe they indicated the main substation is rated about fifty thousand KVA capacity."

"Roger, roger, dodger," I acknowledged reluctantly. "That's a lot of generators, what, about twenty at twenty-five hundred KVA. That's maybe twenty-five grand a crack to put them in place not including fuel. That's a half million plus, just to get the clocks spinning again."

"Get that wand fixed, and have a nice day, Ben."

What did he say, Murphy's Law? The nice part of the day had departed a couple of hours ago when I had walked into the john. It took another two hours to review all the data we had received, to get hold of the electrical engineer, and to have a nice long joint conference call with All American and the array of contacts we had been provided at the plant. Another forty minutes was wasted getting online and making my own travel plans through the corporate system. Traveling from Cleveland to St. Louis to Atlanta to Louisville did not make much sense, but I could have saved twenty bucks with a twelve-hour longer flight schedule. *Don't forget to explain why you declined the cheaper fare, Benny. Oh, and explain why you declined a hotel that is thirty bucks cheaper and only forty miles farther away from the plant.*

I didn't have a chance to complete all the other claim notes and correspondence I had lined up for the morning before getting hit by this new loss. It was tough enough just getting the new file up and running. The good old days of having clerical support were long gone—so as goodbye, dictation, and hello; endless hours on the keyboard; and printing and assembly of letters. Thank goodness, many of the clients accepted email delivery, although it was always prudent to follow with a hard copy delivery by Uncle Sam. At least the mail room had not been exiled, and the company still kept an ample supply of toilet paper in the johns for nose blowing, etc. So the work would back up as usual, and now I had this big mess on my hands. To boot, I had the biggest problem of all glaring in my not-so-smiley face. What the hell was Frances F Murphy up to at this particular time? Or what had she already done? Murphy's Law.

When I had tried reaching her by her cell phone number, it went where most calls go, straight to the deep dark cave we call voice mail. The two lines at her restaurant were also busy, dumping me again into the vast land of electronic nothingness.

I had taken one last glimpse of the phone, shook my head, and again, kicked back the chair. I hightailed it out for the elevator. I avoided using a Claim Department pool car. That would have taken another hour of form and report filing, plus at least one trip to the gas station and another expense report. When I arrived at Ms. Murphy's restaurant a half hour later, I was greeted by an entourage of spectators and flashing lights. *F. Now what?*

F

There was an ambulance, a fire truck, and three cop cars lined up, facing the front entrance of the restaurant—an impressive stone archway stretching out about twenty or thirty feet from the doorway. Murphy's, as the place was so aptly named, was a popular hangout for the elite, politicians, celebrities, high-powered attorneys, and in general, any other affluent or born-wealthy, entitled locals whose pockets were loaded with cash eager to depart ways.

One officer stood guard at the door, while a group of restaurant employees were huddled nearby, nervously filling one another's ears with their individual accounts of what they saw and heard and what they had not seen or heard.

It was late March, and a beautiful morning was greeting a forecasted warm day. Frances F might even need to use her relatively new air-conditioning courtesy of BestEver. Dressed today like a typical field-business guy in a light-blue long-sleeved shirt, gray polyester slacks, and a dark blue sports coat, Benny unloaded himself out of his '95 blue Chevy. With notebook in hand and pen flashlight in shirt pocket, he headed for the doorway. His mind kept repeating, *What the F did she do?*

The officer spread his legs in front of Benny's path. "Would you please identify yourself?" the tall, burly barrel-chested officer with short brown hair inquired.

Benny produced his BestEver identification card. "I am Benny Johnson, officer, of BestEver Insurance. I was speaking with Mrs—uh, I mean Ms. Murphy earlier this morning about her claim with us. The line seemed to be abruptly interrupted, and I was subsequently unable to reach her, so I was concerned. May I speak with her?"

"I doubt that," he replied. "Wait here, and I'll fetch Lieutenant Baker. The lieutenant might want to talk to you."

"Is she okay?" Benny asked, fearing the worst.

"Lieutenant Baker is fine. Wait here," the officer replied, turning and entering the restaurant. Puzzled, Benny just looked at the cop as he walked into the building.

Benny got a brief glimpse of what had greeted the kitchen staff when they reported for work earlier in the dark, empty, and tranquil entry. But now the place was swarming with bodies—people with notepads, cameras, and briefcases of varying sorts. A minute later, a comely woman in a dark blue suit greeted him, inviting him inside.

"Mr. Johnson, I'm Lieutenant Baker." Her black hair was short and worn in a pageboy style. She was trim but barely reached the shoulders of the six-foot-two officer who had followed her back to his station at the front entrance. Her pleasant hazel eyes probed Benny. They were more yellow than brown. While she was no Angelina Jolie, she carried the woman's lips and was modestly attractive. "Follow me, please."

Benny's thoughts told his eyeballs not to follow her ass, a common male and personal trait, so he focused them at her shoulders, smiling at the guard as he passed through the doorway.

There was a short hallway in the entrance leading to an attended coatroom on the left and a reception stand as it opened into the main dining area. The entrance was located at the center of the room and a semicircular stairway dropped to the main floor, with three, four-inch-high, six-foot-wide steps. The lieutenant stopped at the top of the short stairway and turned to observe Benny's reaction. If a man was dexterous enough to touch his belly button with his chin, Benny would have accomplished the feat. Baker confirmed that his level of surprise approached astonishment.

As Benny looked out in the room, he noted there was a short balcony, about six steps high, encircling the room, and banisters ran along the perimeter between openings in each of six sections. Straight ahead at the back of this platform was another hallway leading to four rooms at the back of the building used for private functions. To the right of the reception stand was a burgundy-carpeted hall that led to the manager's office and the powder rooms, as described by Ms. Murphy. Renaissance era portraits lined the walls around the entire room on Gothic-style wallpaper colored black and deep purple. On the main floor, there were semicircular burgundy high-back booths situated around solid ornate dark oak tables covered in white linen and lined with Baroque-style black-and-burgundy-striped high-back chairs, at least thirty booths by his count. From past claims she had made, Benny was aware that the main room could seat two hundred. Four-foot diameter Waterford crystal chandeliers hung from the stucco ceiling, encircling the platform and interior of the main room. A large chandelier twice diameter hung at the center of the room. He had not seen the restaurant before; his prior meeting with Frances F was held at her accountant's office. Benny doubted he could afford the place, even with his big bucks salary.

The room was undisturbed from the previous night's cleaning, with one exception. From the center chandelier hung Frances F Murphy. She glared directly at Benny. But even if alive, Frances would not have seen him, for both eyes were completely burned through. Remnants of gray matter and blood had oozed from her eye sockets, and matching holes burned through the skull at the back of her head down over her deep maroon ankle-length dress. Based on the room furnishings, Benny figured the white pearl necklace she wore was not a cheap imitation. Her left maroon short-heeled shoe had fallen to the floor, and the other dangled from her toes.

"Follow me," instructed Lieutenant Baker. "Maybe you can explain something."

Benny was a bit startled. He had seen corpses before like dead soldiers, attended funerals, and even pulled bloated bodies that had been submerged in the Ohio River throughout the winter and ascended to the surface in the warm spring water flow and snagged by a freaked-out fisherman. These bodies bloated twice their size, more saturated than submerged sponges. But he had never seen this kind of death. She actually stared at Benny, without any eyes, just the two charred black holes in her face. The dead woman had been suspended by a jointed meat hook; the lower part of the S-shaped iron had punctured through her neck at the bottom of her cranium and the upper section was carefully placed on the framework of the chandelier so as not to damage any of the precious crystal components. The double-jointed hook allowed Frances F Murphy free rotational movement once she had been suspended in all that elegance. But at the moment, she was quite motionless . . . and very silent.

"Please, Mr. Johnson," Lieutenant Baker repeated, pulling him from his latest trance.

She led Benny down the hall to their right, past the office on their right and beyond the men's room, which was also to his right, stopping at the ladies' powder room. Benny followed her as she shoved the swinging door open to reveal toilet stalls straight ahead. There was yet another crystal chandelier in this room, and the light it provided was extremely bright, comforting him somewhat. There were four short-back chairs matching those in the dining room. They were set in front of a long mirror mounted on a wall, again to their right. A gold-plated facial mirror sat in front of each chair to the right of four washbasins, which displayed brightly polished antique-style gold-plated fixtures. Tissue containers, hand lotion, and down feather powder puff kits were neatly displayed in a row behind the facial mirrors. It was the wall-mounted mirror that grabbed Benny's attention.

In large letters across the length of the mirror was Benny's handwritten first name, although it appeared as would a mirror image. It was as if someone had written his name on a large placard and held it up facing the mirror . . . or as if they were standing behind it when they scribbled his name on the back side.

It appeared his name had been written with a red fluid of some sort because it had collected and oozed down the mirror glass slightly at the bottom of some of the letters. His first thought was *Oh F, blood.* But something else was wrong. Lieutenant Baker approached the mirror as she had done earlier, shortly after being called to the crime scene. She stood at the center of the mirror, grabbed a tissue, and wiped it over the middle letter *N*. Nothing happened. None of the red fluid rubbed off the mirror. She turned her head back to Benny with question marks protruding out of her eyeballs. Aghast, he stared at his reflection, which was overshadowed by the scribbling.

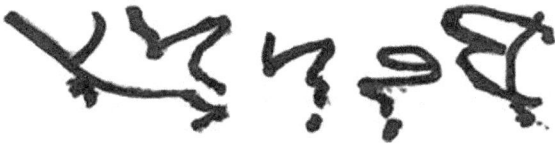

"Well, Mr. Johnson? Or should I say . . . what's up, Benny?" She glared at him but not with the same hollow deathly glare from Frances that had stared him down. She was looking for answers.

"I don't know what to say," he said in defense. "I was just talking with Ms. Murphy a couple of hours ago. How could somebody write something on the inside of the mirror? Is the men's bathroom on the other side of the wall? Maybe she . . . maybe somebody did it from the other john."

"The men's room is on the other side of this wall, Mr. Johnson. Would you care to look? You might find it interesting, but it is hardly amusing," she added.

Benny nervously followed her out and into the second john, which they had passed earlier, back down the hall to their left of the ladies' powder room door. It was not decorated so lavishly, but it did display the gold-plated fixtures, tissue and hand soap dispensers, and hand blow-dry machines on the wall adjacent to the mirror. The mirror sat on the wall facing the ladies' powder room off to their left. Clark Kent could comb his steel hair while admiring women on the other side dusting their cheeks and moistening their radiant lips with fresh lipstick to tidy up their rosy complexions.

Once again, however, without the x-ray vision, the same bloody mirror image inscription slapped Benny square in the face.

"Could there be a room between the two bathrooms?" he meekly asked.

"If a person were made out of cardboard, he might fit, Mr. Johnson," she concluded. "By the way, where were you between, let's say, seven and eight o'clock this morning?"

"Well, I certainly wasn't between these walls painting a mural. I can tell you that much," Benny replied, feeling he was being implicated.

"Don't get me wrong, Mr. Johnson. I'm merely trying to trace her tracks. We believe she arrived here between six and six thirty. You mentioned to Officer Denning that you might have spoken with her shortly after that time."

"I'm sorry, Lieutenant Baker. It's been a trying morning. This is too crazy," he apologized. "I got a call right about seven o'clock, a little after the property manager walked into the office. I generally get in around five, five thirty, so I can get catch-up work done before the phones start ringing. I was having a short chat with one of the girls in the office when Ms. Murphy called. She was hot under the collar, a bit more than usual. Did you know her?"

"I never met the lady," Baker replied. "And who would this 'other worker' be, Mr. Johnson?"

"If you had, you would know what I mean," Benny started. "I'm not sure how she spoke to her employees, but when it came to the insurance company, she could be downright mean. As much as she verbally abused me though, when she had a loss of some sort, she would ask for the claim to be assigned to me. Maybe she just got some kind of a kick out of picking on me. She could be mean, but I don't think she was a mean person." He glanced back at the mirror. "Can we get out of here? This room gives me the spooks."

Baker led him out the door down the hallway and stopped at the platform overlooking the impaled woman. *Not far enough out of here,* thought Benny. Three men clad in white coveralls, goggles, and masks over their mouths had erected rigging and were lifting Frances F to dislodge the jointed hook.

"Try not to disturb the hook, gentlemen," directed Lieutenant Baker. "There might be prints." She looked back at Benny. "The other worker, Mr. Johnson?"

"Oh, I'm sorry. That would be Trudy," he acknowledged. "Trudy. Trudy Perkins, Lieutenant. Just like the pancakes?"

"Certainly," she agreed, "just like the pancakes."

She turned back to Benny, continuing the interrogation. "So how long did this discussion with Ms. Murphy last, Mr. Johnson?"

"Please," he said, "you can call me Benny. I guess it might have been ten minutes, maybe fifteen at the most."

"That might put the clock hands at about seven thirty, if that, would you agree, Mr. Johnson?" she emphasized the *mister* part of the name.

"Yes, ma'am, about seven thirty," he answered. So much for trying to be nice.

"And you said she was upset"—and looking at her notes on the handheld pad—"and hot under the collar as you described. What did she complain about, if that is a correct characterization of her call to you?"

Benny figured their conversation would eventually lead down this path. Maybe he should just confess that she saw a monster in the mirror and thought it was him. They could stick Benny in a straitjacket for the balance of his life, and the case would be solved. But he figured he could tell her enough of the truth without inserting too much about the hard facts, the small details that would land him in the loony bin.

"She believed I had planted a microphone and speaker in the restaurant somewhere and I was talking to her. She thought maybe I put in a video camera or screen somewhere too." Not totally inaccurate, but Benny was being honest.

"She heard you talking to her. And what did you say?" Baker asked.

"Nothing," Benny replied emphatically. "I didn't plant any microphone!"

"I meant, what did she hear when she thought she heard you speaking to her?"

"She said she heard me speak her name. That's it, her name, and she did not really say a whole lot more than that. I guess she was too . . . you know."

"Hot under the collar?"

"Yes, ma'am," he agreed.

"Please, Mr. Johnson, it's Lieutenant. And where was this microphone?" she probed.

"In China, for all I know," he told Baker. *She's getting closer*, thought Benny.

"I meant to ask, where was she when she heard this voice call out her name?"

F, thought Benny. "Well, she didn't really tell me exactly where the voice she heard was."

"Well then, Mr. Johnson." There goes that hard *mister* again. "Where was Ms. Murphy at when she heard someone sounding like you calling out her name?"

"She was in the ladies' powder room. She apparently thought it was somewhere in the room." No sense in trying to hide it anymore. "But she never really saw anything."

"You said earlier, Mr. Johnson, she saw some kind of video. So I suspect that would fit in the category of anything," she fired back. "Would you not agree?"

"I meant she never saw any microphone. She just heard something sounding like it might have come from one. She didn't actually see it," he explained rather truthfully.

"Then what did she see, Benny?"

Benny could not figure out if this was a sarcastic remark or the woman was bending a little bit, maybe relaxing a touch, easing off the old "I got me the perp on the line" routine. Maybe she was playing the good cop, bad cop by herself. She crossed her arms, and it seemed to Benny as if she leaned into him, again staring him down with that not-so-friendly glare.

"Come on, Benny. Give," she ordered.

"She never really described it to me, Lieutenant," he conceded. "But she was somehow convinced it was me dressed up in some kind of suit."

"And what kind of suit was this person she thought was you? What kind of suit was this person wearing?" she prodded.

"She never said." He was not lying. "She just said, 'Nice outfit.' That's all." He didn't understand why he had called it a suit. To the monster, ghost, phantom, or apparition, maybe it was a suit. The thing, whatever it was, probably wore the damn thing day in and day out, most likely day out. He almost wished he had seen the face, if that was what the cloak had concealed. But then he thought twice about it. Frances F Murphy had apparently tried to stare it down and look what it had in store for her.

"Mr. Johnson," Baker said, interrupting his daydream. "So this wasn't actually a suit? Was it a costume of some sort?"

"I don't know, Ms. Baker," he began, "but she must have thought it was a costume, an outfit, but she never really did say that she saw me. She just thought it was me because she recognized what she thought was my voice."

"That's Lieutenant, Mr. Johnson. Interesting, an outfit, a voice, and a bloody signature on the inside of a mirror," she commented. "Make that inside two mirrors."

She turned back to the crew who had placed the body of Frances F Murphy facedown on a gurney. The S-shaped hook stretched out over and beyond her head toward the front of the wheeled cart. "Guys, when you're done over there and get her off to the cooler, we'll need to begin extracting the mirrors. Make sure you have some sharp glass cutters. And let's make up some wooden cartons to haul them out of here. And keep an eye out for a mike and a camera."

Keep an eye out, thought Benny. She was just like Frances F Murphy. They wouldn't find anything behind those mirrors. They were nothing more than doorways, portals. She would have more luck finding a mike up Ms. Murphy's ass or behind her belly button. And Benny knew the damn thing had at least one more portal to get through, unless . . . unless it never went back in and was still out there in the restaurant—somewhere . . . waiting.

"Mr. Johnson," Baker concluded, "we're done here for now, but I'd like to keep in touch, just in case. Do you know if she had any relatives?"

"Not that I'm aware of, Lieutenant. She was divorced, no kids."

"Your cell phone number?" she asked, as she held out her card.

Benny withdrew a packet of company cards, and in exchanging them, he placed one in her right hand. "Here is my office number, Lieutenant. The company doesn't issue cell phones, and I am still stuck in the Stone Age. I never had much use for one. I'm on the darn phone all day long as it is, and I never felt I was important enough that people needed to be contacting me around the clock. I have to laugh when I stop for gas and some moron is on the cell phone with his ol' lady asking her if they need milk."

"Excuse me, Mr. Johnson," she interrupted as her cell phone rang. She lifted it to her left ear. "Yes? Oh, hi, honey." She listened. "Why, it's funny you should ask." She glared at Benny, but then smiled and said, "Why, sure, honey."

"I'm sorry," Benny started as she ended her call.

"That's okay, Benny," she replied, giggling. "It was the moron, all right, but he wanted to know if I would like a bottle of wine tonight."

"Besides being locked up in the trunk of a car, that's the next best use of a cell phone. You have yourself a moron with a class there, Lieutenant Baker."

As Frances had already departed the scene of the crime, Benny followed Lt. Susan Baker out of the restaurant. This time, he did check out her ass, although half of it was mostly concealed by her suit coat.

F

Benny

Well, I got out of that mess without landing in the clinker or some detention center for the clinically insane. And unless I dreamed the entire sequence, Frances F Murphy was as dead as dead could possibly get. I wished I could turn the clock back in time and could have left the office before Harry picked up the phone, or somehow, I might have possibly convinced her not to go back into that powder room of hers. But as stubborn as she was, she seemed to have already made up her mind at the time. As stubborn as she was—that was it.

I couldn't understand why she flew off the handle like that. Frances was always hard to deal with, but without exception, she would always back off, calm down, and get our business done. I knew she had a nice side. I guess everybody does, but it is always the other side that seemed to be the one facing me. Why the hell was she so convinced it was me in the powder room and it was me in the video? What video? There was no video. I could attest to that part of it. Whatever was in the mirror was real and alive, even if it was a ghost or a phantom. So it must have been just as real to her.

I imagined the coroner should be able to pinpoint the time of her death. I wondered how close it could be calculated. How should I know?

I was only an adjuster calculating the cost of repairing crankshafts or estimating the amount of time to rebuild five-thousand-ton hydraulic press cylinders or the amount of overtime to make up two months of downtime at a foundry blessed by the underwriter's generosity in providing coverage for electric furnaces. Furnaces equal fire, Mr. Underwriter. Fire equals property insurance. Well, they had their job, and I had mine. I guess you could write a policy on a burning house, as long as you exclude fire. It was not my money. I didn't get paid the big bucks like everybody thought I did; I just paid them out when and where they were due. How could Frances be so naïve, so stupid to get the idea that the aberration standing in the mirror was a video? Or it was me, of all people.

Wait a minute. If she was anything, stupid it was not. Like her or not, Frances built and operated one of the finest and most successful restaurant businesses this city had ever known. And she did it apparently without the help of the so-called twerp she had divorced. A pocket-picking money grubber, she had once called him, after her dough, not the pasta variety either. So she decided to give him a pastry in the mouth and send him back where he was raised, back yeast.

The thing in the mirror—it had spoken to me. But I had not confronted it. I was lucky enough to get around the bend in the room and escape my reflection in the mirror before it burned a hole through my rear end. What if our john had been long and straight the way the johns were built at Murphy's Restaurant, with wall-to-wall mirrors on one side instead of the room being L-shaped? What if Frances never made it out of the john? What if Frances was already dead when she made the call to me" What if it wasn't Frances on the phone? What if the woman hanging from the chandelier wasn't really Frances? What if it was only a mirror reflection of Frances? What if Frances was really still alive and stuck somewhere on the other side of the mirror? Or between them? Maybe I dreamed this whole mess up somehow.

Why was I suddenly calling Frances F Murphy by her first name? I must be F'ing nuts. But what if all those what ifs were actually true? If the thing in that mirror had found a way somehow to get out through a doorway or a portal, then maybe—just maybe—there was a way to reverse the pathway. If there was a way out, there must be a way to get inside the mirror, wherever inside might be, and I doubt if anybody could do it with a glass cutter.

Now I knew I was F'ing nuts.

Ah, my house was right up ahead. Wait. There was a car backing out of the drive. It looked familiar. It was John J Cooper, the financial adviser. The *J* is for jerk-off. The driver's door had his company logo in the panel, IBS. I thought we dusted this guy off months and months ago, like maybe a year at least. What the F! Did this guy have some kind of hot tip or was the ol' lady cashing in all my dough? I must be the one getting BS'd.

F

Trudy

Benny had looked really hot when he got back to the office a bit earlier, and I meant mad, not sexy or anything like that. I was standing on the aisle shooting the breeze with Helen about a water damage loss when he walked in and skipped his usual smile and "Hi, Trudy" when he eyeballed me. He not only looked hot; he was hot and not in a good way. The expression on his face was one of exasperation, like don't even think about offering him a straw. It would be the last. I had seen him

30

when he'd been through a tough day or had taken a beating from a client or had five or six emergencies to get under control all at the exact same time. It got tough when the phone would just not quit. By the time your hand put the receiver down, it was blasting in your face again, and you could see the person on the other end taking in a huge breath to dump it all out in a single, twenty-minute, nonstop diatribe.

"Helen," I said, "I'm going to check on Benny. Something's up. I'm expecting a call and don't want it to go to voice mail, so flag me down if it comes in, okay?"

"Will do, Trudy," Helen had replied. "He looked so pissed I thought his eyes turned yellow. Make sure you wave a white flag."

"Like maybe waving my panties might cheer him up," I said.

"You nasty girl," Helen responded, laughing at my gutter talk. "Wash out that mouth!"

I peeked into the aisle and found the coast was clear. Sondra had her office door closed. She was probably sleeping or dreaming up new and improved methods of managerial behavior measurement mechanisms. More crap to provide all the employees with opportunities for improvement. *Opportunities for improvement? Kiss my ass. Just more ways to keep our annual performance evaluation results down below meets minimum requirements and delay salary increases for another year, while packing the coffer with bucks for her own office management bonus. Kiss the other side of my ass. I'm too busy with a claim inventory of over 120 files to worry about your silly compliance criteria crapola. Kiss it again, sweetheart. Let your sweet juicy lips take it all in.*

After working myself up, I tiptoed my way up the aisle to Benny's cubicle. Although tempted, I restrained myself from grabbing another chocolate. I called him Benji, which I'd do sometimes when we flirted around. I asked him what was up. He half smiled and asked me why I always looked so good. I told him that was hard to believe as the day was just about over. Then his smile departed, and he unloaded.

He told me I had probably noticed his day didn't start so well, which was so, so true. From there, it went to hell. He didn't get any catch-up work done this morning, got a big F'ing claim down in Kentucky, and ran over to Murphy's restaurant to find Ms. Murphy hanging from a chandelier and his name plastered on the john mirrors backward and was apparently written in fresh blood. He didn't bother to explain why he thought it was fresh, but he was sure the blood was authentic. He got interrogated by a hot-looking cop who apparently was the opposite sex and then headed his way home to pack up for the trip tonight to Kentucky. And then, when he walked in the door, he discovered his ol' lady had been screwing somebody else for over a year. *Goodbye, marriage. Goodbye, Frances. Good F'ing bye.* His life was over, so he might as well jump in the F'ing toilet. I just love it when he talks dirty to me.

I told Benny I would jump in with him, but I doubted if both of us would fit at the same time. So if he would be a gentleman, I would jump in first. That was when I got another half-smile. And then I touched his left cheek. I guessed it was spontaneous. I'd never done before. He gently grabbed my right hand, squeezed it—how electric that was—and told me I needed to make him a promise.

"Sure, Benny," I said. "What is it?"

"Don't you dare go into the john before the lights come on in the morning, neither one of them. And you probably shouldn't go in alone or without me, at least not until I get back from this trip. It's just a one-nighter, and I'll get back late tomorrow. So I'll be back here early Friday morning."

"Why, Benny?" I had said so in a teasing kind of way. It was not the kind of promise I was expecting he would ask me for, but an invitation to go into the john together presented some possibilities. "Is this an opportunity for improvement?"

"I'm not kidding. Promise me, Trudy," he demanded. "There's something horrible in there."

I told Benny it sounded like he was serious, and it was a little scary to hear him talk like that. He said I better be scared, to just stay out of the johns when they were dark. And if I got into the office before eight o'clock, I should keep any of the other girls out until we were all sure that the lights were turned on. The only three who usually came in early were Helen, me, and Sondra and maybe a couple of the guys when they were getting ready for a field investigation.

He confided that even though Sondra was a bitch, nobody deserved what Frances got. I couldn't believe he was calling her by her first name. It was always Ms. or Mrs. Murphy, Frances F, or F Murphy, but not plain old Frances. Benny did not really want to describe what had happened; only that she was found hanging from a chandelier. Just hearing that was enough to make me want to go to the john and let something out of my stomach backward. After making me double promise him to watch my guard, Benny packed up his computer and headed for the airport.

I headed straight back to my cube and made Helen go with me to the john. I cracked open the door slowly and peeked in at the mirror. When you open the door during the day, some kind of sensor automatically turns on the light. Benny knew how that stuff works. He knew a little about all kinds of mechanical and electrical things, even how they made those little skinny rectangular chocolates the restaurants pass out.

He went out of his way to explain how things work when we got claims involving boilers or maybe air-conditioning things. He called them compressors. He would make drawings and try to put complex things into simple terms, like how a diesel engine works without spark plugs. I didn't care much about it beyond the gas pedal, but it was fun listening to him. And Helen could even understand him. She could even replace the spark plugs on her old Chevy!

Well, the lights flashed on nice and bright, and there was nobody in the john. "Avoid the mirror," Benny told me, so I held my hands over my eyes, and I walked through the doorway. Helen followed me, shaking her head and asking what all the fuss was about. I told her I would explain in the morning, but she should not go into the john before I got to work. I made her promise through her silly giggles. I wished she would have listened.

F

"Hi, Frank," greeted Benny at the Southwest Airport gate. "I'm in the *B* group, so try to save me a seat. I reckon you got in the *A* group."

Frank Resetter or Reset, as Benny had nicknamed him, acknowledged he did indeed upgrade to get a good aisle seat. Warren Tetherman got hold of Frank by cell phone and was making his way to the gate. There had been plenty of time for them all to grab a brew and set a game plan before boarding was announced. Frank, an electrical engineer, would assess the electric arcing damage and research as might be necessary in locating replacement equipment and/or repair options. Frank would also pair up with the engineer hired by the property adjuster, compare notes, and try to reach an agreement on the type and scope of damages.

Warren, highly skilled in air-conditioning equipment and process controls, was not a professional photographer, but he knew what the adjuster wanted to look at, capture, and document. He always did a fantastic job of putting a pictorial story together in identifying damages. Warren would photograph all the electrical damages, focusing in particular on the separation between electrical arcing and fire or smoke damage. He would identify what equipment was controlled by each switch in each panel. Some panels could have one or two main circuit breakers, while other subpanels might have as many as a dozen or more circuits, so he could identify what process equipment was affected by the electrical arcing damage.

Benny would buddy up with the All American general adjuster, Betty Bleau, who had been beating the large loss path for about twenty years. She and Benny got along fine on their phone conference, so Benny hoped the two carriers would find some common ground to make the adjustment go easy for the client and for the people writing claim checks. It did not always work that way, and so far, at this point, nobody was coming into the investigation with a predisposed "this is your loss, not mine" attitude.

The dollars would fall where they should fall, both agreed. But Benny was fairly sure the bundles of cash he was carrying would weigh a lot less than the bag Betty would be towing down the road, partly because of the disparity in deductibles each would apply to their separate payments and any overlapping common coverage to be be shared equally by the two carriers. The B&M deductible was substantial, being based on the average daily income of the plant, currently estimated at over a quarter of a million dollars.

The flight was on time, and Benny checked into his room at the Holiday Inn about eight thirty at night after grabbing a quick sandwich with Frank and Warren. They would convene at the plant at seven the next morning, so they would be out the door at six thirty sharp. Benny was up until two in the morning doing catch-up work on his computer, almost forgetting to process the electronic $100,000 advance payment he had promised another client a day earlier before all hell had broken out of the mirror.

When the back of his head finally hit the pillow, the vision of Frances F Murphy paid him a visit somehow on the ceiling of the dark room. *Hard to believe,* the inner side of his eyelids told him as they shut down for the day.

In his dream, Benny was standing at the entrance to his cubicle with his eyes on Trudy. She was walking very slowly, methodically toward him. He had not seen her before wearing clothing as tight as her outfit appeared. The smooth black pants she sported were so tight he could make out her flexing thigh muscles. The material seemed to be made from some kind of spandex that could stretch from here to eternity. Otherwise, how could she possibly walk without ripping them at the seams? It stretched with each stride while her thighs snapped and flexed tight.

The purple tight silky blouse pushed her modest breasts together up and outward. The employee manual might have something to say about the cleavage, but Benny would not tattle. He noticed an abundance of mascara, plus dark eye shadow had been painted on her closed eyelids, and her lips were also painted black.

In his dream and in his sleep, Benny was becoming aroused. Then Trudy opened her eyelids. Her eyes were gone. Two large holes appeared in place of her eyes, and Benny could see right through them and out the back of her head.

And then he heard the scream, "Benny!" Trudy turned gracefully around, spinning from her right to her left, now facing the opposite direction. Beyond the holes tunneling through her head, Benny could see the face of another woman. She was clutching and pulling at her curled light-brown hair. Her face was frantic. She screamed, "Benny!"

Benny sat up in bed. Now the woman whispered, "Benny."

"No," he said, rubbing at his eyes. "I didn't hear that." But he called out her name anyway, "Helen?"

And then Benny fell into a deeper vision-free sleep, wiped out from his exhausting day, but his body pulled him out of his deep shell automatically at five thirty in the morning, a good two hours beyond his normal wakeup call. He recalled nothing about the dream or Helen speaking his name. He slapped away his erection and headed for the bathroom, giving the mirror the finger as he stepped into the shower stall. In reverse mode, apparently due to Wednesday's trauma, he shaved after the shower. He figured his upside-down life needed some new order.

He met Warren and Reset in the lobby after picking up a jelly donut, cartons of milk, and orange juice plus an apple. He never could adjust to the taste of coffee. He dressed in his dark-blue jeans, solid light-blue jean shirt bearing a Chief Wahoo logo, and his trusty brown tweed sport coat. It bore thin lined patterns of deep red and blue and carried dark-brown patches sewn over the holes he had worn through the elbows. Being a favorite of his, it could get dirty without much recognition, and with the smoke and debris he anticipated, this would work fine. It didn't smell yet under the armpits. Benny stepped out into the brisk cool sunny morning with his team and met the day in a head-on collision.

After a tour of the damages and the plant process line, Benny left Warren and Reset with the other insurance team engineers and huddled in a conference with Betty Bleau and the key plant management personnel, all twelve of them. They were able to whittle their contacts down to a single manager in finance and another in engineering. In a separate sidebar, Benny met with Betty. The two agreed the loss was mostly fire damage, but B&M would play a significant role with the temporary power measures and other mitigating expenses, such as expediting costs to make temporary repairs and accelerate delivery lead time for materials.

Betty would take the lead role and Benny would piggyback, determining their prorated distribution of dollars toward the repair, rental costs, and income losses. Once all the damages and repair costs were determined, they would meet again to evaluate what the costs would have been on a what-if basis—meaning what if there had been no fire after the initial electrical fault occurred? Easier said than done, the numbers were big, but the process of divvying up the dollars was elementary stuff. *Just a little math with a lot of bucks, right, Benny?* Easy as finding your face in a mirror. No surprises, depending on which mirror you were facing at the time, and maybe whether or not it happened to be resting on a wall in a dark john at five in the morning.

But there were a couple of surprises lining up for Benny while he sat at the airport bar with Frank and Warren over drinks and Mexican food during the three-hour departure delay for Cleveland. He was glad he had skipped traveling to Hopkins Airport by taxi and had parked at a lot nearby, because when his flight finally arrived home, he discovered all the taxis had gone home for the evening. At two o'clock in the morning, Benny wheeled his Chevy into the driveway and activated the garage door opener. It was almost time to wake up for tomorrow's workday. The garage appeared unusually clean.

F

CHAPTER TWO

BENNY

When I entered the house through the garage entry door, I was not too surprised to find my wife missing, nor was I too disappointed, especially after learning what had been going on for all those months. Her legs had been squeezed together tighter than the skin across Ginger Baker's favorite snare drum. Any love I had felt for the woman had departed some months ago. Even before that, when we were still having sex, we had little else. There was nothing to talk about, and anything she had to say, I really didn't need to hear. Nag, nag, nag.

But the living room furniture? The bitch had to take the furniture? How could she pull that off in one F'ing day? She was not even kind enough to leave my recliner and the television. I was surprised to find the phone was still hanging on the F'ing wall. In place of the bed was a blow-up mattress we had used early in our marriage when we went camping a few times. But we stopped using it after we got kicked out of a state park for having beer in our cooler. The damn thing would deflate anyway before we could even get to sleep, let alone think about screwing in the morning. *Thanks for the thought, honey F, but I miss the confiscated beer more than I miss you.*

I had constructed a wall-to-wall shelved closet with four folding doors for our clothing. While my underwear, pants, shirts, and what have you were spread all over the room, the closet was otherwise empty but had been spared from being torn apart. No evidence of her was left behind, including photo albums, jewelry, clothing, or anything that could have left trace evidence of a fingerprint or a scent.

My record albums—CDs, DVDs, tapes, you name it—were gone. Thank heavens I had bought and paid for this house long before I had met and married her and before falling into her bear trap. Apparently, I didn't make enough money fast enough for her to survive. I guessed I could blame my hot pants. I just couldn't get enough when I was a bit younger. I should have kept moving on to the next one and left her behind. At least I would still have a recliner and a mattress. TVs are a dime a dozen these days.

I said a short prayer before opening the refrigerator door and another once I found my supply of beer cans had not also betrayed and abandoned me. I sat at the kitchen table where I thanked the man in the same heaven above for the salvage and slam-dunked six beers while I put together my notes from the tribulations of my visit to the glass plant. I prepared an acknowledgment letter to the plant confirming receipt of its loss notice and also informing our contact that we had liability for some of the damages under certain portions of our policy.

I explained how Betty and I would be working together to mutually help them out of their mess. I wondered if they could do the same for me. If I would have known this was on the horizon, I might have checked their warehouse for a slightly used smoke-free mattress. I went back for the last beer in the first twelve pack and pulled the empty carton out of the reefer, discovering the divorce papers underneath in a plastic bag. Once again, he thought, *How thoughtful, honey F. How considerate.* She got him a little buzz going before she gave him the body slam.

I woke a few hours later. Sitting at the table, the computer was still humming and staring at my head from across the opposite side of the place I had actually shared some halfway decent meals with my vindictive honey F. The sun was creeping over the horizon and invading my space in the dimly lit kitchen. *F. When does it end?* Two days in a row now I missed my morning workout. I deduced I would not be sleeping in on Saturday morning. I needed to purge myself of some anxious aggression. Being as pissed off as I was, I really needed to piss on something, maybe honey F, if I knew where to find her lame butt.

Through all the fatigue, I almost forgot about my big problem.

F. The clock on the oven read seven thirty-five. And it was morning; otherwise, the sun would be slapping the opposite side of the single-story ranch—the one with the bikini-clad, sunken living room.

I jumped up and over to the phone, dialing the office and punching Trudy's extension. Then I tapped my right foot, and in time with the foot, my right hand slapped at my hip. *Come on, Trudy,* I thought, but once again with the help of that genius of a moron who created the invention, the call dumped straight into voice mail. I thought maybe, just maybe, she had decided not to come in early and would not show up for another half hour. I left a voice mail telling her I would be there as soon as I could.

I resisted the thought of changing clothes and skipping a shower, but the smoky scent still persisted. I believe I had done my share of sweating throughout the day in the dark, musty powerhouse checking out boilers, generators, and other essentials. So I disrobed in the kitchen right where I stood and headed for the pantry to dump the smelly clothes into the washer.

What the F? The bitch took the washer and the dryer. At least the washbasin still stood in its appointed spot. I cranked open the two valves and dropped the clothes in after putting the drain stopper in position. I opened the cabinet door above me. Lordy be, the big F'ing *C* left the soap behind. She must have been in a rush. I dumped out a generous portion of liquid Tide and sloshed the dirty clothes around, including my favorite jacket. I figured after giving them a good soaking I could drop them off at the cleaners or head over to the Beer-N-Suds on Saturday—maybe before I went furniture shopping or maybe after a visit to the locksmith or maybe after I planted a shoe up my not-so-true love's F'ing fanny.

But my priority right now was Trudy, the girls, and that damn mirror. I hauled my naked ass toward the shower, shuddering at the thought of the linen closet. Gone. Everything. I gathered a bunch of T-shirts and headed back to the shower, finding Head and Shoulders to be as loyal as my beer cans. I was so ecstatic I almost drank some. I dressed in my duplicate blue top and gray bottom office garb and headed out the door at eight twenty. At this time of the day, I had a fifteen-minute nerve-racking ride ahead of me. Trudy's line still dumped me into the dark dungeon we hail as voice mail on my way out of the house, but this time, I merely politely told it what it could do with itself.

As Benny headed down Lake Avenue toward the suburban Lakeview field office, traffic was slowed by the passing of an ambulance and then a fire engine . . . and then several cop cars. Benny shook his head. More delays. He had been on the path to the office for twenty minutes already and still had another mile to crawl through the rush-hour mob. At quarter to five in the morning, there was no such thing as traffic jams or, as far as he was concerned, traffic laws. He usually drove fifty miles per hour nonstop from his home to the office, rarely paying much attention to all the stupid things, such as traffic lights and stop signs. He had to slow down, in case a drunk was still out partying, but otherwise, he drove full steam ahead.

When he finally made the left turn off Lake Avenue onto Corporate Drive, Benny was met with the destination of all the flashing lights earlier passing by on their way responding to the emergency call Trudy had placed.

After sneering at the car parked in his special parking spot, normally waiting for him near the north rear entrance, a stone toss from the doorway at his usual five a.m. arrival. Benny circled back and forth and finally found an empty remote parking spot in the lot off the east end of the building. He grabbed his computer bag and headed back across the packed lot toward the crowd gathered by the fountain outside the three-story building. The clock was closing in on nine ticks of the short hand. Benny figured the building must have been evacuated for some reason. It could not have been a scheduled fire alarm. Those were always announced ahead of time and usually occurred later in the day or early afternoon conveniently at the peak of the busy workday. No, this evacuation was not planned. Those did not include emergency vehicles. Maybe there was a fire.

Benny meandered his way through the small groups of office workers huddled in conversations. Most of them were unconcerned and welcoming of the extra coffee break, at least those who ever had time to take them. Others were inquisitive about why they were pulled out of the building in the first place. He positioned himself at the perimeter of the assembly scattered around the fountain near the front of the building at the center of the paved circle. On his way trailing the hospital crew, but out through the revolving doorway instead of the pull doors, was the big burly cop he had encountered at Murphy's Restaurant on Wednesday. He could not recall the man's name, but he remembered the guy was really big.

The inquisitive crowd's questions were answered when Helen was wheeled out on an ambulance stretcher. She was buckled down with restraint straps around her ankles, thighs, her chest, and head. If she could reach her head with her hands, she probably would have pulled out all her hair—at least the hair still clung to her scalp. Her mind had apparently already been pulled out and left inside the building.

The gauze wrapped around her head was already soaked in blood. There was an apparent laceration from her left shoulder down across her breasts to her right hip. Her pale-blue dress revealed evidence of bleeding from the slash. But there was blood all over her body, and eventually, x-rays would disclose a variety of broken bones from *A* to *Z*, and close examination of her flesh would reveal hundreds of tiny red spots, small pinpricks in her skin allowing immeasurable amounts of blood to transfer from her vessel to another belonging to something else. She had been screaming so wildly that the attendants finally had to gag her at least long enough to give the tranquilizer time enough to, well, make her tranquil.

When the attendants wheeled her out, the crowd had drawn silent. Most of the women gasped and reached for their mouths simultaneously. There were a number of *oohs* and *ohs* and *aahs* throughout the startled crowd. And then, just as quickly, they were at it again. Now all were conjuring up their version of what they believed could possibly have happened to the poor woman. She was raped. She was beaten. She lost her rocker. Now we're getting close.

Following the hospital crew out of the building, but again, through the revolving doorway, the burly cop, Sergeant Denning, bore no expression and no smile. But what would he have to smile about, being a daily escort for the recently deceased or otherwise departed souls? Behind him, once again, waltzed Susan Baker. She was an admirably accomplished woman, but Benny was not really inclined at this juncture to become a close friend or associate. He started to backstep just as Lieutenant Baker lifted her right hand and beckoned him forward with her right forefinger. *What the F?*

Benny pointed with his own right forefinger at his chest, lip-syncing, "Who, me?"

A satirical smile and a nod of her head replied, *Yes, you, Mr. Johnson.* She waved him forward while turning back through the revolving door for a private conversation.

Double what the F. What could she possibly want with me? he thought. "Good morning, Lieutenant Baker," greeted Benny once inside the spacious lobby.

A set of three elevators faced them as she continued walking toward them, again with a nod telling Benny, *Follow me, Mr. Johnson.* "It's a not-so-good, good morning today, Mr. Johnson," she replied, pausing. "We meet again."

"Yes, ma'am," he said. "That was Helen Jones. She works up in our office in Property Claims. What happened?"

"We have a forensics team working on it right now. We are trying to gather a clear picture of the chain of events." She added, "We received a call this morning about an emergency."

"You got a call? Was it from the security people in the building, or maybe was it Helen? She looked beat up. Was she attacked or something?"

"No, the call came from Ms. Trudy Perkins. You know . . . like the pancakes? She seemed to be disturbed when the call came in, but not to the degree in which we found Mrs. Jones."

"Is Trudy okay? Where is she?" he asked. "I didn't see her in the crowd outside," he added.

Baker looked back at Benny as she pressed the button for floor number 3. "She is up in your office lunchroom, a bit shaken, but she should be fine." She gathered in Benny's response. "The medic provided her with a mild sedative approved by the hospital physician. Are you okay, Benny?"

That's a relief, he thought, *maybe I'm not the chief suspect in this calamity.* "I'm fine. It's been a crazy couple of days. I got back from Kentucky at two this morning to find my house mostly empty, and now this."

"Robbed?"

"No, ma'am . . . I mean, Lieutenant," he confirmed, "not exactly."

"Oh, I'm sorry. I hope it's not wife problems," she consoled.

"No, it's not a problem anymore, Lieutenant. She's gone, along with most of the furniture. I'll mail her the memories with a five-pound bag of sugar. They're not very sweet. I guess I saw it coming, just not this quick." Pausing, he turned the conversation back to the present problem. "So what did Trudy have to say? What happened?"

"Apparently, Mrs. Jones arrived at the office earlier than Ms. Perkins, who herself had arrived at about six forty-five," Baker confirmed. "She heard some noise coming from the ladies' room and then again from the men's room."

"Noise? What kind of noise?"

"We eventually determined it must have been Mrs. Jones. But Ms. Perkins thought she also heard someone else."

"Someone else?" he asked.

"Guess who, Benny," she replied.

F

Trudy

I decided I would get to the office a little early on Friday and hopefully beat Helen. She was just so, so crazy enough to get in and then just jump right into the john because she was probably thinking Trudy, as in me, was the one who was way too much on the goofy side of the street. When I thought about it, I would probably react the same way. *Oh, Helen, honey, if you have to go, don't go! Just hold it for an hour or two. It's like, Helen, you might not make your way past the big mirror hanging over the sinks to get safely to the toilet stalls. Whatever you do when you get here, Helen, don't go in there alone, and especially don't go in there when it's dark, before the lights go on in the morning.* How dumb did that sound?

So I got to the office at about quarter to seven, even before Sondra, the whip caster, paraded through the door. But when I got to the third floor and used my security card to get into the office side door, I found all the lights in the office were already lit. Benny hates that. He would rather work in the dark, bending over his desk under his little fluorescent desk lamp like a curmudgeonly old miser counting his shiny pieces of gold alongside his bowl of cold porridge. He told me the dark and the quiet helped him concentrate. They scared the crap out of me, alone in that big old office, with any little creaky noise sounding like some kind of ghost or funhouse spook out of a Dean Koontz novel. *Puh-leeze, give me the bright lights.*

As the office door was swinging closed behind me, I thought I had heard somebody's voice coming from the ladies' room. Something like, "I'm sorry" and "Please no." But I was eager to get to Helen's cube and see what she might be up to this morning, so I ignored it. She didn't mention anything about coming in early today. I hoped she didn't blow a brain fart and was thinking she would try to do something sneaky. She should have known I wasn't fooling around when I told her to stay out of the john. I was so serious, and she promised me she wouldn't.

I swept through the aisle to our cubes, and they were all emptier than a bag of popcorn on a Friday night, not even a trace of an unpopped kernel. Then I figured I must have really heard something in the hallway before I came into the office. After withdrawing the Coleman monster flashlight I'd brought to work this morning from the carryall bag Benny brought me back from Mexico, I did the unthinkable and made tracks for the ladies' john, hoping Helen hadn't been crossing her fingers during our promise exchange.

Even more careful than yesterday afternoon, I approached the door more nervous than Don Knotts on his way into a haunted mansion. I knocked on the door loud enough for someone to hear even through a closed toilet stall door. I thought either nobody was home or Helen was sitting on a crapper silently laughing and shaking her head again, just like yesterday afternoon.

Then I heard the screams. At first, I could not recognize the voice, and then the second time, it sounded like Benny. Even though I had never ever heard him really scream, I could pick out Benny's voice in the dark. But I didn't expect him to be in the office so early after his overnight trip to Kentucky or wherever. Maybe he didn't even get back last night. But it was Benny, and he was yelling at someone. He was yelling really loud. But his voice sounded like it was being amplified, really amplified, like maybe through a speaker or something, and it sounded as though he was in some kind of a metal drum or something because his voice was echoing.

I quote what he said, "How dare you enter my asylum!"

Asylum of all things, I thought immediately. The word reverberated. "Asylum-um-um-um-um-um."

Benny could be weird sometimes, but that was way weird. And loud? How could it possibly be Benny? And now it wasn't coming from the ladies' room. It was bellowing out of the men's john.

"How dare you!" he followed. Again, with the "you-ou-ou-ou-ou-ou" echo in a drum sound.

I had never heard Benny sound so creepy. He was scaring the hell out of me. If he was in there, he must have had some kind of sound system with him, or else, maybe it was some kind of recording. But it was way too real sounding. Now I was in heavy-duty competition with Don Knotts; the damn flashlight was shaking in my hands. The batteries inside the thing would not stop vibrating. I even yelled at my hand to just stop it, but it just ignored me.

That was when I heard Helen. Her scream was so gut-wrenching, I thought she was on a rack and her four limbs were being pulled out of her body by ropes tied to four teams of Clydesdale horses.

"Benny! Beneeeeeeeeee!"

Then the flashlight just jumped out of my hands. By this time, my whole body was trembling more than it would if I'd been trapped in a deep freezer for two or three hours. "Don't go in or alone," Benny had told me. He didn't need to remind me or tell me again. I would not dare touch one foot inside of Benny's asylum, Joe Blow's asylum, or anybody else's asylum, and I damn sure wasn't going to put my feet in that john.

Whatever was happening to Helen and whoever was doing whatever they were doing would surely be double dipping on me. One person violating the sanctity of the asylum's border was more than plenty. God forbid, I was helpless; there was nothing I could do to save Helen. Over and over and over, the screams just came pouring out of the john, the asylum, or whatever was currently on the other side of that door.

At that particular point, Helen was the appointed screamer; in my frightened and heightened state, I was fine and content on just being a regular old scream-ee. Feeling guilty as hell, I wished I had overslept. Perhaps the screams were floating silently away in an empty forest never to be heard by a human soul or any other soul out there for that matter.

"Ben . . . eeeeeeee! Beneeeeeeeeee!"

Teary-eyed, I turned and ran back to the office door. I was no Kate Beckinsale fighting off vampires or werewolves or whatever monster of the day she was currently fighting. When I came upon a terrifying situation, I didn't don a cape or cyclone twirl into a cloud of dust and exit away in a superhero costume. I looked for a big tree, a big bush, or a big man with big balls and big fists to hide behind. I was a woman, a cowardly one at that, and I was damn proud of it. Heroes are made in

Hollywood, not in my bones. They like to shake, rattle, and roll.

It took me three tries to dial nine for an outside line and then another three to hit nine-one-one and call the police, the ghost hunters, or anybody who could translate whatever gibberish was about to fly out of my mouth. The damn flashlight had passed the shakes into my hands and my legs and, quite frankly, my entire body. My stomach was flipping pancakes like they were spinning chunks of pizza dough.

After my frantic plea for help on the hotline, I made fast tracks for the far end exit door close to Benny's cubicle to avoid passing the men's room and the nonstop screaming flooding the hallway. I didn't bother waiting for the elevator; the screams were terrifying. I ran down the stairwell as fast as my Adidas tenny runners would carry me, with wobbly thigh muscles and all. I paced back and forth in the lobby, rubbing my shoulders, my arms, and my legs. I was trying to heat them up, trying to get the flashlight shakes out of them. They wouldn't go away. *Just go away! Dammit! Please!*

Finally, I heard the sirens, so I ran outside, not believing what I had heard from Benny. At least it sounded like Benny. I thought. Maybe. It was really loud.

F

Benny

On our way up the elevator, Lieutenant Baker told me what Trudy had told her as they rode the elevator up to the claims office on the third floor. She was really upset. And, when the elevator door opened, they found Helen was still at it, screaming like crazy and calling my name. Baker escorted Trudy through the office into the lunchroom from the back door rather than the door straight down the hallway past the johns. Trudy wanted no part of that.

So Officer Denning was instructed to investigate the noise with the two subordinate officers who had accompanied them.

Baker stopped at my cubicle to have a quick look-see, but Trudy wouldn't cross the boundary of the aisle and wouldn't even accept a piece of chocolate. Everything was neat and tidy, just the way I had left it.

Trudy said she thought she heard me screaming from the men's john—me, Benny, of all people—something about my asylum. Asylum? She swore it was me, but she swore she didn't think it was me. Really? But before that, she thought she heard somebody, not me, from the women's john. Then she really heard Helen screaming away, but she was in the men's john . . . apparently with me, Benny, of all people.

F

"Lieutenant, how could I possibly be here if I was at home with my head on the kitchen table?" asked Benny.

"Can anyone corroborate your whereabouts this morning at, let's say, seven?" Baker replied with her own question.

"Well, no," Benny confessed. "Certainly not my wife, as she was out humping somebody else."

"Then you cannot verify that you came to the office early, left, and returned, say, an hour or so later?"

"Whoa," Benny cried, "you think I did that to Helen? She's an associate, but more than that, she's a friend. I'm about as violent as a worm in a mud puddle, for crying out loud. I would never hurt her. You think I could scare somebody enough to make 'em nutso?"

"I don't know you well enough, Benny," Baker explained. "Could you?"

"Wait a minute," Benny remembered. "Check Trudy's voice mail. I called her when I woke up this morning, oh, about seven thirty, I think."

"It happened to be seven thirty-four, Mr. Johnson," verified Lieutenant Baker. "I asked Trudy to check for any messages before we sat her down in the lunchroom while she calmed down. Her hands were still shaking. I knew she had nothing to do with what had happened."

"So you knew all along," Benny said dejectedly, "but you had to prod. Were you baiting me or something?"

"I apologize, Benny, but I need to be thorough. I've not seen a case like this one in my experience. There's nothing like it in any criminology text or even a damn science fiction novel." She was puzzled. "I'm going to show you something, but you have to keep it confidential. Can I trust you?"

"Again, Lieutenant," he promised, "I'm as silent and trustworthy as that worm in the mud puddle."

"I almost wish you were a worm, Mr. Johnson," Baker now confessed. "I could use some good old-fashioned bait."

F

Earlier, Sergeant Denning and the other two cops could not coach Helen out of the stall. She would not stop screaming long enough to listen to their words of comfort. And, because of her propensity for scratching and biting, they were unsuccessful in trying to pull her off the stool into which she was standing and try to pin herself down on the floor. So Denning had called for the medics.

When he had first approached the bathrooms, Denning had cautiously entered the ladies' room. It was silent and empty, but he found the long mirror facing the entryway to be shattered, and the basins below it were filled with shards of broken glass.

Upon entering the men's room, the first words out of his mouth were "Holy Mother of Jesus." It appeared the mirror in that room had exploded outward. Both the busted pieces of glass and the fragments of drywall revealed evidence of blood, apparently Helen's. Her face, arms, and dress were covered from the flow out of her fresh wounds.

And *Benny* was not the only word coming out of her mouth. Her speech was broken and distorted, but Denning could make out a couple of words fairly distinctly. One was dark; another was dungeon. Denning also thought she had muttered at least on one occasion something about the evil man Benny in the long black frock—the phantom Benny. But he later admitted that she wasn't speaking with any sensible structure, so he had attempted to deduce through the barrage of mumbles what she was really trying to say.

"Nice work," Baker had told him after jotting down the words he had been able to comprehend, "but leave the detecting part to me, Sergeant."

Baker had also complimented Officer Denning on his observation of the broken mirror in the men's room. At first glance, it did appear to have exploded; at least it definitely appeared it was broken from behind. It was as if something, or perhaps someone, had been thrown through the mirror out into the room across the washbasins, as opposed to the mirror in the ladies' room that appeared as if it had been broken from the reflective side of the mirror. The walls behind both mirrors remained spotless. But the wall opposite the mirror in the men's room revealed evidence of a collision with a large object and was spotted with blood, most likely from Helen Jones.

Baker called for the forensics team once again to verify whether or not Helen was indeed the source. She certainly had lost enough fluid from her body. Some of the blood loss from her skull had apparently been self-inflicted. When Baker had first laid her eyes on the woman, as the medical technicians were raising the bed of the wheeled stretcher after they had strapped her down sufficiently, she had appeared to be . . . stark . . . raving . . . mad.

Denning explained in order to get the crazed woman out of the stall, he had the other two officers reach over the sidewalls from adjacent stalls as they balanced on the respective toilets. The two men each grabbed one of her arms, pulling them away from her hair and lifting her upward as though they were going to mount her on a crucifix. Then Denning wrapped his arms around the woman's thighs, but he had trouble lifting her out of the toilet because her left foot had become jammed in the toilet drain after she had broken her ankle. He could not differentiate her screams of pain from those of her deranged state of mind.

He ended up pinning her against the back wall while a medic squeezed into the stall and managed to land a needle at the bottom of her left triceps. She was overpowering the officers, and they could not keep her still enough for him to accurately and methodically inject the antipsychotic tranquilizer into a vessel in her forearm. The men struggled for a while, but eventually, the drug took effect significantly enough that they were able to pry her and her broken foot out of the crapper and load her onto the gurney. The hair lying in and around the toilet was left for the forensic people to bag as evidence, along with samples of the bloodied mirror shards and droplets pasted to the wall opposite the sink basins.

Not having any proper gags or rags available, Denning stuffed a number of paper hand towels into Helen's mouth, and he wound up pressing his bulky palm over her muffled screams in attempting to shut her up after she had spat out the towels two times. Finally, after she became groggy and settled down, Denning set her neck-based loudspeaker free again. Afterward, although she did fall into relative silence, she began to murmur unintelligibly. That is precisely when the officer started jotting down notes and compiling a list of her rambling utterances. "Benny the phantom." Or perhaps it had been . . . "Benny! The phantom!"

F

Benny

When Lieutenant Baker escorted me into the men's room, she pushed the door open and held it there, waving her left arm in a pseudo practice golf swing. "Step right in, Benny. Gents first."

I had not seen too much in the ladies' room other than the broken mirror. Part of it remained intact, and the big section that had been busted out left a somewhat oval opening similar to a football, but it was fatter. And, of course, it was a whole lot bigger, enough for a person Helen's size to fit through in a prone position. *What the F.*

"Are you sure you want me to go first?" I asked Baker. I meant to imply that I was not the detective, and I was not the one investigating whatever the hell happened this morning. I was just the little ol' claims adjuster sitting on the sideline, minding his own business. But if I could believe that, I'd be fooling myself. Somehow I felt everything going on since, when, yesterday? Somehow it was all about me. What did I do?

"Please, Mr. Johnson," Baker had replied. "Just take a look and tell me what you think. Don't worry. The room is clear."

The first thing I noticed was the mirror facing me was mostly gone, and other than some blood splattering on the wall toward the center where it been trashed, the wall was in perfectly fine shape. It was nothing that a coat of primer and one or two coats of paint wouldn't fix. There was very little debris in the basins underneath the mirror. That seemed a little puzzling. Why would somebody smash the damn thing and then sweep all the scraps away? To wash his hands?

I carefully took a couple of steps on my tiptoes. I always wore my tenny runners to the office. It made the toll on the feet more bearable through all the miles back and forth to the copier, fax, and printer, not to mention the john, lunchroom, stairwell, and lunchtime walks around the neighborhood to just get the heck away from the phone for a few precious minutes. It seemed the blood pressure spiked at least ten points every time I sat down in front of the monitor and glanced at the headset and telephone. *Who the F is next?* I ask myself.

I turned and focused on the wall opposite the mirror. There appeared to be a bloody streak on the wall, kind of diagonal, running down a bit from my left to right. Little trails seeped down along the streak, suggesting there was a whole lot of blood that struck the wall. A sloppy painter with an overloaded enamel brush could not have reproduced a better stroke. "Holy sh—"

"My thoughts precisely, Mr. Johnson," Baker cut me off. "And as you might notice, there appears to be a trail of splattering leading from the wall here"—she pointed—"into the stall where we found Mrs. Jones, in what I would characterize as a somewhat frantic state. And look at the length of this bloodstain," Baker explained, running her left forefinger along the path of the diagonal stain. "It seems to match the length of the cut across Mrs. Jones' body."

"How could she possibly fling herself up onto the side of the wall?" I asked, amazed. "For one thing, she's no athlete, and for another, I doubt if an athlete could even do something like that. There's only about four or maybe five feet from the sinks to the wall. No room for a running start." *And she was bleeding worse than a slaughtered pig,* I thought. "You don't think that—"

"We'll be having x-rays taken," she interrupted again. She was always one step beyond. "I would not be surprised to find a few ribs either badly bruised or broken."

"You mean—" I started to say, but I stopped midsentence. I realized Baker was ready to cut me off at the proverbial pass once again, so I let her ride right on through unobstructed.

"As crazy as it seems," she began, "the evidence suggests Helen Jones was thrown out of the mirror. How she recovered and why she seemed to barricade herself in the toilet stall are questions remaining to be answered. Considering her state of mind, the woman was apparently horrified, like the old saying, 'Scared out of her mind.'" Lieutenant Baker looked me straight in the left eye and focused. "Maybe, just maybe, something or someone was chasing her."

"If somebody huge enough could toss her against the wall," I replied, "they could easily have busted their way past the door on the stall and finished her off with one swat."

"Plus the mirror, Benny." She was moving toward my side of the field again. "Nothing adds up. Nothing makes sense. Behind this mirror is another set of basins and another mirror for the office workers at the back side of the building, not to mention the walls and whatever wooden structures hold them in place, not to mention piping or conduits for wiring, water mains, and whatever. Nothing has been disturbed except this mirror. I doubt if a circus cannon could blow her through both of those walls. What's even stranger is that most of the broken pieces of the mirror have blood on the back side, not on the mirrored surface. This would suggest something bloody, such as Helen Jones struck the back side of the mirror before it hit the wall. And oddly enough, the mirror in the ladies' room appears to have been broken from the front side, as if a large object, such as Mrs. Jones, was hurled toward it. But the mirror here in the men's room is not situated back-to-back with the other broken mirror, and the walls are undamaged."

"It does look like the mirror was broken from the back side," I added. I was trying to avoid any thoughts of the dark image confronting me just two days ago. I didn't want to go there, as I could foresee something mushy hitting the fan and me winding up in a room next to Helen somewhere in the isolation section of an insane asylum.

Baker withdrew her notes. "Mrs. Jones was rambling, but we were able to decipher a few words, although none in the context of what I might call an actual sentence." She looked up as she recited the first word—of course, it was my name.

"I have no clue why Helen would be calling out my name," I defended.

"Me neither, Benny. But she wasn't just calling out your name. She was screaming it in bloody horror. And she obviously saw something. What, we don't know. We hope to speak with her once she recovers from her wounds and the trauma of what she has been through. That is to say if she recovers."

"What else did she say besides Benny? You know I'm not the only Benny in the world. Maybe she was hollering Jack Benny or Benny Goodman." I had to ask, maybe throw this discussion off course. And I was already thinking about what some of those other words might have been. Like maybe a big hooded cloak with some monster inside with laser beam eyeballs?

"Nice try, Mr. Johnson. No, she wasn't laughing or singing. She did say things like, let's see," she said, glancing at the notes again, as if that was necessary. "Ah, phantom?" She put her gaze on me again like she knew what was going through my mind, like she knew every thought. That little word struck hard right on the bull's eye. I tried to swallow the damn walnut shell that suddenly appeared and became lodged in my throat, while at the same time, I was praying my eyeballs weren't poking out of their sockets too far for Baker to notice.

"Dungeon? Dark?" she looked up again. "And, of course, the other voice," she emphasized, putting on the three-quarter press. "Trudy seems to think it was your voice, but at the same time, she cannot believe it was you. Odd, don't you think?"

"Me?" I asked meekly. "I surely couldn't be here when I was at home using the kitchen table for a down-filled pillow. We already established that little tidbit. Plus, I'm fairly sure Trudy knows me well enough to fathom the fact I'm not a maniac—a little crazy, maybe, but not a maniac." *F, I shouldn't have said that crazy part.* And the fathom part was way too close to phantom. *F. She's going to think I'm a crazy phantom.*

"It was loud and clear, so says Trudy." She looked up again. This was becoming monotonous. "In particular, very loud. 'How dare you enter my asylum?' That's what she heard. Loud and clear, screaming loudly in fact. She said it sounded like some kind of sound effects were being used, like an echo chamber or something, a big amplifier."

"Did the officers find anything, any evidence of somebody else being here? like maybe sound equipment or maybe some kind of weapon used to cut her up like that?"

"You are looking at what we have, Mr. Johnson." It seemed as though Baker was crossing the field again to the visitors' section. "But there is something I am curious about, Benny."

Oh, boy, I thought, *she's playing both sides of the field now. Do I punt or run out of the stadium faster than Forrest Gump?* "There is a lot to be curious about, Lieutenant," I suggested. "Nothing makes any sense. I mean, it's like nobody was here except Helen, but she couldn't possibly inflict that kind of torture on herself. And the mirrors, the blood?"

"What I'm curious about, Benny, is why you asked Trudy to stay clear of the johns, as she put it. 'Don't go in there alone,' as she put it. 'Especially when it's dark,' as she put it."

Oh, F, I thought when she dropped that bomb. I sure as hell didn't know Trudy put out so much. My fantasies of Trudy had never been about her putting out information. *Now what the F do I do?*

"How about we take a ride, Benny?" Baker insisted. "Let's get all the answers to these questions off our chests."

Oh, F. Now Baker is looking for me to put out.

F

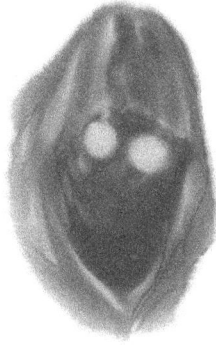

CHAPTER THREE

"You're not going to leave Trudy up here alone, are you?" directed Benny to Lieutenant Baker. He was following Baker out of the men's room to be escorted to the police station for some more apparent and intensive interrogation. He was worried about his present circumstance, but even if he spilled the beans and was on his way to the nuthouse, he wanted to make damn certain Trudy wouldn't be headed to the coroner's office.

Broken mirrors or not, the phantom, ghost, or whatever apparition was behind them just might be able to pull the same trick again through what scant portal remained in them. Benny didn't want to take a sliver of a chance at that happening, and he sure didn't want Trudy to be left alone on the third floor. The monster might be hiding in the office or in a closet or a storage room somewhere. Who knows, maybe even the air-conditioning ductwork, a pencil sharpener, a keyhole, or an ice bucket.

"Certainly not, Mr. Johnson," Baker assured him. "I called in a female officer who is with her in the lunchroom. Actually, we are going to give her a ride home, you know, because of the sedative she has taken and all she's been through. Would you like to see her?"

Benny's first thought was *F, she must think I'm some kind of monster.* And that was exactly what he told Baker.

"I'm surprised you would say such behavior" she replied.

"Well, considering what she told you I was screaming or yelling or up on a stage somewhere chanting about my asylum through some microphone. What am I supposed to think she thinks, Lieutenant?"

Baker responded, "What she told me, Benny, is that she thinks you're a little crazy. You like your fantasies, she says, but you're no maniac. She told me it couldn't possibly have been you in the restroom. Either you two think alike, or she can read your mind."

"Wow," Benny said. He himself was surprised. "She said that?" A minute ago, he thought Baker could read his mind.

"You two have something going on, Benny? I know they didn't put you on the rack yesterday, but even I can tell you've got a good shelf life."

Benny couldn't believe he was blushing. Not unlike him, Susan Baker also enjoyed looking, but not touching. "Of course not, Lieutenant. I'm married, or at least semimarried. I don't mess around. Trudy's a lot younger than me anyway. We kind of fool around with each other in the office, teasing and stuff, but we don't, you know . . . fool around. And I have never made any kind of unsolicited advance. If anybody tried that, she would plant her knee down below the belt. Besides, fraternizing with a fellow employee in any manner other than professional behavior in the office setting is against the BestEver Insurance employee conduct policy."

Besides that, every time Trudy stepped near his electrical field, the proximity where their body odors and heat intermingled, he froze, and the nerves in his stomach vibrated harder and faster than the rattle on a diamondback. It somehow scared him and made him feel like a thirteen-year-old kid.

"I can understand how such behavior could affect company matters," she replied somewhat sarcastically. "Come with me, please. Let's check in with Trudy to see how she is coming along. It's been an hour or so since she was sedated, so I'm sure she has calmed down."

Benny followed. He was as nervous as a tween, as if to ask a red-haired, blue-eyed freckled girl for his first slow dance. He was unable to understand what was going on inside him. Right now, he would rather face the mirror again. *I'm too old for this,* he thought.

F

Benny followed Baker into the lunchroom. They walked past the sink and wall cabinets facing the room situated to their left and one of three refrigerators set against the wall to their right. The rear door on that wall at the far end of the room led to the back of the office. Benny felt an urge to hide in one of the ice cube bins that he so often filled at five thirty in the morning only to find them and the trays empty when he strayed back later in the morning to recharge his juice cup with ice, water, and a splash of orange juice. He eventually had resorted to bringing in his own daily cooler of ice and juice and kept it at his desk. He had pondered pissing in the half-gallon container to garner revenge over the missing juice he had usually stored in a reefer, but he quickly dismissed the reality of doing so. The fantasy of seeing the masked scumbag throwing up in the middle of the room was an ample reward. Payback would eventually visit the rude, ill-mannered F-head.

Lifting his eyes from the light-gray and blue spiral-patterned tile floor, Benny found Trudy being consoled at a table at the middle of the room by none other than Sondra, the opportunist. The hem of the manager's dark-blue skirt climbed well above the midsection of her thighs. Her matching jacket was draped over the chair she had pulled in front of Trudy, and she leaned forward, cupping Trudy's hands with her own. *How cute,* Benny thought. Her white blouse was unbuttoned down to the Grand Canyon gap of her cleavage. How could the woman possibly sit with a stick jammed up her ass? And why would she be so eager to hand over a slice of her peep show to Trudy?

Trudy was having no part of it, peering over Sondra's right shoulder and shaking her head. Trudy saw right through the ball-busting manager whose chief concern was getting everybody's ass back to their desk.

Lieutenant Baker cut off Benny before he could greet Trudy with his "Are you okay?" icebreaker. "Ms. Smith," she began, "Mr. Johnson and I would like a few moments with Ms. Perkins." She broke into a slim sarcastic smile for Sondra.

Sondra turned back, and Trudy took the opportunity to withdraw from the woman's grip.

"In private, please?" Baker added emphatically.

Sondra's jaw dropped open, as though her authority was being undermined.

"Now?" followed the further undermining. "I'm sure you have plenty to do in your office. I'm certain Ms. Perkins isn't the only person needing a bit of consoling. Would you care for something to help settle you down, or maybe you'd like to speak with a professional? I'm certain this could be arranged. Maybe even counseling for the office staff?"

Sondra stood without a word, pulling her skirt down, at least as far as it could stretch toward her knees. She swooped up her jacket and stick-walked her way out of the breakroom through the back door. "I'll be fine," she said as she tripped on her way through the doorway, closing it behind her.

F

Trudy

I almost busted my gut when I saw my boss pull an I Love Lucy on her way back into the office. The sedative I was given to help calm me down had kicked in, and good old Trudy had a really good buzz going long before the pretty police lady came back into the lunchroom with Benny trailing her. She was really nice and wasn't real pushy with the third degree. I didn't do anything, so I really had nothing to hide anyway. Somebody or something else was doing all the doing. I took the moist tissue in my right hand and again wiped away the mascara my tears had washed down along my cheeks. Benny looked really concerned and worried, but I couldn't hold back anymore. As soon as the door shut behind Sondra, I let out a whoop or a cackle as sharp and as loud as you could expect coming out of Phyllis Diller.

Benny started to giggle a little, and I caught myself and slapped my hand over my mouth. I was not sure if it was Lieutenant Shaker or Laker or whatever her name was, but I was pleasantly surprised when a big lovely smile lifted her cheeks. I meant, like she only met the bitch about an hour ago or whatever.

The police lady greeted me with "A real jewel of a boss you have there, Trudy." She did get it!

"I'm sorry, Officer Raker," I replied. "It must be the pill I took."

"It's Lieutenant Baker, sweetie," she corrected, and she got down to business and the smile disappeared.

She had Benny sit at the left side of the table; she took my seat and moved me across from Benny at the head of the table. As she moved her head back and forth, she fired away. I stretched my arms out to reach the folded hands Benny was pointing at me from the elbows he had rested at the edge of the table. The first thing she did was to have me tell my story. Well, it wasn't really a story; it was just me telling what I could remember exactly as closely as I could recall. Like I really gave a fat F. I was flying. I was thinking I remembered some details I thought I already forgot or something like that. *Wow, whatever the crap was they gave me, it was really good shit. Now what am I thinking about? Or am I talking? Whatever! Wow again!* Benny's hands closed around mine, and suddenly, a keg full of words flooded out of my big trap.

F

"So," confirmed Lieutenant Baker, "let me get this straight, Trudy. The first voice you heard was the strange one you could not identify. Then you went into the office to look for Mrs. Jones. Then you heard what sounded like it might have been Benny, but his voice was somehow different and sounded like it was in some kind of a drum or was amplified."

"Yes, Ms. Maker," reconfirmed Trudy. "Then all I heard was the screams coming from Trudy, from the men's room."

"It's Mrs., sweetie, Mrs. Baker," replied Baker. "And it was Helen Jones in the bathroom, not you. But don't worry—you know, the pill? You would be amused to hear how Benny got me to remember your name."

"Oh no, not the pancake routine," pleaded Trudy. "None other." confirmed the Lt.

Trudy pulled her hands free and playfully slapped at Benny. "Bad Benny." The sedative had taken its toll on Trudy, and soon she would begin to tire and lose attention. But nevertheless, another Phyllis Diller cackle erupted. She lowered her head, shaking it, laughing, and repeating, as her long black hair flung about side to side. "Like the pancakes, like the pancakes, like the pancakes."

Baker grabbed her attention once again. "Now I'm not certain how important this might be, Trudy, but do you remember where the first two voices were coming from, the unfamiliar one and the one like Benny's?"

"Oh, my dirty, wrinkled laundry, Lieutenant Baker. I was wrong," exclaimed Trudy. "The first voice wasn't a scream. It was Helen, and she was saying something like 'Please no' or something like that. And then I heard the weird voice coming from the same place, the ladies' room. And then it started getting louder and louder and that's when it started sounding like Benny."

"So it started getting louder," Baker repeated, "and it was changing into Benny's voice, and then it moved into the men's room . . . along with Helen?" She shifted her gaze to Benny. "What do you think, Mr. Johnson?"

"Me?" he replied, pointing to his chest with his right forefinger.

"None other," she responded flatly.

"It's too insane, Lieutenant," Benny began. "But it could explain Helen being in both rooms. And it could explain the other voice or voices also being in both rooms. And the mirrors . . . but that's too crazy."

"What it does explain is what seems to be apparent. Something went into one mirror, and something came out the other." Now Baker was shaking her head. "What it doesn't explain is what went on between the mirrors, wherever the hell that might be."

Benny's forefinger now pointed toward Trudy. "That was fast." Her head was resting on her forearms, and her eyelids were closed. "Which brings us back to the beginning," he added. "It looks like I'm the only one around who came out of the johns in one piece."

"I've been meaning to get to that, Benny," Baker began. "You seemed to be intent on keeping the office girls out of those rooms. What happened to Ms. Murphy and Mrs. Jones does not appear to be a mere coincidence. You saw something. Trudy seems to believe you quite strongly. Ms. Murphy saw something, and she heard something, quite possibly the same thing as Mrs. Jones, who was fortunate enough to make it out alive, at least for the time being. Unfortunately, her prognosis does not give us much optimism. Now maybe you can share with me what exactly it was that you saw, Benny."

Benny folded his hands and began twirling his thumbs around each other. He took a deep breath. "I didn't really want to say too much to Trudy about what I saw Wednesday morning." He hesitated. "By the way, did Trudy see anything, I mean, like, did she see Helen?"

"No, she was really shaken by all the commotion going on in the bathroom. We avoided taking her past the johns in the hallway when we came up to investigate the scene." Baker now folded her hands and twirled her own thumbs. "Please continue."

"It was dark and really early. I came in before the mad rush so I could catch up from the previous day. I like working in the dark, with just the light from the desk fluorescent lamp. It helps me concentrate. Sometimes

I put a jazz CD in the computer and play it nice and quiet." He stopped the thumb twirling and leaned back in his chair. "I usually hit the john for my morning constitutional about quarter after or five thirty. The automatic sensor is set to start about six thirty or seven o'clock, so I usually feel my way back to the stalls and—"

"You can spare me those details, Benny," she interrupted. "So, after the constitutional, what then?"

"Well, I actually never made it that far, at least not at first," he explained. "As I was walking by the mirror, I saw something. I thought it looked like kind of a shadow. But then something happened. There were these haunting eyes. And they were bright, intense, but they were dark, like a deep red or scarlet. Whatever, or whoever, it was had a hood of a cloak covering its head, and the eyes were set deep into the hood, concealing the head, the face. The hood kind of circled around the sides of its face and then downward. The light from the eyes must have illuminated the cloak. The cloak covered its body down to the edge of the sink. I couldn't see anything else. Boy, I sure could use a drink, and I don't mean water."

"Maybe later, Benny. What next?"

"The eyes got brighter, like some kind of really bright flashlight, or maybe even a laser. Then these beams started moving toward me, not like a flashlight—you know, that immediately sends a beam jetting out. They moved slowly, deliberately. And as my reflection passed out of the mirror, they must have stopped or turned off or something. I thought they were going to hit me in the rear end."

"So, when your reflection dropped out of the mirror, this thing you describe, it also went away. Is that true?" she asked.

"I wasn't sticking around to find out, Lieutenant," he said. "I skedaddled for the stall and, you know, my constitution."

"Can't say as I blame you, Benny," she agreed. "When you gotta go, you gotta go. And what happened next?"

"I wasn't about to invite it back. After a couple of minutes, I crawled my way out and avoided looking back at the mirror, just in case it was still lurking there in the mirror. I was a little spooked at the time."

Baker twirled her thumbs again, thinking. Then she said, "In hindsight, probably a good decision, Benny, considering all that has happened."

"So when do they deliver the straitjacket?" he asked.

"I'm beginning to think I might need one," she replied. "Nothing about this whole affair makes any sense. Nothing fits together with any logic."

"As long as we are in the asylum together, as this phantom had suggested, think about this, Lieutenant."

"Go ahead, Benny," Baker invited. "You insurance adjusters must write a lot of reports to document your files. How would you write this one?"

"Well," he attempted, "Ms. Murphy was found out in the dining area outside the ladies' room. But Helen—she never made it out of the johns, that is to say the two of them. Does that seem to tell you something?"

Baker sat for a moment, back to thumb-twirling. "I think I see where you're headed. Whatever this thing or this being seems to have come out of the mirrors at Murphy's Restaurant. The mirrors there were never damaged. That would explain how she was found hanging from the chandelier. But Helen, Mrs. Jones, was found in the men's room. Trudy had heard her voice coming from the ladies' room."

"I think Helen was pulled in by our phantom, into this asylum, this dungeon place Helen was rambling on about when you found her," Benny surmised. "And when he was done with her, he, or it, tossed her back out. But with Ms. Murphy, he just moseyed out and back in once he was done doing his thing."

"That would explain the broken mirrors. And it would explain the hook Ms. Murphy was hanging from, some kind of instrument it, or he, uses to torture his victims."

"Or hang them from it when he's done so he can admire his work," Benny added. "Who knows what other kind of instruments this guy or thing has up his sleeve . . . or I should say up his cloak? What I don't understand is why I was spared. Was it taunting me? Why did it come out for Ms. Murphy and Helen, but it let me go? And the mirrors up here are destroyed now. If they are some kind of portal, I wonder if it, too, was destroyed.

"We still have another portal, Benny," she reminded him. She glanced to her right and found Trudy stirring, awake from her short nap. "Are you okay, Ms. Perkins?" she asked.

"As good as sprain in the pain," Trudy replied, still feeling the effects of the sedative. "Did I miss anything, Officer Taker?"

"Oh, not too much, sweetie. Benny and I were just planning a date." She glanced at Benny with a stern glare.

"A date? Benny's taking you on a date?" Trudy said, surprised. "Not without me!"

At that point, Baker reached for her intercom and called in Officer Denning and arranged for an escort for Ms. Perkins and her vehicle back home where she could get herself to bed and sleep off the effects of the sedative. She could be interviewed again if it became necessary. Fast asleep by the time they reached her apartment, Officer Denning carried her up the stairs to her second-floor unit, led by the female officer. Trudy's keys were placed on the kitchen counter, and the door was locked and closed securely behind them on their way out.

Meanwhile, Lieutenant Baker and Benny continued their conference.

F

Benny

When Trudy came out of her trance and Lieutenant Baker gave me that look, I tried telling myself I had no clue what she was thinking. But shortly after the big burly cop was able to pry Trudy's address out of her, find the keys for her apartment and car, and then join the lady cop leaving the lunchroom with Trudy in tow, the look returned. And it wasn't the kind Dean Martin had once crooned about in one of his popular tunes. There was no romance in this look.

I had replied, "I'm not sure what you're thinking, Lieutenant, but if you're thinking what I think you might be thinking, I think you might want to think again."

Baker confided she was thinking the corridors, or portal, through which this phantom being had passed back and forth at Murphy's Restaurant might still be, well, open. Maybe the thing, whatever it was, had not attacked me because maybe I posed a threat somehow. I asked her how the phantom could be afraid of me when I was the one almost crapping in my pants.

She replied some things like, maybe, snakes or other animals, such as a coyote, are just as afraid of us as we are of them. They only attack because they become threatened or cornered and do so in self-defense. I had replied sure enough, but snakes have venom that can poison, coyotes have big sharp incisors that can rip one's flesh to bits, and this monster had laser beams powerful enough to burn the holes through your head. I had to keep a positive attitude about the whole affair. We were both falling off the edge of sanity.

Baker then replied she carried a Smith & Wesson Model 625, six-round and double-action revolver chambered for the .45 ACP cartridges, and a lot more hardware at her disposal. But I did not hold much confidence about the effectiveness of bullets passing through a ghost, if a spirit was what we were dealing with. A poltergeist maybe? But even those were supposed to be invisible, although they apparently would interact with the physical world, like maybe hurling boulders around or collapsing walls or quite possibly shoving a hook up the back of somebody's skull and hanging them from a chandelier.

Baker insisted she also had access to night vision devices (NVDs) able to detect the presence of the phantom and might possibly filter some of the infrared light. Might? Some? My confidence was not heightened when she suggested mirrors could be used to reflect laser beams back to their source, if lasers were indeed what the deep red beams had been. I doubt the goggles would have helped Frances F'ing Murphy.

Lieutenant Baker provided me with another one of her "business" cards and asked me to get in touch with her at the end of my day. At that point, it felt as though I had already approached the cusp at the end of my world. So I returned to my cube and approached the telephone and its fifty-five-gallon drum full of voice mails. The johns had been boarded shut, and signs were posted directing those with an urge to use the services on the second floor. A handful of faithful soldiers, more diligent than the US Postal Service carriers, and not too shaken by the ordeal, had returned to duty and staffed their stations to keep BestEver Insurance steady and ready for action.

I pushed the lingering vision of Helen's beaten and battered body at the back of my mind and struggled through the messages left by Reset, Warren, and All American Insurance. Frank confirmed he had located surplus electrical switchgear that could be purchased at a reasonable cost, tested and calibrated, and then installed to replace the smoke-damaged gear. The smoke-damaged equipment could then be repaired and put back in place of the destroyed equipment while remediation of the fire and smoke damage was continuing.

Warren was confident he and Reset had pinned down the area of the electrical fault's origin and immediate arcing damage to related switchgear and cabling. Betty Bleau provided an update on the installation of rental generators and miles of temporary cable being acquired to power the twenty substations throughout the glass plant and get its wheels for glass floating rolling once again. At a quarter million dollars a day, the income along with the corresponding dollars for rental and property damage losses were piling up. If only LNN could see us now, as Betty and I both prepared to pen checks for a quarter million dollars.

F

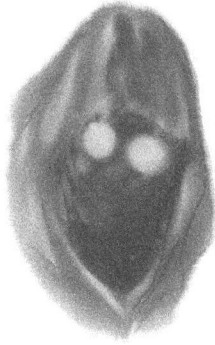

CHAPTER FOUR

Helen Jones drifted in a sea of dreams, none of them sweet, as she lay in a hospital bed. An array of IV drips plugged her veins into bags filled with an assortment of drugs to keep her sedated, to deaden the pain, and to keep her alive. Her head had been shaved to stitch her broken cranium back together and attend to the lacerations and near scalping of her skull. Over and over in high-speed film, the story played again and again. It began on Friday at 5:45 a.m. when she had kissed her husband for the final time that morning and possibly for the final time in her life. Hank sat at her bedside, carefully brushing at her left hand so as not to disturb its IV and wondering if her mind had leaked out of her head with a portion of her brain. With her eyes wide open, her nightmare, a cinemascope of horror in a three-dimensional film, rolled on—once again.

"Gee, honey," Hank had begun, "you're up with the crows this morning. You trying to compete with Benny or something?"

"They have been beating us up with new losses because of the latest catastrophe," Helen replied as she buttered their morning toast. "I'm losing count. Cat 15, 25, who knows anymore?"

"So Sondra, the fire-breathing skeleton, lines you up for a good pep talk to work extra hard during the latest storm catastrophe down south and get all the extra workload done as if nothing happened," Hank confirmed. "Same damn story every time, and they never give you guys any credit."

"Or money," Helen added. "Just the overtime the bitch has to pay us because of the law. And nothing extra for the Saturday or Sunday shifts either. I'll have my toast on the way to the office, huns. I want to get the computer cracking by six. And there's something I want to do."

"Okay, buns. Gimme a smooch."

And that was it. Their lips flexed a one-second smack, and Helen was out the door. She was a woman on a mission she would regret—no more huns and buns.

F

Helen exited the elevator and followed the dimly lit corridor past the two bathrooms on her left and used her security card to unlock the latch on the side door to the office. She pushed open the door with her left hand, carrying her handbag in the other. She looked back at the johns behind her and giggled, muttering sarcastically under her breath. "Don't go in alone. Whew," she added, twirling her right forefinger and keycard in the air.

She flipped the four fluorescent light fixture switches on the wall at her left and paused for a second while they lit up the entire office. When she didn't hear Benny's voice barking from the right end of the office, she released the door resting on her rear end and walked in toward the aisle at the center of the big room. She figured Benny was either working at home, or maybe he was on the road somewhere. She wondered why Benny would tell Trudy not to go in the johns until the lights came on in the morning. As Lieutenant Baker would later declare, "When you gotta go, you gotta go." And she had to go.

But first things first. She headed for her desk and turned on her computer before stopping to power up the fax machine and high-volume printer. As usual, when she checked the paper trays, two out of three were empty, and the third had barely a quarter of a tank full. "Thanks, everybody," she mumbled. She ripped open nine reams of paper and filled all the trays, then she headed back to her desk to log on to the BestEver electronic claim system and to grab her coffee cup. She checked her email and found five voice mails had popped up overnight. *They never stop,* she thought. She would click on the messages and listen to them after brewing a batch of coffee. She noticed one of them was from Mrs. Hartman, her third claim in eighteen months for the mysterious disappearance of jewelry.

Helen just shook her head and paced her way through the back door into the lunchroom, turned on the lights, dropped her lunch bag into a near refrigerator, and headed for the coffee maker. She stepped to the sink, ran the hot water until it wasn't too cold, filled the pot, stepped back to the coffee maker, and dumped its contents into the top reservoir and flipped the switch to the on position. She moved her cup in position to be filled and started tapping her fingers on the counter.

"What the hell!" she thought out loud. Looking at the clock on the back wall, it read thirteen minutes past six o'clock. Might as well get the morning do-do out of the way. *Alone my ass.* Having a second thought, Helen replaced her cup with the coffeepot and headed back to check those voice mails and return any email messages while the coffee brewed.

While moved out of the way for other coffee traffic, Helen's cup remained waiting to be filled and drained down her throat, waving later in the morning as Trudy was being escorted out of the lunchroom.

F

I am the dark of night. I am the preyer of the prey. I am the voice of your nightmares, and I beseech your pain. My kingdom is your fear, and it breathes in the caverns of my dark bloody soul. I am the shiver in your cold, cold bones. Come to me. Come breathe fear with me. Enter my asylum and deposit your breath, your fear, and the shredded remnants of your mind. Enter the chamber of your most ghastly horror and excite me with your screams. Come to me, and let me claim your sweet, sweet soul. I am the dark of night. I am the preyer of the prey. Your soul is my claim. What, prey tell, is this? Alas . . . I have a visitor. Perhaps a soul to claim.

F

Knock, knock. "Who's there?" asked Helen on her way to check emails. She pushed the door open to enter the darkness of the ladies' room from the dimly lit hallway. She reached to her left, but there was no switch to turn on the overhead lighting, only a motion sensor activating the lights when someone entered the room. It would not be enabled for at least another half hour or so near seven o'clock. She thought about propping the door open but had nothing handy to wedge under the door, so she let it swing closed behind her. It was an irregular occasion that she had been to the office this early, given her normal morning routine at home prepping kids for school and breakfast for huns.

"Jeez," she said out loud, "how does Benny do this? It's really fricking dark in here." She planted her left hand on the wall at her side and felt her way back to the stalls lined up at the opposite end of the room. Across from her, staring at Helen's face through the mirror was a quietly dark entity. The cloak covering its head revealed no reflection. Helen glanced at the mirror and saw nothing but the thickness of a black cloud. "Jeez!"

Beneath the cloak, the phantom entity smiled and grinned; its apparent razor-sharp teeth were gleaming under its dark lips. The smile vacated the monster as Helen's image disappeared across the room beyond the mirror.

She felt her way to the middle stall, lifted her dress, dropped her panties, and bent down for her morning do-do.

Click, click, click came a tapping sound from outside the stall. As she was flexing her lower abdomen to let loose, she suddenly lifted her head. "What's that?" she called out to the dark. "Who's there?"

From the phantom, a smile returned in anticipation of what would follow. The entity slipped below the mirror and waited in silence. A taste of fear to initiate the process, nurture the inquisition in the mortal's mind. Let it grow.

While the phantom waited, Helen's abdomen returned to its appointed task. She felt around for the toilet paper roll and wrapped a few turns around her right hand, ready to be folded with care for its journey down below. A minute had passed since the tapping. Helen grunted, releasing last night's pasta dinner.

Click, click, click.

"Stop that," Helen said as she wiped at her butt. She then folded the paper, but she was unable to see what she had in her hand. She uttered, "Shit."

Click, click, click. The phantom reached up at the back surface of the mirror with one of its tools, one of its toys—a very sharp device, a dagger with a slightly curled tip. *Heighten her curiosity, heighten her pulse, heighten her senses.*

"If that's you, Trudy, stop it right now," Helen demanded. "You're starting to scare me."

Ah, thought the phantom. *Fear has taken its second nibble.* The phantom lifted its ogre head above the counter of the sink and peered to its right, but the mortal was not yet in view.

Helen reached back, gritting her teeth while flushing the toilet. She could swear she heard something coming from the area of the sink basins.

Click, click, click came the tapping at the back side of the mirror as the power flush and fill mechanism quickly came to its silent resting point. "Helen" followed a whisper Helen recognized. She exited the stall and turned to her right, extending both arms outward until they met the wall. "You were warned not to enter this room . . . alone . . . in the dark."

It's definitely Trudy, thought Helen. She crept forward; her fingertips were feeling their way in the dark gloom along the cold wall to meet her sneaky friend. Suddenly, Helen's left shoulder collided into her.

"Oops, I'm sorry," whispered Helen. "What the heck are you trying to do, turn the crapper into a haunted house?" She waited, but there was no response.

Out in the corridor, the office door began to swing closed behind Trudy, but she was entering the office, not leaving it. Helen felt for Trudy's shoulders. They were too tall, and as she felt her way down her arms, she found them to be too big, too long. Trudy was covered in some kind of coat. *No, the cloth is too silky smooth to be a cotton fabric. It must be some kind of shawl.*

"Trudy," she whispered again, "answer me. If you're trying to freak me out, you did a good job. Now stop it."

Helen's breath grew deeper and hesitant as she reached for Trudy's forearms and hands, finding they too were covered. Sweat sprinkled her forehead. Her fingers told her it must be some kind of cloak. *My god,* Helen thought, *no one could have fingers this long.* "Please, no—"

Before Helen could utter another word, one of the hands swiftly darted upward and across her mouth. The nail on its right thumb, or digit, poked into her left ear, puncturing her eardrum. Simultaneously, the nail on the forefinger, digit, likewise burst through her other eardrum. As the announcement from the phantom tore its way through the blood gushing from her ears, the clock on her world was suddenly suspended, and Helen was lifted high in the air over its head.

"How dare you enter my asylum?" it screamed.

Helen was then hurled through the mirror into a timeless black cloud of silence. In shock, drifting in and out of consciousness, Helen could neither see nor hear anything. When, finally, she woke, Helen found she was strapped down on a stone slab in a cool eerily still room lit faintly by oil-filled lanterns held in fixtures on tall dark walls. The flickering flames cast ogre-dancing shadows across the room.

F

The phantom had screamed as the woman's body was thrown toward the mirror, smashing the portal. As she crashed through and into the long, steep hall to its dungeon below, its words reverberated back and forth between the steep walls of the canyon until the portal slammed shut. Meanwhile, the dark figure stepped through the door of the ladies' room into the hallway, pausing shortly and breathing in the sweet yet faraway familiar scent of another mortal woman. *There will be another time.* The evil being dashed for the men's room, with its cloak sailing behind as it vanished through the door and into . . . and far beyond the mirror above the sink basins.

The dark being continued to sail and fly through the universe and down the twisting, turning passages of the cavern toward its asylum, deeper and deeper, ages below. It reached the mortal before she had dropped down into its large chamber of toys. Helen was carried to a large waist-high stone slab in the middle of the room. After strapping Helen down, the phantom released the beasts to guard against any attempt at escape. It disappeared through a double set of doors to another chamber. The spiritual being floated its way horizontally above a long coffin, with its contents adorned with black silk lining and matching pillows. The lid closed over its entity as it, too, came to rest. Exhausted from the passage into the world of light, it slept while time here in the phantom's ancient world stood still around it.

As dark clouds lifted from Helen's eyes, she became aware of her surroundings but heard only a low humming sound from her punctured and deadened ears. The ceiling must have been twelve feet high. The torched lanterns were spread about fifteen feet apart along both side walls. "One, two, three, four, five," she counted. It was about ninety to a hundred feet long. Something was hidden in the shadows beneath them. There were also torches on both of the end walls—one on each side of tall wooden and iron strap–reinforced double doors. She attempted to grab her aching head but discovered iron strap bindings attached to chains that prevented her arms and her legs from much movement.

Lifting her head as high as she could, Helen saw two of the four animals sneering at her. They were not snarling or growling, but their sharp canines were bared and their lips curled open. There was no activity from any of their tongues. She was forbidden fruit. Their fur was long, wavy, greasy, and dark brown. They resembled dogs, but Helen had never seen any that looked so ferocious, and they were huge. Each stood four foot tall from forefeet to shoulder. Their necks must have been a foot thick, and their muzzles were ten inches wide. Helen figured she was in a nightmare, a hallucination. She was a victim of a very narrow-minded hoax, or maybe Benny knew what he was talking about when he gave warning to Trudy. But this was just plain and simply impossible. Was it some kind of a dirty trick? Where was this place she had been taken to and chained down on a slab?

She cried out, "Benny!" The beasts started to growl, but she could barely hear them. There stood two tall beasts at each end of the room. They were held to the end walls by chains long enough to defend the doorways but not long enough to reach the mortal pinned down at the center of the room on the slab, although, at the moment, they were all positioned as close to her as they could get.

Helen lay on the slab for what she felt was hours. Her head was still dizzy from something she could not recall. She also felt pain on the left side of her back, again, from something she could not recall. She slept, she woke, and she slept again. Each time she woke, her dread intensified. Finally, she thought she heard the dogs or beasts barking or growling, but she could not discern clearly what was happening. The chains attached to the beasts retracted, and they were pulled back toward the walls. Then Helen did hear something and felt something. It was the loud slam of a very heavy door. It boomed and echoed across the hall.

When the dark entity moved, it did not walk. It floated across the stone floor, with its cloak dragging behind. If there were arms contained within the cloak, they were folded across what would be comparable to a mortal being's chest. The being floated smoothly around Helen from her left. Her eyes followed as it drifted around her, past her feet at the end of the slab, and back toward her at her right side. The cloak covered what would be its head, with its neck apparently bent forward. Behind Helen once again, the spirit moved closer and hovered directly above her head. It bent over.

Helen stared into the opening of the cloak, seeing nothing but the blackness of her darkest night. It was exactly what she would see, what she would not see, in a deep cavern absent of every morsel of light. The spirit moved closer, with its cloak surrounding her head.

"Who . . . who are you?" she asked, trembling.

The reply from the phantom spirit surrounded her. It came from every direction; it came from none at all. "I am the dark of the night." Its voice was low and deep—one she had never heard before and one she never wanted to hear again.

"Wha . . . what are you?"

Its deep, dark voice replied once again. This time, it was echoing all around her. "I am the preyer of the prey. I am the voice of your nightmares, and I beseech your pain."

As the word *pain* echoed all around her, Helen's eyes were suddenly exposed to a glimpse of the universe. She felt as though she was floating in free space, weightless. Suddenly, a dimly lit star faraway began to race toward her and became brighter as it approached, although it barely increased in size. Closer and closer, it raced. Then, just as suddenly, it decelerated to a screeching halt only inches away from her face. She closed her eyes to fight off the bright light. Outside her eyelids, the light went out. She opened them to find Benny staring her down.

But this was no ordinary Benny. His eyebrows were thick and black. His grin was maniacal; his eyes and the cackling laughter erupting from his mouth convinced her that Benny had become a fiendish madman. Benny screamed, "How dare you enter my asylum? Leave this place and leave your soul behind! It is mine to claim!"

Helen had no problem hearing Benny. His message was loud and clear. She took a deep breath to scream, but nothing came out of her lungs. Suddenly, the universe returned but was eerily quiet, although Benny's throat continued to vibrate under its blanket of calm. She could read his lips.

"Your soul is mine to claim!" The stars in the universe abruptly vanished, and then Helen found herself again down in the deep dark cavern. But now she had Benny's company—mad Benny's company, the man under the cloak. He circled around her, from left to right then from right to left, and then she found her head twirling around with him. Helen slammed her eyelids closed, but Benny would not go away.

He moved in closer and screamed silently, "Your soul is mine to claim! Your soul! Your soul! Your soul!"

Benny's devilish grin revealed teeth filed to razor sharp cones. Red saliva was oozing out of both sides of his mouth. His eyes now glowed red.

Her lips released her scream, but the dark cave was silent. She screamed, "Benny!"

Then, just as Benny had appeared from a distant star, he was drawn back, still screaming his claim to her soul.

The universe and the cavern disappeared, and Helen found herself once again peering into the empty dark cloak. The deep, dark voice returned, "I trust your appetite for fear has been whet. We have much to do."

"Who are you?" Helen asked again, trembling. "What are you doing?"

The dark cloak of nothing replied, "I am the dark of night, and I am claiming your soul. Come, see, and . . . play with my toys."

Then Benny reappeared in the cloak. His hair had turned red, and strands of it seemed to crawl around his skull, as though they were thick writhing worms eager to bleed on a hook. "COME SEE MY TOYS!"

"BENNY!" Helen's silent shriek called for help; then she collapsed and fell asleep once again. When she woke, the universe and cavern were gone, and she found herself back in the dungeon. The restraints on her legs and arms had been released. A mug had been placed near her left hand. *Water,* she thought. She rolled to her left and pushed her torso to a sitting position, reaching back to grab the water. Helen found the mug filled to the brim with white slithering maggots. She screamed silently once again—her voice an empty forest. She dropped the wooden maggot mug and rolled off the slab. Her left wrist cracked from the sudden fall; it had broken.

F

When Helen woke, she was on her stomach lying on the floor. Her head was facing the doorway from which the phantom had earlier paid a visit. The chains on the dog beasts had again been released, and two of them lay with their huge heads propped up and their black eyes bearing down on her. She attempted to press herself up to a sitting position, but the pain in her left wrist reclaimed her consciousness, and she fell flat on her face. She rolled over on her back from her right side and cradled her left arm. Eventually, she was able to get upright by manipulating her right arm beneath her and rolling over to her right side, twisting and pushing with her right arm. She leaned back against the cold stone slab, closing her eyes for several moments while catching her breath and preparing to survey her surroundings.

When her eyelids opened, she began to study the shadows. Against the side wall stood what appeared to be a cage, and it was made of what appeared to be thick wooden slats rather than iron bars. A door with a metal latch stood open. On the inner surface of the door, attached to the slats, were a series of sharply beveled spikes forming the shape of a human torso. If she had been able to discern what made up the back wall of the cage, she would have found matching spikes. A chain was hung at the top center of the cage. Attached to the chain was a round metal collar built in two sections with a hinge and a locking pin joining the two pieces together. The collar stood open. On the bottom of the cage were two devices intended for inserting and strapping one's feet firmly against the floor of the cage. There were also devices halfway up the cage for strapping wrists against each side wall.

My god, thought Helen. *Is this Benny's sick idea of a joke? He must have drugged me. How did he drug me? It must have been LSD or something—a hallucinogen. And where the hell am I?*

Just then, the phantom floated across the floor from her right, stopped, and turned. It moved in toward her, as though propelled on silent invisible wheels by a silent invisible motor. It spoke in its deep, dark voice within Helen's mind. "This is my asylum. This is the chamber of your most ghastly horror. Come excite me with your screams, and let me claim your sweet, sweet soul."

The huge hand that had punctured Helen's eardrums returned for an encore, wrapping its long digits in a circle around the top of her head, down around her face, and the back of her neck. The phantom dragged her to the cage, stuffing her inside and playfully lifting and swinging her back and forth until both feet caught the restraints on the floor. The straps slammed shut, and the shoes closed in from the front and rear, curling her toes up and backward, breaking her right big toe. Helen screamed above the cry of pain already gripping her at her wrist and neck. Her hallucination was delivered with three-dimensional pain.

Helen resisted but could not move her feet, and it hand-held her head in a vise grip. Her head was pulled upward, and Helen felt the collar wrap around her neck and lock tight, a half size too snug. She struggled to breathe and to vent her silent screams through a trumpet blast of her lungs. Her head was pulled upward, stretching even farther as the chain from the collar retracted. Both arms were simultaneously pulled outward into the restraints locking around them.

The phantom stepped, slid toward her, and leaned into the cage, and it again moved the cloak close toward her face. The universe was back glaring at Helen. But this time, millions of planets were exploding, and she could feel fragments colliding against her face. Benny's face stood in the midst of the bombardments, with his fiendish scowl in a maniacal roar of laughter. Suddenly, the display went blank, and the phantom slammed the door. Now the spikes became illuminated in a dull, bluish-black color. They began to grow closer. Helen attempted to move her body backward but was then poked by spikes on each side of her buttocks.

"Aaahhh!" she screamed. This time, her scream became audible. *My god, what's happening?* thought Helen.

Progress, thought the phantom in reply.

Then the door opened and quickly slammed shut again and again and again and again. Each time the door swung closed, the spikes inched closer to Helen's body, and each time Helen thrust herself backward, she was pricked from behind in her rear, her legs, her back, and her shoulders. If Helen had enough sense to maintain her faculties, she could have counted the door swings to ward off the growing terror. *Bang! Bang! Bang!* Had the time clock been moving, it would have recorded one hour and three minutes, and Helen's counter would have registered 370 raps at her door and another eight more for good measure.

The tears from her eyes under the screams of pain and horror left them bloodshot and swollen. Helen was drenching wet from the sweat streaming down her body. Dreary from fatigue and pain, she lost consciousness once again. When later Helen woke, she found herself the subject of another one of the toys this Benny replica had in store for her.

Emerging from yet another deep sleep but frightened half to death, Helen was nearly delirious and not yet fully conscious. Her attention was immediately drawn to the pain in her foot from her broken toe, the cracked wrist, and the swelling and bruises around her wrists, ankles, and neck, not to mention the punctures at her back, thighs, breasts, and shoulders. Her eyes were closed but open to the universe and the raving lunatic, Benny's head, with his worm-infested red hair, his freakish eyes, honed-down teeth, and cackling laugh. This couldn't possibly be the real Benny. Fearing near death and delirious, Helen's mind began to wander far away—far from the universe.

F

Helen

He had tried to warn me—at least he had tried through Trudy. He probably knew I would have just laughed it off as some kind of hoax or joke. Benny must have seen the monster or whatever it was beneath its black cloak. Apparently, it hadn't been able to capture Benny, or maybe he was just lucky. It was taunting me, wanting me to think it was Benny doing this to me, wherever the hell it had taken me, if not hell itself. If I had any hope of getting out of here, which I sincerely doubt, it would be Benny to do it. He might be my only salvation. I didn't believe in ghosts or spirits, but here I was, living the real deal.

I had been a relatively good person all my life; I got a good man and good kids. I didn't do anything really bad to go to hell. I was not what you call a very religious person. I got my kids on the way, so they could make up their own minds when the time would come for them to decide for themselves. But for now, I had them on the Catholic path, so at least they could be exposed to other people's faith. Myself, I guess I was not smart enough to figure out the whole religious thing, you know, the creation of humans and life and all that stuff.

Well, God was just sitting around one day and decided he would pop a bunch of people on earth, which was after he created the universe, of course, and figured out a place to put them all. And I would guess after that, he— or maybe she—needed to make a heaven and a hell, kind of like a vacation resort compared to prison. You had to have a place to put all those people after they die, right? And before all this stuff happened, where did God come from? Faith, I would guess. Either you would have it or you don't. But then, tell me who the hell the devil was in this great big scheme. Where did he come from?

If there was one out there, I mean the God of us, why would he have this thing, whatever it was, bring me here to hell? I was sure there were lot better candidates standing in line to get front-row seats. And the damn thing wanted my soul? Ha! You had to have one to give one. Maybe I just never got myself enough faith. That was what it was. Faith. I was not sure how far faith would get me now, but knowing this monster, this phantom had a lot more in store for me sure had me thinking. I should have collected myself a healthier dose of faith a long time ago.

I must be thinking this way because I knew I was about to die. And it had me scared. No, I was terrified. I didn't know if I could fight anymore. I might as well give up and die. Then let us see what happens. I wondered if heaven had a shower and underarm deodorant. I found it hard to believe Benny had anything to do with what was happening to me. But it was troubling that I could hear him, and I could see him. What the hell was that all about?

If you can hear me, or better yet, if you can get inside my mind, get me out of this mess, Benny. Please, Benny. The phantom.

F

"Benny," whispered Helen as she struggled to open her eyelids. She did not feel any of the restraints on her neck, wrists, or ankles, but they had left their marks behind. Helen was lying on her back; her bed was not stone, and it was not as cool as the stone slab. She went to raise her arms to rub the pain out of her wrists, but they struck the lid of the wooden coffin before she could cross them over her breasts.

Then Helen felt another sensation competing with the pain, and it, too, was all over her body. And this sensation did feel cool against her sweaty, smelly skin. At first, she thought it might be perspiration, but something seemed to be moving around in her hair. Shocked at the realization she was trapped in some kind of a wooden box, Helen started to scream again. Her lungs and vocal cords had recovered their functionality; the coffin flooded with her deadened shrieks. As she was wailing, something dropped out of a small hole in the lid of the coffin across her mouth. She quickly spat the young brown short-tailed snake away. It slithered from her chest, around her neck, and up on top of her head with the others gathered in her hair. Her hands fell at her sides and landed on a bed of the snakes gliding back and forth along the bed of the coffin. Then another snake dropped onto her face.

Helen could not see; she could only feel the cool, slimy snakes crawling all over her body. The coffin was filling with the short-tailed snakes enveloping her entire body. Her legs were already drowning in them. Fearing she might swallow one of them, her screams were muffled through the grinding of her teeth. Again, Helen tried to lift her arms over her chest to rip the snakes out of her hair. She struggled to press them behind her in the tight compartment, but she could not even reach her ears. Her fingers were struggling, wrestling to wipe the reptiles from her face and head. Another dropped—and another and another.

Her eyes closed; the universe reappeared. It was filled with snakes whose eyes were illuminated. They wiggled and crawled and slid in toward her. She struggled to close her eyes even tighter, tighter, but more and more snakes appeared. Helen began to shake and squirm, slamming the back of her clenched fists and her knees at the lid of the coffin. The pain was radiating up through her left arm and down to her right foot.

Suddenly, the lid of her containment burst open and dropped to the floor from the coffin resting on the stone slab at the middle of the dungeon. Helen reached up to grasp the sides of the box; her arms were covered with creepy crawling snakes. She struggled and finally brought herself to a sitting position and rolled to her right, tipping the box over and falling out of the coffin. She bounced off the slab this time, with her right wrist breaking her fall, and it, too, breaking before the coffin landed on top of her. She tossed it aside and wriggled around on the floor, grabbing at the snakes on her hair and around her neck. She sat up again, fighting off the snakes and screaming for help. "BENNY! BENNY! BENNY! THE PHANTOM!"

Helen rolled over on her side and pushed herself up to her knees, screaming in pain, screaming in horror, screaming at the snakes, ripping them out of her hair, and ripping her hair out of her head. She began to run away, but the chains restricting the dog beasts had again been released. She ran head-on into one of them, and it leaped up on her shoulders, knocking her down at her back. The salivating beast stood over her on all fours, roaring at her, with its milky spit pouring out of its mouth onto her face. Helen continued to rip at her hair, roaring back in fright and desperation. She was oblivious to the clutch of the devil dog.

Then suddenly, something grabbed her hair from behind and dragged her back toward the slab. She was unable to fight off the pull, but she vainly slapped at her body, wriggling and kicking her legs. Then Helen was lifted above the phantom and slammed facedown back into the coffin beside the slab, with her arms over her head, breaking her nose. Immediately, the lid crashed down in place behind her, and again, she was locked in the silent tomb. She wailed and wept as she felt more snakes dropping down onto the back of her head and neck; the coffin was once again filling to the brim. The universe, the snakes, and the maniacal Benny all returned to the silk screen inside the surface of her eyelids.

Losing the will and strength to struggle any longer, Helen's mind momentarily left her body and drifted into space, mingling with Benny and the snakes in a timeless eternity. It would return to Helen for a brief but final encounter in the rationale of her sanity. This could not be happening. It was all in her mind. *What kind of mind would do this to me?*

F

When Helen woke some timeless hours later, she was again lying on the stone floor. One of the beasts stood over her head and glared at her. This time, a long black tongue reached out of its muzzle and licked its lips. The blood all over her head and throughout her hair had dried in a honeycomb of curls. Her mouth was half open, and her eyes stared right on through the beast, unaware of its presence. She lay there with her tongue resting at the left corner of her dry and bloody lips. She had thrown in the towel, raised the white flag, and surrendered her sword. Helen's mind blended with the remnants of a pine tree cut down, sawed to pieces, sent through a wood chipper, marinated in a digester, and beaten to a pulp.

Helen offered no resistance when, once again, she was dragged across the stone floor around the slab and tossed headfirst into a tall wooden cylinder. Her arms trailed behind her, void of any motor functions and any mobility. They dropped down as far as gravity would allow in the tight enclosure. At the bottom of the cylinder was a rim upon which her shoulders had collided, imparting a slight fracture of her left collarbone. Her tongue meekly drooped out of the center of her mouth, her head was suspended in the open cavity below the wooden rim, and her limp lower body and legs wedged in the cylinder.

Barely conscious, Helen's hypnotic gaze captured nothing below her head. The universe and Benny were apparently in hiding, waiting for the perfect opportunity to reappear. She heard nothing, especially not the small spiders marching in through a small hole at the bottom of the drum in which she was trapped. Teensy-weensy spiders were climbing up the wall.

The ordinary house spiders began collecting at the bottom of the drum and migrating up the wall, reaching Helen's shoulders. She didn't feel them until they started creeping back down her neck toward the clumpy patches of hair on her head. Then the spiders began to explore her face, causing an itch Helen could not scratch. Suddenly, the drum illuminated, and Helen was exposed to a close-up view of them. They were already four layers deep, and their numbers were rapidly increasing. The light flashed on and off. Five layers deep and counting. The light extinguished again and illuminated only seconds later. The small spiders had collected on the entire inner perimeter of the drum and were three layers deep, moving in closer to her face, which was already completely covered.

She closed her eyes and began screaming again; her dry throat was raw from her cries. Two of the spiders entered her mouth, and she spat them out. She closed her eyes, and again, her howls of horror were muffled through her tight lips. The universe was restored, and crazy Benny with his worm-infested red skull was joined by millions of spiders. Soon, Helen's head was swarmed over by thousands of the little crispy, crawling brown creatures restricting the flow of air through her nostrils. They had crept their way over the dress that had dropped down over her rump and forged paths back down her legs to her panties. Soon enough, her entire body was covered with the harmless, innocent, little arthropods, and they migrated up the inner wall and out into the dungeon, taking with them teensy-weensy bits and pieces of Helen's mind.

Her eyes wedged shut; the universe was spinning out of control. The Benny thing with the slithering wormy scalp was silently laughing, whirling, and twirling in the opposite direction of the rotating solar system. Terrified, Helen's curled lips were being crushed by the teeth above and below them in a vain attempt to hold the breath desperately needing to exhaust itself into the maze of spiders. Her lungs were dying to swallow another breath of the sweet, life-sustaining elixir of oxygen, but it had evacuated from her upside-down drum. No longer able to fight the involuntary movement of her chest about to pass out from the lack of air, Helen's mouth flew open, blew a path of hot air through the suffocating mass of creatures, and sucked in a deep breath of the invasive insects. Following a short blast of air, the spiders filled Helen's mouth and flooded her throat, causing her stomach to launch into convulsions. Just as she lost consciousness, the all-too-familiar hands locked around her ankles.

Whipped out of the wooden drum, Helen was tossed across the dungeon hall, colliding halfway up a wall adjacent to another toy used in pulling limbs from torsos. Her curled back crashed first, breaking another rib. Her head followed; the wall imparted yet another concussion to the brain containing a vast vacuum of emptiness. The force of the impact pinned her against the wall for a second split in one, two, three parts separated by infinitesimal periods in time. Helen slid down the wall, landing face-first, rolling over and gagging, spitting out the contaminants lodged in her throat while grappling at her scalp, and pulling and tearing out more bloody hair, as she attempted to swat away the spider nest. She began to dry-heave, expelling the remnants of the cinnamon toast she had hastily consumed on her drive to the office. The slurry of half-digested raisin bread was quickly swarmed over by hundreds of spiders.

Helen rolled over several times, working her way back to the stone slab and squashing hundreds of spiders along the way. She slapped at her face and somehow managed to stand, painfully wobbling while bent over. Her gut was expelling more bread and more spiders. She tried to free them from her back and to sweep them away from her breasts, thighs, and legs while they continued to feed. Having moved beyond coughing and vomiting, Helen again began to scream. She screamed the only word left in her starved memory bank, "BENNY!"

She ran back and forth between the wall and the slab, bouncing off both of them in rapid succession, until finally she collapsed between them. The ever-amused phantom slid out of a corner of the dungeon and stood elevated over her motionless body. Its empty hood was slowly shaking back and forth, as though frustrated by the pathetic excuse of this mortal being.

A cloud of milky gray smoke drifted out from the hood and down over her body, encapsulating it from head to toe. The being below was broken. It was time to collect its ransom, the mortal's soul. A stream of the smoke floated into her nose through her body, probing and searching. Hovering over her, the cloud waited. Nothing. The cloak stood silently; the hood was still pointing down at the seemingly lifeless, stagnant creature. A second swath of the liquid smoke five feet in length aligned in a small stream and split apart as it entered both nostrils. For a period in the outer world of perhaps twenty minutes, the smoke hovered, but again, nothing happened.

The mortal woman was void of spirit, void of faith. She was void of any resemblance of a soul. Or so it seemed. Perhaps it was not welcome, not dark enough.

Evacuating from the motionless body, the smoke reversed its course and streamed back into the cloak. The long fingers of the hands materialized and grabbed Helen around her neck and right thigh, hurling her toward the doors from which she had entered its domain. The doors flung open as she sailed above the salivating beasts across the hall through the open doorway back into the long spiraling corridor.

"How dare you enter my asylum!" it screamed. Within seconds, Helen's body met the back side of the mirror in the men's room, crashing through and landing against the far wall, bouncing to the floor. Lying and bleeding on the floor, Helen screamed for her savior . . . again and again and again. Blindly, she lifted her beaten body off the floor and trudged her way toward the toilet stalls, still screaming and tearing more hair from her bloody skull. The image of the dark universe would not go away, spinning and turning. She collided with the corner of the first stall side panel and ricocheted backward against the opposite wall, collided again, and coincidentally and dizzily, bounced her way into Benny's center stall. She tried to climb the wall separating her from sanity and the starry universe, the deep dark and wonderful universe.

Her tongue hung loosely from the left side of her mouth, rambling whispers between her screams for her savior. "Bennnyyy! Bennnyyy!"

Helen stepped on the front end of the commode and reached up and outward, but her clawing fingernails could grasp nothing on the pale white wall, although she did leave behind scratches and bloody lines. She turned to the left side of her dark universe; her head was spinning from the twisting skyscape and twinkling stars on the backside of her eyelids. In doing so, her left foot slipped off the china toilet bowl's edge and dropped down, lodging in the drain and dislodging the foot from her ankle bones. While turning in tune with the universe, she also broke several bones in her foot. Her screams continued, but they were indistinguishable from that of pain or the loss of sanity. Helen's mind had become a part of the universe, from which it would never return. It had found its heaven, or perhaps its eternal hell.

After the team of police and emergency medical technicians had arrived and managed to sedate her, Helen finally collapsed and stopped tearing at her hair, her face, and her eyes in vain attempts to escape from the dark universe. But she continued to mumble garbled messages about her distant memories of the dungeon, the asylum, the phantom, and her savior, Benny.

Now just hours from entering the restroom, lying in the hospital bed with her huns Hank at her side while clenching her limp right hand, Helen's eyes opened momentarily and captured the forlorn look on his face, with tears at each of his cheeks. And with a final deep breath, she exhaled her last whispered words before a very deep sleep took her away. "Benny, you saved my soul."

The clock chimed at 7:00 p.m. as the universe once again appeared on Helen's eyelids, and she floated in space . . . smiling . . . free as a bird. Once again, as she had known it to be, Helen was at peace with the universe. It was wonderful, beautiful.

I am the dark of night. I am the preyer of the prey.

F

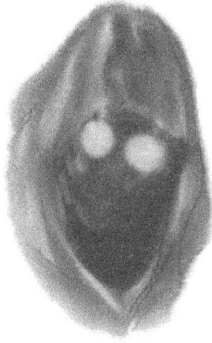

CHAPTER FIVE

With the office excitement now subdued and after getting back in touch with the experts and All American Insurance, Benny spent two more hours in compiling electronic notes and a file memo to be distributed to the underwriter, branch manager, and other concerned parties, such as his boss and the field engineer who services the glass float plant. Now Benny picked up the phone again nearly exhausted. Another typical day spent at BestEver Insurance. It was five minutes before five o'clock—ivory tower time.

"Harry," he responded. "It's me Benny. Glad I caught you before the chimes called you home."

"I was just looking over your notes and printing the file memo," Harry replied. "It's too late to get a manual check out tonight. We don't need a big boy signature for that much, but he'll want to know what's coming before it happens. Good job on your file rationale for the advance. We'll schedule a meeting out at the plant with All American once things settle down."

"They want us to get them a fund transfer, Har. Betty is going to get the routing info for us, so we should have it in the morning. Too bad they don't have their corporate office in Honolulu. I'd volunteer to hand-deliver a shopping bag full of cash."

Harry then replied, concerned, "I have seniority on that one. You had a really hectic time out there today, I hear. It's all over the building up here. How are you doing? Hanging in there?"

Hanging, thought Benny. It brought him straight back to square one. "It's like getting a one-two punch in the face, Har. First, it's Mrs. Murphy, uh, I mean Ms. Murphy, and then *bam*, this crazy thing with Helen flipping out in the john, or should I say johns. I sure hope this isn't one of those bad luck strings happening in threes."

"We didn't hear much detail about what took place, so I'll spare you for now." After a short silence, he continued. "But as long as we're talking about threes," Harry came back, "I put a couple of losses on your roster. Both are Claim office transfers. One involves a Dowtherm hot oil boiler in California starting to escalate. It might not hit a hundred grand, but it's too technical for Phyllis out there in Sacramento. The other is something Property Claims screwed up. They should have notified us a month ago, and now the claim contact is screaming. You'll need to jump on this in the morning and calm her down. It's a graphic printing press loss."

"Super! I really love those kinds of losses—you know, the ones you need to put a towel over the earpiece? I'll make sure I put on my bull's-eye outfit."

"It's right in your backyard, so you can talk to the property rep in the morning. I put some notes in your new file, and you can catch up with their file notes and see what's been taking place. They just never recognized B&M was involved and called the contact last night to let them know BestEver was going to deny coverage and have them notify the B&M carrier, which is us, of course. The client is a little bit pissed off. Oh, and just to warn you . . . you're the fourth file handler on this one."

"Great," Benny added. "I double love these kinds of losses. Don't tell me Helen or Trudy was involved. They're too smart for that kind of screwup. They would have been over here asking me questions a long time ago."

"Roger, started in the Cincinnati office and eventually made it up to Lake Erie via Pittsburgh," Harry agreed. "You have those two trained really good. You even have Trudy calling me. This went to one of the newer Claim guys. You'll have to work on him. Meanwhile, go home and catch up on some sleep. Don't work all weekend."

"I'll check on those two new ones before I get out of here, but I also have one more call lined up with Detective Baker. I guess she has a theory about what's been going on here and wants to talk to me about it. Why, I'm not sure." *Huh,* Benny thought, *Trudy calling Harry?*

It was not exactly a lie coming out of Benny's mouth before his afterthought. He knew why Baker wanted to talk to him about her theory; he just didn't know what exactly she had in store for him. And Harry had no clue about what exactly Trudy had in store for Benny.

"Okay, good luck," he replied. "And hang in there, Benny. Good night." *Click,* and Harry was gone. The last remark left Benny thinking, *Thanks, but I'd rather not.*

After another two hours of reading files and printing notes and compiling his own electronic notes, Benny left a voice mail for the contact on the out-of-control file, assuring he would sort it out just like Val Kilmer did with *The Ghost and the Darkness*. But Benny would leave the long-barreled rifle behind. He then powered down his computer and picked up the phone again. A glance at the clock on the monitor before it blacked out told Benny it was creeping up on 7:00 p.m. After a swallow of ice water laced with a couple shots of orange juice and a deep breath, he dialed Baker's cell phone number while belching as loudly as possible to see if he could get an echo in the silent, empty room. As her phone rang, he thought, *F, now what?*

F

"Baker here," she replied, lightly pressing the cell phone to her left ear. The caller ID told her it was Benny Johnson.

"It's Benny from BestEver Insurance, Lieutenant. Hope I'm not too late. As you might imagine, it's been a really crazy day around here."

"I see you are still at the office. I just happened to have your card in hand when you rang," she replied. "I'd like to meet with you tonight, if at all possible. You must be tired, but this is really important. Have you had anything to eat?"

"I had some cheese crackers a while ago, but to be honest, I could probably handle a couple of beers. You know where Rita's Pub is, on Lake just a few blocks west of Corporate Drive? They have really good wings there."

Baker, in her unmarked squad car, was just approaching the stop light at Corporate Drive. She had rung his number a few minutes ago, but it went directly to voice mail. So she had guessed he was still pounding away at his office desk and thought she would pay him a visit. "I'll be there in a flash," she replied. "Want me to order?" She continued through the streetlight toward the bar.

"Busch Light," Benny answered. "Cheap but good enough for me. I'll be there before it gets warm."

"I meant order something to eat like wings?" she said.

"Come on, Detective," Benny joked, "you need something to pave the way first. See you in ten."

Benny disconnected before Baker could answer and packed his computer in its bag, looked back at his desk with a sigh of relief, and shut off the fluorescent lamp. As he headed for the stairwell, Benny licked his lips, imagining the taste of his first beer.

Ten minutes later, Benny passed through the back door of Rita's from the rear parking lot; and as he passed into the lounge area, he saw Baker wave from a booth at his right. His beer stood in front of her on the table, unlocked and loaded. "Thanks, Lieutenant," he acknowledged. He lifted the bottle in a short, swift toast on its way to his lips and took a double swallow. "Yummy!"

"You seem to have a reputation here," greeted Baker. "Rita has placed your 'regular' on order. I like mine hot too." She sipped at a glass of semi-cheap Chablis. "This place might not be Murphy's, but it's nice and homey. And it provides a bit of privacy too. I see they have a small band coming in two hours or so. We need to get our business taken care of before it gets too crazy."

She decided to wait to spring the news she had learned right after her call with Benny. The precinct had left her a voice mail informing her that Mrs. Helen Jones had expired at precisely 7:00 p.m. She hesitated to pass the sad news along to Benny, at least until sometime after she had divulged her plans and discussed them with him, as he was to play an integral role. Breaking the news now might influence his decision.

There were about twenty to thirty happy-hour customers celebrating Friday night in the dimly lit bar. Baker was lucky enough to grab the last available booth at the back end of the bar, away from the front right corner area where the jazz trio would be setting up their gear.

"It gets really packed in here on Friday nights," Benny agreed. "I'm not sure what I can do for you, Lieutenant. I've told you all I know, at least all of what I think I know. The thing in the mirror . . . I just can't explain it. I have no clue what it was I saw. It was really dark, and the hood covered whatever was inside the cloak."

"For some reason, Benny," she began, "you seem to be an integral part, a piece to this maddening chain of events. Somehow this thing, this entity, seems to be trying to get at you but only indirectly through your acquaintances, people you know. Maybe somehow it senses it cannot get to you, cannot harm you like it did the others. God knows where it came from or where and if it might have stricken someone in some other distant place. But it's with us, and the thing is here right now, stalking, hunting its victims. We need to do something to stop it."

"I have a bad feeling about what you're thinking and an even badder feeling about what you have up your sleeves," Benny suggested.

With her jacket off, Baker leaned forward, crossing her exposed lean but muscular arms covered with short light-blue sleeves on the table, giving Benny a boxing foe stare down. "Number 1, Benny, *badder* is not a word. And number 2, there is nothing up these short sleeves but biceps, triceps, and a couple of shoulders. If there is anything badder, it's what comes next from this thing, this monster. Do you really believe this thing is just going to stop, retire, and go home to its nice little asylum in the sky?"

Baker leaned back on her seat as the blond waitress set a platter of hot wings between them.

"Hi, Sally," greeted Benny. "I'll have another please. Ms. Baker, uh, I mean Mrs. Baker?"

"Why, Benny?" replied Sally with a sneaky grin. "Ma'am, care for another Chablis?"

"We're business associates, Sally," offered Baker. "Right, Mr. Johnson?" She stared him down again. "And yes, I will have another. Thank you."

Sally winked at Baker mischievously, picked up their empties, and headed back to the bar. "My, oh my, Benny," Baker said as Sally retreated, "you do have your fans."

"Sally likes to, you know, kid around, and I'm not sure I could describe you and me as associates, business or not," Benny began. "But willing or not, ready or not, here I come, Lieutenant. You're the boss. Now show me some shoulders, biceps and triceps, and let me know what kind of firepower you got up there in those short sleeves."

Still smiling while staring down at Benny, Sally returned with another round, and then Baker shared stories with Benny about their careers and family life, likes and dislikes, while the two of them marbled their fingers in a mixture of Louisiana hot sauce, Parmesan cheese, and spices. Benny was famished, and while stuffing his face silently, his eyeballs grew with envy and admiration and then, when Baker revealed her plan, they grew wide open with incredulity. The woman was off her rocker, crazy. She had cracked her nuts wide open.

F

"You want me to do what?" asked Benny, still in disbelief. He wiped his lips, his cheeks, and his fingers with the Wet-Nap provided as a side dish to the hot wings. He took another swig of this, his third beer.

"You might want to slow down on those beers," suggested Baker.

She switched to ice water after the second go-round with Chablis. "Awesome wings," she added. "The ol' man would love this place."

"They go good with Browns games, unless you got a pot of frijoles going for burritos." Benny took another swig of beer. "So you are suggesting we just nonchalantly walk into Murphy's and then dive right on through the mirror in one of the johns," he continued. "Your parents' lineage has a long history of insanity, right? Did you learn that from one of those fake-ass research companies who finally stumbled on something actually true? Or does your whole family happen to reside in the local crazy hut?"

"Some of us might belong there, including you and me, if anyone caught wind of our conversations on the subject. What would you suggest, Mr. Johnson," Baker countered, "we just wait for this monster to pop out of another mirror somewhere, like at your house?"

"I'm not sure if my F'ing ol' lady left any mirrors behind when she and her tongue-wielding bed bunny cleaned the place out," he replied. "And he or it or whatever didn't attack me like it did the two women."

"Your F'ing ol' lady? Oh, I get it. But precisely," she concluded, "it didn't attack you, but it did attack people you know. And it attacked women you know—people who somehow are connected to you at work. Women who you know are connected to you in some fashion at work.

This has something to do with you and with women, as though it is trying to get at you from your association with other people, women in particular so far."

"For all I know, it could be my ol' lady, or my ex ol' lady, I should say," he began. "But she spends all her time in front of mirrors, not behind them. Maybe she joined some kind of cult or something. Hell, I don't know."

"Think about work, Benny," she led him. "I think this thing, this entity or whatever, already has another target in line. You get where I'm coming from?"

"Oh, sh—" he thought out loud, alarmed. "Trudy. We have to warn Trudy. She could be next. It might have sensed her out in the hallway while it was beating up on Helen or maybe even saw her through the ladies' room mirror. God, I hope she doesn't have any mirrors in her apartment."

"Really, Benny? A woman without a mirror? And an attractive woman at that. Do you have her home number or a cell?" asked Baker. "I remember her home address, but I must not have jotted down her cell number in my notes. Denning would have it, but he's off duty as I am, at least officially until Monday morning."

"All I have is her office number," he answered nervously. "We never really contacted each other outside the office, besides maybe a lunch with her and Helen on a payday Friday or maybe a retirement thing at a bar, you know, something like that."

"This monster didn't wait too long before claiming its second victim," Baker surmised, "and I doubt if it is going to wait much longer for the next one."

"Then let's get over there before something happens. We have to make sure she's not alone," Benny added, now clearly distraught.

"Dammit," uttered Baker. "I should never have left her alone. Dammit. Things just didn't seem to piece together. We were thinking we were dealing with someone, something tangible, real, not some damn spirit." She reached for her wallet and credit card while waving at Sally and then grabbing for her jacket.

Benny plopped a twenty and two ten-dollar bills from his wallet on the table, shouting, "Sally, this should be plenty! We gotta run!"

My, they're in a rush to get under the blankets, thought Sally. Her eyes followed the happy, horny couple making a mad dash for the rear door. And as disappointment surrounded her lips, Sally thought, *And I thought I had first dibs. I knew his marriage wouldn't last. I could tell she was a cheater. He might as well be one too. I wonder what Mrs. Baker has up her sleeve tonight.* Sally smiled then wiped the table clean in preparation for the next rendezvous.

F

Earlier, as Benny had been picking up the phone to ring Baker, Trudy had been filling her second tall glass of Bordeaux.

She had not yet changed or even removed the clothing she had worn Friday morning. After Officer Denning dropped her off on her couch at her apartment and, as a precaution, investigated the premises for any signs of peculiarity, he bid her goodbye. Trudy then found her way to the bedroom, sleeping solidly for four hours.

She had dreamed of what she thought was a prince, a man dressed in clothing Robin Hood might be wearing, minus the pointed, feathered cap on his head. She saw she was behind the man, and looking down, she found she was dressed in a long silky breast-revealing deep dark-blue gown, her second favorite color. Trudy saw the brave man engaged in a deadly sword fight with a villain dressed in all black, with a cloak covering his head. Robin of Lakeview had plunged his sword into the villain's stomach, but the evil man did not fall. He just laughed hideously, dropped his sword, and then vanished in a smoky mist. Robin turned away, back toward her, in disbelief. His familiar face was briefly revealed, but then it was blurred from view by the mist floating between her and her Robin. The man spoke. It was Benny's voice, calling, "Trudy, where are you?"

Frightened out of her deep sleep, Trudy woke, and although aghast at the lingering image of the villain, her body felt refreshed. "Holy F, Benny," she whispered, "I never knew you had it in you." She had not remembered him calling for her.

Glancing at her bedside clock, she saw it was closing in on 6:30 p.m. Food could wait; she headed for the chilled bottle of wine in the refrigerator and turned on her TV to the local evening news. Trudy was reminded of the horrible ordeal once the headline story brought her back to the hallway and Helen's screams. The woman's condition was poor, and the news anchor would keep everyone out there in TV land informed up to the minute. "You can put your faith in us," he promised. "We are always up to the minute."

You're up to my ass, she thought.

Reclining on her sofa, she propped her head on a couple of fluffy pillows, holding the wine in her left hand. Her middle right finger told the anchor how much she cared about his up-to-the-minute news. All she cared about at this minute was Helen. She pulled herself off the sofa to refill her glass as the sports commentator began his nightly summary.

Spring training was wrapping up and the Tribe would be opening up against a Central Division foe in another ten days during the first week of April. Optimism was always high on opening day. For most teams, it was usually the following day when reality struck home.

Trudy rolled off the sofa, noticing for the first time that she had never removed her Adidas tenny runners, although the laces had been loosened. She did not bother removing the black cotton socks she wore. She kicked the rubber shoes off toward the TV as she made a U-turn toward the small kitchen, which was tucked in a cutout at the head of the beige-carpeted hallway on her left leading straightaway to the bath and to the bedrooms on either side. She filled the glass, took a sip, and walked down the hallway to the full-length mirror hanging on the outer panel of the bathroom door, which was closed. Trudy stood in front of the mirror, staring at her image. She wore full-length black slacks; a neckline and short-sleeve purple silk blouse over which she had a knitted long-sleeve black sweater. Her earlier tears had washed away most of her dark mascara, but a hint of blue eye shadow remained. She felt rested from her long nap, but despair was creeping in and was beginning to wear her down.

"Oh, Helen," she whispered softly, "if only I had gotten to the office earlier and stopped you. If only I had—"

Trudy was suddenly interrupted by silence of maddening amplitude. The TV had shut off. A shrill chill slid through her chest down to her stomach as she turned back. The power to the apartment had not been interrupted. Dim light still poked its way out of the kitchen into the dining and living room area, with one room separated by a four-foot-tall bridge wall topped with polished oak trim, which ran parallel behind the sofa to the wall opposite the kitchen.

"Damn TV," she uttered under her breath. She started stepping slowly back up the hallway but made only two strides when the kitchen light extinguished. The minute hand on the wall clock in the kitchen was straining to strike the numeral XII.

It was barely 7:00 p.m., not completely dark outside, but with the drapes closed in the living room, the apartment was dark.

"Damn power," she whispered, hoping it was nothing but a power outage. *Please not tonight,* she thought.

Her thought was followed by another whisper, "Trudy." But it did not flow from Trudy's lips. It came from behind her. And the voice was familiar. Again, there was whisper, but it was long and drawn out, almost as though he had been singing her name, soft as though in prayer or chanting mode.

"Truuuu-dyyyyy."

"No, it can't be," she said, alarmed. It was louder than a whisper this time.

Trudy stood steadfast in her tracks and began to tremble.

"Truuuu-dyyyyy," it sang again.

"Benny," she pleaded, "please do not do this to me. You're scaring me. Please."

This time, he yelled at her, "TRUDY!"

Startled, Trudy jumped forward a half step, shivering, frightened to turn around. It sounded as though Benny was standing right behind her. He could probably touch her. The thought had her ready to jump out of her skin. Had he been hiding in the extra bedroom? Why would he be playing such a mean and nasty trick, especially after what she had been through earlier that morning and after what had happened to poor Helen?

"Benny! Stop it!" she screamed. Trudy turned to face him and give Benny a piece of her mind.

But, unfortunately, for Trudy, it was her entire mind that was in desire—her entire mind and her soul. There was unexpectedly something else.

Facing the mirror, she headed down the hall slowly to confront him, still clenching the barely sipped glass of Bordeaux. Benny was nowhere in sight. The universe was not in sight. Her own image was not in sight. Nothing was everywhere in sight. Her shaking right hand, by habit or some autonomous command, lifted the wine to her trembling lips. Just as the rim of the glass came in contact with her lower lip, an image appeared in the mirror. Barely visible, Trudy saw two very small dim and reddish orbs spaced apart far enough to be a set of eyes. Trudy dropped the glass. It bounced off the carpeting, spilling the contents, splashing wine on her slacks and socks, and rolling away. She tried to move, back away, but her feet were frozen to the floor. Trudy attempted to shout, to scream for help, but her lips were also frozen. Terrified, fully awake, fully conscious, Trudy could do nothing but watch and wait . . . for what would follow.

A hand reached out of the mirror toward her. Another hand followed. Both of them draped with dark cloth—the long loose sleeves of a black cloak. She watched as her own hands slowly reached out for the foreign fingers and hands calling to her. In amazement, she could only watch and observe her own hands placed in the palms of the strange being reaching out from inside the mirror. Trudy could not resist the slight pull, the slight tug at her hands, coaxing her to step forward. The hands were warm and inviting; she could not feel that the fingers were extremely long and bony. Her shivering stopped. She was suddenly filled with warmth from head to toe. Her mind fell to ease, at peace. Willingly, Trudy stepped forward toward the phantom's asylum, into the mirror and what lay beyond.

F

Benny

I stood nervously at Baker's right side as she pressed the buzzer button for Trudy's apartment, waiting for another buzz at the security lock on the ground floor vestibule. "Damn," I repeated.

Baker pressed the buzzer for the third time. I didn't know what to do with my hands other than roll them around in a jittery ball. My fingers were panning for gold in the palms of my hands. After following Baker to Trudy's apartment complex, I had confronted Baker about Helen as we strolled in double time across the parking lot. It did not immediately dawn on me about the meaning behind reference to a phantom or whatever claiming its second victim.

I knew Helen had been mostly beaten to a pulp, but I wasn't sure how bad she was suffering internally. Now I knew Helen was dead and was killed in a really gruesome manner. It must have toyed with her and slowly tortured her beyond sanity, as it had appeared. I didn't want to even think about what it had in store for whoever might be next. I kept trying to put Trudy's image out of my mind. Maybe the damn thing was inside my head, lurking there, reading my thoughts, and picking out images that looked appealing and acquaintances who could be pursued.

I was getting worked up, angry.

About the time I was ready to start banging on the glass security door, I saw a pair of legs traversing down the steps directly in front of it. The clock must have been creeping up between 7:30 and 8:00 p.m. It was a young dude, either getting ready to go out on his Friday night prowl or to pick up his girlfriend—who knows, maybe his boyfriend. Baker swept me off to the left with a brush of her left hand, and as the ponytailed man-boy opened the security door to retreat from the building, he was greeted with her badge.

"I'm sorry to bother you, sir," she led, "but we are trying to reach Ms. Perkins. We know she's at home, but we don't seem to be getting an answer."

"Ms. Perkins?" he asked shyly.

"Yes, Trudy Perkins?" she replied.

"Oh, yeah," he responded, waking up. "Trudy," he said with a bit of excitement. "Everybody around here knows who Trudy is."

What a wise guy, I thought to myself, deciding he probably wasn't out to meet a boyfriend. It made me a little bit irritated, but after I mulled it over for about, what, a millisecond, I realized I wasn't the only guy on the planet who might get his eyeballs stuck in place for a second or two when she walked by, maybe three seconds.

"Then please let us pass through, if you would?" Baker asked politely. I was sure she would toss the guy on the floor if he even showed her a hint of resistance to the suggestion.

"Sure enough, Officer," he agreed. "She's up on the second floor, second door down on the right." He swept the sandy hair that had popped out of his rubber band away from his right ear and smiled while holding the door open. As Baker passed into the hallway, he cut me off while getting a good look at Baker's profile in the process. Now the feeling of irritation got the stopwatch moving again. However, I resisted the temptation to grab his neck in a twisting motion and let the weasel pass by undisturbed, undamaged.

As I followed Baker up to the landing and the second flight of stairs two steps at a time to the second floor, my thoughts turned to the next problem—getting inside Trudy's apartment. I doubted if Trudy could have slept through the racket we made pounding on the door, especially after ringing her apartment buzzer three times, for at least ten seconds a crack on the last two attempts. Before stepping in front of her and jamming my shoulder against the wooden door, I tried the door handle with my right hand. It didn't budge when I turned it to the left, but it turned with ease in the opposite direction. I then gave it a slight push with my left hand, and it swung open.

I started to advance into the room, but Baker waved me off using her left arm as though she were a school guard holding back a bunch of fidgety rug-rats at an intersection. I was ready to jump in and face off with whatever would confront me, but I had second thoughts. The lieutenant was the one here who was armed and dangerous. I relented and stepped back a half pace.

The cautious cop pushed the door forward and fully out of the way. I could see the glimmering light of the television and also a glow emanating from the kitchen at the far right of the big room. If Trudy was lying on the couch asleep, I knew I had miscalculated her. She would have to be a real power sleeper or have her own stash of downers to make it through the noise we had made.

Regardless, Baker called out her name, "Ms. Perkins? Are you there? Can you hear me? It's Lieutenant Baker." She paused, continuing to hold up the stop sign. "I'm with Benny, Ms. Perkins. Trudy?"

Then the lieutenant pulled out a Smith & Wesson .45 caliber handgun from a shoulder holster. No stop sign was needed on my end. I held my ground, nervous but safe. She took two quick steps inside, then as graceful as a gazelle, she stooped, twisted, and turned back toward me, quickly scanning the hidden parts of the room on either side of the door between us. Those TV cops had nothing on this lady. She turned back just as swiftly, cautioning me with her left hand behind her to hold my position while she continued to investigate the premises for anyone, anything.

Slithering forward slowly and scanning the room from left to right, she progressed toward the dimly lit hallway leading to the back rooms. As she passed by the kitchen, she waved me inside. I accepted this invitation as a generous privilege. I proceeded toward the TV to turn off the damn game show currently broadcasting. Trudy was not on the couch, but the zapper was sitting there waiting for my hand. *Click* and the apartment grew silent. Baker turned with a scowl. Oops. She quickly turned back to her canvassing.

I saw the tenny runner office shoes Trudy usually wore resting on the floor near the front of the TV. My own detective work told me she must have kicked them off because they were not neatly placed in front of the couch.

What Baker saw before she turned back must have convinced her the place was void of Trudy or any other presence. She turned back, approaching me again out of the hallway with that familiar stop sign while holstering her cannon at the same time.

"She's gone," Baker announced. She looked around the walls and found a switch for the hallway light and flicked it on.

"What do you mean?" I had asked. "What about the back rooms? Did you check them?"

"No need to, Benny," she replied. "But we'll check them anyway for evidence. But she's gone, and I mean gone. She spilled her glass of wine in front of the mirror hanging there on the bathroom door. And wait until you see this." Susan Baker flipped off the light switch and passed me a grim-looking expression. "Denning must have left the door unlocked," she murmured. "I'll have to thank him when I see him again, but tell him I'll castrate him if he ever pulls something like that again."

I figured she could probably handle the big boy and pull it off if she really wanted to, I mean, with the castration part. I never thought someone else might have left the door unlocked. Checking for her approval, I slowly stepped forward to proceed down the hallway. As I reached the lieutenant and approached closer to the mirror, which she had been blocking, I hesitated and stopped dead in my tracks. I could not believe what I was seeing. There was a message inscribed on the mirror, but there was something behind the scribbling much more sinister, much more incredible.

I screamed, "Trudy, where are you?"

F

"No," the lieutenant cautioned, "don't touch it. And I wouldn't spend a lot of time staring into it at this point."

"This is crazy," Benny responded. "It looks like it's . . . alive." He was standing in front of the mirror in awe. He shook his head, grabbing his temples with the thumb and middle finger of his left hand, massaging them. "The writing was just like in the john at Ms. Murphy's place. It's backward. But it doesn't look like it's written in blood. Maybe chalk, but like it's just floating there in midair. I can't even tell if there is any glass on the mirror anymore, but the letters aren't moving. The writing looks the same, although it's a lot smaller this time, and it still looks like it was written from the other side. I'm not sure if I enjoy the joke." There were two lines of the message, each with two words apparently written in haste, but the greeting was clearly legible.

"Well, it certainly is no joke, Benny," she replied. "Welcome to Benny's asylum. If that's not an invitation, I've never been to a wedding."

"Welcome to hell is more like it," he added. "What or whoever it is, it's teasing me, taunting me. And it looks like we could just step right on into it—whatever it is."

"I've seen the midnight sky out in the desert away from the city and all the lights," Baker said, "but never so majestic, so . . . close. Just as you said, it looks alive."

They turned, facing each other in the flickering glimmer from the mirror, and for more than a moment, Benny became lost in the allure of the yellow tint in Susan Baker's hazel eyes.

He could imagine how she had conquered the man in her life with the deep universe in her own eyes.

"Earth to Benny," she began, waking him.

"It's funny you should say that, Lieutenant," he said, cutting in, "standing here in the middle of a hallway, looking out at the universe. So now what?"

She reached into a jacket pocket, pulling out the squad car keys. "There's a cardboard box with some tactical equipment in the trunk," she said, extending the keys to him. "How about you retrieve it while I check out the rest of the apartment, see if there are any clues?"

"Like maybe a spaceship and a map of the universe," he suggested. "So what happens if you're not here when I get back, Lieutenant? I mean, you better stay away from this thing. Whatever is in there seems to have a knack of coming and going, you know?"

"If I'm not here, I guess that leaves you in charge, Mr. Johnson," she replied. She then winked her left eye. As crazy as the situation was and as apprehensive Benny was at the moment, he could not dismiss the thought of how this woman just kept looking better and better. Good ol' Benny . . . always in fantasy mode.

"Whatever you say, boss," he said, yielding a half salute. He stopped at the kitchen to grab a paper towel, which he planned to wedge in the security door below. "Officer Johnson at your service," he said, waving on his way out the door.

When Benny returned with the box prepared by Lieutenant Baker, he knocked on the unlocked door and announced himself. "Officer Benny back with the goodies, Lieutenant."

There was no reply. Benny deposited the box he had pulled out of the trunk on the spot where Trudy had been fingering the newscaster just about one hour earlier and called for Baker again. "Lieutenant?"

There was no reply. Benny found he was standing in the apartment all alone. *All by myself,* he thought. The light in the hallway remained off, so it was lit only by the glare from the kitchen stove's digital clock and the stars at the far end still glimmering through the mirror. He rapped at the bathroom door, making sure he didn't touch the surface of the mirror, if there was a surface at all, or interrupt Baker, if she was in the bathroom investigating or otherwise.

No one was home in there. He backstepped two paces, now noting the door to his right was slightly ajar. Studying the scene further, he found the officer's Smith & Wesson lying on the wine-stained carpet about two paces away from the bottom edge of the door. He pondered picking it up to determine whether or not the barrel was warm, hot, or otherwise, but let it lay there undisturbed. Further discovery led him to the single shell casing lying below the mirror at the threshold of the universe. He had not heard the weapon discharge while executing his materiel retrieval sortie at her car.

Benny pushed the door open a bit wider. The spare bedroom was dark. As the door swung open, a light from the floor beamed up toward him. It was a cell phone. Benny checked the universe at his left to make sure there were no visitors standing by the portal, and then he bent both knees to lower him and both his arms to retrieve the gun and the phone. The barrel was not hot, but it was not cool either. Asking questions, collecting evidence. He figured this was just part of another routine day in the life and times of a boiler and machinery claim adjuster.

The phone did not belong to Trudy. He verified this fact after checking the other bedroom in which Trudy had been sleeping earlier. Her purse had been left in there, and from it, he had discovered her cell phone. And besides, the directory display staring him in the face from the other phone belonged to Lieutenant Baker. While the contact list for the phone display was alphabetical, directly on the bottom of the page was the keyword, Denning.

Baker had told Benny if she was not in the apartment when he returned he should consider himself to be left in charge. Well, decision-making was a big part of his job, and with $100,000 in claim check draft authority, Benny had quite a bit of leeway, although his decisions must always be made in good conscience and must always be supported by the facts underlying the circumstances being investigated. And they must always be supported by the terms, conditions, and provisions of the policy. In this particular situation, Benny did not have a physical manuscript in front of him to review. Nor did he have a supervisor a phone call away to bounce the matter off for a second opinion about the decisions being made. His supervisor in this instance, Baker, was on temporary leave, somewhere wandering about out there in the universe beyond the mirror.

The sudden reversal of fortune left Benny in charge, with full authority. He doubted if Harry would be able to provide him with guidance and support on this one; it was a bit out of his realm of expertise. But he did have a good idea how his current supervisor would have proceeded. And he had a hunch the Lieutenant had already set in motion her idea before she was so rudely interrupted. With this thought in mind, Benny made an executive decision and pressed the call button.

F

"Denning here, Lieutenant. What's up?" answered Paul Denning. "A bit odd for you to be calling on a Friday night." He and his wife had ordered pizza delivery, and he had just finished putting the dishes and silverware in the sink, pondering about another freehand slice. He had been reaching into the reefer for another beer when his cell phone rang.

"Who?" Denning asked surprised. "Benny who? And what are you doing with Lieutenant Baker's phone?" His dander was quickly rising.

"Oh yeah, you're that insurance guy," he confirmed. "So what are you doing with the lieutenant's phone?" Paul Denning tuned in again. The man on the other end of the line sounded nervous.

"Did she tell me anything about what case?" he asked. "What are you talking about anyway? Put the lieutenant on the phone. Now!"

"What do you mean she's not here?" he demanded an answer. "She's always got her phone at hand."

"You just said that she's not here? Just where in the hell is here?"

Paul turned to his wife, who was tapping him on his Clint Walker left shoulder, motioning him to calm down. She was a petite woman, half his size, and called the bear-sized man Gentle Ben. They had been married six months, and she had not yet sprung it on him that she was with child. She had planned to spring the news later in bed.

"It's all right, honey," he said. "It's a call from the office."

Back to the cell phone. "I wasn't talking to you. Now tell me where Lieutenant Baker is!" He paused. "Why in the hell would I call you honey?"

Denning listened astutely, briefly. "Okay, then tell me where the hell she was already!" he demanded again.

Denning's wife decided to retreat and let him deal with the office. Hopefully, this would not result in a late-night duty call. She gently squeezed both shoulders, swept back her long blond hair, and tiptoed her way to the bathroom to give him a moment or so of privacy.

"Trudy who?" he asked, calming down a bit. After a pause, he replied, "Oh yeah, that pretty little girl from the insurance office. She was kind of a bit out of it. How is she doing? Is Baker with her?"

Denning listened again. "What do you mean probably, but they're both gone?" He listened as Benny tried to explain without giving away too much of the truth, as he feared the Lakeview's white suit squad would show up at Trudy's in place of Denning.

"Listen, Officer Denning," Benny pleaded, "Lieutenant Baker told me to get something from her squad car, and if she was gone when I got back, she said in a roundabout way, I . . . I should get in touch with you and get you over here. That's not exactly what she told me, but she didn't want to make a big fuss and have a bunch of flashing lights and screeching wheels and sirens and things. She kind of told me indirectly to get hold of you and keep it quiet. That's why I have her phone. She kind of gave it to me."

"What do you mean, kind of told you this and kind of told you that and kind of gave you her phone?" he asked and paused. "You'd better explain. I'll be there in twenty . . . maybe thirty minutes."

Now Denning had some explaining to do. He didn't have time to change from his jeans and corduroy shirt into his uniform, and he was off duty anyway. So he just collected his boots and grabbed the keys to his Chevy. Originally an Oklahoma ranch boy, he knew his way around bronco busting and still clung to his Western gear. He had second thoughts about retrieving his service revolver from the safe but left it behind. This was weird, but he was off duty, and Baker knew how to handle herself. Even so, it sounded as though she was in a jam.

F

Benny

I was really relieved to have gotten through the call to Officer Denning unscathed. I imagined if I had been talking to him face-to-face, my neck would have dropped about two collar sizes. I couldn't really tell him what was going on over the phone and who knows, maybe the cops' phone calls were all recorded by the department.

I was getting a little spooked in the apartment all by myself, and I didn't feel like inviting LNN into the living room through the TV. Why would I do that when I had the entire universe to keep me entertained? So I gathered the lieutenant's car keys and the cardboard box and headed back down to her car, leaving Trudy's door unlocked and jamming the paper towel back in place at the security door so we wouldn't get locked out.

I opened the trunk of the car and placed the box back inside, then I spread the flaps apart to see what Lieutenant Baker had in her repertoire. I found a couple of hand-sized mirrors I didn't think were wide enough to actually block a couple of steel-piercing laser beams from blowing out your eyeballs, but holy moly, the lady had really been serious when she had made the suggestion. I also discovered four more handheld devices, but rather than being reflective, they were destructive or, more precisely, explosive. Grenades. I figured she either had a connection at an army surplus store or maybe borrowed them from the evidence locker.

Then I happened to stumble on a couple of handguns, with four extra clips, later learning they were Glock G26, 9 millimeter, fixed sight, 10-round concealable weapons, you know, pocket pieces with blunt ends. I was still not convinced bullets, hand grenades, or even atomic bombs would match what this phantom thing, randomly floating in and out of mirrors from outer space, had in its arsenal. I think Helen and Ms. Murphy might have agreed with me on that point. But both were dead, so it was a little too late for me to solicit their input.

There were a couple of small high-powered flashlights with a few spare batteries rolling around and some other devices in the box, which I could not readily identify, including perhaps several smoke bombs, maybe the insect extermination kind, for all I knew. Once out of the armed forces, I had never aspired to educate myself in the art of Rambo-ism. I was always a ladies' man. I had always been mostly content with letting the macho kind of guys shoot 'em up, or get shot 'em up, for that matter.

When I saw headlights approaching Baker's vehicle, I closed the lid of the trunk as far as I could without locking it and prepared myself for Sergeant Denning and maybe what, some Rambo-ism in action on me and my body?

F

Denning pulled into an empty spot at the back of the parking lot next to Baker's vehicle. Pulling down the lane, he noticed someone was stirring around in the trunk of a car and closed the lid as he was approaching. Sure enough, it turned out to be Baker's unmarked squad car and none other than Mr. Insurance Man. *What is this dude doing messing around in the trunk of her car? Dumping her body?*

Denning pulled his way out of the seatbelt harness and rolled his double extra-large body out of his old Chevy. It was a 1985 Chevy Silverado—a short bed pickup with a 305 cubic inch, V-8 engine Paul had rebuilt in his spare time, along with just about everything else in the vehicle, replacing the three-speed transmission with a four-speed and keeping a spare 411 positraction rear end for use at Thompson Drag Raceway when he had an itch to blow some carbon off the valves. It was primed and ready for new paint. He had yanked out the eight-track player and installed a combo stereo and CD player about a week after buying the used vehicle he had located on an internet ad. He needed good tunes when he drove around.

"Well, Mr. Insurance Man," Denning began as he approached Benny. "What are you doing messing around in the trunk of Detective Baker's car?" He pulled his shoulders back, flexing his neck and trapezius muscles, as he reached the back of Baker's car.

Benny stepped back and raised both arms, with his hands at each side of his head, stepping back one more pace. The car keys hung from the lock below the trunk. "Whoa, Officer Denning, it's me, Johnson, Benny? We kind of met at Murphy's Restaurant and at my office. We just spoke on the phone."

"Yeah, we spoke all right on the lieutenant's phone," he verified. "And now you're snooping around in her car with her keys. What else do you have? Ms. Baker, maybe?"

Benny needed to urgently tone down the conversation, as precious time was flying past them. "Mrs. Baker, I believe," he started with not much confidence. "The box, the box." He pointed toward the trunk with his right thumb, not yet being authorized to lower his hands. He stepped back to make room for Denning.

"So what's in this box you're talking about?" Denning inquired. "Body parts? I think you need to take a couple of steps back."

Benny was really getting frustrated. "Well, there will be body parts and plenty of them if we don't get our asses back up to that damn apartment. Both Lieutenant Baker and Ms. Perkins have gone missing, probably kidnapped. And we're wasting time down here dicking around. I suggest you grab the box and we hightail it upstairs right now." Benny recalled Lieutenant Baker had left him in charge, not Denning.

"You do?" Denning asked. He kept his eyes on Benny as he lifted the unlocked lid. The trunk's dome light lit the top of the box.

He shuffled the flaps around and then looked back at Benny. "Holy crap! She must have been planning for something. Let's move."

"I'll fill you in, Officer Denning, once we get up there," he said. "But I hope you're really hungry because you're gonna have a lot to swallow."

"I just ate," he answered wryly, wishing he had grabbed the last slice of pizza.

Once Denning and Benny breeched the doorway to the apartment, Benny stopped him and gave him an earful of fantasy, explaining how he and the lieutenant had pieced together the conclusion that the culprit or, in cop terms, the perp, was most likely something not necessarily earthly and just possibly some kind of spook out of this world. Denning looked on in disbelief and skepticism, shaking his head up and down and smiling as he absorbed the wild tale.

"I can see you don't believe a word of what I'm saying," confessed Benny. "But neither did Lieutenant Baker or me at first. I mean not completely at least. We had some wild ideas until we made our way up here about, I don't know, maybe an hour, hour and a half ago, if that. And then we figured they weren't so wild."

"Like you said, Mr. Insurance Man," replied Denning, "it's a lot to swallow." He scanned the room beyond Benny, who had him somewhat pinned against the door.

"Please, Officer, the name is Benny," he pleaded. "Well, get ready for a real healthy spoonful of reality fantasy." Benny turned, keeping his eyes on the cop, motioning him to follow him down the hallway. He flipped the hallway switch, which he had turned on before he left the apartment for Baker's car, and the bulb snuffed out as he led Denning down the path, then he stopped and motioned him ahead.

"Holy crap!" Denning exclaimed. He started to reach for the mirror and its universe beyond.

"No! Don't touch it!" Benny warned. "It might pull you in!" He reached for Denning's shoulders, felt the bulging muscles, and gently urged him to back up.

"What the hell is going on here?" asked the sergeant. "What is that writing? What is going on here?" He looked closely, reading the message backward. "Come . . . on . . . in . . . Benny. Come on in, Benny?"

Benny replied, "Yeah, but the message changed a little bit since I first saw it. Last time, it said, 'Welcome to Benny's asylum.'"

F

Benny spent precious minutes, a solid half hour, explaining to Denning where Lieutenant Baker's investigation was heading and what he thought she had in mind. He carefully laid out all the evidence supporting the crazy theory about the perp in the two cases being one and the same, and whoever or whatever it was came from the opposite side of the mirrors at the restaurant and the insurance office. The cop kept shaking his head but continued glancing at the starry night glaring back at him from the mirror at the end of the hallway.

"Impossible," the sergeant kept murmuring under his breath. And then he glanced back at the weapon stash Baker had collected. "She's always three steps ahead of everybody," he confided with Benny. "She usually keeps me up to date on cases I've been on with her, even when I'm relieved. No wonder she's been keeping me in the dark. And she left you in charge? That's a bit of a stretch."

"For some reason, she thinks I might be the clue to solving this thing, like somehow I have a connection with whatever is behind this … craziness," surmised Benny. "I think what she was trying to say was if she did go missing, I had to make some decisions and find her before it was too late for her and Trudy. I had to follow her. And there's only one place she could have gone." Benny pointed back toward the mirror.

"Well, she isn't around here anywhere," agreed Denning. "And her weapon has been fired." He shrugged his broad shoulders. "What did you have in mind?"

"We go after them, maybe hold hands or something when we first go through, you know, so we don't get separated," he said, with a question mark imbedded in his forehead. "Believe me. I'm straight, Sergeant," he added. "Everything I told you is on the up and up, no BS. Plus, like I'm married, you know? At least I was until today."

"You're not—" started Denning.

"Straight as an arrow, Sarge," Benny said emphatically. "I like my fantasies, but I think I still have my sanity after all these years."

"What about all this stuff?" Paul asked, pointing toward the box of goodies.

"To be honest, I'm not sure if any of it will do any good. Look at what he, or it, did to Ms. Murphy. The lieutenant seemed to think the mirrors might be some kind of protection against a laser beam, if that's what cut through Ms. Murphy's head. I don't know about the guns and grenades."

"Wouldn't hurt," suggested Denning, "but the grenades might be stretching it. We'll leave those behind."

"I'll stick with the mirrors," replied Benny.

"You better take one of the Glocks and an extra clip, along with one of those flashlights. I hear dungeons and chambers can get really dark." Then he took a deep breath. "Mother of—I don't believe this crap—what the hell am I doing?"

Benny took Denning's advice, even though he felt guns were probably useless against whatever they would be facing. He grabbed one of the small hand-sized mirrors. It was encased in a brass rim and furnished with a matching chain attached to an eye on the frame. Clutching the mirror in his right hand, Benny slipped the chain around his neck and nervously made a miniature sign of the cross at the center of his chest. *Like that will really help,* he thought. Maybe it was a sigh of the cross.

Moments later, Paul Denning, apprehensively clutching the bathroom doorknob with his right hand, grabbed Benny Johnson's right hand with his other hand and followed the insurance man toward the door and lower rim of the mirror. He lifted his left leg through and followed Benny for a walk on the wild side. The universe closed behind them, as Denning's fingers slipped off the brass knob and away into the darkness beyond. His first thought was that he could have really used the crapper at the moment. On the television, now bright and colorful again, between the same daily obnoxious commercials, the weather forecaster broke in, mentioning a possible storm. Details would follow at eleven.

F

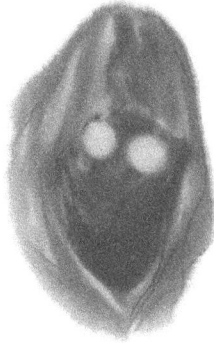

CHAPTER SIX

LORD LAWRENCE MEETS THE PHANTOM

So who is this phantom creature stirring the proverbial pot of excitement in Lakeview? Could it be a man or possibly some kind of creature beneath the hooded cloak? A woman? A mutant? Or is it just the mere creation of the mind, something deep, dark, and sinister? Could the phantom be a figment of someone's imagination? If so, this figment most certainly must be a very . . . big . . . fig. Whatever lurks beneath the hood is evil. And one fact of fate common within man's long history on planet Earth is that evil has survived the test of time.

Evil has retained its presence from the beginning of time, throughout medieval times, and remains with us today, and it will be at our side for all the morrows to come. There is evil everywhere; we all have had a taste of its temptation. What a wonderful scent. In the struggle of good versus evil, sometimes the bad prevails above all else, no matter its size, large or small. Even the gardens of utopia have produced a rotten seed or two.

But what of Lord Lawrence? What was his special gift? Or shall we say, what *is* his special gift? And how was it acquired?

Where was the evil stirring within this phantom acquired? Traveling back in time, we might discover some clues. We need just to close our eyes and drift back through the ages. Let our minds wander into the unconscious realm of thought where dreams are our saviors, our salvation from the horrifying grip and dread of reality.

When our eyes open, we find our Lord Lawrence had orchestrated his quiet reign of terror during the midst of the Black Death pandemic in the Late Middle Ages, also a time when upheaval and splitting factions of the Catholic church competed with the punishment waged against the Jewish religion. Wars raged in Europe to further add disarray to the turmoil of the times. Set in a remote western region, his castle provided Lord Lawrence with a haven of protection against these hazards and the freedom and secrecy to practice his own religion, unencumbered.

As a young man, the male witch shielded his pernicious deeds under the false pretense of what was considered white magic being used for the purposes of good, fighting the ravages of disease and peril to spread good fortune. After a series of failures and frustrations, the death of all his family members initiated a remarkable stroke of good fortune and wealth. Their timely demise opened an unabated path to his darker side where he studied the practices of demonology and satanic rituals. He sought to hone his skills with those he acquired in servitude. A captive of his own twisted mind and under its spell, his wandering thoughts were free to practice their devilish ways.

In frustration and anger, his wavering libido led him to sin and torture. It was in the year 1350 our Lord Lawrence had forged a final path to his own demise and ill fortune, a victim of his own curse at only forty-two years of age. He was destined to wander for all eternity in the annals of time, standing still deep in the caverns of his own chamber of horrors he had left behind. Here lay a dwelling of no place and suspended in no time, Lord Lawrence, an entity of no being and no flesh, left to dwell in the sentence of the dark magic. It had all begun with an act of hate and an unfulfilled love. And the unintentional yet self-imposed curse placed on him could only end with the fulfillment of what he had been forever denied—a darker soul.

F

One fateful afternoon, Lord Lawrence was dallying with creations of playful phlebotomy in the dungeon of his castle, ingenious methods of extracting blood. It was not a huge castle as one might perceive when thinking of King Arthur and his Round Table. But it did contain a small courtyard, a pinnacle tower at each corner, a rather large great hall for entertaining, and two stories containing an additional six rooms, most lost in their loneliness. There was no wide moat or large, tall drawbridge. But Lawrence's privacy required a deep pit surrounding the semicircular fortification wall enclosing the front boundary of the courtyard and extending around the sides and rear of the castle walls. A small bridge, wide enough to convey servants on errands passing by one another on horse-driven wooden carts, led to an entrance gate strengthened by thick wooden double-planked reinforcement.

Outside Lawrence's private domain stood a large barn and stables for horses and other livestock. Here, he set living quarters for his busy staff and another three-room building where animal slaughter, leather tanning, and smoking of meat and fish took place. A wide walking bridge was provided at the left side of the courtyard service entrance for workers to access the kitchen, supply storage rooms, and facilities for brewing his wine and ale. It was important to keep those who supported his lifestyle busy while he played in his dungeon.

In the midst of the courtyard was a square flower garden surrounded by a hedge and enclosing a circular shallow pool in its midst. Lord Lawrence relished both his red and white roses, which filled the garden. It contained wormwood, valuable as a repellent, and mugwort and marigolds for their medicinal and cookery usefulness. Blue iris was cultivated for use as ink, a necessity for the many drawings Lawrence prepared and discarded in the design of his dungeon toys. Ground cover of periwinkle, violets, and daisies spread around the stone walkways in the garden concealed the shallow graves. The garden had been assembled during construction of the castle at a time when Lawrence was practicing his craft on an array of animals. It was here in the garden where Lawrence spent many late-night endless walks in circles, dreaming of his designs and methods before putting them to parchment.

The pool held significant portent for Lawrence, as beneath it lay his first kill, one of accident, the family pet that had survived a great fire but not a blow to the head in a fit of angered frustration, a kill of great pleasure merely tickling his thirst for kills by other means, other methods. The pet was a pest, always jumping and dancing in front of his master, begging attention. The ignorant animal never did digest much of the English language beyond *sit,* and the mutt had never even acquired the taste for blood or made a kill of any sort. It was the feral cats running amok throughout the grounds who kept rats and other vermin in check. The dog's absence from the garden was no great loss.

His mansion was constructed at the former site of his parents' dwellings at an early age after he had gained his fortune through inheritance—the untimely surmise of his mother and father, a younger brother, an older sister, two uncles, and three childless aunts during a festival fire at a faraway village. *A shame,* he had thought through a sinister smile while observing the debris field left behind by the fire. He grieved, albeit quite briefly and impatiently after his sudden but exhilarating exposure to this newfound freedom to do as he pleased, answer to no one.

As Lord Lawrence matured and his darker inner side won favor over the miniscule sense of guilt lingering in his mind, Lawrence decided he needn't grieve for them any longer. It was their misfortune, not his. Their fortune was his. It was shortly after their passing when the grounds were excavated, and his castle was constructed, along with his asylum four stories belowground, accessible through either of two hidden passageways spiraling their way down opposite ends of the castle.

However, he did have the forethought of building a secret escape passageway from the lowest level of the castle mansion out to the back of the building. Its doorways were constructed with the same stone used in building the outer and inner walls. They were kept locked in place by a latch midway up the door that could be manipulated open and shut from either side of the door. Sturdy iron hinges ran the entire height of the doors. Only a keen eye familiar with their location could detect their presence, or locate the latches hidden behind and operated by small round stones. In time, this passage would serve purposes for Lord Lawrence much more meaningful than escape. It was there in the asylum

Lawrence would consult with his inner being through long periods of fasting, contemplation, meditation, and eventual experimentation. He enjoyed his long afternoon naps where he dreamed of new toys in the comfort of his black silk-lined oak coffin.

During these three years of construction, Lord Lawrence shed the body fat of his youth and had developed into a rather pleasant-looking young man, although his mind grew ugly with self-adulation. His addiction to power over others not as fortunate and a lust for mastering the arts of the occult served to teeter the balance of his sanity, feeding his insatiable appetite for prophesying the future, making it happen.

Lawrence's eyes of brown matched his shoulder-length wavy hair. He was not an extremely large man in stature but tall for the times, standing near six feet tall and bearing a solid muscular structure. He was pleased with the images reflected in his blown glass mirrors, although a bit clouded and distorted due to their composition and slight conical shape; they concealed the sinister being beneath the skin. So he dressed the walls of his castle with many of them.

He dressed himself with trim, tight-fitting tunics of the day, colorful shirts flaring out at the waist but not one being very fashion-minded. He preferred long trousers over short stockings and fancied out-of-date tall leather boots, usually black. Lawrence was especially fond of long-hooded silk cloaks and black leather gloves. Lord Lawrence loved black. And most of all, he loved the crystal amulet that remained a staple around his neck almost from the day it had been discovered.

Avoiding social circles, Lawrence kept to his castle, only infrequently venturing far beyond the borders of his realm during daylight hours. As he had progressed into his darker side, Lawrence would venture to villages and taverns under the privacy of night when he engaged in a specimen hunt or was seeking feminine company from a woman of the night, whom he would use and quickly discard. On these ventures, he left at the sight of dawn, traveling the many leagues to these communities and returning on the dawn of the morrow, on occasion with company in tow, willing or not.

Not in want of sexual ambitions on this coming eve, Lawrence was focused on perfecting one of his tools, making modifications to seek the effect he desired. What type of mechanism could be employed to separate all four limbs simultaneously without the necessity of having to corral and feed animals in the bowels of his asylum? They required much too much care, created a mess, and if not kept washed down, smelled obnoxious. Their smelly excrement would only serve to burden Aldred with chores Lawrence hoped to avoid. The poor man had more important duties to tend, such as ridding the dungeon of waste from his master's experiments, the corpses, or parts thereof, and waste from their own excrement, innards and bloodletting. Plus, Aldred had the castle to keep; the maids, servants, gardener, stableman, and watchman required oversight. This kept him busy.

No, Lawrence needed a mechanical remedy of some sort. Possibly an arrangement using wheels and rope or chain could be employed. Perhaps a barrel of some sort on which the attendee could be strapped on his or her belly, with arms outstretched and restrained at either side. The restraints could be wound in circles at opposite ends with hoist mechanisms, such as used to raise buckets from a well. But, of course, the feet must also be well secured in place with blocks. While the barrel revolved, the arms could be drawn farther aside. This might require quill to parchment, along with a good bit of ale, to qualify a proper design. Why not strap them to the barrel itself by their wrists, down on their backs, and rotate the barrel? Forget the hoists. Break but don't bend.

Management of the castle was Aldred's assigned vocation. He no longer had any conscious memory of the rooms below in the dungeon, not to mention its undertakings. Lord Lawrence made that certain, hypnotizing him to rid his mind of any knowledge about his dark activity belowground. He was Lawrence's most valued asset. Children growing up together, Aldred's parents had held his current position and managed the former dwelling and grounds upkeep under the employ of Lawrence's parents. That is to say they did until they, too, had perished in the horrible fire. *Another shame,* Lawrence had thought for a fleeting second, but it was a great opportunity.

Aldred's parents were not only servants under their direction. They were also considered a part of the family, at least in the eyes of the parents. The two children were born only months apart; the parents spoke more than once about how the future might have looked if one of the two boys had been a girl child. How rosy it would have been, at least in the eyes of the parents. In truth, one of them was spoiled rotten, lazy, jealous, and spiteful. But for a healthy relationship, Lawrence had supplanted very rosy childhood memories and recollections in Aldred's mind.

The lord had mastered the art of hypnotism, which he often employed when visited by unexpected or unwanted company or prostitutes whose special skills warranted other opportunities to please him. In secrecy, he had learned the art from an old man, a white witch who had sought shelter in Lord Lawrence's castle. He was being sought by accusers of a nearby village for practicing sorcery. His vain attempt to aid an ailing young woman of a stomach ailment was followed by her demise. How could he have known she had suffered an appendicitis attack, which by the will of her god led to its rupture and the internal bleeding that followed? The old stranger was no man of medicine. He was nothing more than a kindly old white witch.

Lawrence had kept the man sheltered for a year, sharing life stories while dining nightly and learning the man's secrets, brews, potions, and craft. And finally, upon his graduation, long after the search for the old man had been abandoned, Lawrence had instructed him involuntarily to seek out the village and confess his sins. Two weeks later, Aldred, having himself returned from the village after a two-day venture to acquire provisions, commented on something he had noticed, hung and rotting from an old oak tree at the outskirts of the village. It was not a yellow ribbon; it was the old man. A sign, hanging from his lifeless body, had read WITCH. Aldred had never before seen the man. "Why should anyone practice sorcery, my lord? They might should have burned him at a stake."

But this was not Lawrence's first walk on the evil side. He mistreated Aldred at any occasion presenting an opportunity. He had done simple deeds, such as hiding his own clothing in Aldred's quarters and then blaming him for theft. Aldred was often the target of punishment, ill thoughts placed in the minds of others. The boy needed a good whipping.

On a horseback ride through the country one afternoon, Lawrence jumped at the chance of opportunity, just as an athlete would grasp his skill in hand and take it to the next level. He came upon a sorrel horse grazing at the side of the pathway. A man was lying on the ground nearby, obviously in pain and in need of assistance. Lawrence was eager to rush to the injured man's side. With his leg broken, the old man explained through winces and deep breaths that he had fallen when his horse came upon vermin slithering across the path. Until the boy spoke, the stranger was unaware the slimy reptile was not the only snake in the grass. It had appeared to Lawrence the injured man was some kind of a holy man. He had been wearing a dark-brown cloak with a hood partially covering his face. Kicking his injured leg and laughing at the helpless vagabond, Lawrence had inquired if the man was some kind of a monk.

"Not the kind you would expect, fat BOY," replied the injured man. Clearly in severe pain but sound of mind, the man quickly recognized the evil being standing over him.

Lawrence had countered to inform the man he was about to die, either from the fall, old age, or the dagger waving in front of his wrinkled face.

"True," he replied, "but not before my life's final task is complete, fat BOY." He grimaced from the sharp pain in his wound inflicted by the rotten little fat boy.

"I have been seeking someone such as you to bestow a gift to last a lifetime."

Then the old man smiled as he pulled the hood from his head. He displayed crooked teeth through a scraggly gray-bearded face. His hair was swept back and held in a ponytail by a brown leather string. "And far, far, beyond, fat BOY!" His voice elevated as he pulled an amulet strung about his neck. Then he began to whisper an utterance the fat boy could not discern.

Tired of the insulting fat-boy references, Lawrence placed the dagger he had drawn in position and swiped the blade across the not-so-holy holy man's neck. After cutting the amulet loose from his neck and setting off with the sorrel's reins in hand, he heard the man uttering another unintelligible curse he had mistaken for a prayer. He turned back and dismounted, kicking the man for clarity.

The man laughed at Lawrence and lay his bleeding neck and head down on the ground. "You have not seen the last of me, fat BOY."

Lawrence had been thirteen years old at the time. And the curse was growing within, nurturing. Lawrence was reminded of this from time to time when the images of the not-a-monk-of-his-kind monk would suddenly appear, in a mirror, in a pasture, and out at the shoreline across the lake. Five years had passed before the not-so-holy holy man first appeared. It was there out at the lake where he had been persecuting Aldred with his commands and threats. The man's image appeared on the surface of the lake, standing over Lawrence while he sat at the lake's edge admiring his own reflection. When Lawrence confronted Aldred about the not-a-monk-of-his-kind monk standing over them, Aldred just looked back at him, puzzled. "What monk? What holy man?"

F

But here and now, on that fateful afternoon, Aldred summoned Lord Lawrence by drawing the rope hanging on the main castle floor outside the door to his master's bedchamber. He could not be found in the great hall, solar, or kitchen area, and he had not ridden to the lake. The rope ran across pulleys through the bedchamber ceiling and extended deep below from bells hanging in the bedchamber to bells hanging near the ceiling of the dungeon where Lawrence was currently in contemplation. Aldred had been prescribed not to ring the lord unless warranted by visitors at the doorstep, unknown or otherwise, or some matter requiring his immediate attention and authority. When called on in such rare occasions, Lord Lawrence would surface from his bedchamber at the south end of the castle. Patiently, Aldred waited for Lawrence to emerge from the locked door of the room.

Several minutes later, Lawrence unbolted the door and opened it slightly after viewing Aldred from a peephole in the door. "Yes, Aldred," he began, "you have a matter of import at hand? I am quite engaged."

"Sire," Aldred replied in a concerned voice, "I beg your forgiveness. We have an unannounced visitor. A lady, if you will."

"Humph, a lady, you say," Lawrence said with disappointment. His utterance was more of a nervous throat-clearing than any word he muttered when he was irritated or disturbed. His attention was disrupted from its current task. "Who might she be? Why would a lady call on my castle devoid of invite?" He poked his head out of the door to examine the hall beyond Aldred. "Where is this lady you speak of?"

In order, Aldred replied, "A mistress in distress, sire. A quite handsome lady, master. She travels from France to seek out her uncle in Sorwich, seven days' travel hence. Lady Catelin—she is so addressed."

"Hmm," Lawrence interrupted, "French. And handsome, you say?"

"Quite so, sire," he agreed. "She travels with a coachman and one guard. Her carriage has come to peril three leagues north. A wheel broke free in two. The guard has become impaled beneath the carriage in his fervor to haste with remedy. She seeks shelter for the eve at hand for her and the coachman."

"And where does she wait?"

"At the foot of the main gate, sire," explained Aldred. He was never to allow entry without approval.

"Show the coachman to the stable," Lawrence instructed. "Humph. And present the lady to the solar. Bring goblets and mead . . . ale for the coachman. Plenty of it. He will likely bring his hunger. See to it."

"As you wish, Master Lawrence," acknowledged Aldred.

"I shall greet this lady presently," Lawrence relented. "Humph. Has the sun fallen, Aldred?"

"No, but soon."

"And the guard?"

"Perished, I fear," Aldred added.

"Humph. I suspect there is game in the woods afflicted with hunger, as have I." he commented nonchalantly. "Have the kitchen prepare a suitable meal for our gracious Lady Catelin. Lest she thirst for wine, see to it. Now go and see to it you are fed. Dress your bones with a bit of meat, Aldred. I need you alive. I would not see the sun again, but not for you."

Aldred would have been wise to heed this advice and store the words in pocket for future recollection.

F

When Lord Lawrence next appeared in the solar, he found Aldred with Lady Catelin. Their backs were turned to him while they were standing in front of a portrait, admiring Aldred's parents. It was set among others, including Lawrence's family members and another of several of the two men when they had been young boys and portrayed as best of friends. In this portrait, they were kneeling close to a pond while admiring a frog between them. The next snapshot would have shown Lawrence grabbing the frog by its hind legs and ripping it in two, straight up the middle, as though they were segments of a wishbone. It had been an uncanny act for the child at the time, but it was merely a preview of greater things to come and the man who would evolve. He could only explain to the astonished Aldred he did not believe it could be done with such an air of ease. It was just a frog.

There were others to admire.

Lawrence cleared his throat as he approached the couple quietly from behind. Their two heads turned in unison; Catelin's over her right shoulder and Aldred's at her right side. Their cheeks were within striking distance. Bright smiles painted their faces.

"My lord," greeted Aldred. He stepped back two paces and bowed with his left hand stretched across his lower back. He then rose and extended his right hand to the beautiful woman and accepted her left hand. "I am pleased to present Lady Catelin, niece to Lord Baldwyn of Sorwich."

Catelin wore an open light-blue surcoat with a matching long gown hanging to the floor. She curtsied and then released Aldred's hand to unfasten her long black cape and remove her blue bonnet revealing an exposure of cleavage from her well-developed breasts. Aldred accepted the clothing and removed himself from the solar, as Lawrence's glare would have him do.

Catelin's ocean-blue eyes followed Lawrence around the table set at the middle of the room bearing the small feast prepared for them but not before leaving Aldred's trail out of the room. "My lord," her soft voice appealed to Lawrence, "I am in certain debt for your kindness."

Lawrence had never been to the ocean shore, but he found himself swimming in the depths of her eyes. Never before had he been so captivated in the presence of a woman. Never before had he fallen victim to hypnosis. And he was such willing prey to the gaze of her magic. The radiant young woman wore her hair in an unusual fashion. It was long, silky, black, and free. Most fell behind her, but strands of hair were tossed over her left shoulder down onto her bosom. She felt his eyes captured in her rapture, drinking in her silhouette. Lawrence pulled himself out.

"My lady, it is with pleasure I accept your company with no question. Your presence brightens the day."

Lawrence knew at first sight he could not let this woman leave him. He was falling and falling quite rapidly. As they sat to dine and drink, the gears in his mind were already devising a scheme to delay her stay. Aldred could attend to the burial of the guard and the repair of her carriage. Although this repair could be accomplished at his own stable, he would send Aldred to the village to collect stores while the wheel was repaired. He would take the coachman along, giving Lawrence more time to think about how the coachman would be efficiently dispatched. And the uncle must be considered. *What to do about him?* He was certain if he could delay her stay long enough, she would succumb to him at her own will, with no restraint, no reservation. She would be his forever and ever. He would need no power of hypnotism. He would not have it; she must choose him of her own free will.

His mind began to overload as he thought about his secrets; they must remain secrets. And what if she desired to wed? How could he keep his dungeon a secret? But what if she felt the same desires and needs as he did, the same hunger as he? What a blessing. If she did not, then she must stay until she did. He must take her to the dungeon and share with her his life passion. These thoughts flooded his mind in an instant hypnotically.

But first things first. His mind was racing far ahead of common sense. Long afternoons in the garden, moonlight, and romance. Long walks while holding hands and exchanging dreams of future times, of past times. Such a pitiful waste of time but . . . necessary. The coachman must die. Then all events would unfold for him and transpire smoothly, such as with the frog, accompanied by an air of ease.

***

After three hours of indulgence, Lawrence summoned Aldred to escort Lady Catelin to a guest chamber on the main floor. She had nodded twice into a light sleep, as she courteously paid audience to Lord Lawrence. He appeared to be a rather cordial man, but there was something odd about him, not such with the other gentleman whom she, at first, thought was brother to Lawrence. Aldred was his name. He was kind and gentle, but she felt he was troubled. It was not an oddness he had but a burden, hidden. Catelin could read these things. It was a gift she had rarely ever shared in her youth, certainly not with strangers. A person who could read minds was said to hold court with the devil. Death came to those who held such a gift. And it was not just the mind Catelin could read; it was something else even she could not understand. It was not necessarily a reading but more of a knowing.

She had first learned of this knowledge when she was a young child. One afternoon while with a playmate, she noticed a third young girl lying on the grass next to a stream in which she and her friend were wading. Barefoot, she approached and discovered this girl wore the same dress as her playmate. Her mouth and eyes were open. A blank stare covered her face, and her skin was pale and blue. Although hardly recognizable, the girl seemed familiar. She was not breathing. Her playmate had called to Catelin, noticing her sudden distraction. Catelin looked back to acknowledge and then back down at the girl's body lying in the grass. But it was gone. Two days later, so was her playmate. Drowned.

As the years passed and Catelin grew, she began to nurture this manifest capacity to know the unknown, to read what was not written, to seek out that which was hidden in the minds of others. She learned to confide in her secrets with only the highest of confidence. And usually the benefactor of her knowing had no desire to spread the wealth of her knowledge. In fact, their purses were offered in exchange for her private confidence, her silence. Circumstances had led her on a path to battle evil ways with conscience and guilt. She had learned to control minds, not through hypnosis, but through her own will.

F

And so, as planned, Aldred set out with Rodney, the coachman, at his side on the large cart, wondering why they were not merely instructed to repair the wheel in the compound but having his suspicion. Something other than beauty about Catelin was alluring. He knew Lawrence, too, had her on his mind. And with Aldred's current station in life, he also knew he must keep his distance. She was out of his reach, far above in the heavens. And Lawrence was his dearest friend, although due to his own station in life, he was obligated to conceal his true affection. Nevertheless, Lawrence had provided him a home at a time in his life when he would otherwise have been placed in destitution. And for Lawrence's generosity, Aldred was most grateful and would honor the man for the remainder of his life.

"And so, young man," began Rodney, "what is it there on your mind? You have not spoken for a league and more since we buried me dear friend." Rodney had a full head of graying brown hair and was a bit stoop shouldered in his middle age. His voice was low and rough, and his nose and cheeks were red, possibly an attribute from his fond love of ale. "My lady, perhaps?"

"Upon whose mind would she be not?" answered Aldred. "But I also have other thoughts."

Rodney kept the conversation at Catelin. "She has her way with men. She does. I have not seen one get too far beyond what they have up in their mind though, lad. But they all seem anxious to enrich her purse. They do."

"You say she sells herself?" Aldred replied. He was startled that this seemingly refined woman could do such a thing.

"No, no, son," Rodney explained. "She is as pure as a newborn rose petal. She is as unblemished as she was on the day I brought her into this world, some twenty and seven years past." He looked upward, as though in deep thought.

"They all want her," Rodney continued. "But in the end, they all want her gone. A bloody game she plays. It is and a dangerous one. She knows their secrets, and they share their gold to keep them corralled. They do."

"Why does she persist?" asked Aldred.

"Been that way since her mum and father died," he said. "Together, they did all right. On the same night, they did. One knife, two hearts."

"Murdered?"

"Not so. Mum had both her hands on the knife when I found 'em. Her heart must have broken, me thinks. So she done used it for to cut his out then stuck the blade in the shattered pieces of her own. Ten years past, it was."

"So she now heads to her uncle? Ten years later?" asked Aldred.

"Her uncle? If so, I say she must have a hundred of 'em." Rodney sighed. "She is looking for something. What, I don't know. Maybe because of what her father done to her . . . or woulda had he his way. She has us on the road, and when her game has played, we return to France. Once each year, ten in all by me count. We return for the autumn harvest in her orchards."

"She must bear much pain," Aldred said and snapped the reins.

"That and a lot of gold coin in her purse," agreed Rodney. "For revenge against men, me thinks." But Rodney did not explain how Catelin herself had been tricked, swindled, left pregnant, penniless, and abandoned by another man as twisted as her father. She earned her way out of the poor house amassing a fortune and now owned her own mansion and orchards filled with grapes and fruit trees. "Now you said you bear troublesome times on your own mind. What might it be?"

"Dreams," Aldred replied. "Bad dreams."

The friendly wise man and Aldred spoke of these dreams along their travels. The chores prescribed by Lawrence kept them away so he would not have need to share her beauty with others while he laid his trap. Aldred spoke of his dreams, some far too vivid to seem imagined. Between them, Rodney shared stories of Catelin and her imaginary Lord Baldwyn of Sorwich. To Aldred, it seemed both he and Lady Catelin were on trails leading them nowhere. Both were victims of dreams imprisoning them in circles of infinite wandering, wondering, and yearning for avenues of escape. And now their trails were converging, to what end, he knew not.

"These dreams," Aldred went on, "they come and go from me but seem to have a pattern. In the end, another soul is taken horribly." Aldred attempted to describe the most recent recollection of the recurring nightmare as best he could recall.

F

In his dream, Aldred floated above his own body, which was fast asleep in his quarters far down the hall on the second level of the castle, somewhere above the bedchamber of Lord Lawrence. He was awaken by the ringing of two small bells hanging beside each other. They chimed from beyond his bedchamber above the door out in the hallway, three sharp rings; the trigger was calling him to action. Aldred's body rose from the bed, awake but yet fast asleep. A blank stare was on his face. He watched his body while it reached behind a stand at his bedside to retrieve a long key hanging there on a wooden peg.

Methodically, his dual self-dressed in his work clothing, lit a candle, and marched out of the room to a door at the end of the hall beyond the stairway. Aldred had never consciously breeched its boundary and sensed it had always remained locked. He had never inquired about its contents. It was possibly a memorial for his lord's fallen family, or perhaps it was a mausoleum containing the remnants of their incinerated bodies. There had never been burials.

Aldred's eyeballs raced under their lids as they followed from behind and watched his body pass through the doorway to a small landing containing nothing other than a tall mirror on the wall opposite the door at the head of a spiral stone stairway. The rolling balls under the lids of his eyes watched the sleeping image mindlessly glaring back at him. Cautiously, Aldred sleepwalked, descending and following the glow from the candle he carried in the dream.

Aldred counted ten and more complete spirals as he twisted and turned his way down the dark passageway to finally reach a second landing in a small solar bearing no fixtures, other than a sole mirror and a small stand holding a lantern and a fuel container. In a corner were two buckets filled with water and a mop standing between them. A stack of large sheets was tossed on the stone floor in front of the buckets. To the left hung a long body apron to be strapped around one's neck. His prone sleeping body watched as his own image rolled up his sleeves and donned the apron along with elbow-length gloves.

Mechanically, Aldred retrieved one of the sheets and dragged it through a set of double doors left open and waiting for him. A pretty, young, and slim woman, stripped of clothing, lay sideways across a long stone slab set in the middle of the room. Four devilish-looking beastly dogs paraded around the slab, as though they were on guard. They all stopped in unison and sniffed at the air above them. Finding Aldred's scent, they gathered together and trotted to the far end of the chamber and lay at guard before another set of tall open double doors.

The young lady's head and what remained of her long curly blonde hair hung down over one side of the slab, as did her legs on the opposite side. Missing were her hands and feet, and a section of the top portion of her skull was all collected in yet a third bucket below her empty head. Blood had drained from her neck into the bucket from her slashed throat. A large hole cut into her chest suggested her heart was not in it, apparently deciding to join the other missing members of her body collage.

A familiar voice broke the silence from the opposite side of the large hall. "Dirty hands, dirty feet . . . dirty mind. Let us leave them all behind. A poor specimen, Aldred. Rid the place of it. It carried no soul of any use. How I tire of this nonsense. I need more. Something dark."

The command came from a figure dressed in a long black hooded cloak. The man inside was unrecognizable; his features were hidden by the curvature of the black hood and mask covering his face. He wore matching silk gloves gracing his hands, which both bore long sharp scalpels wiped clean of blood over the dead woman's abdomen. In a sweeping motion that lifted the cloak, the figure turned and vanished beyond the devil dogs now sitting alert, ready for another command. The doors closed behind him.

Aldred stepped forward and advanced to the task of ridding the room of the poor specimen, placing the sheet over the corpse, and rolling it and her missing parts inside. He tossed the body over his right shoulder and *turned back to his point of entry, picking up the candle he had placed on the slab with his left hand. After disposing the body in a shallow grave, he returned to the chamber of torture in order to cleanse the operating table and the stone floor surrounding it. He left the room again with the bucket in hand. The dogs returned near the slab and awaited the return of the sleeping man on guard until Aldred reappeared with two buckets of fresh, soapy water.*

Done with his chores, Aldred raised his head for permission to dismiss. Recalling the bored look on the face of the man when he had earlier lifted the mask momentarily with a scalpel, terror washed over Aldred, and he woke . . . every time the dream repeated.

F

On the trail back to the castle, Rodney brought their chatter back to Aldred's dream. Every element taking place in the sequence of Aldred's footsteps from the time he removed the key, left the room, and walked down the hall through the door, past his reflection in the mirror beyond the door, and down the spiraling stairway, had been described in great detail, even the description of the tortured woman and the color of her bloodstained blonde hair. There was one exception. "Do you recall the face beneath the mask, lad? Familiar to you, was it?"

"As plain as day, yet dark as night," answered Aldred. "I follow the path of my dream, yet when I approach the man in the cloak, my mind goes blank."

"Me dad once told me a man must follow his dreams if he wants them coming true," began Rodney. "Me, I never carried much luck for dreams. But you, lad, you are a young man. You should be having good dreams. You have many leagues ahead of you and many forks in the road to choose from. You say you follow the path of your dream over and over in your sleep and in your mind, but have you really tried to follow the path?"

"What do you mean, Rodney?"

"Start from the beginning," Rodney said. "Look for the key. Maybe 'tis a bit more real than you think."

Aldred was startled. He pulled the reins and brought the two horses and wagon to rest. He turned to Rodney; a puzzled look was on his face. "Why did I not think of that?"

"A good question, Aldred," replied Rodney.

"I mean, why? I mean, the very thought never ever had entered my mind. Lord in heaven, what if there is a key? Could that mean—"

"Then it could very well be a bit more than you think," repeated Rodney. "If there be a key, there be a door, and if there be a door, there be the man behind the mask of the cloak."

Aldred snapped the reins, and the two draft horses jerked the wagon forward. He tried to shake the thought of the large dark door set at the end of the hall. He thought he had climbed up and down the stairway to the great hall thousands of times, paced himself in and out of his bedding chamber, walked, skipped, or ran down the hall toward it. However, he had never given it a thought, never given it a glance. In his conscious mind, it did not even exist. It was forbidden. The very thought of the door was forbidden. For all he knew, it was not even a door. It was not even real. It was a painting, a portrait, something only imagined, something existing only in the dream, the nightmare that haunted him. It was dark down there at the end of the hall—oh, so dark. Could it be real? Could the stone wall in the dark hall actually contain a door? He realized he could not answer the question. He did not know what was at the end of the hall.

"Are ya with me, lad?" asked Rodney. He slapped Aldred on his right knee. Aldred had seemed to slip into a trance.

"Oh, I was just thinking," Aldred replied. He smiled. "What was it you were saying? Something about the wheel? It should fit up fine, I should think."

"It was the key, Aldred," said Rodney. "The key."

"What key?"

"Why, the key in your dream. It hangs from a stand beside your bed," said Rodney.

"My dream? Bedstand? I have no bedstand," replied Aldred, confused. "What dream would that be?"

The hypnotic spell Lawrence had cast over Aldred was taking hold again. His recollection of the key, door, and the man behind the mask had slipped away.

Rodney was perplexed. Lady Catelin's carriage was in sight, so he knew the castle was not far away. He knew something was wrong with the poor lad, something out of his own control. One minute, Aldred could describe in vivid detail the sequence of events occurring in the dream tormenting him, but in the next, the slate of his memory was wiped clean. He could not even recall something as simple as a stand next to his bed.

Something had to be done to help the young man. Rodney decided to pocket the conversation for the time being. What if it had something to do with the proximity of the castle? Perhaps a bad experience from the past, some event or type of occurrence that subconsciously he could not face when he drew close to the place where it happened or scenery or images triggering the memory lapse. Or maybe even someone. Rodney figured the lad needed help. Perhaps he could investigate.

He wondered if Lord Lawrence knew about the nightmares. But, if Aldred had no memory of them when he was near the castle, he couldn't possibly have consulted his Lord Lawrence about them. It might not be a good idea to approach Master Lawrence about the subject. Something in his manner did not fit right. Aldred's room seemed to be a more appropriate place to start. He would need to exercise extreme caution in finding an opportunity to steal his way up the well-described stairway and down the hall to his room. He must choose a time when he would not be discovered. Perhaps a time would arise when Aldred was attending to the needs of Lady Catelin and Lord Lawrence. But then what would he do if there was a bedstand? What would he do if there was a key? What would he do if the key fit the door at the dark end of the hall? If he was right of mind, he would then grasp Lady Catelin by the hand and run like hell.

"Why, yes, lad, the wheel," said Rodney. "I should think it be fine. I should think it would all be fine."

After they reached the coach and replaced the wheel, Rodney stopped by his old friend's graveside and prayed he would not soon be joining him.

F

While Aldred and Rodney were on their chase of a wild goose Lord Lawrence had set them on, he was busy spinning his web, hoping to ensnare the beautiful young Lady Catelin. As innocent as the young lady appeared, however, this would not be the first time she was exposed to the bait of spinning silk held to lure her into a net of devious desires. She had squashed more than one spider, although never one so deadly poisonous. Catelin led him on with flirtatious conversation. "You are so charming. I have never met a man such as you. You have the depth of soul in your eyes."

Lawrence had soul in more places than his eyes, and at this particular time, his thirst for another could not be quenched. He must have this woman. He must have all of her. He treated her to the best of wine at evening in the rose garden. Each afternoon, she was taken for a ride in the countryside and a light lunch by the small lake. On the first such outing, she insisted on a swim, disrobing behind a bush and shooing his eyes from her with a provocative smile, and lift of her delicate right hand while she held her dress over her bosom. Who was it holding the bait and casting the web?

It was the afternoon of the day Aldred was returning to the castle when Lawrence first exposed Catelin to the crystal amulet he wore around his neck. He had, up to that time, kept it concealed beneath his blouse. His power of hypnotism worked great magic when combined with the rays of the sun, the moon, or certain candlelight projecting into its prism-like shape. It was the oscillating slow motion and refraction of light that captured his victims' minds and stripped them of free will. The sun flickered through the swaying leaves of an oak tree under which they sat on a blanket overlooking the lake. Lawrence pulled the crystal over his chest and toyed with it a bit. The amulet waltzed in the glimmer of the undulating reflections of rainbow-color bands. Catelin began to stare at the beautiful patterns; her eyes were becoming dazzled. It was the first step toward strings of silk-wrapping around her helpless appendages and bringing her down and under the control of Lord Lawrence.

But suddenly, Lawrence withdrew the amulet from her gaze and shoved it back under his blouse. *What am I doing?* he thought. He had her in the clutch of his hands, and for the first time in his life, he was struck with apprehension. *Fear? Certainly not. Fear of what? What do I, Lord Lawrence, have to fear? Lady Catelin? Certainly not,* he thought. *I fear nothing, no one.*

"What is it, Lawrence?" Catelin asked. She reached toward him; her left hand was approaching his neck to retrieve the shining crystal. She wanted more of it, another taste of it.

"Humph, why, nothing, my lady. Humph, nothing," he said. He quickly stood, with the amulet now well concealed under his blouse, and grabbed her hand. "Come. We must return. I expect Aldred and your servant approach the ebb of their journey."

Back in the horse-drawn buggy, Lawrence thought about what had happened. What was he to do? He must have this woman, but again, for the first time in his life, he actually felt apprehension, guilt, about placing someone in a spell to gain control over them. No. He felt guilt about placing *her* under a spell. He must have her, but it must be of her own accord, her own volition. He must not lose her, must not let her go.

It was the coachman. He was the key. He would open the door. With his sudden death, the second tragedy in such a short period would certainly cause her to lean on Lawrence. He would become her savior. He must not lose her. She belonged to him and him alone. No one else could claim her, Lady Catelin.

On their return to the castle, Lady Catelin gently placed her left hand on his right thigh, tapping her fingers, weaving her own little web. "I love what you have around your neck," she said.

Perhaps it will be mine soon, she thought, smiling, weaving.

F

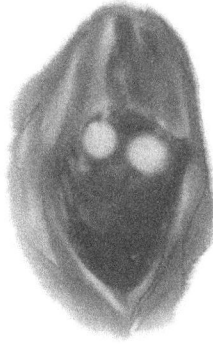

CHAPTER SEVEN

"Aldred, be so kind as to fetch some port for our Lady Catelin. I will be joining her presently in the garden," instructed Lawrence. "And see to it a fire is set in the pit."

Aldred and Rodney had returned earlier in the day, collected Catelin's team of horses, and went back to retrieve her carriage. They had returned to the castle grounds near dinner, then they set off to the stables to care for the teams of horses. Aldred returned to the great hall, where Lawrence had finished dining, to inquire about any further instructions for the day. His limbs were tired, and he was ready to retire for the evening.

"Why, Aldred," Catelin began, "you should join us for a spot of wine and enjoy the light of the moon. It is so romantic."

This irritated Lawrence. "Humph, I believe Aldred has other tasks to perform, my lady, and he looks worn from travel. I am certain he is ready to rest for the night. Are you not, Aldred?" Lawrence said this not as a question, and looked him in the eye.

"I should retire, my lady," Aldred replied. "Would you like your port heated, Master Lawrence?"

"That would be pleasant," Catelin interrupted. "And I insist you have one small taste before you are off to your chamber."

Again, Lawrence found this distressful, but he relented. "Humph, yes, Aldred," he said. He forced a smile. "One short taste before you are off. Come, my lady." Lawrence rose and offered her his right hand.

Catelin was stunning in her gown of light violet. It appeared to be an evening gown worn for social gatherings or a grand ball. It was one of fashion Aldred was not familiar with. It fit tight against her slim, rounded figure and fell straight to the floor from her hips. He wondered what kind of undergarment could be beneath the gown, if any at all. He caught her ocean-blue eyes cast directly sighting his own and froze in his footsteps, treading water and drowning in them. His tongue could have been drooping to the floor along with her hemline, and he would have been oblivious to the embarrassment.

"Aldred!" commanded Lawrence. "Be off with you." Then he rushed her away, although Catelin kept Aldred in view, eyeing him over her shoulder. She, too, was in the ocean but only wading.

As Lawrence escorted Lady Catelin past the stables toward the garden, he withdrew the amulet. The moon was full and bright. The flames in the firepit around which they sat flickered merrily. He was ready to continue what he had begun. This time, he would not retreat. She must learn not to flirt with another man, especially not with one of such low stature. The man would be a beggar if not for him. She would learn. She would be trained. How could she do such a thing? Why would she do such a thing?

Rodney watched them as they passed by the stables and through the gate beyond the corral to the rose garden, not his cemetery in the courtyard, which, too, was surrounded by tall hedges to keep livestock from devouring the bush and flowers. And shortly thereafter, he watched again as Aldred passed by from the service entrance with a platter containing two pitchers and three wineglasses.

This presented an opportunity Rodney could not let slip by unattended. He waited until Aldred passed through the garden gate and paced himself as quickly as his wobbly legs could carry him, more skipping than running these days. He looked cautiously in both directions before passing through the double doors of the mansion. He entered and passed through the small solar into the hall, leading him to the staircase at its opposite end. The doors leading to the great hall were at his left. He knew just where to go and followed the stairs up to the path well-worn in Aldred's daily labors, in Aldred's dreams, in Aldred's nightmares. He paused at the top and turned to his right to check for a door, but the far end of the hall was hidden in shadows. *Drat, I should have brung me a candle,* he thought.

He quickly turned around and headed the opposite direction toward Aldred's room. He reached the door and turned to look back. Nervous as a bug in a bird's nest, he reached for the door handle, which was a straight handle rather than a round knob. *What's the diff?* he thought. He pressed down, but it didn't move. *Locked? No, why would Aldred lock his door? He has nothing to hide. Rather, he didn't know he did have something to hide.* Rodney gave the handle a good slap, and it shot down, releasing the latch.

He leaned his head through the partially open door and inquired, "Anyone be at home?" *Of course not,* he thought.

Rodney pushed the door fully open and stepped in, but having no window on any wall, there was no moonlight to pass through, so it was as dark as the hallway with the dead end or door yet to be discovered. He could see the form of the bed to his left and tiptoed toward it, reaching out with both hands in front of him, hoping they did not come in contact with another breathing figure or otherwise. He took one tiptoe too many and plopped face-first across the bed.

"My lord!" he exclaimed, tempering the volume. He crawled forward until he reached the other side and dropped his hands down onto the stone floor and wiggled his body forward until he rolled off the edge.

Now Rodney was really getting nervous. "Got to get this done and get me outta here," he whispered aloud.

Rodney crawled forward on hands and knees until his head crashed into a solid silhouette, something made of wood. He pushed himself upright on his knees and felt the face of it. It was open at the bottom and solid on both sides. He found his head had collided into the bottom of a drawer, the top of which would have been level with the top of the bedding mattress. "I got me a bloody bedstand. That's what I got me," he concluded in a whisper.

Rodney crawled around the right side of the stand and reached behind with his right arm. Up, up, up, it dragged on the back panel. "Lord be," he said to himself and began shaking. "Ain't not no bloody dream."

The key was long and skeleton shaped with an oval loop or ring forged into it at one end. It was made for a big lock in a big door. "Legs, get me outta here." Rodney had second thoughts about grabbing the key, but thought otherwise, as he needed to act forthright before his courage waned away to the size of bread crumbs.

As he crawled around the bed, he also thought about what would happen if the dream returned, and when Aldred reached for the key, his fingers found nothing but a short wooden peg on the backside of the stand. If Aldred did not show up to clean the bloody mess, the masked man just might come looking for him. Would Aldred just stand there all night long in front of the door and be discovered by the masked man? Provided, that is, there was a masked man, and provided, that is, the key belonged to the door at the end of the hall, and provided, that is, the key actually fit the lock, and provided, that is, the door actually had a lock. Aldred's door had no lock, so why would the door at the end of the hall have a lock? Provided, that is, there actually was a door at the end of the dark hall. His curiosity was killing him. As he turned to crawl back to the bedstand, he tried to convince himself there was no one else to do the job. No one knew. He had to know.

Rodney figured someone needed to investigate just where the key would lead, just what would be found behind the lock, wherever that would be found. Again, second thoughts invaded his mind, questioning Rodney as to whether or not he really felt up to the job. How could he ever explain his actions if he was discovered snooping around all the doors and locks in the castle? Aldred had free rein of the place, so it would only be fitting for Aldred to be the one doing the snooping. Somehow he would need to get the key in Aldred's hands and somehow convince him to keep Lord Lawrence's hands out of the picture.

Rodney reached behind the stand and fetched the key, plucking it between his remaining teeth as he crawled back toward the door. When he reached the door, he clumsily got up to his feet and tiptoed his way back down the hall, but this time, he did not stop at the stairway. He scurried straight head-on into the dark entryway. He kept the key clenched in his mouth and reached out to whatever would be found when it terminated, hoping it would not be a free fall down to the pits of hell.

Holding his breath, his fingertips found wood. They finger-toed their way around its surface and found a latch. He pressed it down, but it was held fast. The fingers of his right hand explored the surface around the base of the latch handle. The latch had been discovered on the right side of the door. On the right side of the latch, his fingers unveiled a lock. *It must be a lock,* he thought. The iron thing protruding from the door was formed in the shape of a circle, and there was a hole at the middle. Keeping the hole located with his right forefinger, the fingers of his left hand elevated toward his mouth and retrieved the key. They slowly descended to join forces with their mates by the keyhole. But as they converged, something started nervously shaking them. *Calm down, Rodney,* they pleaded.

He seemed to be ignoring them. Frustratingly, they fumbled around to and fro, unsuccessfully poking jabs at the door itself. If they had not been tethered to the man so tightly, they would be free to exercise their own will. Finally, the man standing over them, apparently shaken by its wobbling legs, took a deep breath and held it fast. The right thumb and forefinger grasped the back end of the key, and its partners on the left guided the key home. They twisted to the right. Deadlocked. They twisted in the opposite direction. With a resounding, muffled clank, the lock was freed.

Quickly the twin fingers backtracked, twisting the lock closed and begged the man to take another breath and get his shaking legs moving in the opposite direction. They were unaware of a village named Dodge City would someday exist in a land yet to be discovered, but nevertheless, they wanted out. The duo surrendered the key to an appointed pocket as the nervous man's wobbly legs began hustling their way in the direction of his first thought back toward the bedstand, but instead, the man ordered them to retreat in a hastened detour back down the stairway.

All this and barely a half glass of port had passed Lady Catelin's lips. Rodney found his way back to the stable and collapsed on a pile of hay, catching his breath while his heart raced along at a frantic pace. His fingers reached to brush themselves clean through his mussed graying hair, but the key was not among them. Could they have abandoned it in a jail cell door back in Dodge City?

F

"So tell me, Aldred," petitioned Catelin. "You grew up here with Lawrence. Is this not true?" Her lips kissed the rim of the glass, over which her eyes wrapped over him. She could not will her dazzled eyes to look away. *Why does he please them so much?* she asked herself.

Aldred looked at Lawrence for approval before he spoke. Lawrence cast a stern look in his direction, wondering how the woman could have known such a thing. Aldred's name had not crossed his lips since he had been gone.

Catelin answered his silence. "I saw your names carved in the large oak tree at the lakeside."

"Humph, we try not to dwell on the past, my lady," injected Lawrence. "That was a long time ago, was it not, Aldred?"

Aldred nodded but did not speak. He had not been given permission. Lawrence toyed with the amulet, trapping beams of moonlight in its crystal eyes and casting them in Aldred's direction. He thought perhaps it was fortunate she had invited Aldred. He could work on them both at the same time. *If only she would look my way.*

The three sat on wooden high-back chairs; two of them provided cushioned seating and angled backrests. They were arranged in a triangle around a circular firepit in their midst. Firelight sparkled in Aldred's eyes, moonbeams in Catelin's, and sparks were about to ignite in Lawrence's. Roses surrounded them on three sides: climbers, teas, and floribundas of red, yellow, white, and pink.

"Please," Catelin asked, "indulge me." Lawrence relented. "Humph, proceed, Aldred."

"As children, Lawrence taught me to fish there," he began, setting his eyes on Master Lawrence. "Together we carved our names there on the old oak. Mine was placed at the lower end of the trunk and my lord's at the higher station, as is our stations in life, of course. It was the day Lawrence found his beautiful amulet he wears to this day."

These were also lies, of course, with the exception of their current stations in life. Jealous, Lawrence had carved his name weeks after discovering Aldred's carving. The man had never caught a fish in his life. The labor of it all was too demeaning. He would watch Aldred make the catch and eat the fish he made Aldred cook over an open fire after beating him with a switch. The lake belonged to him, not Aldred. Lawrence had not precisely actually found the amulet; he had stolen it off the man of cloth he murdered, the not-so-holy holy man, the not-a-monk-of-his-kind monk—the reappearing monk.

"Why do you look away?" asked Catelin. The question was directed to Aldred. But both men had turned away. While Aldred looked at Lawrence for approval, Lawrence looked for the shrouded flash of an image he had clearly seen standing, glaring at him from across the dancing flames.

"Humph, I believe he tires, my lady," interrupted Lawrence back at attention. "Do you not, my childhood friend?" The image of the not-a-monk-of-his-kind monk wrapped in his hooded brown cloak had irritated him. *Where do these images come from? Why do they appear?*

"Yes, my lord. I should retire by your leave," said Aldred. He could not look in Catelin's direction. Something forbade him.

Lawrence waved Aldred away with a sweep of his right hand. Reinforcing the spell he kept Aldred under had over time become a second-thought task. The man just seemed too willing. Once he could separate himself and Lady Catelin from Aldred, he would place her in his forgotten memories. Catelin watched Lawrence's wicked smile, as Aldred stepped away and out of the garden. The not-a-monk-of-his-kind monk angered him, and her attention to Aldred festered the wound; the images ate away at his mind, his consciousness.

"Strange." Catelin found Aldred's behavior odd from a man she thought of as so charming. Her gift told her Aldred was indeed troubled, not in control. Something about the man seemed to change when he was in the close presence of Lord Lawrence. It was Lawrence, not Aldred, who was in control. She found her attraction to Aldred . . . unusual.

"I am sure he will be about his wits on the morrow," said Lawrence. He turned to face Catelin, grasping the amulet to catch a beam meant for her eyes only. "Now," he said, "let us begin."

Catelin smiled as Lawrence played with the amulet, attempting to arrest streams of moonlight and focus them in her direction. Catelin played with Lawrence, he within the grasp of her hands.

"I would love to touch it," she said.

Lawrence was caught off guard, his attention paid to harnessing the amulet's magic. "My lady?"

"I wonder. Does it throb when held in one's hand?" Seductively, she lifted her left eyebrow.

Lawrence was not quite certain what Catelin meant. He was becoming aroused, starting to flush with blood . . . down below.

"I would love to hold it, squeeze it, and feel its warmth, its heat." She closed her eyes and began to hum under her breath, as if dreaming of stroking the amulet, raising her right hand, cupping it.

My god, thought Lawrence, *what is this woman doing to me?* He could feel her hand wrapped around the amulet, wrapped around him. Sensing uncontrollable stimuli approaching, Lawrence quickly stood, released the amulet, and turned away from her, gasping for air while his heart nearly beat out of his chest. He held back, fearing he would spoil his trousers. He took in slow deep breaths, calming himself. Was the woman already under his command, or was she driving him mad? He did not know. Or could it be both? She had not even touched him.

He turned back to face her. Catelin's lips were back to the wineglass, and under its own lip, she wore a broad smile. "Can I be of service?" she asked. She had pulled her gown up high on her thighs and crossed her exposed legs, swinging her right leg over the left.

Lawrence squeezed his eyes shut tightly. *I must be dreaming,* he thought. *This cannot be real. She is so . . . pure. I must be hearing . . . I must be seeing . . . things.* He opened them again. Lady Catelin sat silently, staring into the firepit. Her wineglass was resting on a small wooden table at her left; her beautiful legs were bent at the knee but not exposed. She hadn't said a word.

"Yes, maybe he tires," she said. Then she watched as Lawrence withdrew the amulet, holding it by its chain, slowly stepping toward her.

F

As Aldred passed by the stable, he heard a shuffling behind him. It was Rodney. He was half walking, half skipping, awkwardly trying to be quiet, popping his head up and down as though he was imitating a chicken pecking for bits of feed. "Rodney?" he asked.

"Master Aldred," Rodney said, approaching him. "I beg of your indulgence, lad. But I must have word. I fear for you. I fear for us all."

"It is a calm, beautiful evening, Rodney. What have you to fear? Do you sense a wild animal?"

"Far worse, I fear," he answered. "Perhaps the devil's servant or even the devil himself, me thinks. There is great evil around this castle."

"What kind of tricks does your mind play with you, sir? This is no place of evil. Come with me, and we shall have us a mug of port. It will settle your nerves and help you rest. We both tire from our journey. A good swallow will put us both to bed."

The two men retired to the kitchen where Aldred heated more port wine and filled two large wooden mugs. They sat at a rectangular table on opposite wooden benches.

"Now tell me what troubles your mind," said Aldred. He took a long drink from the mug. "My, how your Lady Catelin's eyes sparkle and shine. You know, I have never seen a woman so lovely in all my days. I have never ever been so near someone so lovely or actually spoken with one. And she actually spoke to me."

Aldred had actually been close to one young woman once or had at least become infatuated ever so briefly but never intimately, not even with a prostitute. But he had engaged with one young girl, full of active hormones and eager to gain more experience with Aldred. Penelope had been an orphaned, peasant girl he had met some months ago near the same village he and Rodney had visited. They had kissed once one evening and sometime after he brought her back to the castle. She had been awarded a position in the kitchen. Lawrence had observed their closeness and their evening rides to the lake and put an end to it, awarding her a higher position on his stone slab in the dungeon. She was among his most recent victims and among Aldred's missing memories. If the flood of banked memories had been restored simultaneously, it could overwhelm Aldred so badly he might just lose the conscious part of his mind completely.

"Me thinks my lady has an eye for you too, lad. I took liberty in stepping into the garden shadows. I seen you both, like you was a couple o' lost puppies," confirmed Rodney. "But she is not what we need to have word about, lad. 'Tis your dreams. The ones you have over and over."

"I do not recall any dreams. What dreams do you speak of?" asked Aldred. He took another swallow of wine and stared at the ceiling. "She has an eye for me?" he added.

"Get your mind right now, lad. 'Tis the dreams which ain't no dreams. They be real. You told me all about them, but you cannot remember nothing when you get close to this castle and your Lord Lawrence."

"What did I tell you, Rodney?" he asked.

"I can do better boy. I can show you," Rodney said. "But we got to be awful careful. We do, lest we be caught."

"You seem to be spooked by something. What could you have to show me?"

"I can show you where the dreams which ain't no dreams happen,"

Rodney replied. "And maybe then you can start to remember what goes on down those stairs. Something very evil."

"Evil?" Aldred asked. "What stairs are you talking about? I think you need a bit more port. Or maybe you might have been into the barrel a bit too heavy already?"

"'Tis the steps leading down to the dungeon where the lady's body was cut apart. Those be the steps me is talking about, lad. Murdered and cut apart. And you take 'em out and bury 'em some place in the woods me thinks. You do. Cleaning up the bloody dirty work. And me does mean bloody." Rodney took his advice and took a long swallow of wine. Then he went on to tell Aldred step by step the recurring dream Aldred had described to him again and again.

"Preposterous," said Aldred. "A key leading to a dungeon? A woman cut apart in pieces? I do not even have a bedstand. How could there be a key on such a stand?"

"Well, I went up there, and I got me the key what was hanging on a peg on the ol' bedstand what ain't there," said Rodney. "Let me show you what ain't there is there."

"If that is what it will take to set your mind right," began Aldred, "then show. I would genuinely appreciate seeing this what ain't there is there you seem to be talking about."

"We will need us some candles, lad," suggested Rodney. "'Tis awful dark down in that hall."

As Aldred and Rodney were making their way up the stairway to check on the bedstand that wasn't there that was there, Lord Lawrence was making his way into Lady Catelin's mind. And even under hypnosis, Aldred remained present in her thoughts. Lawrence was intent on removing and replacing them. It was not very complicated. She would not love another. She would not think of another. She belonged to Lawrence and only Lawrence.

F

"I do not believe this," Aldred said. He removed his right hand from the peg at the back of the stand along with the fingers clutching nothing, not even a shadow of a memory of what hung from the peg. "I must see this every night. How could I possibly not remember?"

Rodney stood at the doorway; his right arm was extending a candle into the room. "Tricks of the mind. Me seen it once at a traveling fair. People told to do things they do not remember being told. They do them, and they do not know why. They be told to forget things."

"But where is the key?" Aldred asked. "You said the key was hanging here on the peg. What happened to it?"

"Me fingers left it in the door. They got a fright and run without it. Come. I will show you the key. We can find it in the door be stuck to it." Rodney backed out of the doorway and waved with his free hand, inviting Aldred to follow.

Aldred retrieved a lantern from atop the elusive stand and contemplated gripping the key, which did not yet quite exist, in his right fist while gritting his teeth. *What other surprises lie ahead for me?* he thought, nearly biting his lip, holding back the verbal expression of frustration. He struck a match to the lantern, then he turned to Rodney's wave and followed it out of the bedchamber, taking one last glance at the stand before closing the door behind him.

Aldred took charge, passing Rodney in the hall while holding the lantern ahead of him. He reached the stairway, stopped briefly to listen for any chatter or movement below, and stepped into the dark hall beyond. Rodney blew out his candle, as the lantern cast plenty of light for them to navigate. He stepped beside Aldred, pointing to the key.

"There it be, Master Aldred," said Rodney.

"I am no man's master," Aldred replied. "And in this venture, we are companions, explorers of the unknown. If what you tell me lies beyond the door becomes truth, then we will have much more to discover." He grasped the oval ring at the end of the key and freed the lock. He removed the key, placed it in a trouser pocket, pressed the latch handle down, and pushed open the door.

There he stood, observing his reflection in the mirror as he had done so many times in his dream, although on this occasion the blank stare was missing. Rodney cupped his left hand around Aldred's right arm for security.

"We should pass, lad, and close the door behind so we not be seen, me thinks," suggested Rodney.

"It is the mirror you spoke of," Aldred confirmed. "I have passed this door a hundred times, but I never gave it a thought. I never realized there was a door. This seems insane. Am I insane?"

"Not you, Aldred," Rodney said, "but I imagine the man who made you this way has a few wobbly marbles rollin' 'round his head."

Aldred moved across the threshold with Rodney in tow who then closed the door behind them. The lantern's reflection helped illuminate the landing. Rodney stepped to Aldred's side when he turned to extend the lantern over the spiral stairs leading down toward their left.

"We must do this," Aldred said. He moved forward, and without hesitation, he began to descend the stairs, just as he would do every morning at sunrise, down to the main floor of the castle to meet with the kitchen crew and see about tending to the day's chores around the castle grounds.

"Wait for me, lad," Rodney said, losing his grip.

"Wherever this leads us, it is quite far below," said Aldred. They had rounded the tenth circle of stairs.

"Two or three more turns, lad. You told me a dozen turns round, but I'm not sure if they be a baker man's."

Finally, Aldred reached another landing and stepped into a small solar. There, in a corner, sat the buckets, a mop, gloves, and sheets, just as Aldred had described to Rodney and Rodney had described to Aldred.

Aldred did not hesitate. He stepped to the double doors and pushed them open. The room was dark and cool. It felt dank and held a sour odor. Aldred held the lantern high and stepped forward beyond the doors. He could see shadows of structures in the room, and the large stone counter or slab Rodney described was straight ahead of him in the middle of the room. He held the lantern out to his right. Its flame illuminated the shape of a large animal. It stood at a stone pillar's attention, with its ears lifted high. The huge animal bared its incisors as it sniffed the air. Hearing a low growl behind him, Aldred turned the lantern. Another animal stood; it, too, was chained but investigating the scent.

"Do not move," he warned Rodney.

"Me thinks not, Lord Aldred." Rodney needed no suggestion.

Aldred whispered in reply, "I am no lord, Rodney." He paused and added, "But I pray tell the beasts . . . they know not."

"You told me not of them, me thinks."

Aldred waved the lantern back and forth once more. The devil dogs both approached him cautiously and raised their snouts; each was grunting, then growling lowly. With his left palm open, Aldred raised and lowered his forearm up and down—first, at the beast to his left and then the other. Rodney began slowly retreating back through the doorway, wanting no part of it. But then the beasts fell silent and sat down as though yielding to a command. They had been trained to recognize Aldred. Obediently, both animals then stretched their forelegs outward and positioned their heads down upon them. The dogs, if they were dogs, were mutants, something grown out of experimentation, bred with the devil in mind.

Aldred stepped forward several paces, turned, and waved the lantern once again, finding the animals had both closed their eyes. He walked to his right toward the far wall and motioned Rodney to follow. "Me, me lord?"

"No, Rodney," he began, "the beastly dog standing behind you."

Rodney sprang to his tiptoes and swiftly trotted to Aldred's right side. His arms were folded halfway in a curl but held outward at his sides, praying not to make a sound.

Paying no attention, Aldred found the wall held more lanterns. However, because the occupant was currently away, none were lit. He then made his way to the stone slab and ran his left fingers across it, as he made his way around its full perimeter. "A young woman?" Aldred inquired. He saw Rodney's eyes were pinned to the animals. "They sleep."

"I trust they remain in their dreams," Aldred replied. "And the woman? Young, you say?"

"Yes, young, so you said, not I," agreed Rodney.

"Blonde of hair, fair looking, and slender, you say?" Aldred asked.

"Yes, again, so you said."

"Blue of eyes? Was she blue of eyes? I seem to recall a young girl. But I cannot remember why or from where. But she was fair and blue of eyes," said Aldred.

"You did not say, lad. In your dream, maybe you were afar or turned away."

"Then if I should have this dream of horror again," Aldred began, "I should take note." He turned to look at Rodney. "This young woman. Here, in this place. Butchered. Could it still be a dream? A nightmare?"

"'Tis hard to tell," began Rodney. "The slab—it seems to be stained. It could be from an animal."

"Animals are butchered in the yard, beyond the stable," said Aldred. "Why bring them here? To experiment? For what purpose? Unless it be these beasts before us. They are quite uncommon. We have no physicians about. No, not animals. Not here. There would be others around, other species perhaps. Look beyond. Another set of doors. You say the man— the man with the mask. He stood beyond this stone counter. Is this so?"

"Yes. But you wake as he tips his mask with a scalpel. Every time you do, you say." Rodney looked at the doors at the opposite end of the long hall. Two more of the chained devil dogs were at rest. "The doors behind us lead to you. Them doors there beyond," he pointed, "they must lead to the man and his mask."

"Then let us find this masked man," Aldred replied. Anger was beginning to build inside him. His dream was becoming reality. He could not accept himself willingly participating in an act of such despicable savagery . . . humans, dogs, other animals, or not.

"We've no weapons, lad," said Rodney. "How do we defend us against his scalpels?" Worry and fear enveloped his face.

"The lion is not in its den," replied Aldred. "He would be here now. The room would be alight with his presence, his cloak, and his mask. These lanterns about us would be alive."

"Lad," Rodney started, "you are beginning to sound like you did when we were away from this place, when your head was right. When Lord Lawrence is about, you talk quite like a puppet, I must say. But you sound a bit more like the man you should be, you do."

"I had not noticed, Rodney."

"You wouldn't, not when you ain't you."

Aldred shook his head. "As strange as it sounds, my friend. It makes complete sense. If I am not me, how would I know I am me?" They both chuckled. Rodney was nervous, and then Aldred shook his head toward the other double doors. "Let us explore."

Rodney saw the other two beasts stationed at the opposite doors. Suddenly, they jumped to their feet and began running toward them, not quite barking, but not quite roaring. Rodney hustled to the back side of the stone slab, bent down, and covered his head with both arms, muttering some kind of prayer. It ended with, "I promise. I promise."

Once the beasts entered into the field of Aldred's scent, they dropped their hind legs and skidded to a stop, each of them bumping into one of Aldred's thighs. He stood his ground with an uncanny confidence he knew not from where it came, but he knew the beasts would not harm him. "These beasts," he said as he kneeled, "they know me." They both rolled on their sides as he reached out and brushed each on their massive shoulders. "Do I feed them?" He thought about it briefly. "I care not to know where they acquire nourishment. My heaven!"

"Me thinks maybe the man behind the mask, me lord?" He, too, cared not to know, or even think the beasts fed off the victims. "And me thinks otherwise, Lord Rodney."

"These animals are not normal."

"Best we depart, Aldred. We would not want to tease their appetite now me thinks." He was back up on his feet again, working his way around the slab to Aldred.

Before proceeding forward, Aldred shone the light toward the wall at his right. It was another contraption Lawrence had been designing and constructing, not near completion; it was a deviation from his original plan. Eventually, it would become the confining restraint used to trap Helen when bound by all four appendages, collared around the neck, and plucked repeatedly with spikes around her entire body. It would be perfected with modification and a number of practical applications on test specimens.

"A cage of some sort," said Aldred. There were other devices, chains with cuffs on their ends, supported and hanging from the wall. There was also a tall barrel set in a corner of the room. "Not suited for a dog, my thoughts tell me."

The companions moved forward toward the double doors, with Rodney nervously doing so. The beast to his left had risen to a sitting position as he passed, leaning his head toward him, revealing its huge fangs, which were sharp enough to rip off the man's arm with one chew.

Nice puppy, thought Rodney.

At the doors, each grabbed a handle and pulled. The unlocked doors easily swung open. Another solar appeared. This one was twice the size. It contained a variety of carpenter's tools stored on shelves to their right. Directly above them were two small bells attached to a rope and pulley system. The pull cord was used to call Lord Lawrence from outside his bedchamber. To their left was another set of shelves upon which was stored many sorts of knives, scalpels, clamps, and devices for pulling, smashing, hanging, and ripping. On a stand in the opposite left corner were containers of oil for the lanterns, matches, and a lighting instrument. In the right corner hung several black cloaks and masks; black gloves and boots were stored below them. Cleanliness is next to godliness.

Directly opposite was another threshold leading to another smaller solar and a second landing leading to a spiral stairway. A stand in one corner held a spare lantern. On the wall to their right was another door. It sat closed.

"Them steps lead to the mask and the man, Aldred," said Rodney. "And I know it ain't you and it ain't no company what's spending a night or two. Ain't but one man it could be."

"It does appear to be so," Aldred said. "But if we had just a bit more."

"We got the knives and scalpels. We got the contraptions and the slab. We got the beasts. What more do we need, lad?" Rodney asked.

"A body," Aldred said.

"Well, you weren't too clear on that part, son. But I guess we might find us one or two out in the woods somewhere. Ain't nowhere to put bodies down here, what was left of 'em. And you did say you wrapped 'em up nice and tidy. You did." Rodney looked for approval. "I'm not so sure I'm eager to climb these stairs, Aldred. Not right now. It could be Lord Lawrence might be on his way down to his chamber soon."

"Tomorrow," agreed Aldred. "We'll take a walk into the woods. Gather a shovel. Might be the graves be shallow. Maybe so wildlife could get what remained. On the morrow. Let us return whence we came. I will come fetch you in the kitchen when Brita is preparing and serving the early meal for the staff."

"I hope me can sleep," said Rodney. "Me mind is spinning 'round."

Backing their tracks past the sleeping beasts and up the long stairway out into the hall above the staircase, the companions bid their night farewell. Aldred returned the key to its appointed peg. Rodney returned to the stable, and bidding his goodbyes to the castle would soon follow.

F

Lord Lawrence was not making his way down the spiral stairway to his dungeon. He remained in the garden, making his way toward Lady Catelin. She was not falling easily. He had never before had such difficulty. Catelin read through him and knew he was attempting to gain total control over her mind. She could almost see the thoughts spinning around his mind, but they were swirling in frenzy. The man had been practicing this art for quite some time. He had a special place for the women he had possessed in the past, but she could not picture its location.

It was not his bedchamber. She felt he had many women pass through, but some of them lingered. His hunger did not lie in the bedchamber; it was somewhere much darker, something much darker. His hungers lie for something within these women. She sensed he might be confused about his intentions toward her. It was different, but dark nevertheless. He battled an internal struggle, opposing desires. Believing her will was stronger, Catelin decided she would succumb to his flirtatious whim, set his mind at ease, and explore the secrets he held he would unconsciously share with her.

"I will submit," she said. "You cannot deceive me. I will follow you into your darkness. But do not toy with me, Lawrence."

Lawrence felt once he was able to place her in a hypnotic state, he could easily win her over. She would no longer have control. None of the others ever did. *Look at poor Aldred, my sweet,* he thought. The allure, infatuation she had for Aldred would be wiped clean. And once he had eliminated Rodney, he, too, would fall below the shadows of her memory. He stepped closer, dropped to one knee, and rolled the amulet in his fingertips. The reflections of moonbeams were trapped in her eyes. As she fell into a trance, her last thought was of Aldred's image.

"You will no longer think of Aldred," Lawrence commanded. "Wipe him from your thoughts. And your coachman Rodney, he will go missing. You will think nothing of his departures. The man takes leave at will and always returns within a fortnight. You will have no concern when he fails ever to return. His memory will fade away with the setting of the sun. You will have no desire to leave my castle, no desire to leave me. It is I you truly love. I alone will dominate your thoughts. I alone will be in your thoughts from this day to come and those forevermore."

"You alone," Catelin said. Her eyes were lost in the flickering light of the amulet. She was down and under. Her conscious will was compromised. "On the morrow, at midnight, you will come to me. You will come to me at my bedchamber. From there, we will enter the dark. We will enter my asylum."

"On the morrow, at midnight," she repeated.

"When I snap my fingers, you will wake. Your thoughts of Aldred will be gone. You will tire, and without word, you will retire to your bedchamber." Lawrence stood and tucked away the amulet. Then he snapped the fingers of his right hand.

Catelin's eyes came back to life, and she yawned, placing both delicate hands over her mouth. She stood, curtsied, and began walking back to the mansion. She paused, turned, and smiled sensually at Lawrence, then she walked away.

"Sweet dreams," Lawrence said, smiling away. He watched the sway of her graceful body as she passed through the gate. He poured another glass of port and raised a toast to himself and his garden of roses. *One more picked,* he thought.

Dreams of Aldred, I pray, Catelin thought as she picked up her pace. Once Catelin was well out of the garden and approaching the boardwalk to the castle mansion, Lawrence followed, but instead, he made a detour for the stable. The coachman, the dear faithful man Rodney, was nowhere to be found. Lord Lawrence waited.

F

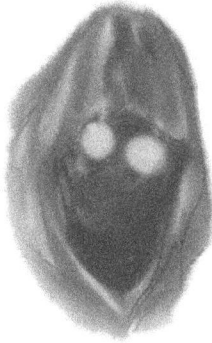

CHAPTER EIGHT

"Mother Brita," said Aldred. He approached the heavyset brown-haired woman. She was the head cook and master of the kitchen. All the staff addressed her as such. Don't mess with the hands feeding you. She wore a large white apron hanging from her huge bosom down past her knees. It was dusted with flour.

"Top of the morning to you, Master Aldred," she replied.

"Oh, Brita, you are almost my mum. I am no master. Have you seen the coachman Rodney?" he asked. Aldred seemed to be concerned. He had already made a round through the stable and had earlier canvassed the kitchen, but Rodney was nowhere to be found.

"His mouth has been the first I see of late, sonny boy," replied brown-eyed Brita, winking. "But I have not seen him this morning."

"Perhaps I missed him in the stable. I will look again, perhaps the corral." Aldred began to stomp out of the kitchen in a rush.

"You need your vittles," she responded. Brita tossed him a warm buttered biscuit just out of the oven. She had been in the kitchen well before dawn. "Keeps the mind full and the tummy sharp."

"Thank you," thinking about what she said. "I would wed you if you were not like me mum." He bit into the biscuit, smiling before he turned away.

"Nonsense," she replied. "'Tis the young one you would have. I see it in your eyes. Now off with you."

Aldred began to leave the kitchen but turned, inquisitive. "Mother," he began, "have you ever encountered me in the yard on the grounds late at night? Just walking? As though in my sleep?" Another bite departed the biscuit.

"I've me own business to tend, Master Aldred," she answered. Back to formalities. "I've no mind to be pinching in on yours." She looked down at the floor, almost shameful, and then she turned back to a mixing bowl, scraping at her right eye with her right wrist while clasping a large dripping wooden spoon. "Keep your eyes on the young mistress though, close I would." She brushed at the tears once more.

He made his way to the stable, thinking Brita must know something and must have seen something. Could it have been him behind the mansion, the castle? Could she have seen him carrying something away into the forest? He would need chatter with her again.

Aldred searched the stall and clump of hay Rodney had been sleeping on, but other than a blanket, it was bare as it had been earlier. He checked all the stalls, but they were fully occupied by horses. No Rodney. Leaning against one of the stall gates was a shovel. Aldred lifted it to find fresh earth, not completely dried. It had been used quite recently. He wondered if Rodney had gone exploring already and either found nothing or made a discovery. If so, why had he not gone straight to the kitchen and waited? Perhaps he muddied himself and went to the lake to bathe his clothing and his body, rather than washing off in one of the horse troughs or a bucket from the well as he usually had done in the morning.

Aldred rode bareback down to the lake but found it uninhabited. He glanced at the oak tree and his name carved at the bottom. He recalled Lady Catelin had noticed his name. His name, not Lawrence's. A second thought he recalled suddenly from nowhere. They did not carve their names together. Why had this memory told him so?

Aldred returned the horse to the stable and again went to the kitchen. There, he found Lady Catelin consulting with Brita. She, too, looked concerned.

"Have you seen Rodney?" they asked simultaneously. Then the two bashfully smiled at each other, but the smiles quickly turned to worrisome frowns.

Lady Catelin was dressed in riding clothing. It was a drastic change from her gowns, but she was just as beautiful, even though she resembled a tomboy but as no other. She had donned tight black slacks and a gray blouse a gardener would wear for a day of digging and hoeing while toiling in the hot sun, dirt, and dust to tend a garden. Her long silky black hair was tied behind in a ponytail with several blue ribbons trailing their way down the long mane, keeping it tight, lest it loosen and shade her sparkling eyes.

"I must speak with you, Master Aldred," she began, "in private, if you would have it."

Once outside, Aldred escorted Lady Catelin to the stable and Rodney's temporary bedchamber. She pleaded, "Lord Lawrence must not see us together, Aldred. I sense he has some evil plan. In the night, in the garden, something happened. It was the amulet. My memory of the eve has left me. Only fragments remain. I played my game as I have done with other men, but I fear I might not have him in my hand. I do recall Lawrence told me Rodney would go missing. I fear something might have happened to him. As the sun rose, I came to the stable, but he was gone. He is like a father to me. He raised me as one of his own. I fear for him so."

Aldred was stunned. Lady Catelin spoke to him as though they had known each other for years. She actually confided in him.

"And I recall being told I must cast you out from my mind, my memories" she continued. "But in my dreams and my mind when I woke, yours only was present in my thoughts. Never have I felt this way. I embarrass myself with these foreign feelings."

Aldred felt his legs start to wobble and wished he had a chair behind him at the moment. "I, too, have the same thoughts, my lady," he confessed. "And I, too, have fear for Rodney. We made a discovery in the dark of night and were to meet on this morning near dawn. We discovered a hidden chamber deep under the mansion, a dark place with dark secrets. Dreams, nightmares I shared with Rodney might be true. I cannot remember them. They are hidden from me. But Rodney confided that on our journey away from this place, away from Lord Lawrence, I had confessed to him dreams of the dastardliest of deeds I had not only witnessed but had placed my hand in and on them. Horrible deeds they are."

"The amulet," she replied. "Perhaps he uses it to capture the mind. It captures my mind and also yours, Aldred."

"But you have memories. The amulet has not yet imprisoned you.

You must leave this place," said Aldred.

"Not without Rodney," she said, "and not without—" She was about to disclose the part of Lawrence's mind she had explored . . . and perhaps captured.

"Then you must leave the castle for the day," he interrupted. "I will saddle a mount for you. Try to avoid Lord Lawrence as best you will and hesitate to be alone with him. If you encounter him, do not gaze at the amulet. Hide your eyes. Look away."

"Impossible I avoid him, I fear," she said. "I will insist you dine with us." The gray clouds in her mind concealed the danger she faced by even speaking Aldred's name. "He makes plain you are his childhood friend, so protest to my bidding he should not."

"My memories here at the castle tell me so, but now I wonder. If he does reject your plea," said Aldred, "I would be close at hand."

She reached forward, and they embraced each other's hands . . . and each other's gaze. Then Aldred turned away to gather Catelin a mount. After he watched her ride out of the stable toward the lake, he turned again to gather the shovel and the waiting exploration, the pending excavation.

F

Aldred's dreams had never revealed to him how or where he had actually disposed of the evidence, the bodies of those who had been brutalized, sliced apart. From Rodney's recall, he sensed there must be graves, and they must be close to the castle mansion. It must be close enough for him to finish his part in the assassinations, the annihilations, and then cleanse his body, hands, and the chamber of the bloody remains and return to his bedchamber before the sun rose. He always woke before the sun peeked over the horizon. The victims would most likely be concealed in the forest directly behind the mansion. And if the remains had been burned, there should be remnants of a large hole or pit filled with scorched bones. Aldred headed that direction, careful not to be witnessed by Lawrence, or so he thought.

Hidden behind the merlons on the battlement surrounding the top of the mansion, Lawrence paced behind and followed the path of Aldred, as he made his way from the stable past the kitchen and along the west wall of the mansion to its back side. Up the hill, Aldred climbed toward the burial ground.

Aldred does not collect firewood, Lawrence thought, *and will do so not with a shovel. He has no cause to go there. There are other servants for such a task, and they all have been given strict instructions as to where the wood is to be collected. The shade of the evergreens is a prohibited territory.* Certainly, the man could have no knowledge of what could be found there, under the boughs of the tall evergreens hidden in the shadows far below. The memory of the place was too deeply embedded in the unconscious, erased from any remote recollection.

It matters not, Lawrence thought again. *Aldred will report any disturbance, anything out of place. Dead animals, dead people, it matters not. Nothing there will be disturbed. Nothing there is out of place. The dead belong where they lie, fodder for occupants roaming the wild. If Aldred does make some kind of discovery, it will be reported, and he will be provided another . . . treatment.*

No matter, Lawrence had more important matters pending. He would follow the path of Catelin. She was certainly off for a jaunt to their favorite meeting place. She, too, might be in need of another treatment. She might be saddened by the sudden abandonment of her servant Rodney, but she would welcome his plan. There was no need for her to return to France or visit this uncle, whoever it might be. She would find happiness everlasting here with Lawrence as his betrothed. His charm was the only treatment she required. As for the servant, he would be cared for later. He was currently and patiently awaiting his fate, tied and gagged down in the chamber of fun, the asylum. *The joy of slowly tearing his limbs apart is too great a temptation,* he thought.

Lawrence climbed down the stone stairs from the battlement and collected a basket of pastries, butter, and jam, plus a bottle of port and his mount, smiling, long before Disney. "Hi ho, hi ho, it's off to work we go."

Lawrence whipped his horse to a gallop and soon joined Catelin. She was sitting under the limbs of the oak tree. "My lady," Lawrence greeted. Dressed in black, dismounting his black stallion, his blouse displayed a wide open *V* down the front. His amulet glistened in the morning sun. He noticed Catelin was tracing the path of a name carved in the oak tree. But when he stepped close to her, he found her fingertips on the name below his own. *Why does she trouble me so,* he thought, *a tease?*

"I have learned of your servant departing our company. Has he been charged with some enterprise, some task?"

"He is not present, but not at my bidding," she replied, not looking back. She kept tracing Aldred's carving, trying to block her thoughts from any distraction, any trap. "He would not do such a thing, less by my leave."

"Perhaps then," Lawrence suggested, "he will return. I offer my comfort in his absence. We will bide the time until his joyful appearance. Until then, I pray you cast worry to the wind. I will be at your side, your servant to redeem your every wish. I am at your command from this day."

Catelin turned. "My wish is your command?" she said. "How inviting, Lord Lawrence." She smiled seductively.

"Please, my lady. I am not your lord. I am your servant, until our souls become one." Lawrence continued, "I wish to have your hand, my lady."

"How sudden," she replied. "We have met only a fortnight past. You would give away to me everything of yours?"

"Time does not move in your presence, Catelin. It remains in space, motionless. As I said, until our souls join as one, there will be no time."

"And what if there is another?" She looked in his eyes, avoiding the amulet, which he now clasped in his right hand, although hidden by his fist.

"Another? Time, perhaps?" He looked surprised, angered by this response. "Humph, there could be no other, my lady. Your soul is destined to be part of mine. No other soul could empower this union. Not for you, my lady, nor myself. Ours will exist as one forevermore."

Catelin was troubled. The man must have taken to port quite early in the day. He was either dazed from a blow to the head, or he was quite drunk with the elixir of himself. She had not read this when she had entered his mind.

"Forgive me, Lawrence," she said. "But I am too forlorn to provide you with the comfort of an answer. I cannot remove my mind from Rodney," she said. With the exception of Aldred, she omitted. "There must be time." She turned away. "If you would allow me, Lawrence, I would have a private moment here at the lake. I have much to think of, much to consider."

"Humph, certainly," Lawrence replied, hiding his sarcasm as best as he could. "I will remain at your bidding, until we dine on this eve then?"

"Yes, Lawrence. And would it not be a shame, should your dear friend Aldred attend?" Catelin reminded herself of the pledge he had just made, his contract of obedience.

"Aldred?" he half-asked. "Humph, why certainly, if it pleases you, should he not be in greater need elsewhere. I would consult with him, my lady. His duties keep him quite out and about, you know."

Quite busy. I am certain, she thought, especially on this day. "I am certain there would be no greater need than my wish."

Frustrated, Lawrence bowed, turned, and mounted his black steed, thinking about whether to seek out Aldred in the forest or release a bit of his fury on the worthless servant man. He kicked the black mount again to a gallop as he headed back to the stable, pondering the deeds taking place in the forest.

F

Aldred feared what he might find on his hunt but was quite convinced these forgotten dreams were nothing driven by the subconscious, portraits of thoughts buried in steep caverns of the mind, brought to life by some daytime stimulus—a bird, a word, an image, or thoughts of days long past. The thought that he truly did have childhood memories was a mere illusion. He had so few of them, and those he did recall were cloudy and gray, seemingly rehearsed and always brought to his conscious recollection by a conversation led by Lord Lawrence. As he traversed the gentle slope through the tall grass and breached the outer wall of the pines, oaks, and maples and walked into the shadows, he suddenly realized he had no memories.

Certainly he had recollection of day-to-day, week-to-week, month-to-month things but only a limited inventory of any reminder of his childhood, his parents, any recollection of how he acquired the small scar he wore to this day on his left knee, anything, anyone other than Lawrence himself. He was becoming exceedingly convinced that any memory he did have was invented—something planted. His memories were nothing more than shadows themselves, obscurities cast by a dark hidden source, certainly not the light of sun but by the darkness of evil.

Carrying the shovel over his right shoulder, Aldred dragged along a canvas sack with his free hand. He looked left to right but saw nothing. Then he abruptly stopped. If this behavior had somehow transpired over a lengthy period, then either he or whoever was disposing of the bodies would most likely have developed a pattern, a routine, and in doing so would likely have chosen a suitable spot, a graveyard. And if there had been an ample supply of bodies, then they might well have left a worn path. And if there had been any recent sacrifices, murders, and there was no actual path to the graves, then there might be some evidence, some kind of trail left behind, as the corpse or corpses had been dragged or carried along to their final resting place.

Aldred turned to his right and began walking parallel to the castle toward the other end, opposite the stable area. Unless there was a passageway he had not yet discovered or had not yet dreamed about, then the shortest course to the forest would be around that far side from the front of the mansion. But if he had carried these victims through the halls of the castle, most certainly there would have been a trail of blood left behind. He kept close to the edge of the woods, keeping his eyes out on the tall grass. Then he found it, almost at the end of the mansion. The grass was not matted down, but some of the tips of the blades were tainted red, blood red. *Damn that man,* he thought.

He dropped the sack and shovel and positioned himself by raising his arms out at his sides and aligning his right arm in the direction of the trace evidence. He turned to the direction his left arm led him. But then he thought again. It made sense that once the body got to this point, the gravedigger probably made a beeline toward the burial site. It seemed probable that the madman followed some kind of pattern, so burying them in random spots was unlikely. So, rather than following an angle of about thirty degrees, he began marching head-on, dead forward, toward what the shadows had in store.

Soon enough, Aldred noticed something resembling a path—disturbances in fallen branches, pine needles, and crumbling leaves. The forest was thick, dark, and dense, becoming darker as he progressed. It seemed as though he had been walking over an hour, weaving his way through new growth—weeds, vines, around stumps of fallen trees—down toward a ravine, across a trickle of water, and back into thick growth, although it was probably less than half that amount of time. Finally, he approached an area ahead where the sunlight had poked its way through the treetops. His heartbeat began to elevate, so he stopped, drawing in deep breaths of fresh cool air to steady his nerves. "Do not fail me now," he begged his courage.

Aldred stepped forward to investigate the clearing. Before he reached it, he came upon an abundance of mushrooms. Hundreds of them were scattered about. He passed through them, admiring nature's bounty. His thoughts momentarily turned to a thick, gravy sauce made with red Bordeaux, smothering a platter of mushrooms and onions. *What am I doing?* he thought, *I should be on a mushroom hunt.*

He dropped the canvas sack and stepped forward, taking in one more huge breath. He broke through into the sun. Slowly he paced; his mouth hung open as he scanned the small field from left to right. He estimated the field of stubble to be about 200 paces across and perhaps 150 from side to side, although it was slightly oval shaped. The field was a mess. The gravedigger had been somewhat orderly, but he did not labor much when planting his crops. The graves were shallow; some were barely covering the bodies. His lips moved silently, as he attempted to count the number of plots. Some had been disturbed so violently by the varmints violating the sanctuary of fallen souls they seemed to have melded into one. Some of the corpses had been dragged out of their graves and torn apart, picked clean by coyotes, wolves, raccoons, and other vermin scavenging the burial site, their feeding ground.

Aldred counted more than two dozen victims he managed to piece together from the debris, some with legs protruding from the earth, absent any flesh. Several skulls were spread around, and bones were scatted throughout the field. It seemed the plots had been arranged in parallel rows; there were five of them set in the middle of the clearing. The center row, the most deteriorated, had probably been the first. Additional rows were then set ahead of it and behind. Apparently, expansion would call for digging new plots in a perimeter around the first twenty-five. Another excavation had been made in what would become the center of the sixth row. Alongside the hole, not more than two feet deep, was a shovel lying on the ground, the blade facedown. The gravedigger had already made plans for the next victim. Shove it under and make way for another.

A deep swath was slashed away from the fear he had carried into the burial grounds. It was the morbid expectation of finding someone he actually knew, finding Rodney, bloody, beaten, limbs and maybe even his head neatly severed from his torso, carefully wrapped in a bloody sheet. He had no remembrance of the prior night, whether it brought him sleeplessness or dreams or another visit to the dungeon. He had woken refreshed, not worn and tired as he did on occasion. Contemplation of the exploration to be undertaken with Rodney had filled him with apprehension the evening beforehand. But it had otherwise been an ordinary night, a sleep filled with emptiness, void of any memories or any dreams. The dawn waking had brought him thoughts, conscious thoughts in fantasy filled with Catelin, but his attention quickly tuned in to the matter at hand, validation of dreams come true.

The newest of the occupied graves had not yet been disturbed. A tuft of bloody blond hair protruded from one end of the pile of dirt. A recent light rain had packed the muck down slightly over the sheet wrapped around the body but had also washed away dirt covering the fair-skinned stub of an ankle, minus the foot, sticking out of the opposite end.

Aldred's hypnotic dream struck home, piercing his heart with a flaming arrow of reality. He dropped the shovel he had carried to the mass earthen crypt along with his body. Down on his knees, he prayed. "My god." And he continued to pray through his tears.

In a short time, the meager half-digested contents of the biscuit in his stomach exploded out of his mouth. Recovering, wiping his mouth clean across his left forearm, he knew he could not leave the young woman be, not in this manner, not for the wolves. And he also knew what he would find when he unearthed her body. Aldred grabbed the used shovel and began to dig; it would be digging a grave for the twenty-seventh time. But this duplicate grave would be properly deep. He swept away dirt from her body and rolled the woman, forever young, outside the perimeter of the burial site, careful not to unwind the linen and expose any more of her brutalized remains, especially her eyes. He felt he could not bear the pending guilt ready to pour out of him from the sight of her dead and blank, pleading blue eyes, begging for mercy while she had prayed to her god that Aldred be her savior. Presuming of course, there were eyes to be found.

Aldred retrieved a yellow wildflower from the far end of the clearing and placed it at the head of her grave. He prayed again and solemnly traced his steps back to the mushroom grove, unable to take his mind off the number of body parts trapped in the linen or the missing parts of her bodily flesh and contents of her skull his dream had divulged to Rodney but currently remained in seclusion from his own mind.

Lord Lawrence would enjoy the mushrooms. If only they could be poisonous . . . or poisoned. Maybe Aldred himself would partake in such a delicacy and rid himself of hidden memories yet to be dreamed. He wanted to rid himself of the horror such recalled memories would accompany.

F

Lawrence decided he need not to follow Aldred into the woods. The man would disclose the events of his misadventure. If for some unknown reason Aldred did not, he could simply place him under and investigate the matter percolating inside his mind. The matter of Catelin, however, was more important. He must act soon and rid Aldred from her mind.

Now the thoughts in Lawrence's own head spun round and round. Thoughts Aldred had already spun seeing himself and Catelin together, holding each other, walking hand in hand, with their lips…touching. Lawrence could not stand it. He would not stand it. How could the woman betray him? How could she do such a thing behind his back? The rage was building. The amulet clung to his neck, but now it hung out of his blouse. It sparkled. The thought of Catelin and Aldred together was blasphemy. The amulet glimmered. Aldred—the man he had taken care of so dearly for all these years. *He would be nothing, if not for me,* thought Lawrence. *And now he betrays me?* The amulet glowed pumpkin orange under his chin. *No. I will see to it. I will show these, these lovers!* The amulet twinkled.

The rage continued to build. The amulet continued to sparkle and glow here in the shadows of the stable. It grew brighter and brighter, stronger and stronger. Lawrence reached for it, reached for comfort, but it was blazing hot to the touch, biting at the tips of his fingers. Rage. Hate. More rage.

Images in his mind would not escape him. Her smile. His smile. Their touching, their feeling, their mooning each other, where do these images come from? The amulet was now flashing bright, dark, then again bright and dark. Lawrence could see the two of them in his fracturing mind; their eyes were locked on each other. More rage. More hate. He would strip them of this adolescent fantasy. He would show them who was master of this household. More glimmer, more sparkle, more glow, more flutter, more rage. They would pay. He would bring them to his asylum. There, they would learn. There, they would pay. There, they could forever be together. The amulet was now so bright it cast intermittent shadows across the line of stalls lined up on the walls of the building. A lone horse neighed nervously and bolted out of its open stall through the rear doorway into the corral.

Lawrence grabbed at the crystal with his right hand. He screamed, as the crystal scalded the palm of his hand. He shrieked and babbled senseless mutterings, falling down onto Rodney's bedding, falling into a deep trance and an even deeper nightmare. His cries were unable to find or capture an audience. A mule wandering into the barn turned back toward him and brayed. An assault from visions of Catelin and Aldred overwhelmed him. In his daze, he stood, turning in circles, blinding his eyes with the palms of his blistered hands. But the visions swept over him as he dropped back down on the pile of mussed hay. *Catelin and*

Aldred. Catelin and Aldred. In a puff of exhaustion, the amulet glittered, flickered, and lay itself down to sleep on the dark-hearted chest of the unconscious evil man while the foray of visions continued to sweep over him. Soon, soon the reward would be paid.

F

When Aldred left the boundary of the woods, he headed directly to the stable, returning the shovel to its station. He found Lawrence, not Rodney, asleep in a stall. Quietly, he stepped by him then placed the clean shovel between dowels on a post supporting the roof near the middle of the stable. The stable itself was quite long and wide, so there was a series of these load-bearing posts throughout the building, lining the walls and each side of the passageway through the middle of the structure.

Half the stable's length contained stalls for horses and mules and others for milking cows. The thought of grabbing the axe hanging between a pair of wrought iron nails on one of these posts crossed his mind, but Aldred thought better of it. He slowly withdrew his fingers, as they slid unhurriedly down the long handle while resisting Aldred's will to pull them away. No matter what he himself had done, how he had participated in this madness, his free will had been seized in the process. He had been made to perform these evil deeds; he was coerced against his will to perform them. He was not an evil person and could never commit such heinous acts.

Somehow, Lawrence must be brought to justice. Perhaps, once he knew everything, he could inform the villagers. They would know what to do. They would form a committee, hold a hearing, and review the evidence. And then at the edge of the village, they would hang the witch of a man from a tall dead oak until he was more rotten than its barren limbs.

Lost in thought, Aldred was brought to attention by the pitter-patter of hooves. Lady Catelin stopped short of the stable and dismounted. Aldred scrambled out of the stable, the sack of mushrooms in hand, to meet her.

"Come," he whispered, "around back to the corral. We can undress your mount there. We must have words." Aldred pressed his right forefinger to his lips and grabbed the reins from Catelin.

Concern swept over Catelin's face, erasing the smile put there by his sudden appearance. Close behind, she followed him silently.

The huge corral was bordered by a fence terminating at the rear of the stable. Built from limbs and trunks of pine trees, it held a variety of animals when they were brought in from the pasture before bedding them in the stable. Separate pens occupied one corner for the pigs and hogs, plus numerous feed and water bins were scattered along the fence borders. Chickens and roosters had free rein of the corral, roaming with the horses, cattle, sheep, and geese. They could easily fly away from and over the fence, but they generally remained near their coop, which allocated them shelter plus nesting areas for harvesting eggs from the layers. Since she had arrived, Catelin had spent time here some mornings, petting and feeding the stock before they were set loose.

"What is it, Aldred?" she asked. She walked around to the left side of her mount where Aldred was removing the saddle and reins.

"Lawrence is fast asleep in the stable, on Rodney's bedding. He might be more than asleep, but not dead, as he breathes quite heavily. His eyes, they are closed, but they race each other in some feverish fashion. Perhaps he is midstream in one of the dreams. I sense maybe even another dream he plans to feed me. This dream would be filled with knives and saws and terrifying contraptions used to torture his next victim." He glanced back at her as he pulled the saddle off the horse. "I discovered something horrible, something Rodney and I sought to find together."

Catelin looked more distressed. "Please tell me Rodney is safe, tell me he has not been harmed."

"I have not found him. He would not abandon us at this hour. It was he who prompted our discoveries. I would yet be numb with my lord's chain round my neck, my mind. No, I did not find Rodney, but I found others, many of them. Your Rodney might be alive yet. The others fell to Lawrence's ill fortune. And I fear I partook in his evil ways. I am certain he has used me, somehow, but I have no memory. God forbid, it should return. Wait here a moment."

Aldred picked up the saddle he had set on the ground and carried it back into the stable through the large and open rear double doors, setting it inside over a stall fence. Returning, he grabbed the sack of mushrooms and Catelin's right hand. "We must speak with Mother Brita. I believe she has seen me late at night when I am under whatever spell has bound me to Lord Lawrence. Come."

Pulling off her stationed feet, Catelin skipped a few steps to meet Aldred's pace, squeezing his left hand. "It is the amulet. He uses it to control your mind. What shall we do? It is there rests his power over you."

"We must feign any knowledge," he replied. "We will wait for our moment. But you must not be alone with him. We must fight his will. I must find a way." His thoughts shifted back to the axe in the stable. "I pray I did not waste it away."

The fingers of both hands clinging to the axe now held the mushroom sack and wrapped around Catelin's hand, as the couple entered the kitchen. Brita had just eaten a generous serving of mutton stew and was cleaning the bowl in a large pot of water. "Now that you have found her, you both must leave this place. Escape while there is time," she warned.

"You have seen me, Mother," Aldred declared. "Tell me. Show me what I have done. If he has control of me, he can gain control of anyone. Everyone here is in danger."

"I fear it is too late, Aldred. His control is everywhere. The crystal he wears on his breast," she began, "it had me also. It did. Until I saw you one night. It was a night I was distressed, fraught with sorrow. I took to walking in the cool breeze coming from the forest to cleanse my worries. I went to the back of the castle, and there you were, stepping out of the wall, carrying a sack or a bag made from white linen over your shoulder. Linen from bedding perhaps." She paused. "It contained no potatoes. They do not bleed juice so red."

F

Brita went on to explain. It had not been long after Aldred had brought the young woman, the blonde, to the castle grounds for her servitude in Lawrence's kitchen staff. It was not far beyond one month past it all happened, bringing back the light of life in Brita's mind. Brita had been training the young energetic girl as a cook's helper. Penelope seemed smart, innocent. She was personable and learned quickly. Each morning, she would wake with Brita's stirring in the building housing the staff long before dawn, but invariably, Brita always found her way to the kitchen ahead of Penelope while the young girl fussed with her long blonde wavy hair. She had been with them barely a fortnight when she went missing. Penelope's bedding had been made up, as she did every morning, but she never made her appearance in the kitchen. Brita thought it odd the girl would run away without a word but be self-conscious enough to make up her bedding beforehand. In truth, she had never slept on her final night.

The moon was full the night after her disappearance, so light was cast behind the castle. Brita heard a rumbling as she was walking along deep in the night, unable to sleep. Thinking about the lost girl, she wandered for a walk behind the castle before she would make her way to the kitchen. Suddenly, not far ahead, Aldred stepped out of the wall. A huge door had cleared the way for his exit down in the gulley surrounding the castle. Aldred then stepped back inside briefly and struggled back out with a large bundle over his right shoulder. Each end of the bundle was tied in a knot.

As she watched him crawl up the side of the gulley with the sack across his back, Brita called to him. "Master Aldred," Brita yelled, "is that you?"

Aldred said nothing, got to his feet out of the gulley, and continued forward up the gentle slope toward the woods. Brita hurried along after him. She caught up with him and tapped him on his left shoulder, but he lumbered forward. It was then Brita saw strands of Penelope's pretty blonde hair hanging out from the bundle. It was unmistakable, but also, it was not unlike the sheet covering her body. It was stained red.

"ALDRED!" she screamed. But again, there was no response. She stepped in front of him, but Aldred merely changed course, as though plotting his movements through a maze or around a large boulder. She waved her hands in front of his face and even slapped him on his left cheek. There was no response. In shock, Brita fell to her knees in tears, just as Aldred would do after the passing of another full moon. Aldred stepped around her, as though she was a fallen stump in the path.

Brita got to her feet and tried to collect herself, to calm her trembling nerves. She lifted her long gray dress at her sides and followed him cautiously. The forest was dark, but the moonlight cast slivers of rays generously sufficient enough to keep Aldred and the lantern he held in his left hand within sight. She shivered and startled with alarm at the ruffle of leaves and snap of twigs as the hidden audience of nightlife kept her in sight, their noses held to attention at the scent of an intruder, one with fresh warm blood, hopeful of a nighttime meal about to be served. When she arrived at the edge of the clearing, Aldred was engaged in his dirty work. In utter shock, Brita turned and ran, tripping time and time again over fallen branches, protruding roots aboveground, and in the shallow stream.

When the balance of the kitchen staff reported to Brita hours after her return to the kitchen, they found her half stewed from a third helping of port from a large wooden goblet. Later that morning, Aldred paid a visit to the kitchen to report Lawrence's displeasure over his morning loaf of bread, a tad salty.

Brita's response was plain and simple. "If it don't fit right in his lordship's mouth, Master Aldred, let him next try it next up he's ass."

Aldred reported back to Lawrence that Mother Brita had been ill and had become saddened over the missing apprentice. Penelope was nowhere to be found, and Brita thought she would never ever be heard from again. *Was it my advance?* Aldred had thought. That morning, Brita had brought Penelope's disappearance to Aldred's attention.

"Who is Penelope?" he replied. "By the way, Mother," he continued, "Lord Lawrence has told me to make return to the village. He feels you are in need of an apprentice, someone to share your burden. He would hate to suffer through another loaf of bread laden with salt."

From this day of awakening, Brita began to remember other forgotten memories. And when Lawrence paid her a visit that afternoon with his amulet tucked away, her reply was just as plain and simple as had Aldred's earlier been. "Penelope? Never heard of her, my lord. I must thank you for seeking me out an apprentice as Aldred has informed, my lord. It would please you. I am certain." And she knew just how it would please him.

F

"I could not see clearly what you were doing out there in the forest, but I can still count to two, son," said Brita. "And I knew something was up with your mind. You could not even remember the girl's name."

"I dug her a proper grave, Mother. But I still have no memory of her," said Aldred. He turned to Catelin. "Today was the second time I put her in the grave, and I could not remember ever seeing the girl."

"Maybe for the better, Aldred," Brita suggested. "But now you know how you got her out of the castle. The door made of stone. 'Tis down there in the gulley near the far end. Where does it lead, your mind tell you that much?"

"Rodney tells me my dream ends when I leave that horrible place. There must be a stairwell," he said. "Catelin, I am going to find it. You should stay behind with Mother."

"But I want to stay with you, Aldred," Catelin implored. She grabbed hold of his left arm with both hands. "What if Lawrence should find me?"

"Put her to work, Mother Brita. I promised you another apprentice. And in my exploration, I have found you a wealth of mushrooms." He held the sack up and extended them to Brita.

"You know much about the kitchen, lass?" Brita asked. "I could use a couple of good hands. I was only just getting accustomed to having an extra pair around when Penelope up and disappeared."

"I know enough to mix up a French sauce to cover those mushrooms. I do so much share your sorrow for the young girl, Mother, if I may address you as such. I feel your pain now, for my Rodney."

"Wonderful, Lady Catelin," said Aldred. "And I was just thinking about a thick sauce made with a French wine."

"Seems she reads your mind, Aldred. And you, young lady, address me as you would, child," Brita replied. "And find that pain of a man Rodney, Aldred. Should have run across that old cuss long ago. You have mind not to share him, wouldya, child? The skinny runt comes 'round looking for pastry. Ha! It's not pastry on his mind."

"Why, Mother!" Catelin and Aldred echoed simultaneously. They all smiled, one of the few, if any, yet to come.

F

Before Aldred returned behind the castle, he hustled his way to the stable, finding Lawrence had not moved a muscle, unless his eyeballs qualified as such. Aldred was not sure. The man's eyes were rolling around under the lids faster than a pair of goldfish suddenly dropped in a small glass bowl. Aldred wondered what could possibly be going on inside the master's mind. But thinking again, he decided he would rather not be privy. The images tumbling around inside there along with his eyeballs were likely too disgusting to fathom. Was he dreaming of just one victim? Did those images involve the manner or manners in which he would torture that poor soul? Did this possibly involve scheming over some new method of inflicting agony? Was this apparition of torment focused on Rodney?

Once again, fleeting thoughts of the axe baited his temperament. He could envision both his hands wrapped around its handle. Under his breath, he damned his faltering courage and instead reached for a lantern hanging above the head he wished to remove straightaway. Aldred fled from the stable, running.

Catching his breath, Aldred climbed down into the gulley about halfway across the rear wall of the castle. His eyes scanned it up and down. He paced nervously along the ditch, dragging his right hand across the wall, as his feet maneuvered their way through the rocky rubble. His fingers crawled along the random pattern of the oddly shaped stones and over the tributaries and streams of mortar meandering their way around them, seeking something out of place, out of the mold, something foreign to the random configuration over which they swept.

Suddenly, his forefinger stung sharply. Instantaneously, it lunged toward the safety of Aldred's mouth and buried itself under his tongue, behind the man's lower teeth. The tiny droplet of blood oozed out slowly. *Ah, the sweet security and warmth it felt.* A moment later, the forefinger was dragged away back to its appointed task. But before it did, it turned toward the man's eyes, begging inspection. Again, it lunged for his mouth but stopped short of it as Aldred bared his teeth and bit down on the splinter. The finger pulled away, but just as the mouth spat it away, it dove in for another cleansing. It, too, was spat away, back to its vocation, its mission. The small sliver of wood had no business swimming in the river of aged mortar.

Aldred looked ahead, dropping his right arm at his side. He could be no more than thirty or forty paces away from the end of the back wall. He stopped and backed away, up the incline of the gulley. He sat and studied the wall, reading the stone pattern block by block. Finally, not ten paces away from where he sat, he discovered a stream of mortar appearing to form a vertical line, and although wavy as it was, it ran fairly straight up and down the wall. About halfway up this curvy line of masonry was a small round stone protruding slightly outward, farther than other stones. He stepped toward it and grabbed it with his right hand; the embattled forefinger wrapped itself behind its form.

Aldred pushed. Nothing happened. Then he pulled, and the round stone relieved itself from the wall slightly as he did, but it did not pull away. It seemed to reach the limit of its travel, but Aldred pulled harder. The door trudged along, as the round stone made a sweeping arc in front of Aldred, toward him and to his left. The light of day illuminated the passage. It revealed a small landing about six paces long and a stairway, not quite as wide as the spiral case leading down to the dungeon. Aldred stepped in and found it, too, was spiral. He stepped back out of the passage, retrieved the lantern, and put it to match.

Aldred scaled down the stairs about four tight turns, what he thought might be about one floor. He came to another short landing and a second door. The stone handle for this latch was not as neatly concealed. He grabbed the stone and pulled. The door opened with ease. Aldred found himself in the small solar he had only discovered one eve ago. Across the room was the familiar stairwell. He knew where to go. The lantern, held shoulder height, led him through the double doors.

He followed the light cast from the lantern toward a mumbling he heard coming from his right, deep in the room. There, he found the contraption and strapped across it was Rodney. The shadows across his face came not from the lantern but his beaten and bloody cheeks and lips. Aldred could not discern the sounds coming from the man. They did not form words, but the suffering was plain enough.

Rodney was laid across the top of a large round barrel; it was quite larger than those used for containment of ale or wine. His head drooped back behind him, and his legs were wrapped down over the curvature of the barrel. His arms were stretched out behind him. Aldred feared if Rodney's back had arched any more, either his back would break under the stress or an appendage would be ripped away, and quite likely both were only an increment away from occurring.

Pulleys below the barrel diverted chains attached to cuffs on Rodney's arms and legs toward a revolving mechanism operated by a large handle beside the barrel. While such a mechanism might be used for hauling well buckets up and down for retrieving water, this mechanism had but one purpose, taking something, someone down. As the lever device was turned and tightened, a heavy rope around its drum and the chains was wrapped around separate drums on either side of the main drum. Then the victim's body was stretched over the large barrel, bending the spine backward, as the arms and legs were drawn toward one another. Had the man been placed over the barrel on his stomach, he would eventually be pulled apart at the weakest joint in his body. But in this manner, his bones would sever and split apart before any external bleeding began.

Aldred quickly ran around the machine and attempted to unwind the main drum. But it was locked in position. Not having time to study its design, he looked for one of the madman's instruments, and finding nothing, he ran back to the parlor in which they were stored at the opposite end of the chamber. He grabbed the first sharp device attracting his eye, a scythe.

Back at the human stretcher, Aldred used the tool as he would a saw, grabbing the blade and hacking away at the rope on the drum. With a loud boom, the drum released the tension on the chains. Rodney rolled over the top side of the barrel, still strung up by the cuffs and chains, but his back now curved toward its intended bending position was relieved from some of the pain. Aldred ran alongside him and supported Rodney's back on his bent left leg, reaching behind for the cuffs at his wrists. There was no lock, just a latch he twisted on each, freeing his hands. Clutching Rodney under his shoulders, Aldred unlocked the cuffs at his feet and carried him away from the dreaded killing implement, with the lantern held in his left hand. Having lost consciousness, Rodney was silent and, for the moment, free from excruciating pain.

Aldred slipped from the dungeon as quietly as he could accomplish back through the open passageway, paying no mind to the evidence left behind. His concern was for the evidence he held in his arms. When he reached the kitchen, Rodney was placed on a large cot in the pantry used by Brita for her afternoon snoozes between midday and evening meals.

Alarmed and horrified at Rodney's condition, Catelin was nevertheless relieved when the aging coot opened his eyes and smiled. He smiled again once Brita placed a cool, moist cloth over his forehead to begin scrubbing him clean of the bloody mess left behind by the horror of all lords, Lawrence.

Catelin and Aldred spoke and schemed. The evening meal must take place with Lawrence just as planned. It would take place as usual meals do, as though nothing had happened. Nothing at all.

Their escape would be made the following day. Brita and Rodney would precede in Lady Catelin's carriage. Behind them would follow the rest of the castle grounds staff; each one of them swearing never to return, never to look back at the cursed place. While Rodney slept and recovered, Brita would stir the pot and alert the staff.

Lord Lawrence and his hellish dreams had other plans for Catelin and Aldred.

F

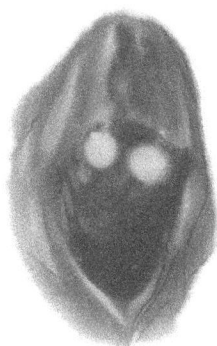

CHAPTER NINE

As planned, Aldred and Catelin had kept themselves busy being out of sight of Lawrence. Sometime in the late afternoon, the lord must have woken and retired to the castle, perhaps to his bedchamber.

When the horses had been brought back to the stable for the evening, Aldred found Rodney's stall empty. The stall itself was a mess; the hay was strewn about as though a madman had tossed it in heaps over his head, as he searched for a golden needle lying at the bottom of the pile. His dreams had provoked movement from something other than his eyeballs.

Catelin had prepared baked mushrooms with onions smothered in a thick wine sauce, while Brita made a fine roast of beef smothered in potatoes, onions, and carrots. With Lawrence nowhere in sight, Aldred oversaw the setting of the great hall table and lighting of the candles and lanterns throughout the room. At precisely seven o'clock in the evening, Catelin made her appearance in a beautiful gown of scarlet red, trimmed with black lace over her shoulders, breasts, and wrists. Her long beautiful, black hair was hanging free behind her, decorated with scarlet ribbons.

Their long ties were hanging down the length of her hair. Below the gown, she wore her high black boots suitable for riding . . . or running.

Aldred met her as she entered the room from the hallway leading from her bedchamber. They exchanged glances and gazes. Aldred was dressed in a fine white linen blouse, tufted at the shoulders and open across his bold chest. He wore tight tan trousers held in place with a scarlet red sash wrapped around his waist and tied at his left side. It was hanging free down below his waist above his thigh. The long-tailed tight jacket he wore matched the color of the sash and concealed the dagger at his left side.

Two servants entered the room and quickly departed after arranging the covered trays of food, the roast and large bowl of mushrooms, and filling three glasses with port, leaving behind two pitchers of the wine. The aroma filled the hall. Back at the stable, Brita was loading a chest of clothing, along with Rodney, into Catelin's carriage.

Lawrence remained inconspicuously absent.

"What shall we do, Aldred?" asked Catelin. She approached the table set off to one side near the middle of the room, and with her eyes set on the stone floor, she carried her left hand around its rim as she circled the table on her way toward him, slowly drawing her eyes up to meet his own.

"We should take our appointed stations," he replied, "and await our host, Lord Lawrence, should we be inclined to feign our appetites. I could eat our master's horse." His eyes circled the room around Catelin, as though sensing Lawrence was close at hand, hidden, observing their behavior in his absence. He pulled back a chair, standing behind it. "Please be calm. Be seated."

"How is your mind occupied with provisions in this hour?" she asked nervously.

The chairs were set in a triangular fashion around the large oval table, equally apart, with Lawrence at the head, Catelin and Aldred at his sides. As Catelin sat, her eyes traced Aldred's steps as he advanced his way opposite her. "Come, Lady Catelin. I propose a toast to our Lord Lawrence, wishing for him a long and happy life," he said.

"Ha, I say, a long and happy life without us, I propose," she replied. "I would toast you leave this place with haste, and free yourself of his grip on your mind." Her eyes searched neurotically around the great hall, and her inner voice told Catelin Lawrence was nowhere near them at the moment. "But I would not hold toast for him," she whispered.

Then something told Catelin he was approaching, but not as the man she knew. Something had changed. He was no longer Lawrence. It seemed to her the man she knew, although aloof from reality because of his overwhelming obsession with her and no longer in a sensible frame of mind . . . somehow he had deteriorated even further. He had become totally consumed, replaced, and removed from the physical being he had been earlier in the day when he had approached her with his wild fantasy out at the lake. She could no longer see any actual physical presence of the man in her mind. She felt the body encompassing his twisted mind had been snatched away, and now some entity, even more evil and sinister, some altered state of being, was approaching them.

"Aldred," she said, "I fear we are in danger. Something is amiss." She lowered her wineglass away from her lips before serving tribute to the toast.

"Indeed, my lady," he replied. He leaned forward to whisper across the table. "But once we have exposed Lawrence, I am certain he will retreat from us, willingly, as we shall from him."

"But it is not Lord Lawrence I fear," she said. "He is no longer with this world. There is something else, a spirit far more hideous inside the shell of the man. It is approaching." Catelin did not attempt to hush her words. "I feel its hatred. It cannot be stopped, Aldred."

Aldred pressed his right forefinger to his lips. "Please be calm. Lawrence will not harm you. I will protect you." His right hand retreated from his lips and reached for the comfort of the blade's handle.

"Listen to me, Aldred!" she demanded. "What kind of being Lawrence has been, he is no more. He has been possessed, but much more than your lord had possessed you. It is hatred approaching, and it is darker than the dark of night. There is no escape from its presence. We must leave at once."

"Lady Catelin, you speak in riddles," he began. "The man could not just disappear into the air. We found the young woman. She did not vanish, even though her demise was the consequence of his demented mind. He cannot vanish . . . the man is made of flesh and blood. He is certainly evil, but his evil is contained in his hidden chamber. He is possessed only by his diseased mind. He could not possibly be possessed by some demon. Such is black magic nonsense. Please be calm. I promise you no harm will come—"

Suddenly, a crash resounded from far down the corridor from which Catelin had entered the great hall which led beyond to Lord Lawrence's bedchamber. The thunder of the doors slamming into their jambs was so ferocious one of them rebounded back open and flew off its hinges, smashing across the hall on the wall opposite the chamber and coming to rest in the doorway behind a dark presence floating its way forward toward the great hall.

Catelin reached to suppress her scream, but it could not be muffled. She looked from the doorway to the corridor leading to the bedchambers and back to Aldred. Terrified and trembling, she was frozen in her chair. She had never faced a foe of such magnitude in her prior encounters and conquests. Her ability to read minds told her Aldred was badly mistaken … Lord Lawrence was no longer a man of flesh and blood.

Aldred stood up, alarmed at the sudden explosion, wondering what had just occurred. He stepped away toward the doorway leading to the bedchambers to investigate.

Catelin begged he cease his advance. "Aldred, please no!"

Aldred stopped momentarily, heeding Catelin's plea. He straightened himself and reached back for the dagger. He looked back at her, motioned for her silence, turned around, and took two warily daring yet authoritative steps forward, when suddenly the double doors to the corridor burst open.

"My god!" he exclaimed.

F

Earlier, while Catelin and Aldred had huddled with Brita and tended to Rodney's wounds, Lawrence had woken to find himself sprawled under a bed of hay. He had rolled over onto his knees and, while breathing heavily, struggled to his feet. Every muscle in his body seemed worn and torn. With his equilibrium off-center, the man teetered and faltered, reaching for the wall of the stall to regain his balance. He had no recollection of what happened or how he found himself in this predicament. But the unfamiliar voice in his mind told him exactly where he was, and a clear set of instructions were laid out in front of him. He reached for the amulet, now glowing dull yellow-orange. Its warmth filled him with satiation no less than a mug of fresh cool water would down the throat of a thirst-starved man. A smile formed below the man's hollow eyes as saliva dripped from the left corner of his mouth. His lips formed the words, "The mirror."

The shell of Lawrence surveyed his surroundings and then stepped cautiously, as his wobbly legs led him toward the stable doors and out into the sunlit afternoon. Strands of straw were still sticking out of his hair. His right hand never left the sweet essence of the crystal amulet. The not-so-holy holy man Lawrence had so viciously murdered in his act of passion to satisfy the early thirst of his young dark soul had left behind a final bequest. *Your recompense shall be your infinite hell.* Both the amulet and Lawrence's dark heart were locked in battle for dominance and survival. At the moment, the not-a-monk-of-his-kind monk held the reins, controlling his physical senses.

Fully aware of his surroundings but unable to maneuver on his own accord, Lawrence traced the well-worn path from the stable to the main entrance of his castle. But even as he followed the step-by-step disposition on his track to the mirror, also burning in his mind remained the conflicting images of Catelin and Aldred, both traitors, both fools.

Lawrence took note of his surroundings as he passed through the solar to the great hall and beyond through the tall double doors toward his bedchamber. The amulet filled his aching muscles with relief, while their thirst was filled with fresh blood from the runaway pulsation of his heart as he progressed. He quietly slipped into his bedchamber and beyond the bed toward his favorite passageway, the stairway leading down to his asylum. The door at the end of the short entry pulled open with ease, and he stepped forward. His legs halted when he reached the mirror on the upper landing at its far side. It was the mirror in which he had so often admired his most cherished reflection of perfection on his way to impart pain and suffering.

For the first time, he also faced the reflection of the amulet. It had always been kept sequestered, tucked away beneath the privacy and protection of his black blouse. But now, for some unknown reason, there it stood blatantly in plain sight, in its full splendor and glory. He felt as though someone was there with him, also clutching the amulet, smiling at him, grinning.

No . . . the unseen presence was smirking. This made him feel ill at ease, discomforted. This made no sense. It was he, Lawrence, who dished out discomfort and in good healthy doses. Well, probably not exactly healthy, but the doses were quite generous by any standard. He did not particularly enjoy the thought of sharing or relinquishing the amulet or its power with anyone.

Lawrence managed to tear his eyes away from the amulet momentarily; even though through its smugness, it remained alluring, hypnotic. Could this possibly be the feeling he conveyed to his victims when they were captured by the power of his magnetic trances? It seemed inviting. Could this unknown presence he felt possibly be in control of the amulet? Was this a trick of some sort? His eyes wanted to run back and plant themselves on the amulet, but they were on a collision course with their own reflection.

What his eyes witnessed was not what they had been accustomed to bearing. Rather than the widely open and shining gaiety of brown that had always greeted him, these eyes seemed dead to the world. They seemed to be too dark, even in the light of the lantern his right hand had somehow, someway magically and suddenly plucked out of thin air and raised to the side of his head. He could not recall having lifted the lantern from its resting place on the small table set below and adjacent to the mirror at the corner of the landing. Nor could he recall having struck flame to a match bringing it to life.

Never the mind, he thought. He leaned forward, lifting the lantern for a closer look. Those eyes, they were wide open, certainly, but they were not shining. They did not seem to be merrily engaged in a gay old time. They were blank, seemed to be set back deeper in their sockets than eyes were meant to be seated, and they were much too dark and motionless. He raised his sight quickly to his forehead and back down, but he caught no comparable movement in the image facing him. The eyes just sat there, blankly staring back at him, reflecting nothing in their own path of sight.

What is wrong with them? he thought. *Never the mind,* he thought again. *Let them sit.* He tilted his head downward and cast his own eyes toward the amulet pressed against his chest.

What pray is this? he thought. The tips of his forefingers and thumbs were delicately adorning the crystal. They were not just touching it; they were carefully caressing it, as though it was his fragile heart. His very own tender black heart. The amulet seemed to be pulsating, expanding, and contracting with each beat of the drumming taking place in his chest. He could see, but he could not feel his thumbs and forefingers or the remaining cupped fingers of his hand dilating and compressing with each pump. The amulet, he discovered, was no longer glowing its dull yellow-orange hue. It appeared to be dark red, perhaps scarlet, and on its surface ran thin black tributaries carrying whatever venom was contained within. Although his lips sensed no motion, no activity, the reflection in the mirror lifted them out of their smirk up and beyond to a satisfying smile, at which time those lips became blacker than the rivers of blood in the dark, dark heart of the amulet.

When Lawrence raised his head and eyes again to the mirror, he was confronted with an image barely discernible. Someone, something stood there before him wearing a black cloak. The man's head was concealed deep at the back of a hood pulled over his head, if it was truly a man concealing its face. The amulet was no longer in sight; it was stored away under the cloak, silent and no longer glowing. Its appointed task had been completed. The human's soul had been seized, and his physical being was stolen, erased, captured in a timeless prison. And then on each side of this hooded reflection, the not-a-monk-of-his-kind monk brought him two images slowly materializing.

Damn their souls—Catelin at his left, Aldred at his right. But they were not looking back at Lawrence; they were looking toward each other through this foreign figure in the mirror. Both were unaware, totally oblivious of the being standing between them. *Damn their souls to hell.*

"I promise you this," Lawrence spoke. "You will live in hell for eternity. You shall forever live in damnation," he promised the reflection.

But there were no images of Catelin and Aldred in the mirror, as there were in his mind. Lawrence's promise, his curse, had been cast upon his own reflection. And then, quietly but succinctly the not-so-holy holy man's voice that would forever control him granted Lawrence his wish, acknowledging he would forever be held prisoner in his new form, incapable of life or breath or time. *Your recompense shall be your infinite hell. Come to me, and let me claim your sweet, sweet soul. I am the dark of night. I am the preyer of the prey. Your soul is my claim.*

But what the not-so-holy holy man had not contemplated was the immensity of hatred manifesting within the young fat boy's heart. And now, fully mature, it would live on in the remnants of Lawrence's mind. Its struggle to survive might entail an eternity of conflict, but it would somehow prevail. While trapped in this inhuman form, Lawrence's yet surviving mind could control its actions, and he knew he would find a way out. All he needed was a soul. But first, he would try existing without one for some time; being rid of body and soul felt . . . refreshing. Perhaps he might collect a few and preserve or discard them until one suitable enough for him could be found, one suitable for his magnificence.

Then, joining the reflection, Lawrence stepped into the mirror, willingly accepting his fate with vigorous anticipation. Feeling the power of the phantom absorb and extinguish his soul, the rendered lifeless being screamed with laughter and stepped back out of the mirror into his asylum.

The phantom had a dinner to attend and must not disappoint his guests. *I am the dark of night. I am the preyer of the prey. Your soul is my claim.* Now he would begin to perfect his new craft.

F

Standing now with the wineglass held in both hands at her breasts, Catelin gasped. The glass fell to the floor and burst into pieces, scattering around her shivering feet. Her fingers found her mouth and suppressed another scream she was too frightened to release. "My god," her silent lips paraphrased Aldred's words.

What stood in the doorway appeared to be a man dressed in a black cloak, with the hood atop protruding outward beyond his forehead, wrapping around under his chin, and hiding a clear view of his head and face. But his eyes were anything but human. Two balls deep in the hood seemed to glow a soft but deep red. While the garment extended to the floor and dragged behind the cloaked man, it was quite obvious his forward motion was not propelled by a pair of feet linked to the man by a set of corresponding legs. The advance of the cloaked man was slow and deliberate, and there was no bounce or sway. It was as if the man was standing on some kind of hidden and silent platform resting on wheels, rolling across the room.

How could it move without being pushed or pulled? The man was gliding as would a swan over a lake propelled from beneath, thought Aldred.

Aldred now cautiously stepped back, keeping distance between him and the advancing stranger. He reached at his side again for the handle of the knife. *This cannot possibly be Lord Lawrence,* he thought. But then, on second thought, he asked the cloaked man, "Lawrence, is that you? Is this some kind of folly?"

Aldred looked back at Catelin and turned back to the menacing figure. "Please, sir. You are frightening Lady Catelin. I ask you to cease, to desist in this nonsense."

Continuing to slowly reach with his right hand to clutch the handle of the knife and relieve its blade from the scabbard, he noticed the dark figure stop its advance.

A voice, foreign to Lord Lawrence, deep and low, addressed Aldred's inquiry. "Folly?" it asked. "Nonsense?"

The cloaked figure raised its right appendage, bent at the elbow, to his waist. The long sleeves covered its arms, but slowly a clenched fist with long fingers seemed to grow out of the open end. The nails on them were long and thick, skin thick and wrinkled. Suddenly, the fist opened, the fingers flexed, and the knife flew out of Aldred's hand, imparting a deep gash in his palm as it sailed on its course to the stranger's hand.

"Folly, you say?" the deep voice asked again. "Nonsense? And what of this?" He held the dagger out toward Aldred. "AND WHAT OF YOUR

FOLLY!" he screamed. "WHAT OF YOUR NONSENSE!"

The phantom's voice was so loud it echoed throughout the halls of the castle. Catelin and Aldred covered their ears with their hands to muffle the sound and grimaced from the shrill reverberation in their ears.

Aldred leaped ahead to charge the thing in the cloak, raising both arms to attack at the man's neck. The phantom's other arm lifted, with a hand protruding through the sleeve with its palm held facing the fool. Aldred was stopped in his tracks, lifted, and flung back across the room, landing flat on his back and sweeping across the table, clearing it of most of the tableware, silverware, and serving trays. A pitcher of wine escaped the collisions.

Aldred got to his elbows to lift himself off the table, but the left palm of the phantom thrust forward again, slamming his head back down onto the wooden surface. Then the palm turned around, waving fingers toward the cloaked entity. Aldred flew back off the table, landing at his knees on the floor and slid all the way on the hard stone floor to the black-cloaked figure. *Now, who is a gliding swan?* thought the devil.

Catelin made a vain attempt to flee from the great hall, but she could move neither her legs nor her arms. Her frozen right hand was still clutching for the wineglass that had fallen and shattered around her feet. Catelin now released a second scream heretofore she had managed to suppress. She had never faced such an evil man. But this was obviously no man.

The phantom looked to her direction; its hidden face would have revealed disgust. "AND YOU!" it screamed. Echoes resounded through the halls once again. "YOU BETRAY ME FOR THIS?" A long crooked and wrinkled finger from its left hand pointed down at Aldred.

Then, as the phantom did with Aldred, he summoned her with his left palm held outward. Catelin was launched forward, slamming her thighs against the edge of the table, smashing her face, and breaking her nose on the oak, as she was jettisoned into a forward roll across its surface on her way to the phantom's feet where she landed flat on her back.

With a twist of the left hand, Catelin was hoisted up onto her knees to join Aldred, side by side, with their arms pinned at their sides and their necks shoved backward by the invisible force. Their eyelids were locked open on the phantom; its piercing eyes were glaring at them from deep within the cloak's hood. Blood dripped from Catelin's left nostril down her chin, oozing its way down her neck and chest. Aldred's blood dribbled from his right palm down his little finger to the stone floor.

"And now," the dark figure whispered, "remember." He motioned both hands, twisting the pair on their knees to face each other.

Suddenly, a flood of images simultaneously entered the minds of both Catelin and Aldred—sacrifices, killings, rapes, and murders. There were scores of bloody body parts, with Aldred collecting them in sheets, dragging them through the woods, and burying them. Tears of horror and shame flowed down Aldred's cheeks, as Catelin, terrified, looked on at the theatre of horror being plastered in front of her for nearly an hour.

Lawrence made sure they saw each victim, one by one, in the living color of death. Hell, he had all the time in the world. Each meticulous operation, extraction, amputation, mutilation, and experimentation in terror vividly rolled across their fields of vision. Then, for one long moment, their minds and the room went completely black. Both of them drew a deep breath, wondering if the maniacal phantom was now going to cut both of them apart and kill them, one by one, slowly and patiently down in his dungeon of terror.

To relieve their apprehension and elevate their fear for the final act, Lawrence revealed to them a look into the future.

As he had done earlier, Lawrence provided them with a three-dimensional, colorful view of what was about to take place. Each viewed Lawrence's plan from above while the stage below them turned slowly round and round. Aldred witnessed he was once again in possession of the dagger, and he was kneeling face-to-face in front of Catelin. Her arms remained locked at her sides, and their heads were rigidly vertical, facing each other directly. Aldred saw himself grab her gown near her breasts with his left hand and run the dagger down between them with his right hand, slicing the dress down the middle to her waist. As it drooped down across her tender bare shoulders and smooth skin, opening the crevice between her breasts and beyond and down to her midsection, Catelin felt the horror of anticipating Aldred's next move in striking her.

She tried in vain to close her eyes, but she could do nothing but helplessly, hopelessly witness Aldred plunge the knife deep into her lower abdomen and lift it as quickly as his struggling arm could convert the phantom's command into a sawing motion back upward through her lower torso, her belly, through her breastbone and up above and between her breasts, this time slicing through what the dress had theretofore concealed.

With the task finally completed, Aldred pulled the dagger out of her chest and shoved it into his own heart. In her final act, Catelin grasped Aldred's fist with both her hands, twisting it to the right and left, as he assisted the plunge with his left hand placed over Catelin's on the heel of the dagger. The two collapsed toward each other, resting their heads on each other's right shoulder, while silently drawing their final breaths on their knees. Then teetering but remaining balanced above the stone floor in their duet of death, blood poured out between them into a pool on the floor as prepared to exhale their final breaths.

After another moment of blackness, Catelin and Aldred saw themselves once again. They were sitting in high-back chairs set close to each other in a dark room. Aldred's right hand was wrapped around Catelin's left hand; their heads both bowed as if in prayer. The pair recognized each other by the bloodstained clothing worn by the two deteriorated corpses.

And then, the two-sided screen playing between them went dark for a moment. Slowly their vision returned while Aldred and Catelin, kneeling, stared at each other knowing they were about to act out their roles in this macabre play of tragedy written and directed by none other than Aldred's lord and master, Lord Lawrence. A look of horror on Catelin's face remained momentarily, but then it changed to hate. She turned from Aldred, breaking free from the constraints holding her rigid to face the phantom figure who was now in control of Lawrence's fractured mind.

"Proceed with your game, you silly wretch of a man. You want my soul, do you? Well, take it! I beseech you have it and put it away with your demented mind. I shall reveal to you what is dark." She turned back to Aldred, glaring at him. Hate was still in her eyes. "I beg you, Aldred. Do it now. I welcome my death. Bring me my freedom."

Aldred was more horrified at her appearance than he had been during the sacrificial display he had just witnessed. The intensity of her hate grew stronger. "Catelin?"

"Damn you, Aldred! Do it now!" she commanded. "He cannot win. He will never win! He is no better than the others. He will learn. Kill me now! Let him gather his darker soul!"

On this occasion, the cinematic display would roll on in real time. And each of them would not only see it; they would feel it. Aldred could not control himself. He lifted the dagger toward Catelin's dress, above her breasts. Her hate relinquished; a devilish smile rose on her face. It was a look of evil Aldred could not reconcile. *Who is this woman?*

"Who you ask? Come, Aldred. Come to me," she pleaded. "Come see what a—"

Then it happened. Their screams, just as those from Lawrence had echoed, resounded throughout the great hall . . . until their bodies fell silent, embraced by each other. A wicked smile was held firm across Catelin's beautiful face.

F

The phantom Lawrence discovered removing the treacherous bodies was not as difficult a task as he had anticipated. He merely had to will the lifeless bodies to move and follow him to the dungeon. The bloody mess in the great hall was a bit more problematic. It even brought forth second thoughts. Perhaps he should have had Aldred clean up the mess Lady Catelin made and carried her down to the asylum before he had him take his own life. Aldred could have set Catelin on her eternal throne before he committed his own suicide. Nevertheless, Lawrence would merely collect one of the staff under his control and have him complete the task. He might be in need of another assistant, now that Aldred had been . . . discreetly discharged from his lord's service.

Lawrence glided his way back up the stairway to his bedchamber, which itself was no longer a necessity, and through the great hall and solar to the main doors of the castle. He commanded them open. This was accomplished with ease. But when he tried to pass through the threshold,

Lawrence found he could not breach the outdoors. He looked out across the yard and noticed a man on a horse leaving the grounds. It was nearly dark, but the man was visible. Lawrence called out to the man, but he also discovered his voice did not carry beyond the walls of the castle. Then he discovered the horse was frozen in midstride, galloping as fast as it could carry the man, with its tail extended backward. It stood there in midair with the man hunched down over the horse's mane, and two of its hooves were suspended in above ground.

Had Lawrence been able to investigate the premises, he would have found it deserted. Brita had not only collected Rodney but also gathered all the remaining staff at the castle and revealed to them what their lord and master had been doing these past years. All of them gathered their belongings and stole away in carts and wagons and on horseback, taking with them a good portion of the stock, whatever they could scavenge from the grounds, and supplies and leaving the corrals open so the remaining abandoned animals could themselves flee.

Most of the staff followed Rodney and Brita to Lady Catelin's orchards in Southern France and settled there for the remainder of their lives. Rodney and Brita had desperately attempted to locate the bastard girl child born under the veil of sin perpetrated by the old man who had kept Catelin in servitude. Fearing the sight of the old man's face would reappear in the baby's image, she had abandoned the child on the doorsteps of a church. From that day forth, Catelin was known never again to set foot under the roof of any sacred grounds. It was then Catelin's appetite for revenge had planted its own seed within her. Fleeing from religious persecution, a descendant of the girl child would one day set foot on American soil, not unlike a descendant of an orphaned boy taken in by Rodney and Brita who would find a way across the pond.

Brita and Rodney had prayed years for the return of Catelin and Aldred but never again heard a word, and both had sworn an oath of secrecy, never returning to Lord Lawrence's feared grounds. It was cursed.

The castle would sit vacant for the ten years following the curse before anyone had discovered the tenant had disappeared or had abandoned the property. No sign of life had been found. His power within its walls was limitless. Lawrence saw to it the doorways to the stairways in his bedchamber and the upper floor hallway had been covered by stone removed from other walls, so the entrances to his asylum were never thereafter discovered. The castle sat unattended for a hundred years before being auctioned. However, occupants soon moved away because of the nightly screams heard throughout the halls. The property passed hands on many occasions thereafter. Legend passed down over the ages theorized the castle was haunted by the original occupants who had mysteriously vanished with no word or trace left behind.

Over the course of the centuries to follow, the phantom Lawrence would find he was stuck in a timeless zone. For him, the clock did not tick. The outside world carried on as it would with or without him. But when he attempted to breach its boundary, he was unable to step into current time. He first gathered a clue months after Catelin and Aldred were put to the throne. He again attempted to wander outside the castle.

Their putrefying bodies were deteriorating slowly but were still mostly intact. When he commanded the front castle door to open, he found the horseman had indeed left the castle grounds. Also, leaves on the surrounding trees had fallen, and a foot of snow lay on the ground. The stain of blood in the great hall remained—a memento.

For several centuries, Lawrence was trapped in the silent confines of his castle. To him, a century could pass in a second or vice versa.

Eventually, he found a bit of magic still remained in the amulet. And then he discovered the hidden world beyond his mirrors; they were a portal to the present. He finally learned to pass through from his timeless prison to the present, even though when he did this, he entered a timeless field. It was fine with him. He learned how to maneuver while on the other side, sneak about unobserved, but also learned he must do so swiftly. He was able to manipulate animated objects while on the other side, bring across select tools of his trade, and he was able to acquire more articles for his arsenal of torture.

He later found he was able to make physical contact with these tangible objects and other physical things, breathing or not. But while on the other side, he had limited physical attributes, and he got tired quickly. He did not spend much time beyond, for he thought if he fell asleep, he might not wake and might not be able to return to his asylum. Company, if any, must somehow be brought to his side; it must be invited.

For two more centuries, Lawrence toyed with his ability and the prospect of such an invitation. But he was unable to bring his victims back to the timeless space in the castle. Somehow, he sensed it must occur of their own volition; they must somehow be willing. His dark heart and the curse remained in conflict. So he did the best he could under the circumstances while attempting to develop his talents. He left his kills behind. But even this caused him frustration.

His victims were caught in a timeless zone, between breaths, between steps. There was no challenge, no excitement in severing the head of a man with an axe when the person could not defend himself, when the person could not even feel the pain, could not feel the terror. They were stripped of their lives with no knowledge whatsoever of the horror he so desired to inflict on them. Ever-present one moment . . . and then vanished. Here today, gone tomorrow. He could not rob them of their souls if he could not frighten them to the brink of lunacy. He traveled throughout the world, killing at random but mourned for the thrill of the experience his memories of torture brought to him.

Another century passed before phantom Lawrence developed yet another vital skill—communication. He learned he could actually observe a person in their current time from his side of the portal and transmit his voice into the world beyond his mirrors. This he could accomplish by remaining in the universe beyond his mirror and locating another portal, another mirror through which his thoughts could be communicated into words. The phantom Lawrence developed this craft through many years of practice and many thousands of mirrors. Ultimately, he developed the ability to imitate other voices, even though his inner voice of the not-so-holy holy man never changed. He placed himself in the universe at the surface to these portals and waited. It was by simple chance that he discovered this new and untapped resource.

He had discovered a fair young maiden, a girl of perhaps ten years of age. Something about her struck him as familiar. He passed through his portal to observe the young girl but hesitated at sacrificing her. He decided perhaps he could observe her growth, so he settled himself at the surface of the portal she visited regularly and witnessed her movements in real time. She was a pretty young girl and spent her evenings before bedtime sitting and facing the portal brushing her hair. It was deep black. Her eyes were ocean blue. He loved the motion of her arms stroking her silky black hair behind her.

As the years passed in her young life, her hair grew longer. Looking for more excitement, Lawrence turned to other portals to observe other humans, thousands of them, but eventually he turned back again and again to this special one. Over her youthful years, he watched as she became a handsome young, teenage woman. One day, as she pressed her image close to her mirror to perhaps examine a blemish, an imperfection in her milky smooth skin, Lawrence met her eyes. He thought it impossible but moved in closer, almost pushing his nose through the portal and breaking the chain, moving the clock surrounding her human form.

There could be no doubt. Why not? He had already accomplished the impossible. So why could she not exist once again in this new world, the world in the future? Lawrence was certain he had once again found Catelin—the Catelin he had lost, the one whose soul had somehow eluded him, the soul she had promised him. Somehow it had escaped the fate levied on her by the hand of Aldred. It was her soul that lived on. Her soul had survived and claimed the flesh and body of another living being. Catelin had been reborn. It would be some time before she had grown into the woman Catelin had been, before she would become the Catelin he had known. But to Lawrence, time was immaterial. He had all the time in the world. And now, all he needed was a soul, and he too could be renewed. He would let her be while he began his search. In time, she would be mature, become ripe for picking, and in the meantime, he would set out to claim his soul. Then he would return to claim Catelin and bring her back to his asylum. Born again, she would be willing.

In the ten years following outside his world, the demented mind of Lawrence deteriorated even further than it had been, as his lust for Catelin deepened. His patience was growing thin; he released his aggression on the innocent, savagely annihilating unsuspecting victims. He taunted them through their portals by projecting his other voice— the voice of the not-so-holy holy man, the voice of the not-a-monk-of-his-kind monk. It was with the landmark first victim when Lawrence discovered this talent. After playing with her on one fateful day, he finally reached through her portal and pulled the woman into the world between the portals and dragged her back through his own mirror to his beloved asylum.

Come to me, and let me claim your sweet, sweet soul. I am the dark of night. I am the preyer of the prey. Your soul is my claim.

The woman had been a prostitute, a lady of the night, a woman of the street. He had discovered her in England. How fitting. He just loved women from England. And he loved prostitutes. They were among the first of his victims in his former existence. He loved tearing them apart. He had observed the woman regularly covering her face, neck, and breasts with powders and essence and applying sticks of varying colors on her large lips. Each night, she had returned to her mirror, apparently worn out from her labors, scrubbing her face and lips. Her bloodshot eyes were attempting to focus on the duty at hand. *Drunk with wine,* suspected the phantom. It was here during her nightly vigils when the phantom Lawrence had first called out to her. Inebriated, she, at first, turned away and searched the room behind her with her impaired vision, apparently thinking a suitor of her trade had followed her home for a second helping.

"Come to me," he had beckoned. She had turned away from the mirror, with moist towel in hand, trying to maintain her balance on the stool on which she sat and surveyed the room. "Come to my chamber." She quickly turned back, looking up, down, and around, unable to locate the source of her company.

"Who ya be?" she had inquired on this first occasion. "Get ya gone now, will ya? I'm needin' me sleep, so get ya gone."

Phantom Lawrence let her be, but then he returned and toyed with the woman nightly until her response became "You again? Just be keepin' yur eyes shut and leave me, me privacy." He just loved the way those cockney London women spoke.

Now accustomed to his familiar voice and nightly visits, Lawrence kept silent on the evening of his breakthrough, or it should be said her breakthrough. "Where'd ya go, sweet?" she summoned. She leaned up close to the mirror to accept his invitation. "And where's this here chamber me keeps 'earin' 'bout?"

"Right here, my sweet, sweet soul," the phantom replied. He then cast his long marbled fingers through the mirror and wrapped them around her neck, pulling her back through the mirror's portal. She did not even scream.

Lawrence did not attend to her until after the alcohol had flushed its way out of her system. He pulled her back into the asylum through the mirror set in the stairway behind his former bedchamber, which to him had ages ago become a useless necessity of his former self. If he needed to recover from too much time on the other side, he had a coffin which was quite comfortable.

He had left the cockney prostitute tied down naked on the slab in the middle of his asylum for weeks before returning, which for him was hardly the passing of one circle by a second hand on a new age clock. The heavyset brown-haired woman had lost considerable pounds, was completely dehydrated, and was nearing starvation, but her senses had been restored. *So much the better for the infliction of horror,* his deranged state of mind had thought.

Phantom Lawrence took his time with the woman. And although moments before she had succumbed to the skinning of her arms, legs, and torso, half eaten alive by a variety of insects and had become reacquainted with her god, she kept calling to him, you know. Lawrence had been unable to collect her soul at the time she died. "I'll be needing a better specimen than this one," he told himself, "and quite a bit more practice."

F

The phantom had concluded in order to collect a soul, it must be one of a special breed, perhaps an acquaintance of Catelin. He returned to the portal mirror the young girl had sat behind in his presence for years, but when he investigated beyond its surface, she and the familiar surroundings were gone. The mirror had been moved outdoors, and it was resting on top of a mound of indescribable waste. He stepped through and found boxes of a material of which he was unfamiliar. Some were filled with books, many of them with very thin paper. Most of which had paintings on the cover page in brilliant colors. There were broken dolls, broken furniture, scraps of food, and metal objects of various shapes and sizes, some with large doors lying next to them sporting shiny handles. There seemed to be no humans around, and if he could smell again, the place would surely stink more than the rotted corpses in his garden of cadavers lying beyond the castle.

So the phantom set out to find her once again. When he did, he found she indeed had blossomed into the innocent and lovely Catelin, who had once stumbled onto his castle grounds. Her voice was the same as it had been, but the language she now used was crude and provocative, much more so than the original Catelin. This he did not mind.

She was standing in front of a long portal in a strange room. There was a door at one end of the room behind her, and another young woman was set at the end of a bare wall. She and the other woman standing next to her were admiring themselves while they were arranging their hair and faces, smiling and giggling with each other, as they posed in front of the mirror, talking about someone named Sondra. They spoke something about it being time for them to get back to the grindstone, although neither one of them had displayed any evidence of dust in their hair, their arms, or their bodies.

At this first sighting, the phantom thought, *How exciting, an acquaintance.* He also thought, *How exciting, a grindstone on a pretty face.* When the door closed behind them, the light shining in the room from above them extinguished.

He had turned to discover nearby another portal. It appeared to be the same shape and size as Catelin's mirror. A variety of men passed through; most of them did not bother to stop at the mirror or the devices resting below them. They just passed by from one side to the other, reappeared, and then disappeared out the door from which they had emerged. But the last man struck a chord in phantom Lawrence. But this man did stop. The hair was much shorter, but the color was precise. Also, the size and shape of the man's body was the same as the man who had driven a dagger through his own beating bloody heart and whose bones now rested silently in the asylum, behind an unlocked door. *Damn his soul to hell.* Aldred survived. Aldred survived and was reborn along with Catelin. *Damn his soul to hell.*

Knowing he could now read minds, enter them, and search their contents undetected, Lawrence knew he could find Catelin's personal portal—one she did not frequently share. He also knew Aldred was within his grasp. They hide behind new names, Trudy and Benny. *Really? Trudy and Benny? These are actual names?* He would take them from their new world.

Their new names could be left behind. But first, there would be a bit of retribution for their treachery, a bit of disruption in their happy and contented lives—something he could take from them. Then the trap would be set, and he would bring them back home, back to where they belonged. And once safely back in his asylum, their asylum, he would collect Aldred's soul and reclaim Catelin.

There were many thoughts passing through Aldred's mind, and many of them included Catelin. It appeared she had been in distress on many occasions, and Aldred had rushed to her side in defense, such as the time he had saved her from the tip of a saber and, again, from the jaws of a powerful beast. He had once stopped a massive machine moving and roaring across metal rails to which she had been tied down and gagged. And on each occasion, their lips had met before the memory was interrupted by another thought. *Where had he acquired these skills? Where had he acquired this inhuman strength?* However, an acquaintance also currently playing frequently on the tip of Aldred's mind would be first in line. Frances F Murphy. *How fitting. F for first.*

CHAPTER TEN

BENNY

"Where the hell are we, Johnson?" asked Paul Denning, all sergeant in his inquiry. His grip on Benny's right hand was suddenly getting tighter.

"Please, Sergeant, it's Benny," he replied. "I have no idea, but I'm really sure something is pulling us along at a really good pace, except I can't feel any kind of wind or breeze blowing on my face. And I don't think my hair is blowing around either. It's like I'm just hanging here in thin air."

"And the stars are flying by like they're all shooting at the same time. I'm getting dizzy." Sergeant Denning's grip on Benny began to fade away. "Don't lose me."

"I see what you mean," said Benny. His grip on Denning also began to loosen, and in a flash, he joined the sergeant in counting sheep . . .

or possibly stars.

When the two men woke, they were lying on a stone floor. There were no more stars shining or shooting past them, and it was pitch black in the room in which they were confined. Benny figured it was a room because when he woke, his head was leaning against a wall. It felt as though it was made of concrete or stone. They were no longer holding hands, but they were both lined up side by side against the hard wall.

"Are you awake, Sarge?" Benny asked. He felt around in his pants pocket for the skinny flashlight he had deposited before their departure from the real world.

As a beam of light smacked Benny directly in his face, the cop replied, "If I'm dreaming, it's the first time it has happened with the actual touchy-feely stuff. This floor or whatever is hard as a rock, and it's a little chilly. Let's get our bearings and try to get up."

Denning moved the light away from Benny straight up the wall behind him to the high ceiling above them, brought it back halfway down the wall to their left, and moved it clockwise around the room. The light beam found a stairwell. As he continued floating the light beam around the room, it found a mirror. They were on a landing at the bottom of a flight of stairs. An old-fashioned oil lantern sat on a small table in a corner of the landing.

"The mirror over there must have been the door or gateway that got us into the room," said Benny. "I hope it works the other way round."

As Denning continued to move the light around the room to the next wall, he discovered a door and then another doorway opposite the stairwell in which they were sitting. A key with a small string attached was engaged in the first door's lock.

"I wonder if it goes outside," said Benny. "What do you think, Sarge?" Benny began to shuffle to his feet but found he was still a bit woozy, so he sat back down. "Wow! That sure did beat any rolly-coaster ride I've ever been on. That's for sure."

"Rolly-coaster?" asked Denning with a funny look on his face. "Even so, I'm not sure I ever want to go on a ride like that again. My head is still spinning."

Pushing his back against the wall, Benny slowly climbed up on his feet while taking in deep breaths and bringing his large penlight to life. "I'm not sure either, but if we're lucky, I guess we have at least one more ticket to use up before this is all over."

"Please don't remind me," Paul replied, as he, too, pressed himself to his feet. "I guess we should check out what's behind door number one." He stepped to the door on the side wall and grabbed the handle. In Aldred's dreams, this was just one more memory Lawrence had not preserved for him. It was merely another memory placed out of bounds.

The handle did not move, so Denning rattled it back and forth a few times until it clacked open. "You ready, Johnson?"

"Benny," Benny pleaded. "We have to start somewhere. It might as well be right here as anywhere. I wonder what's upstairs."

"First things first," Paul replied. "Maybe the girls are tied up or something in here." He pressed the door forward. It offered resistance, but it was not jammed shut from swelling, so it freely swung wide open.

Their two beams of light, bright as a set of headlights, projecting into the room illuminated two silhouettes. Both occupants were sitting in high-back chairs and neither complained about the sudden interruption of their privacy or the bright lights shining in their eyes. They were long dead. Withered clothing and dilapidated boots draped down from their dreary bones. Crudely engraved with a sharp object on separate headrests of the chairs were the names Aldred and Catelin. Bones of their hands were entwined around each other. A dagger had fallen onto the lap of the man, sitting to the right of the woman from their viewpoint.

Benny hesitated before stepping into the room for a closer look. "Another weapon probably wouldn't hurt, you think?"

"I guess not, Benny," said Denning. "This looks like a setup, like they were arranged this way. I doubt if they died holding hands just sitting there. Somebody must have killed them and set them side by side. Lovers 'til the end, I guess."

"It sure didn't happen yesterday," Benny added, as he retrieved the knife and stuck it under his belt at his right side. The Glock occupied the other side of Benny's waist. "They still had their clothes on. What's left of them anyway. They look like rags now. Hard to tell if it was as gruesome as what Helen and Ms. Murphy went through. But it must have happened ages ago. I'm surprised the bones didn't just eventually collapse into a pile."

"Why, Detective Johnson," Denning remarked, "I'm impressed. Forensics would tell us more, but it looks like the guy was stabbed in the heart. Maybe they went quick and didn't get tortured like the two women. Maybe they were put there before rigor mortis set in, and gravity just held them in place after a couple of days because they were probably balanced in that position."

Denning stepped closer. "And so, after their dead muscles relaxed, they just kind of stayed in place, except for their drooping heads, I guess. And look what we have here," added Denning. He was moving his light beam to the right of the two figures. It landed on a coffin set on a wooden platform; the lid was about waist-high to the sergeant.

"I will let you have the honor, Sarge," replied Benny. He removed the Glock. "I'll back you up, just in case we wake up somebody."

"Very considerate of you," Denning said as he pulled out his own weapon. He held it ready for discharge as he lifted the lid with his left hand holding a flashlight. He moved the light beam back and forth. "Nothing here but a black lining, silk maybe, but it's still in good shape, not like with the dead people. The pillow has a depression. Someone or someone's body has been in here. I'm not sure whether or not the depression would have remained in it for as long as these two people have been dead. Maybe it's still being used."

"I'm sure George Washington didn't sleep here, and I'm not too sure what kind of people enjoy skeletons for company."

"Get serious, Johnson. We just might have somebody lurking around here. I'm sure the ladies didn't just step through the damn mirror for a walk in the park by themselves. We need to stay on the lookout."

"This room is a little spooky, like maybe we have a vampire character on our hands who comes out at night. We should probably get on to door number two, no?" said Benny. "Maybe we'll find the grand prize. It's only been a couple of hours, if that, since the women disappeared."

"This place looks like it might never get any light. But there's probably not enough time passed yet for him or it or whatever to do his thing. It looked like he took his time with Mrs. Jones. She took one hell of a beating. I can understand why she lost her mind. And it would have taken a while for this guy to get Ms. Murphy up on that chandelier. Talk about crazy, the guy or whatever is a real maniac. Let's move on out of here." He politely closed the lid on the coffin and turned back to Benny with a smirk spread across his lips.

"Then I guess it's my turn." Benny left the room and approached the next door, and it opened easily, no lock. It opened to a larger room, and in this one, a wall-hung lantern was burning. It did not provide bright light, but it was ample enough to maneuver around without running into a wall.

"Somebody's been here," said Denning.

They extinguished their flashlights, and as their eyes adjusted to the light, the contents of the room came into focus. They had discovered the room in which phantom Lawrence kept his miscellaneous tools of the trade. On the opposite side of the room was a set of double doors leading those who cared to pass through to the infamous asylum of the dark phantom in the cloak.

"Look at all this stuff," remarked Denning. He ignited and directed his flashlight to a shelf containing a number of various-sized cutting tools. There were knives of different sizes and lengths and saws. Some of them were ancient and of archaic design, while others appeared relatively new, including coping, hack and miter saws, plus an eighteen-inch long carpenter saw and several surgical saws. They all had a variety in size and number of teeth per inch, but their one common factor was they all exhibited darkened traces of dried blood.

At an adjacent wall filled with shelves, Benny was observing another collection. "Clamps," he uttered. There was one with a threaded clamp jaw that had been sharpened to a point. Some were wooden; others were made of metal. One was apparently molded with jaws to fit over the upper and lowers rows of a man's teeth and would open to spread them apart, rather than apply pressure to a body part. A variety of hand tools were spread out on a table below the shelves.

"It doesn't look like these are here for woodworking projects. This is sick. And look in this corner," Benny said, directing the beam of his flashlight. "It looks like the kind of mad scientist's white cloak they all wear when they're up to their experiments, not to mention the tall boots so they don't get their feet dirty walking around in the mess they're making. Like the Friday-night spooky movies you see with the hosts dressed up like Ghoulardi."

"Well, at least the cloak and boots are still here, and the girls aren't around anywhere," concluded the sergeant. "And I hope none of these tools are missing. Let's keep moving. There must be a bigger room beyond those double doors."

Both of them put their flashlight beams on the doors. They did not appear to be completely shut, and they were certainly not locked. Benny approached the handles apprehensively. "What the *F* am I doing?" he whispered.

"I could think of a better word than *F*, and you're asking me?" questioned Denning right back at him. "Maybe Lieutenant Baker was here just a few minutes before we got here. I can see she might leave herself an escape route, so maybe she lit the lantern and left the doors open."

"But why would she leave the lantern behind, and why would she come here without me?" replied Benny, "I mean, without us." He looked over at Denning as the sergeant looked back.

"I don't think either one of those girls would be jumping through that damn mirror on their own, Johnson," advised Denning. "I mean, Benny, especially Baker. I mean, she is the best detective in the department, but every now and then, she tends to stick her neck out a little bit too far. But no, I doubt she would ever go this far, not unless something prompted her into some kind of trap, induced or persuaded her somehow."

"You sound a little protective there, Sarge. And Trudy was really freaked out with all the other stuff going on. You know, with Ms. Murphy and Helen. Poor Helen." Benny brought his focus back to the two doors and stepped forward.

"Poor Murphy," Denning seconded. "Baker is my boss," he said flatly. "I cover her back. She covers my ass." He followed Benny, just as cautious, and as Benny's left hand found its way to the left door, his right hand placed itself on the right door. They glanced at each other and pressed forward to find that a couple of lanterns in the huge room had been lit, but the wicks seemed to be on low fire or they were dying. The small flames illuminated a few silhouettes but not much more.

The two men slowly moved forward toward the large slab at the center of the room. Their flashlight beams were falling on each side of it. Sergeant Denning turned off his light and motioned for Benny to do the same with the one he nervously held. The room quickly darkened, but their eyes slowly adjusted to the dim light and shadows filling the area.

Benny pocketed the flashlight and then placed his left hand on the stone slab. It settled on top of a bone fragment covered by a significant layer of dust and was lying in a pool of its former inhabitant's dried-up blood. As vision cleared for Benny and Paul, the layers of bloodstains from the English woman and a number of other victims greeted them. No doubt, a contribution from Helen was among them.

Benny withdrew his hand from the bone, as though he had just pinched a rattlesnake's tail in a game of Pin the Tail on the Donkey. The bone fragment sailed onto the stone floor. He withdrew his flashlight again, clicked it on, and let the beam wander over toward the left of the room where it settled on a pile of bones. Among them, at least two dozen were discernible skulls. Many more were hidden beneath the pile standing the height of a tall man and resembled the shape of a conical Indian mound, less the earth used for the deceased victims' burials. Aldred was no longer present to tidy up the surroundings of the asylum for the master phantom Lawrence, who had been negligent in his own housekeeping.

While the sands of time held fast in phantom Lawrence's world, they flowed freely in the physical world. Lawrence had not experienced time for centuries, but it had not stopped to wait on him or, for that matter, for him. And it stood still for any of those in the presence of his world. The two women they were seeking, plus Paul and Benny themselves, were now in a timeless zone. Should breath leave them, they would join the sands of time.

"Jesus!" exclaimed Benny upon discovering the mound of bones. Then he grabbed his mouth to silence himself and quite quickly spat out the dust back on top of the former prostitute's final berth.

"Who is that?" shouted a female voice. "Is that you, Johnson?"

"Lieutenant! It's me, Sergeant Denning," replied the cop. He turned away from the pile of busted skeletons toward the wall at his right. "Are you all right?"

"Hell, no!" she responded. "Get me out of this thing. It's about to chew me up. And be quick about it, Paul." She had never before addressed him by his first name. "It didn't take you guys very long to get here. How did you get here so fast? Come over here to this darn cage before it chews me to pieces."

Benny and Denning put both of their lights back into motion and quickly located Lieutenant Baker stretched out in a wooden cage suspended from a beam atop a wooden frame. There was a ratchet assembly of some kind operating a series of sharp wooden stakes against spring tension. The stakes encircled her from head to foot and were controlled by a lever on one side of the contraption used to rotate a serpentine gear at the bottom of the cage, which, in turn, rotated and collapsed the radius of the half-pike lances.

Leather straps under her shoulders kept her elevated from above, and others wrapped around her wrists, waist, and ankles were fastened to the top and perimeter of the human birdcage. Interference with the straps and stake assembly served only to tighten her binds. For good measure, a leather collar held tightly around her neck was also fastened to the cage in four quadrants, keeping her in static motion and struggling for air.

When Denning's light found her, it landed at her backside and traveled the crucifix fashion of her arms and legs. He uttered a toilet word under his breath, as he rushed to Baker and approached the door of the cage and her sight, which each faced the stone wall.

"You are a sight for sore eyes, Sergeant," said Baker, somewhat relieved. "And they are sore."

"Talk about being chewed to pieces, Sarge," said Benny. "We have company." Benny was standing at the opposite side of the cage. He moved his flashlight beam to his left.

Four huge doglike creatures were slowly advancing toward them. All of them had tongues drooping from their mouths, just above some very long and sharp teeth. Positioned in a football backfield spread formation, they appeared much meaner and formidable than Notre Dame's infamous Four Horsemen.

"And they look really hungry," added Benny.

"We have to keep them away from the lieutenant," Denning said, as he slowly stepped around the cage to position himself between the beasts and Baker.

Benny followed his move while pulling the Glock out from his belt. "I sure hope these things work, Sergeant."

"What's happening?" asked Baker. She tried to turn her head, but it was too tightly restrained. "Paul! What is it?" She sounded frantic.

"Just a little diversion, lieutenant," he said. "Stay calm. It's all under control."

Suddenly, the quarterback of the group charged Denning. He bent his legs to make ready his aim and fired two rounds, but they were too late. The gun discharged again as the animal's forelegs crashed into his chest, driving him back toward the cage. His head missed colliding with it by a fraction. As the two of them were falling, Benny released two rounds squarely into the side of the beast's head. It was dead before it landed atop the cop.

The other three animals charged side by side, as though they were about to bust open a hole for a delayed quarterback sneak. Benny quickly whirled around and ripped off four more rounds, while Denning collected himself, picked up his revolver, and shot the beast to his right four times, blowing its muzzle apart into fragments. The other two beasts shot by Benny hit the floor and were writhing in pain. Benny stepped forward and put a couple of slugs into each of their brains.

"Holy crap, Benny!" commented Paul. "Where did that come from?"

"I guess it's like riding a bike, Sarge. You might go on living without doing it all the time . . . but you don't forget."

"What the hell was that, you guys?" asked Baker. "You okay? Talk to me, Denning. Talk to me."

"Just a little diversion, Lieutenant. All under control. Now we're going to get you out of this damn cage." He moved back in front of her. "Just be calm and be patient."

"Easy for you to say," she replied. "Get moving, if you don't mind." Benny had followed Denning and made a circle around the cage.

He then dropped to his knees and began crawling around on the stone floor inspecting the gear and ratchet arrangement underneath the cage. He then rolled over on his back following the path of the lever and weird gear with his flashlight. As the sergeant began to open the latch on the cage door, Benny shouted from below. "Stop! Stop it, Sarge!"

"What's Johnson up to, Paul?" Again, Baker addressed him as Paul.

"Detective?" he replied. He was still a bit surprised but, nevertheless, flattered she was addressing him by his first name. After all, he was on duty, and she was in command, right?

"It's not like we need to follow protocol stuck out here somewhere in the damn wilderness of the universe. What's he up to now?" Baker could feel the rattle of the cage below her.

"One second, Lieutenant," Paul began, "I mean, Susan."

"Please," she replied, "stick with Baker and get me the hell out of here."

"Yes, ma'am," he said. "Benny, what are you doing down there?"

Denning aimed his light at the floor and dropped to his knees and leaned over to see what was happening.

"I'm trying to figure out what kind of setup we have to deal with. There is a lever leading up to the door you were about to open. There are two steel springs underneath here, see?" Benny shone his own light above.

"So what?" Denning replied. "We need to get her out of this thing. Those spikes are almost ready to start jabbing her all over the place, even her face. Let's get the door open."

"Not unless we want to kill her," Benny replied.

"What do you mean kill her?" the sergeant asked, whispering. "What's going on, Benny?!" piped in Baker.

"Well, I wasn't the best inspector in the world, Lieutenant," Benny began. "But I learned a little bit from the best of the BestEver Insurance specialists to be a boiler inspector rather than just a boiler looker. Sometimes people can become complacent when they are doing the same thing over and over again every day, miss important stuff, like a sticking float on a low-water fuel cutoff."

"A what?" asked Baker sarcastically. "What does that have to do with this damn trap this maniac has me locked into?"

"A low-water cutoff? It's a simple device. It's something like what you find in a toilet, but if it sticks, the boiler can blow up if the water drops below a safe level, I mean, like in exploding and blowing up anybody in the building when it goes *boom* along with the boiler. Did you know high-temperature water under high pressure expands about sixteen hundred times its volume when suddenly exposed to atmospheric pressure? You know what that can do to a house?"

"Cut the crap, Johnson," demanded Denning. "Who gives a damn? This ain't no boiler, and she ain't in no house! Let's get the lieutenant out of this thing before *my* temperature and pressure start rising."

"If we open the door right now, the second spring is going to pop this serpentine coil here loose, and it will tighten the cage, as in spring it loose all around her body. I don't think we want to blow up this contraption with our boss inside." He placed his hand on the coil. "Paul, we need to borrow a saw from our host, so we can cut loose this other spring from the door."

"I don't know what the hell you're talking about, Benny, but you'd better be right. Otherwise, we'll have two dead people on our hands here, and I can guarantee you I won't be one of them." Denning got to his feet and was back faster than you can recite the old and mostly forgotten Crest toothpaste slogan. He had several tools of which Benny chose a hacksaw fitted with a fine-tooth metal-cutting blade, wondering if it would cut through bone easier than a carpenter's saw.

Benny handed Paul his penlight. "Sergeant, try to focus the light beams on this spring. Mine seems to be losing power."

"Mine doesn't look too bright either, Benny," the cop replied. "Maybe we should have brought some extra batteries."

"I have a suggestion where you two guys can install those batteries," added Baker nervously. "Hurry up and get me out of this thing."

After a couple of minutes of hacking away at the structure, *Pow!* The door cage spring broke free and recoiled. Had it been attached, Baker would have been either crushed or punctured to death in a split second.

"This guy is really sick, Benny," Denning agreed. He got back to his feet to open the cage and then thought twice about it. "Are we okay down there, Benny? Can we open this thing now?"

"Hang on, Sarge. One minute." Benny began to hack away at the connection to the other spring. In a minute, as promised, *Bang!* The other spring recoiled, and the wooden stakes were all propelled in circular fashion back against the inside surface of the cage.

Denning uttered another toilet reference, but this time, it was holy. He turned the latch on the door and opened it. Then he reached in with a knife he had retrieved from the devil's toolroom and began to work on the leather straps, starting with those at Baker's ankles. Then he wrapped one of his muscular arms around her waist and freed her arms and neck. Relieved, Baker collapsed over his left shoulder.

"Jeez, oh man, Paul," she whispered, "why are my feet so sore?"

Benny focused the two flashlights for a clearer path away from the cage back to the slab where Baker could sit and rest her aching muscles and bones. The lumination from the lights was fading fast, and they were dead moments after Denning set Baker on the slab.

"Great," Baker complained. "Now we're just about blind down in this dungeon." She felt for the sergeant's big left shoulder. "Don't go too far, Paul. I can barely see a thing."

"It sure would be nice to have one of those lanterns like we saw in that room with all those weapons and tools this crazy guy has stored back there," said Benny. "I'll bet if we raised the wick, it would light up this whole dungeon or torture chamber or whatever."

Then, suddenly, from behind Baker on the opposite side of the slab, an oil lantern came to life. This time, Baker made a religious toilet reference. She added, "Where did that come from? Benny? Was that you?"

"Well, I don't know, Lieutenant," he replied, "but like I was saying, I was just thinking about lighting up a lantern and seeing how it would light up this room. It's not quite as bright as I thought, but who am I to argue?"

"And you were just thinking about lighting up a lantern?" asked Paul. "I mean, as soon as you said it, the damn thing just popped up out of nowhere."

"And you just thought about it?" Baker said, shaking her head. After a minute of silence, when she caught her breath and senses, Lieutenant Baker thanked both of them and brought the two men up to speed on what had happened in their absence and what might have happened to Trudy. "My lord, those dogs or whatever they were—they were huge."

"Benny here took down three of them, Lieutenant."

"You just continue to surprise me, Benny. And I'm sure glad Benny got hold of you, Paul. Good thinking on your part, Benny F Johnson," she began. "This thing, whatever it is, he's got Ms. Perkins thinking she is somebody else. That is, I guess, if the it is a he. I couldn't identify whether or not it was a man. The thing's face is buried in that black cloak . . . man, woman, or ghost maybe. At first, I thought it might be some kind of holy man, a monk, or something."

"Then I wasn't dreaming or hallucinating when I saw it in the mirror. The black cloak and the weird eyes set way back some kind of reddish color."

"I don't remember too much about him pulling the eyeball stare at me," Susan Baker replied. "But he has other tricks up his sleeves. And the guy doesn't even walk. He floats around the room, for god's sake. He floats! And sometimes he appears in one place, and all of a sudden, he disappears and shows up on the other side of the room."

"Sounds like some kind of spirit thing or tricks maybe with laser lighting. And what do you mean Trudy thinks she is somebody else?" asked Benny. He lifted himself up to sit on the slab at Baker's left side, while Denning stood before them, with feet spread apart and arms crossed over at his chest, taking it all in and trying to reconcile what the hell was happening. He should be at home chowing down on another slice of pizza, for crying out soft.

"Magic tricks with lasers? Maybe you can explain this place, Benny. No, this thing is real. And Trudy thinks she is this Katie or Katy Lynn person or something like that," she said. "I'm not too sure because the cloaked thing, the phantom, had me out for a while, either knocked out or in some kind of trance like he did with Ms. Perkins."

"Catelin was the name," injected Denning. "Did you see the remains of the two people back in that anteroom where the guy in the cloak has all these tools and knives and stuff?"

"No, I don't remember any other room. I think I woke up in here, and besides . . . I was a bit preoccupied in getting my ass kicked," she said. "Ms. Perkins was already out of it by then. Heck, I don't even know how I got here. One second, I was looking at the mirror in Trudy's apartment, and the next thing, I'm standing in front of this slab being stared down by our mystery man."

"You must have gotten at least one round off, Lieutenant," said Paul. "We found your service revolver and one casing back at Ms. Perkins' place."

"You could have fooled me. He is either some kind of spirit, or he knows a lot more about magic than Houdini ever did. She was with him. And she was smiling. I was hypnotized, paralyzed, couldn't move a muscle. Next thing I know, I'm strapped in the cage over there, and the two of them are sashaying out the other end of this room, hand in hand, I might add. But what a hand, I might also add. It looked like something out of a Disney cartoon, but it sure didn't belong to Prince Charming."

"How could all that stuff happen in such a short time?" asked Denning. "I mean, it was at least an hour, maybe even two hours before we got to this place."

"It seemed to me like it was only maybe five minutes or so, although my body tells me something different." Baker was massaging her neck and rotating her head side to side to free the kinks. "I can't explain. I feel like I've been hanging here for hours. I'm physically drained, and I could use about a gallon of water." She looked up at Paul. "You said there were two bodies in that room?"

"Yes," said Benny, "but they weren't exactly bodies. They were skeletons sitting in a couple of high-back chairs, holding hands. Plaques over their heads identified them as Catelin and Alfred."

"Aldred," corrected the sergeant. "And there was a dagger resting on the guy's lap, like it had fallen out of his chest."

"Why his chest, Paul?" she asked. "Couldn't he have been holding it in his other hand or something?"

"I thought about that, Baker," he began, "but his other arm was situated on the armrest of the chair, palm down, just as though he was posing for a 'king and queen' photo. It looked staged. So, when he was still alive or right after he died, the two of them must have been put in those chairs and posed as the happy, loving couple for some reason by this guy or whatever killed them. The knife must have fallen out of his chest once his body began to waste away. It would have fallen on the floor if he was holding it in his hand. It's too late now to run any forensics. There's nothing left to look at."

"Maybe, maybe not, but good thinking," Baker said. "Well, I doubt if we could ever persuade the chief to get a forensics team out here in this twilight zone. She would have us put away in straitjackets if we even tried. I'm afraid we're on our lonesome on this one, Paul."

"We brought some goodies across with us, Lieutenant," said Benny. "I had my doubts about whether or not the guns would do any good, or even if they would work in this place. But it's a good thing we brought them along. We just saw what happened to the flashlights. They died off really quick, so I'm not sure what will happen to the ammo."

"No harm in keeping them ready to fire," said Denning. "They are better than nothing."

"And twilight zone sounds as good as anything for this place. I'm thinking it's what we're dealing with, something right out of another zone. Here, Lieutenant, take my gun, compliments of the sarge. I haven't had the need for a gun in quite a while. I retired mine a long time ago."

Baker reached for the Glock, while Benny played with his back pocket to retrieve the two clips of ammo. "You'll have to fill me in on that one sometime, Benny. You sure as hell know how to use that piece. But you could be right," she agreed. "I'm not sure if anything is going to stop this thing, even if they do work down here. He, or it, just doesn't seem to be human. We're dealing with some kind of supernatural state. We need to concentrate on Trudy and see if we can get her and us out of here before we all wind up in cages."

Then Baker heard a clanging sound behind her. All three of them turned around to see where it came from. Then Baker let out another religious reference about the man many people recognize as the son of God. "Benny! What the hell is this?"

"I'm not sure, Lieutenant," he declared. "But I was thinking we must be in some kind of a castle or something, and you mentioned you could use a gallon of water. Well, I was just thinking back in those days they probably served drinks on a platter with pitchers and mugs. You know, that's about it."

"That's about it?" asked Denning. Now he was shaking his head, staring in disbelief at the gallon wooden pitcher of water around which three wooden mugs also sat on a large platter next to the lantern. "Hold off on the chamber maids and grapes, Benny."

Baker couldn't take her eyes off Benny. "Something is going on with you, Benny. It must be this place. I had a feeling somehow you might be a missing piece to the puzzle. Just be careful what you think up there in that head of yours. We wouldn't want any unwelcome surprises. We've already had to deal with a pack of wolves, or at least something like wolves. Now, where were we?" She reached for the pitcher to fill a mug with water.

"You said they walked out of the room from those far doors at the end of this hall?" asked Paul.

"More like a dungeon, as Benny said," Baker began, "a torture chamber. And she walked, but the cloaked thing floated. It just glides across the floor, like it's on invisible ice skates. I'll tell you what I remember, but there are elements I think are probably missing."

Then Baker took a long swig of water and told her tale, but she was spot-on when she said she probably didn't remember everything.

F

Earlier, although in the space of timelessness the concept is relatively meaningless, the phantom Lawrence had returned to Trudy's portal after she had enthusiastically accepted his invitation and joined him. He had won her over with ease. Lawrence had lured Catelin through the mirror with the amulet. Upon revealing its presence to her from the other side, the woman calling herself Trudy had become immediately enamored.

That fateful day out by the lake when Lawrence had revealed his devotion and his plans to Catelin, she had begun to fall, but for some reason, she had been overcome with apprehension. She had acted strangely. Somehow, she had been drawn away from its allure, and its power over her had been stifled. Then she had betrayed him, even spitefully robbed him of his pleasure when she so eagerly welcomed her death. Now that she had returned, Lawrence would not allow Aldred or any of his silly intentions to interfere.

Once back in his asylum, Lawrence brought the memories of their courtship back to Catelin. While she was experiencing them, living them once again in her mind, Lawrence was careful to orchestrate them while all recollection of Aldred was removed or at least distorted to the extent he could not be identified by her or anyone else. However, in accomplishing this feat, he discovered the rewind of her past experiences was being complicated by the uninvited presence of the interloper Benny, who still occupied her mind, causing an impediment to the process and injecting false memories. Eventually those falsehoods would fade. *Imagine,* he thought, *him, the impostor posing as this Benny, clad in fine, fluffy clothing, wielding a sword against three men dressed in black wearing*

*masks over their faces! Ha! Aldred could not fence his way through an open
barn door.*

Meanwhile, as Catelin revisited her past, Lawrence returned to the
outside world, hoping he would find the impostor Aldred, challenge
him, entice him back through to the asylum, and twice and for all,
eliminate the menace. Besides, there were chores awaiting him . . . Aldred
had a bone or two to pick.

But to his surprise, in his stead, Lawrence found another figure,
another acquaintance. No, it was not the little girl who Catelin's
memories so cherished, but it was a specimen nevertheless. Why do these
women not wear gowns? They seem to wear clothing not even suitable
as riding dress. Some are even cut far above the knees. *Child's clothing,
perhaps?* This woman was wearing dark-colored men's trousers, slim and
tight fitting. He revealed himself to this acquaintance. She stood there
motionless momentarily; her face was painted over by surprise. *Fright,
perhaps?*

But then the woman stepped forward while pushing back the left
flap of the outer garment she wore. The woman withdrew something
from a sheath at her side tucked under her shoulder. It was not a knife.
She reached forward with both hands gripping the iron device she held
and stuck it through the mirror toward the shroud covering his head.
The phantom returned the gesture, grabbing the instrument just as her
forefinger squeezed its handle and shoved it upward as it discharged to
his side. The bullet casing flew back inside the woman's domain. He
wrenched the weapon away from her, tossing it after the casing while
reaching through the portal and grabbing Baker by her neck. He could
now return to Catelin with a gift. The woman's actions, thrusting her
arm into the phantom's world, was her acceptance to join it. The Aldred
impostor would need to wait a bit longer. Time mattered not.

"Come with me, wench," said the monk-looking phantom. Then he dragged her through; his long fingers were easily wrapped completely around her neck. Lawrence would toy with her while Catelin relived the edited version of her former life, and Aldred's image was purged forevermore.

Before the gasp had exhaled with her breath, Baker found herself standing at the opposite end of a large stone slab facing Trudy, but she could not feel her feet on the floor. She was suspended in air. Phantom Lawrence floated at Trudy's right side. She herself appeared lost of emotion, unaware of her whereabouts. Baker stood as rigid as a statue; her face was locked in stone. She was wide awake at the moment, alert, but unable to move her arms, her legs, anything. She could not even speak. The phantom creature Benny had described was staring at her up and down, likely drooling, she thought through foggy eyes.

Small orbs deep in the cloak over its head cast a dull-red color. Then the long plump but stringy fingers she had felt around her neck reached upward from its right side and pulled out some kind of pendant or charm hanging around its neck. It, too, glowed with the same dull color of the phantom's eyes, but a wave of brown was undulating up and down the surface of the jewel or crystal. As her vision cleared, Susan Baker found it comforting; she no longer felt the muscles in her stone-chiseled legs trembling. She heard the phantom speak.

"I am the dark of night. I am the preyer of prey," he began. "You have come to my asylum. It is here you will deposit your soul. Welcome to the horror of your nightmares."

And you, Sir Cloak Man, are the sicker of the sick, she thought.

"She speaks!" replied the monster floating toward her. It moved rapidly, and almost instantaneously, she was gazing into deep outer space, as she had been only moments earlier before she woke up in the dark chamber in which she now stood. "I will yield you no mercy, mortal being. You will feel the wrath of my infliction."

As long as I don't have to smell your breath, she challenged. Baker was a tough bird.

Then the phantom drew away from her, intensified the red glare he held in her direction, and swept end to end without turning around, back and forth, the length of the large hall, coming to an abrupt stop at her other side. Then Baker felt all her toes curl under her feet, involuntarily stretching to reach the heels of her feet. She screamed in pain; this time she could speak. Trudy stood motionless, now smiling at the imagined memories playing in front of her eyes in full wide-screen, high-density color.

Baker's muscles relaxed from their rigid fixation long enough for the pain in her feet to subside somewhat before she felt herself flying through the air. She flew with the greatest of ease, no doubt, until she slammed against the far wall to her right. She bounced off the wall long enough to take a breath and wince before she was hurled back onto her feet, suspended in air again and whipped into a wooden cage. The door slammed shut in front of her as leather straps whipped out of thin air, wrapping themselves around her ankles, arms, shoulders, and neck.

Baker attempted to twist her way free from the bindings. She heard a loud, mechanical click followed by a rattle of the cage. Then she opened her eyes and saw the wooden spikes staring straight down the center of her eyes. Suddenly, she was enlightened with an attitude adjustment, straining not to scream or even think. But the sight of Helen returned to her thoughts, and she did scream.

"What a lovely thought," she heard the cloak man offer. "I do hope you will be as much fun as your acquaintance."

She found she was able to turn her head slightly without disturbing the mechanism her wiggling had provoked. The cloak man and Trudy were standing beside her. "Ms. Perkins?" she asked. "Is that you?"

So rudely interrupted from her reeducation, Trudy's eyes lit up, and she replied angrily, "I am Catelin. Come, Lord Lawrence," she added. "We have much to do, much to prepare." Her eyes did not move from Baker, nor did she wink. But her face held an eerie, provocative smile.

"We must clothe you in suitable dress for this occasion, Catelin," said Lawrence. "Then we will rid our abode of this rubble."

The pair turned, hand in hand, and departed through a set of double doors far at the end of the hall.

F

"And about the time they left this hall or whatever, this torture chamber, that's when I heard her call his name," said the lieutenant. "She seemed to be out of it, but what a smile she had on her face. It was evil, nasty looking."

"His name?" asked Benny. "The phantom or whatever has a name? That would mean maybe he is a man, or some kind of a person. Or at least he was at one time."

"What name?" asked Denning. "Although it probably doesn't mean much at this point. This guy is not what you might call a human or anything like it."

"Lawrence," Susan replied, "Lord Lawrence." She looked at Benny, wondering if it meant anything.

"Heck," Benny followed, "I don't know anybody named Larry, except maybe Larry Doby, and I never did meet him. And he retired from baseball years ago. And I never heard him being called Lord either. Or Lawrence for that matter. Just plain old Larry." *Or maybe the guy from Arabia?*

"We are not doing matters any good by just sitting here," said Lieutenant Baker. She shuffled off the stone slab and shook her arms and legs. "Jeez," she added, "what the hell did he do to my feet?"

"Can you walk okay?" asked Denning.

"I'll be fine. Just a little sore, that's all."

"Should we follow them or go the other way?" asked Benny. "I'm not too sure we want to just walk into the same room. Maybe if we can find out where they're at and what he is up to, we can come up with a plan to distract him and grab Trudy."

"That might be an idea, Lieutenant," Denning offered. "And maybe we can grab some of his stuff he uses to cut up all these people. We know it works down here. Look at all those bones.

"I would like to see if this gun still works down here," Baker replied. "There's no reason to think it wouldn't, although there's no reason to think this place even exists either. You're right, Paul. Let's go get some of the guy's own ammo, so we'll have it if we're firing blanks."

"I think I'll stick with this dagger," said Benny. "Remembering what happened with the flashlights, I'm fairly sure this knife thing works, but I'm not too sure if the guy has anything to stick it into. And if he moves as fast as you said, Lieutenant, then how are we supposed to catch him and hold him down?"

"One step at a time, Johnson," said Baker, "one step at a time. Just try not to think about it too hard right now. This phantom thing has enough of an edge on us already. We need some time to scope out the landscape above."

Oh F, thought Benny, *she's back to Johnson.*

In the phantom's toolroom, Baker collected several knives. Denning grabbed a ball and chain plus a large meat cleaver, wrapping the chain around his bulky right wrist so he could use the spiked ball as an extension to his rock-hard fist. After mulling the situation over a bit further, the trio decided it would be better to take the exit on the opposite end of the dungeon, rather than the path that the phantom had taken where Paul and Benny had entered the asylum. When they passed through those double doors, they discovered a smaller solar containing several buckets, mops, a pile of moldy linen, and another well-worn stairway, but they missed the stone doorway that blended into the opposite wall.

Then they gathered their nerves, passed by another mirror on the landing, and headed up the stairwell, with Baker on the lead behind shadows cast by Benny's probing lantern. Around and around, they went on a path well worn by none other than Aldred. Benny could never, in his wildest fantasy, have dreamed that the collection of bones holding hands with the Catelin skeleton was a connection to a far-distant ancestor, through the orphan boy adopted by Rodney and Brita. Paid-for-hire DNA lineage researchers could not have invented that one. The fantasy he was currently living was fodder enough to keep his appetite in check.

In this space of timelessness, the three reached the landing and the large wooden door through which Aldred had passed on many occasions. Had they entered the castle in real time, they would have discovered the passageway had been sealed in stone, and there would be no exit beyond the door. Conveniently enough for their sake and Lawrence, this stone wall did not yet exist, as they were now suspended in the past. After unfastening the lock mechanism from the inside, they cautiously stepped through one by one. It was dark beyond the open door.

With the lantern held high, Benny and Paul focused their eyesight down the long corridor, but their vision could not reach its end. They followed Baker and momentarily stopped at the top of the wide stone stairway leading down to the great hall where Catelin and Aldred had met their eternal fate. Benny thought it looked similar to the staircase made so famous in *Gone with the Wind*.

He could picture Trudy dressed in a beautiful gown of the times gracefully waltzing down the steps. But then he thought, *Oh F, I'm not supposed to think.* He held the lantern over the staircase and held his breath in anticipation of another daydream creation. The lantern found no sign of Scarlett O'Hara, Rhett Butler, or anyone else from the Tara plantation. And, of course, no Trudy appeared. Benny breathed a sigh of relief.

Absent from Benny's brief escape from the reality of their moment had been none other than . . . Benny. For once, he had not pictured himself. He had not appeared on Scarlet's staircase with Trudy.

"See something, Benny?" asked Denning. "The stairway looks empty to me. Lieutenant, where should we go now?"

"Let's finish our little exploration of this upper level," she said. "Then we can work our way down. Maybe there is another stairwell at the end of this hall leading back to the dungeon or, shall we say . . . Benny's asylum? Lead the way, Benny. Just keep your mind open. And when I say open, I mean shut."

Benny led the trio down the hallway and found the door leading into Aldred's quarters slightly open. He stuck the lantern through the doorway, but the only shadow cast was from the bed. On the last day of his life, Aldred had not made up his bedding. He had had other things on his mind. What remained of the linen was as tethered and deteriorated as the clothing hanging from the skeletons below. Denning discovered the key to the stairwell door hanging at its appointed position. Not knowing its partnered lock, there was no need to retrieve it, but Denning decided to stow it away in his front right pocket, just in case.

"Might as well," seconded Benny.

Finding no clues to the whereabouts of Ms. Perkins, Baker led them out of the room and proceeded down the hall where they found three other rooms. All of them were vacant with the exception of bare wooden furniture. *Guest rooms,* they surmised. Their investigation of the remainder of the corridor led them to a blank wall. It was the hallway's end and had no exit signs or doors.

"There's no other stairwell around here, so our Lord Lawrence could not have brought Ms. Trudy up to this floor," deduced Baker.

"So, if there is another stairwell, it must lead from a room somewhere below, maybe on the main floor," added Denning.

"Let's make our way down that staircase," Baker continued.

"There must be some kind of dining room or main room where people would gather."

Benny turned back and led them, side by side, with Denning doing curls with the iron-spiked ball in his right hand. *It feels good,* he thought, *love to bash a bad guy with it, like the creep who locked up my boss.*

They reached the top of the staircase, and Benny stopped, holding the lantern ahead of him once again, double-checking to make sure Trudy was not leading them down the steps. "Ready or not, here we come," he whispered.

F

CHAPTER ELEVEN

TRUDY

ack in my apartment after I finally woke up, the first thing I headed for was the reefer to get a glass or three of wine. My nerves were still rattled from all the commotion with Helen at the office.

I figured I needed all of it to sink in for a while, and then maybe I could make some sense out of, well . . . nonsense. I got up off the couch and was walking around the apartment when I first heard Benny's voice coming from like nowhere. I thought I might just crap in my pants right then and there. I mean . . . why not? About then is when I figured out what must have been running through Helen's mind when she got attacked. And then, when I saw the thing in the mirror, I said to myself, "Well, Trudy, might as well bend over, shove your head between your legs, and kiss the ol' butt goodbye."

I mean, this guy or this thing was not about to take me out for a night on the town, and from his demeanor, I was really sure he was not out looking for some head. I started shaking really bad, but I was frozen at the same time. I prayed I wasn't going to get the same treatment as Helen. I imagine I would dish out a lot of head to get out of being tortured.

My eyes being plastered to the mirror, I saw something looking like eyeballs, but they were the strangest-looking eyeballs I ever saw. And they certainly were not the color of any eyes I have ever seen. After a few seconds, I started to calm down and I don't even remember his hands reaching out from the inside of the F'ing mirror. But I can remember them touching me. Wow! Now I was totally relaxed . . . I mean like really relaxed. So relaxed, I was ready to tear my black sweater, socks and slacks off. I thought at the time, Maybe this guy *is* looking for some head.

Just about then, I recall the hood thing covering his head kind of fell back a bit, and I could see his face. And I will swear forevermore on a stack of fruitcakes it was Benny. I mean, my Benny, except for the eyes. They were still that weird shade of red, but they were awfully pretty. And wow, they did ever have me locked in. And I'll add another except—for his hair. Benny's hair was the same color, but it was long, I mean, like down to his shoulders. As Benny would put it, just like the old days. Like Benny had any old days. He's not old yet, so how could he have any old days? But he was looking as beautiful as ever.

And then as he was pulling me in closer to him, I saw this thing he was wearing around his neck. It struck me as strange because Benny doesn't wear any kind of jewelry, not even his wedding ring. Although given the current state of affairs, I'm sure he wouldn't have been wearing it then anyway. But, when my eyes caught the pendant or whatever, I started to get a little bit sleepy. I was still horny as hell, but I was getting a little woozy.

It was as beautiful as his eyes, but the color was different. I mean, it was kind of golden brown, maybe with a dash of yellow mixed in, kind of like harvest colors. It's what you see when you're driving through a forest or the county park when everything is in full autumn bloom. But these colors were flowing up and down and around, like the jewel or the stone was filled with some kind of lava or liquid.

So here I was, hot enough to lose my virginity for the fifth time on the same night as I feel myself being carried into the mirror. I mean, like through the mirror, and what do I go and do? The obvious . . . I go and pass out. I imagine the way I was feeling when I lost consciousness. I could have expected to wake up and find myself naked and spread out on a fluffy mattress all dressed up with silk linen tossed all over creation, pillows halfway across the room, and sweat pouring out of my pores.

Well, none of those things happened. What I do remember is waking up and feeling the hands still wrapped around my waist. Whoever had me in their clutch was behind me, and I knew it couldn't be Benny. Benny's fingers weren't twelve inches long.

As my eyesight began to clear, the hazy star things flying past me started to slow, and I could see we were approaching what looked like another mirror. But I didn't see my reflection. I should say our reflection, whoever was with me. I could see something on the other side. Maybe it wasn't a mirror after all; it might have been a window. It was kind of dirty and kind of wavy, like the ones you see in the funhouse at the carnival. But just like the galaxy mirror of mine, I just passed right on through without busting it all to pieces. Like Benny would say, "That's F'ing insane."

As we passed through this window or portal or whatever it was, I started to get a little bit nervous again, but I had a teeny bit of a buzz going from the wine, so I wasn't really scared a whole lot. While those hands around my waist seemed to be really long and bony, they just held me nice and snug. It didn't seem like those hands wanted to squeeze the stuffing out of me or dig the claws probably attached to them into my guts. I thought maybe something else long and bony was about to start coming at me.

And I felt like maybe I was in outer space or in one of those antigravity chambers. I was just floating around with those hands, just as safe as a bug taking a dump on a scoop of mashed potatoes. About that time is when I remember the movie started. But this was no ordinary flick. It was like I was smack-dab in the middle of it, and when those sweet hands turned me a little way, the whole movie screen was turning, and I could see what was over to the left of me. But nobody could see me. And then all of a sudden, right then and there out of the blue, or whatever color it was, there was me.

I know a lot of girls would love to be a movie actress or queen, and I had my princess daydreams when I was a little girl, but I never imagined me being in a movie. And in this movie, the people were not on film, they were real and alive. I thought I could just reach out and touch them, even feel their hot breath. I was tempted to try to touch them, but I found I couldn't really feel anything, not even my own hands. All I remember is I could hear and see everything playing out in front of me. And I was one of the main characters. *How cool is that!*

This was unreal. There I was in this castle, and I was with this strange man. He was kind of handsome, and he dressed like he was one of those old-time movie actors in one of the swashbuckler thrillers or something. His hair was long, about the same length Benny had when I saw him in the mirror. He had presented himself to my other me in this movie as Lord Lawrence. I guess this guy was kind of attractive, and it sure looked as though he was filthy rich, but I didn't seem to be horny or enamored of him like I was with Benny a while earlier. Then I thought, *Wow, Benny would look really neat dressed up like this guy, with the long hair and all.* In fact, I was trying to imagine it, and all of a sudden, the screen became really blurry. I cleared my mind of the thought, and everything started up all over again. I mean, not from the beginning, but like a little later when I was sharing a glass of wine with this mannerly gentleman. You know, the semi-handsome Hollywood guy.

I must admit I thought I looked really awesome dressed up in this wonderful blue gown and the pretty bonnet sporting what looked like white flowers. I got the feeling this guy thought I was looking really hot. And after the conversation went on for a spell, I got another feeling my character wasn't really me because I don't really flirt around like this woman did. I mean, maybe with Benny, but that's okay because it's just a little game we play between the two of us, more or less to get ourselves through the grind of the day at work. Claims, claims, claims. Phone calls, phone calls, phone calls. Letters, letters, letters. Reports, reports, reports. Sondra, Sondra, Sondra. Those things made me think of Benny again. And then the damn movie blurred out again. So I just waited. As Benny would say, "What the F?"

And then I figured, *Oh well, it's just a movie, right?* When it started up again, I was being escorted to my room or to my bedchamber as the host was telling me. How romantic did that sound? I remembered climbing into bed really tired, and the next thing I knew, I was out by this beautiful lake sitting under a tree. There were names carved into the trunk. There was Lawrence, and underneath it was the name Aldred. I never heard of that name before. This guy Lawrence was playing around with the pendant thing I thought somewhere along the line he called an amulet. And there I was again, making moves. I was thinking at the back of my mind, I mean, her mind, she had something else going on and was maybe playing a little game with the guy. This girl was not really acting like I usually did. But then again, I figured this was some kind of movie thing, so I just played along and watched my character.

And then I was really stunned. When this man, Lord Lawrence, had become distracted for a second or two, my character looked back at me. I never, in all my life, realized I could put a snarl on my face like my character did right then and there. I mean, she was staring at me blank in my eyes and had the meanest, nastiest, dirtiest snarl on her face. I thought she was going to bite my face clean off. I was horrified. She was moving her eyes up and down, apparently checking me out. Her staring me down felt really weird.

Imagine that. I was the one who was supposed to be watching the movie. I couldn't figure out what the hell was going on. As I was looking at her looking at me, I saw everything around her had come to an abrupt stop. It was like somebody put the movie into a freeze frame or something. With those old movies on the projectors, if somebody did that, the film would just go into flames and melt right there on the big screen. I could remember Benny telling me why the film just burns up because of the heat from the projector lamp. So why didn't she?

Well, anyway, Lawrence was perfectly still, having turned to look out at something across the lake. There was someone on the other side who appeared to be dressed in a long brown hooded robe. The guy's arms were crossed, and he was looking back at the two of them, or should I say him and me? But remember, the movie projector had slammed its brakes on a single frame; even the leaves on the trees stopped shaking from the gentle breeze.

This character of mine I was playing was looking more and more malicious by the second. She was apparently really pissed off at something. What did I do? I was just watching the damn movie or whatever was playing out in front of me. Well, there and behind me too, I should add.

I decided to turn and look back, thinking maybe there was somebody behind me in the movie getting the evil stare down. Nobody was there, so when I turned back, the look on her face got even more intense. Her eyes started to burn into my own. I thought she was about to get up and start strangling me or something. Why would I want to go and strangle myself for crêpes Suzette sakes? Her glare started to make me dizzy.

All I could think of at the time was Benny. Where was Benny? And then everything went blank, like the film in the projector just broke. I couldn't even think anymore. Now, here I was, floating around in a starless space of white light, wishing the projector would start up again. *Where am I? Where is Benny? Benny?*

F

Catelin

Who was the woman in my body? Where did she come from? Where did she get the strange clothes she was wearing? Could those be for riding? She did not seem dressed or inclined to set herself upon a horse. Why did she impose her will on my scheme? I had a claim on Lord Lawrence, not her. Who invited her out to the lake? I was the one who would have his purse. *It is I, Lady Catelin. My work is not done. My revenge, not complete.*

Where was she when I was a child, orphaned and taken in by a soul who wanted nothing more than my dignity, my youth, my innocence? It was I who suffered, not her. No one tied her down to those bedposts in the old man's repulsive den of sin. I was but a child of fourteen when that sick and deranged old man took me . . . again and again and again, night after night, until I became sick with child.

I took my revenge. One fateful night, I bid him to free me from the binds on my wrists and ankles so I might please him more. Oh, he did find joy in my beseeching. I did bind him to the posts, and I climbed atop the old, wrinkled, worn-out man. And then I took him . . . again and again, through the night, until his heart beseeched I stop. And I laughed and laughed . . . until screaming beneath his feathered pillow, he could breathe no more.

Where was she when I was alone and abandoned? I was saved by Rodney, who became the father I had never known. He had saved me and saved the orchards when I had become heir to the holdings of the dead, old wicked man. But he could not save me from the curse. I could not stop. I could not stop taking men, having them. And I could not stop taking them down . . . along with their purses. I spared Rodney the truth. I had been cursed. Revenge was my curse. I must have it. I had it. But I had never attained its pinnacle, so I kept looking for the next man to persecute.

I could not let her interfere. But who was this she spoke of? Who was this Benny? What a strange name. Could it be a pet? A dog? Certainly not a man.

I must occupy her mind. She had unsettled mine. *Come closer, wench. You'll not have Lawrence. You'll not have his pockets. They are no more. What is left of him to claim is mine. See my eyes, woman? Come, see my eyes. These are the eyes of Catelin. Step into these eyes. Come see what a whore can do.*

Show me this . . . this Benny. In exchange . . . I will show you Catelin.

F

As their brief life together in the past played out in the reincarnation of Catelin, Lawrence felt he was beginning to reach her. The look of apprehension and fear had abandoned her face. The woman calling herself Trudy was discovering her true identity. He could see this by the smile appearing on her face. *My sweet, sweet Catelin.* What disturbed him was the recurring thought of the impostor hiding behind his shield name Benny. It would take time, but Lord Lawrence had all the time in the world. He would purge Aldred from all her memories and then purge the impostor.

He left Catelin in his bedchamber, setting her down on the bed and using a bundle of rags as a pillow for her beautiful head. Something must be done about her clothing. It could wait. But for now, there was business needing tending. He went back to the mirror in the stairwell and stepped through. He would once again approach this portal of Trudy and seek out an associate. This other woman who he had seen in her thoughts was also wearing strange cloth but apparently cloth of the times. For now, until Catelin returned in her full form, it was time for play.

After retrieving the other woman, Lawrence had left her unconscious on his operating table and returned to Catelin, who remained in his trance. But her eyes were wide open, and her smile was broad across her face.

"My lord," she spoke after he lifted her off the bed. He entered her mind and saw the vision of him who she had acknowledged wearing the face of the impostor. Once again, he brought her thoughts to rest and purged the image. He lifted her and floated down the stairwell together to join the new specimen.

Lawrence had found the acquaintance to be insolent, rude. She had no respect for her superiors. She needed be taught a lesson. He would return to this wench and treat Catelin to a display of his cleverness. He would not dispose of this Baker woman quickly, as he had planned. He would toy with her. It might even take a bit more torture than the last woman to bring her to the brink. The screaming, hair-pulling woman brought him much joy but displeased him when she failed to relinquish her soul. This one he could claim. He had earlier thought of entering her realm to make quick work of her but recalled the last venture had left him winded. He tired rapidly when time moved around him. So he merely reached through and pulled her back to his asylum, but it was not before revising his message for the impostor on the inner face of the mirror. *Come, Benny, the impostor. Join me,* he thought.

Lawrence set Catelin on her feet beside him at one end of the slab where the woman lay. He pulled the unconscious woman out of her trance, and using the long fingers of his left hand, he levitated her body into the air and then set her at the opposite end of the slab. After tossing her around a bit and putting a little scare into her mind, Lawrence left her locked in the spiral cage, hoping she would slowly squirm and twist, progressively tightening the jaws of death surrounding her. Once he heard her screams, he could return to free her and dally with her in another one of his toys, perhaps after severing a few limbs. It would please him when she finally succumbed to his tease with quite an oral display of pain. Perhaps he would just break all those pretty little bones and see how they fit in her pretty little shoes.

Throughout this demonstration, Catelin continued to witness the story of Lawrence and Catelin play out in a 360-degree display of animated action. This was the love story Lawrence was planting in her mind, and it would end as they were about to wed and consummate their eternal life of glee by engaging in a fun-filled killing spree, beginning with the impostor. But this seed in Catelin's mind had company. It had been put there by the strange woman who had been occupying Catelin's body. Whenever the woman had placed an image of this Benny person in her life story, Lawrence had it obliterated.

But unknown to Lawrence, Catelin was assuming her own control, and she could enter this Trudy's thoughts in private. Sweet Lawrence would have no objection. We must all have our own little . . . privacy.

'Tis my mind and my body, thought Catelin. *The woman is impersonating me, not Lawrence. I shall remove from this woman what is mine and leave the shell for Lawrence to dawdle as he pleases. What is mine is mine. Now . . . where is this Benny?*

After Lawrence locked the woman in his cage, she turned slightly and addressed Catelin as Ms. Perkins. Catelin politely corrected the woman; she needed no lesson in manners, as did the caged wench. Catelin then turned and directed her twisted smile at Lawrence, bidding they return to their chamber and make preparations for their ceremony. And then she began to think and to search. *Benny? Come out, come out . . . wherever you are.*

F

"Benny . . . are we okay down there?" asked Baker quietly.

Benny had begun their slow procession down the staircase. He held the lantern out in front of him, silently praying it had a bottomless oil reservoir, and he had a brand-new wick and an extra pack of matches in his pocket. Before he could answer the lieutenant, he felt something move in his front right pocket, and it was not the small mirror he had deposited before his walk on the wild side. He was beginning to understand something about his wishes, his fantasies.

"I can't remember being this nervous the last time I had to testify in a deposition. And those can be nerve-racking," said Benny.

"At least you know you'll get out of those alive, Benny," whispered Denning. He was still doing curls with the spiked ball, ready to wield it at the drop of a pin or a hammer or an anvil.

Then Baker and Denning stepped down to Benny's level, and Baker patted Benny on his left shoulder. "Let's just keep our senses alert, guys," she whispered. "And play along. Trudy might not recognize any of us."

Benny turned to her. "But this guy in the cloak, this phantom or whatever he is, he's going to know you and me, that much I know is certain. I'm not so sure about Paul. And I'm fairly sure he probably doesn't know we made it through to this place, 'my asylum,' as he put it. But like you said, he sure did extend an invitation."

Slowly, step by step, they descended the staircase, a journey seemingly taking Benny forever. Once they reached the landing halfway down, Benny took several deep breaths in an attempt to slow his pulse. It wasn't working.

"Don't worry," supported Paul, "it's a good thing to be a little nervous. Keeps you on your toes."

"I would think toenails," replied Benny. "Last time I was facing the enemy, they had blood running through their veins. I've never heard about a ghost having blood."

"Look down there," interrupted Baker, "to the right. It's a big doorway. And straight ahead, those doors must lead outside."

Benny's wish for a bright lantern had come true. The light was a bit dim, but it reached across the small room they were approaching. The solar leading to the exit was straight ahead, and the great hall was toward their right. Baker led them, heading down the steps for the big room, scanning the area back and forth as she did. Once they entered this room, his lantern became a bit brighter. It cast shadows around the room and, on the dust, covering everything.

The room was exactly the way it had been the night Lord Lawrence and his temper extinguished the lives of Catelin and Aldred. The huge table remained in place, and the chairs were set around its perimeter. There were place settings remaining on the table, in addition to those sent flying to the floor alongside Catelin. Vermin had long ago feasted on the dinner spilled across the floor and left their tiny balls of feces behind.

"Look, there are some candles left on the table," said Denning. "It would be nice to light them, brighten up the place a bit."

"Well, Paul," began Benny, "I just happen to have a pack of matches." Benny handed them over, and Paul Denning set about lighting candles. There were six of them remaining on the table; four more broken candles and fancy holders were spread out around the floor. Baker grabbed one Paul had lit and set about examining the room.

"Benny," she said a minute later, "over here. Bring the lantern. I'm fairly sure we have some bloodstains on the floor."

Denning finished lighting the candles and joined them, holding one with the hand from which suspended the spiked ball. "That's a really good stream there," he pointed out. "Are you thinking what I'm thinking, Lieutenant, I mean, Baker?"

"If you mean our skeletons in the closet?" she replied. "I sure do.

You didn't, by the way, see any blood on those chairs our lovebirds were sitting in, did you, Paul?"

"No, ma'am," he answered. "Not that I noticed. They had some remnants of clothing left on them, but the rags were too deteriorated to even give us an idea of their original color. I did not see anything on the chairs either, other than the two birds holding hands."

"So you think this is where they were killed?" asked Benny. "And then the bodies were moved down below?"

"Maybe to hide the evidence," Baker began. "But maybe not. He didn't seem to bother cleaning up the mess. It could be he spends a lot of time down there and maybe wanted them close by."

"Strange company, I mean, it's not like they would be running away or anything, Lieutenant," added Denning back to protocol. "But the pile of bones tells me you're right about his favorite habitat. I guess his asylum. And that coffin down there seems to suggest to me this guy could be some kind of Dracula character. I should have brought a crucifix and some garlic along with me. What next?"

"We keep looking," she said. "I have a blessed cross I'm wearing around my neck, but this is not Hollywood, and we're not in a movie. Ms. Perkins has to be around here somewhere. I don't think this phantom was planning to take her back to her apartment. It sounded like he was planning for some kind of ceremony. And I doubt it was a funeral."

"But why would he pick on Trudy?" asked Benny. "There are millions of women in the world and millions of mirrors too. That seems to be his modus operandi. He could have picked anybody, anywhere."

"As far as we know, Benny, you were the first one this thing, this phantom killer, came to visit. Maybe it's a connection between the two of you, something about the two of you. And he has Trudy thinking she is this woman, Catelin, one of our lovebirds down in the asylum."

"Maybe this guy actually thinks Trudy is this Catelin," suggested Paul. "Maybe Ms. Perkins looks like she did when she was alive. Like a double or something."

"You could be on to something, Paul," she agreed. "And maybe that's where Benny comes into the picture."

You mean Alfred?" Benny asked.

"It's Aldred, Benny," reminded Denning again.

"Benny," started Baker, "I'd like you to try something for me, if you don't mind. How about it?"

"Whatever you say, Lieutenant. You're the boss," he replied.

"I'm starting to think you're the boss around this place, Benny," countered Baker. "We could use another lantern. These candles don't seem to put out much light. How about going over to that table and getting us another lantern?"

"There are a few hanging on the walls, but I didn't see any lanterns on that table," Benny replied. He turned to look back and raised his lantern, but its broad reach revealed only the four remaining candles, all aglow.

"You didn't see any lanterns down in the torture chamber either," said Denning. "I think you just remembered seeing the one we saw in the little room we woke up in when we got here."

"Just imagine you walking over there and picking up another lantern, Benny," suggested Baker. "Think about it. Try to picture yourself doing it."

F

Benny

Well, I always thought Benjamin F Johnson could fantasize with the best of them, but I never thought I could pull off a Houdini stunt one. Me. Benny. Hell. Like Baker said about the phantom guy, Houdini himself could not have done something even comparable, not unless there was some kind of trick involved, like mirrors or somebody behind the curtain pulling off the old switcheroo.

I actually did close my eyes, and I did think about seeing me in my mind, just walking over to that old table and seeing a bright and shiny lantern loaded with oil and all fired up. It didn't scare me or anything, but when I opened my eyes and saw the damn thing burning brighter than a Fourth of July firecracker, I almost had to crap in my F'ing pants.

I turned back around to the lieutenant and the sergeant with this face of amazement plastered all over my blushing head. I didn't even get applause from them, let alone a standing ovation. Well, they were already standing, But the thought was beside the point. I had just pulled off an authentic F'ing miracle. They just stood there, shaking their heads again.

Baker reminded me about needing to keep my head on straight and not to let the gas inflate the brain too much, as it just might go into overload and maybe explode. I needed to keep the situation in perspective because the phantom thing currently held the upper hand. He was the one pulling people back and forth from one dimension to whatever dimension we were currently held captive. And captives were exactly what we were at that point. But that did not deter me from thinking I was ready to kick some good old ass, even though I had never really been an ass kicker my whole life.

And I didn't consider the things I had to do back during my time in the war as part of my life. Back then, I was not me; I belonged to somebody else. I didn't make decisions; I was told what to do and when to do it. And when you were doing those nasty things, you did not really have a lot of time to think about it. Those who did stop to think were usually the ones lying on the ground, either blown apart or with a hole in them from one side clean out the other. When I left the war behind me, I left my guns behind and that part of my life.

I was not an ass kicker, but I was by no means a pussy either. I guessed I was lucky because I was able to put it out of my mind; a lot of other people were not so fortunate. I didn't even know why the hell I was even talking about it. Maybe it was part of the reason I fantasized so much; it helped keep the real stuff out of my mind. If I kept thinking about those years, I would probably lose my mind. When I go to sleep at night, I plan on dreaming about some good stuff, like maybe half-naked chorus girls hurdling beer kegs with long-stemmed red roses clutched between their teeth.

With my head back intact on my shoulders, I asked Baker what she thought we should do now we were able to shed a little more light on the subject. We had a fairly good idea Trudy and I were some kind of target. Maybe this phantom character's plans had been rudely interrupted way back when, so he knocked them off. He must have had his own plans for this Catelin character, but this other guy Alfred or Aldred must have squeezed him out of his own fantasy. So what better solution could there be than to get rid of them both and let them see how they would feel spending eternity together, dead, dead, dead.

Baker probably hit it on the head. Somehow this phantom guy was thinking Trudy and I must be the two people who spoiled his plans, so now he was going to set matters straight. He would get Trudy as his

Catelin and good old Benny, the Aldred, would get another knife in his gut or wherever it had been deposited in the first place.

We had to find Trudy, who was apparently thinking she was Catelin, and convince Catelin she was really Trudy, all hopefully without encountering our host of honor, good old Lord F'ing Lawrence. It sounded easy at the time. I just needed to figure out how my daydream fantasies could help us out of this mess and get us back to Trudy's or to the office or, gosh forbid, to Murphy's Restaurant. If we could find another mirror, I was hoping it would take us back somewhere in Lakeview, rather than the Sahara Desert into another dungeon in Timbuktu. But I didn't think too hard about that part. One dungeon was enough.

So off we went on our way to do a little more exploring in Lawrence's castle. We headed toward the opposite side of the big main hall we entered toward another pair of double doors and what lay beyond. My heart was not racing anymore, but its beat wasn't slow enough for sleep. Baker had her Glock stuck under the belt of her slacks at her left side next to a couple of knives, and the three of us walked side by side. Baker was holding the bright and shiny new lantern, and Denning was curling his spiked ball. I wasn't sure if we were in a Veterans Day parade or marching toward our execution.

F

Once phantom Lawrence had escorted Catelin back to his bedchamber, she continued to watch the display of their budding mutual love for each other. Although irritated with the persistent interruptions, the hazing of Benny in particular, once they had returned to his quarters, the intrusions had essentially subsided. Beside Lawrence's intervention, Catelin had discovered she could explore the censures by invading the mind of her impostor, this Trudy woman, while providing Lawrence with the satisfaction he had finally purged Catelin of Aldred's existence. This pleased him, so he left her—in search of a proper wedding gown—on her pillow of rags and floated to the bedchamber Catelin had occupied centuries earlier. She had left two chests filled with clothing, but when Lawrence opened them, he found mildew and mold had wasted them away to scraps and dust.

Not disappointed, Lawrence decided Catelin could dress in another hooded cloak. They would be perfectly harmonious. He returned to his bedchamber. After their wedding ceremony and reception party, in which these mortals would be put to death, the two of them could explore and acquire whatever suitable clothing she desired.

Being satisfied Catelin had been well educated in the history of their romance, Lawrence woke her and set her feet on the floor. "My child," he spoke, "are you willing . . . are you ready . . . for our vows?"

"My Lord Lawrence," she replied. "I have waited, and I am more than willing, more than ready . . . for your vow . . . and much, much more." She smiled, but she sheepishly looked down at the floor.

"Come," he said, "we are to gather a witness for this glorious occasion." He held out the long bony fingers of his left hand.

Catelin accepted the offer with her right hand. "A witness," she agreed. Together, they floated and bounced their way down the stairwell.

If Lawrence was capable of drooling, he was doing all the dribbling at that moment.

At the bottom landing of the stairwell, Lawrence collected another hooded cloak. This one was white. Lawrence held it open for her, as she slipped her arms into the sleeves. The left side wrapped around and over her breast to her left side. Brown leather loops fastened over leather buttons from her neck to below her thighs. There were five buttons in all. Catelin pulled the hood over her head, concealing the devilish smirk on her face.

"A witness," she repeated.

Lawrence had anticipated Catelin would be experiencing lingering effects of the trance he had subjected her to earlier, but Catelin was responding very well. It was wonderful. Teeming with excitement, he led her into the asylum to fetch the wench, exchange vows, and then slash the insolent acquaintance woman to bits and pieces, bunches of chunks.

But when they reached the hanging cage, they found it empty. Lawrence was appalled. No one had ever escaped his wrath. No one ever had escaped from his dungeon, his asylum. *Who is this woman?* he thought.

"I know this woman," replied Catelin. She answered his thought. "She is called Susan. Susan Baker."

You can read my thoughts, thought Lawrence.

Silently, in thought, Catelin replied, *Of course, Lord Lawrence. You made me in the spirit of your vision.*

From this point, the two held most of their communication in thoughts. Catelin had learned much from Lord Lawrence. Much more than Lawrence had anticipated. And Catelin had learned much more about Lord Lawrence than he had anticipated. Catelin had also learned quite a bit from the other woman Trudy. She was quite helpful in restoring other memories—memories lost in centuries of dust. Catelin had found Benny and placed him deep inside her mind, a place reserved for her most private of thoughts, a place where even Rodney had dared not to go.

We must find her, communicated Lawrence silently. *No one can escape my asylum. I am the dark of night. I am the preyer of the prey. I will have her soul. I claim it to be mine.*

"You deserve to have many more, my lord. Let us find her. No one escapes you, my lord."

"You have read my mind. Then you know of the great hall. Return, and go there. I shall seek her from the other stairwell and meet you there. It is fitting we would find her there."

Our minds are one, she thought to him. *Except for my private spot,* she thought to herself. Then to Lord Lawrence, *We shall meet in the great hall.*

Catelin did not float to the stairwell. But she did scurry, hesitantly looking back as she reached the double doorway to the landing. Lawrence paid her no mind. He had already vacated the asylum and was floating up the opposite stairwell. Lawrence was satisfied Catelin was well under his control; her mind was washed clean of any contamination. There would be a slight delay in the ceremony, in their celebration. She would pay no mind to it.

F

With Baker leading them in their midst, Benny and Paul followed closely through the tall double doorway and down the corridor on their procession in search of Ms. Trudy Perkins. They found the door to the first chamber they entered had been left open. Inside, they discovered a bed; its linen was also decrepit from age. And they found two chests had also been left open but exhibited a dank odor, as if they had been opened recently. There was no evidence of Trudy having been in this room, and her captor had apparently left nothing else behind, including bodies or bones or stairwell passages.

They left the room and slowly marched down to the far end of the corridor where they discovered another chamber on their right. This one had double doors of normal size, unlike the huge, heavy doors they had passed through entering the corridor. These doors were not closed, and they were not locked. But one of them had broken free from its hinges. A depression in the corridor wall opposite the doors indicated this door had collided with it. This door lay on the floor in the midst of the doorway.

With his right hand, Denning grasped the door to his right. It was dangling precariously from a single hinge and appeared as though it would break loose with the slightest bit of force. He pulled at the door and it did bust loose, crashing down in front of the trio. Denning jumped backward, colliding with Benny. The loud bang it created as it landed square on the floor resounded through the corridor and into the great hall.

"Oops," declared Benny. They all stood silent for a moment investigating their surroundings, hoping they had not woken a sleeping giant.

Then Baker poked her lantern through the doorway. Benny pushed the fallen door out of their way with his right foot while he extended his lantern beside Baker's. With both lanterns shining into the space, the room lit up. All three noticed what appeared to be another short hallway beyond a wall jutting out from the side wall a few paces directly beyond the bed. This led to a second doorway hidden at the far left corner of the room, the second stairwell they were intent on finding. Benny doubted people in medieval castles made use of walk-in closets. The edge of the open door was visible to them as it peeked out of the stubby hallway.

"It must be the other stairwell," Denning said, saying what Baker was thinking. "If they came up here, they must have gone back down, or we would have run into them."

"Nobody is hiding under the bed," said Benny. He was now stooping low to the floor and craning his neck sideways.

"Great observation, Johnson," remarked Baker. Sarcastically, it was back to Johnson. She was approaching her get-ready-to-rock-and-roll mode. Strictly business. "We're getting close. Stay alert."

Then they heard some shuffling through the far doorway, but they heard no boots or shoes pounding the stairs. Someone, something, ghost or not, was approaching. Baker pulled the Glock, set the lantern down on the floor, and did a semi-squat, raising both arms erect and bracing her right arm with her left, ready to fire at will.

Then Trudy rushed through the doorway into the light. The hood on her head had fallen back, and her long hair was draped and waving behind her. It settled back down as she skidded on her black woolen socks to a not-so-screeching halt.

"Holy crap!" shouted Baker. "I almost shot you."

Trudy responded in surprise. "Benny . . . that's you, right? Benny?"

She said it as if she was not sure of herself. Then she hesitated, caught a breath, and added, "Ms. Baker, Lieutenant Baker? Is that you?"

"It's us, all right," said Benny. "And this is Sergeant Denning. We've come to get you out of this place."

"Yes, Trudy," said Baker. "We need to get to one of those mirrors. We all came in down in that damn torture chamber he calls an asylum. Do you remember how he brought you here? Where did he bring you through?"

"I," she hesitated again, "I really don't know. I don't remember. It's all so hazy." Trudy was lying, or after being subjected to hours of the feel-good motion picture, she really was a bit hazy, although she wasn't so hazy a couple minutes ago.

"Maybe we should head down to the asylum through this stairwell, Lieutenant," suggested Denning.

"I don't think you should, Sergeant," said Trudy astutely. "He is down there right now. Lord Lawrence is down in the dungeon place. Maybe you should go the other way." Now Trudy really was lying, or she really was really, really hazy.

"We need to try to avoid this guy at all cost," confirmed Baker. "Okay, let's go back to the way we came in, down to the main hall and then back up the staircase. We're halfway home, boys and girls." She accepted Trudy's word about the phantom thing being otherwise occupied at the moment. This much of it was in fact true.

"Come on, Trudy," urged Benny. "You look really good in white. I never saw you wear clothes with that color before. Although I'm sure you'd look good with nothing at all."

"Benny!" said Baker. "Now is not the time to fantasize. You want her running around here naked?"

"What?" said Trudy, confused. She walked across the room to meet them, and Paul stepped toward her, offering her his left hand. He had wedged the handle and part of the blade of the ten-inch cleaver-type butcher knife under his belt.

Baker led the way out of the room, followed by Denning and Trudy, with Benny at the tailgate. Trudy could not have known they were on a collision course with Lord Lawrence, if indeed she really was Trudy at this particular moment. Lawrence, having reached the great hall, was already patiently waiting for the reappearance of Catelin and Baker, whom he surmised Catelin had fished out of the pond.

F

When the party of four arrived at the huge double doors to the great hall, Lawrence was there at the center of the hall, ready and waiting. He was standing, floating on the spot where Baker and Denning had examined the bloodstained floor.

"My," he greeted them. He was pleasantly surprised at the gathering. "Look what we have here. None other than Ms. Susan Baker and Mr. Benjamin F Johnson." He moved forward a few floats. "And what is this, pray tell? Why, it is an unannounced guest. And one quite uninvited I might add. But if it would please Lady Catelin, we might find room for him at our table, I should think."

The four of them were assembled just inside the doorway. The lanterns had filled the room with light as they entered, and all four came immediately to attention, pondering their next move. Baker made a move to turn and run back through the hallway, but the large doors slammed shut before she could take a step. The booming collision of the doors in the jamb resounded throughout the room around them. The three brave warriors froze in their footsteps.

"Please let me share with you my . . . accommodations." The phantom floated in a bit closer. "My, my, now where should we begin?" The three listened in utter awe to Benny's voice.

The cloak hid his eyes, if he possessed any in the darkness shrouded by the hood. His right arm lifted, and he extended the foot-long fingers of its hand, which scanned them up and down, one by one.

"Catelin," he said, "please join me. Join in the fun and merriment while our guests become acquainted to our surroundings and enjoy some of our old-fashioned hospitality."

Trudy began to slowly step forward, but Denning held her back, grabbing her upper right arm. "Stay put, Ms. Perkins," he advised. He was ready to take a swing if the phantom thing floating there moved in any closer. He was slowly loosening the chain wrapped around his wrist, allowing the heavy ball to descend down the side of his right leg.

"My goodness," replied Lawrence. He was now speaking in a voice foreign to them, even to Trudy, relinquishing the vocal cords on loan from Benny Johnson. "Not yet invited, yet Mr. Denning shows his host ill manners." Lawrence was quite familiar with the voice of the not-so-holy holy man.

"How did you know my name?" Denning replied. "And who the hell are you? This is no banquet dinner, and you are no damn diplomat."

"My sergeant," the not-a-monk-of-his-kind monk continued, "you are a feisty one. Is that how they put it in your world? Or should I address you as copper? Or how about pig? That's what you were called when you were the little fat boy on the playground. Pig? Little piggy? Well, you grew up all right, and now here you are . . . a very big . . . pig. How do you put it in your world? Am I in the ballpark, Sergeant Piggy?"

"You son of a—" began Paul Denning. He was clearly ticked off. How could this son of a mother of a dog know about his childhood? Long ago, he had come to the realization he had become a cop because of his mistreatment as a kid. Tired of the beatings and humiliation by his peers, he had worked his ass nearly to the bone, becoming a weightlifting fanatic by the time he got to the summer break after his third year in high school. The day came when he kicked the stuffing out of the class bully who had been beating him for years. He walked tall in his senior year when he came back from vacation sporting a body that had exchanged twenty-five pounds of fat with solid muscle. And he never stopped taking care of his body. He was about ready to put it in action.

"Careful," warned Baker. "Don't lose your temper, Paul."

"Come now, Piggy Paul," answered Lawrence. "Demonstrate how well you can swing the little ball around your head. How is it said in your world, Piggy? Give it a shot?"

Denning released Trudy, urging her to step back by extending his left arm across her access to the cloaked man. He then took a step forward, dropping the ball free from his wrist. He pulled the butcher knife from under his belt with his left hand, and with his right hand, he gripped the chain and began to swing the spiked weapon back and forth, behind and in front of him, as though it were a pendulum. Then he started to whirl the ball in a great circle, extending his right arm forward then up and over his head, over and over again.

"Come now, Piggy. GIVE IT A SHOT!" screamed the phantom. "COME NOW, PIGGY!"

Suddenly, Paul's arm began to swing uncontrollably, increasing in velocity, creating so much wind Trudy's hair was blowing in the breeze behind her shoulders on top of the cloak's hood. A look of dismay blanketed his face as he dropped the butcher knife at his left side.

Baker yelled at Denning to stop, but the grimace on his face told her he was unable to do so; he was not in control anymore. The phantom Lawrence stood there, exposing his long right forefinger. His wrist bent at a right angle. It was twirling and twirling and twirling in synchronization with the orbit of the spiked ball.

Then he held the huge digit in place momentarily. The ball froze in the air directly over the cop's head, and the chain was fully extended and became as rigid as an iron bar. Then Lawrence freed the chain from the man's hand.

"Pigs do not stand on two feet. DOWN ON YOUR HANDS AND KNEES!" the phantom screamed.

Now the ball and chain began swirling in the air without Denning's arm to guide it, but it started rotating in the opposite direction. So the ball was swinging from behind Paul up and over his shoulders and out in front of him at his right, with his arm held fast against his body and upper thigh. It whirled faster and faster and faster. Paul was then forced down on all threes because his right arm remained pasted at his side. He could do nothing to resist what was happening; he could not move his head, his legs, or his arms. He was stuck, cemented in a three-armed wrestler's kneeling position, seemingly waiting for his opponent to grasp his left elbow and wrap his other arm around Paul's back and waist.

Then suddenly, the phantom twisted his finger ever so slightly toward Denning, toward his chin, but continued twirling. The spiked ball followed his command, altered its course as it swooped from behind, around, and over Denning's shoulders and then swung upward, making impact squarely under Sergeant Piggy's chin.

Denning's head flew backward, as the lower set of his teeth and part of his jaw were blasted out of his mouth. Baker and Benny stood in shock, and their faces squirmed as they heard the snap of his vertebrae when his upper spine was split apart by the impact. Denning was lifted up to his knees by the momentum of the heavy ball as it proceeded upward through its long arc. He began to teeter, forward to back, side to side, while blood gushed out of his busted mouth. His head dangled loosely behind him between his shoulders as the iron ball braked at the top of its arc.

"These are *my* toys, Sergeant Piggy," explained Lawrence, "and I have had plenty of practice in their . . . application. My, my . . . such . . . poor . . . etiquette."

Then Lawrence motioned the finger once again in a slow circular arc in the opposite direction the ball had been flying. It took flight once again, spinning faster and faster. Then when the phantom's finger reached the bottom of the arc for the fifth time, he quickly flipped it upward. The ball again followed his command, again altered its course, and collided with the back of Denning's head. This time, it sheared the flesh and bone around his neck free from the man's torso.

Lawrence quickly elevated five feet in the air as Denning's head rolled on the floor below his cloak and beyond him and through the great hall doors leading to the staircase. Denning's body went into convulsions momentarily, then it dropped to the floor. The blood pouring out of the cavity atop Denning's body oozed its way along the floor to join the pool left behind by Aldred and Catelin ages ago.

Stunned by this display, Baker finally pulled out of her immediate shock and reached for the Glock. She pulled it ahead, dropped into her firing stance, and pulled the trigger. Benny raised his hands to plug his ears but to no avail. The weapon did not fire. Baker repeatedly pulled the trigger, then in frustration, she threw it at Lawrence. The gun stopped in midflight short of the phantom and dropped harmlessly to the floor.

"My, my" said Lawrence, "temper, temper. Now, Catelin, you may proceed to my side and enjoy the exhibition."

Trudy pulled the hood of the cloak up and over her head. Her smile was hidden from Benny's view. Besides that, he was too taken aback by Paul's cruel demise to move at the moment. He did not notice Trudy was now floating.

"Ladies and gentlemen," spoke Lawrence, "let us be calm. How do you say this in your world? Ah, let us not lose our . . . heads?"

"You call this senseless assassination an exhibition?" asked Baker. "In what? Insanity?"

"The mortal violated the sanctity of my asylum," replied Lawrence, "and in exchange, he has provided me his remittance." Benny's voice was back on loan. "And now, what are we to do with you, Ms. Baker?"

That would be Mrs. to you, she thought. Baker leaned down to place the shiny lantern on the floor, thinking, *Come on, Benny, do something.*

"I'm trying to think, Lieutenant," said Benny.

As Trudy approached Lawrence, he had extended his left long-fingered hand. When she accepted, she floated next to him and turned to face the audience. Both Trudy and Lawrence shifted their focus sharply to Benny when he had answered Baker's thought.

"What?" said Baker. "You heard me thinking? Benny, you can actually read my mind?"

Benny had been thinking he wished it was a bit brighter in the room. "I was thinking we could use some more lanterns in this room, to make it lighter so we could see what we're dealing with here. It's too dark, just like it is inside this guy's hood."

Suddenly, around the room, lanterns hanging from iron brackets began lighting up. They illuminated a number of centuries-old paintings also hanging around the room; some of them were stately looking men and women in their finest dress, others of landscapes, and one of the lake visited by Aldred and Catelin. There was another that seemed familiar to Benny. It was a portrait of two young boys sitting together on a broad, high-back scarlet-colored chair dressed in the same clothing. Huge round white collars wrapped around their necks, and a fluffy blue bow was tied under their chins. Their white blouses had large puffy sleeves, and their blue trousers were tight and held up by suspenders, matching the blue bows. Their lower legs were suspended in air from their knees bent over the chair cushion.

Now back in her Catelin mode, Trudy responded in kind with Lord Lawrence as the hood of his cloak traced the perimeter of the room in time with the lighting of the lanterns. Nothing ever surprised or astounded him, but everything happening in his world was a result of his own action, his own creation. And Lawrence did not command this to happen. He preferred the dark of night. He was the dark of night.

Taking the opportunity of this diversion, Baker tiptoed toward Paul's body and picked up the cleaver knife. It was a better choice than the knives under her belt. She made it safely back in her place before Lawrence turned back, holding the heavy blade behind her back with both hands.

"The painting there"—pointed Benny—"with the boy on the right side of that chair. You see him, Lieutenant?" asked Benny. He seemed to be blanking out Lawrence, ignoring him, ignoring their dire situation.

"I hope you're not trying to be funny at a time like this, Benny," she said. "What about it?"

"It looks like me when I was a kid," he said. "Except I never wore those kind of clothes, not even when we dressed up for plays and stuff in grade school, like our class pictures."

"It is time we ceased with your silly pretense, impostor," said Lawrence. "You know very well you are the boy. And the other boy is yours truly, your lord and master. And now, Aldred, I shall rid you and your charade forever from my world."

"I think not," replied Benny. "Because you don't have a world. You don't even exist. You, master of deceit, are nothing more than a figment of some dead man's imagination. You hide under your silly cloak because there is nothing left of you. You are the fantasy of all fantasies. You cannot harm me."

Benny was not sure if the bluff would work, but he had to start somewhere. He had to think. No . . . he had to fantasize.

While responding to Lawrence, his eyes had been scanning the room. He saw a shield suspended on the wall displaying a rather plain coat of arms. Two swords were hung vertically on either side of the shield. The coat of arms was a hand-painted simple design. The shield was faded, but the background appeared to be gray in color. There was a red heart at the middle, and on each side, it bore white wings, angel's wings.

Trudy's Catelin could not take her eyes away from the portrait of the two boys. *Benny,* she thought.

Benny answered her thought. "No, the boy is not Benny. He is Aldred. And the man you see in your mind is not Benny. It is Aldred. I am Benny, not Aldred. Aldred is dead, killed at the hand of your lord and master, Lawrence."

"My lord," she said out loud. But she was not talking to Lawrence. "I see him," she spoke. This time, she was talking to Lawrence. "Have I not been the victim of deceit?" She turned to face Lawrence. "Swear to me what I see before me is not true."

Lawrence reached for the pendant with his right-hand fingers and held it out in front of her. This could not be happening. He had purged the man's image from her mind.

"My Lady Catelin, the man is an impostor. He plants a seed, and it grows. Rid yourself of this man." He focused the pendant toward her hidden eyes. He must bring her back under control. How could this impostor reach her?

Benny grasped the opportunity. He held out his right arm toward the shield and swords. The double-edged longsword at the right suddenly broke free and sailed across the room into his hand. He grasped the long cruciform hilt in front of him and reached for the small mirror he had moved from his neck to his left front pants pocket.

In turn, Baker drew the butcher knife from behind her back and hurled it at Lawrence. Just short of striking Lawrence at his chest area, the knife stopped and was hurled back at Baker. The blade landed squarely at the middle of her forehead, splitting it apart and driving her backward where, after two steps, she collapsed on her back.

Then suddenly, Lawrence directed his glare at Benny. The familiar scarlet red beams grew out of the cloak's hood, stretching their way toward his head.

At the same time Baker had hurled the butcher knife, Benny had taken two steps forward, holding the mirror out in front of him. As he progressed, the beams reflected away from the mirror, back toward the portrait, only seconds earlier capturing Trudy's attention. Or was it Catelin?

The hot beams collided with Benny's double and the young boy seated next to him, causing a small explosion. As the portrait and the two boys burst into flame, Benny reached forward and swiped at the leather strap from which the pendant was held through a ring at the top of the solid gold rim around its circumference. Benny's aim was as true as his fantasy. The pendant dropped out of the phantom's fingers, falling to the floor.

Benny saw the meat cleaver flying past him while he was lunging forward to strike at the leather strap. After seeing the jewel fall, he turned back to find Susan Baker stepping back and falling herself.

Now he had lost them both; he was responsible for their two deaths. He was mortified but knew he would be joining them if he did not act quickly. He turned again and lunged forward once more, dropping the mirror and grabbing the hilt with both hands taking a mighty swing across his shoulders at the phantom Lawrence's neck. The blade struck the phantom at the left side of his neck as it was swooping down and through him, although it met no resistance. As it cut through Lawrence, the fabric merely clung to the blade and was swept away with the sword while Benny completed his roundhouse swing in a square dance twirl.

Benny picked the cloak off the tip of the sword with his left hand and shook it several times, wondering if part of Lord Lawrence was stuck inside of it. Nothing fell out. Benny turned back and surveyed the room in front of him. No phantom. The man, or the thing, had vanished. He looked back at Baker and hustled his way toward her, but he found she was clearly dead. Her face, head, and hair were drenched in blood; her mouth was open, exhibiting the look of shock and disbelief her last thoughts must have registered when the huge blade of the butcher knife sped toward her face and embedded itself into her forehead. Benny covered her body with the black cloak. The phantom was gone; he would not mind.

Benny walked back toward Trudy and the spot the phantom

Lawrence had been standing. The hood of Trudy's cloak was back down, and she was apparently coming out of her trance again. Just as the phantom had disappeared when he was separated from the pendant, so too had the pendant when it was separated from Lord Lawrence. A coating of dust or ash was floating on top of Paul Denning's fresh pool of blood.

"What just happened?" asked Trudy. "Where are we, Benny?"

Benny tried to console her, stepping close while dropping the sword at his right and grasping her shoulders gently. "I guess we're about as close to hell as anybody can get, Trudy. I have a feeling this place is going to start falling apart. And if this 'Lawrence phantom' thing comes back, he's going to be really pissed off. Lieutenant Baker told me he has a way of moving around really quick. Maybe he made himself invisible or something. "

"Phantom? Lawrence? My god," she said, "what happened to these people? All this blood? What happened to his head? I think I'm going to be sick."

He dropped his hands to point them out. "It's Sergeant Denning and Lieutenant Baker. Don't look at them. The way he killed them, it was horrible to see. I can't believe what happened. It all seems so surreal—this whole place. I can't believe I'm not down there on the floor with them. It was all about you and me. This phantom thing, Lord Lawrence, thought we were these other people. Their skeletons are below in his asylum, the torture chamber. Their names were etched in the chairs they were sitting in, or at least where someone had planted them. He even had the skeletons holding hands. How morbid. Their names were Aldred and Catelin."

"Some phantom thing?" she asked. "Who is that? Who is Lord

Lawrence?"

"He must have had you under hypnosis or something, maybe a drug. Sounds like you don't remember too much. You're probably better off. But you were the first one to pass over into this house of insanity. The three of us followed you, kind of, at least the sergeant and I did. This Lord Lawrence guy pulled you and Lieutenant Baker through. You would not want to witness what just happened. I cut this medallion he was wearing around his neck. It must have had something to do with all this. You thought you were this other person, and you were remembering this other guy. I think he was trying to hypnotize you again or get you back into his trance. I cut the thing off, and he just vanished, *bang*, gone. And now here we are . . . but not for much longer, I hope."

"Lord Lawrence," she said. "Sounds creepy to me, Benny." She lifted up the white cloak, grabbing it at her breasts, revealing her black socks. "Where are we? Where did this thing come from I got over my clothes? I think you're right. We should get the *F* out of this place."

"Now you're starting to sound like Trudy," Benny replied. "I'm not sure where the cloak came from, but like I said before, you would look good in black, white, or nothing at all."

"What?" she asked. "You said before . . . before what?"

"Never mind, Trudy. Come on. Let's head to the basement place. There is a mirror there that should get us back, hopefully to your place. It's some kind of passage or portal that takes us through space somehow. It's impossible to explain or even understand. I still don't believe I'm here, or all this just happened. And the way the phantom guy disappeared. It just seems all too easy, like it's not really over in like two seconds. *Bam*, once I cut the thing he was wearing around his neck, if he even had a neck, he just turns to dust. I don't understand it. Too damn easy."

"He was wearing something around his neck, a necklace or something? You want to go to my place?" Trudy asked. "What mirror thing? You are really confusing me, Benny."

"You must still be out of it. Maybe you should stay this way for a while," suggested Benny. He grabbed her cool right hand with his left hand. "Come with me, Trudy. Come see what Benny can do. There are a lot of stars out there waiting for us."

"Stars?"

"Come on, Trudy," he continued. "Let Benny take you home with him."

"I would love to do that, Benny," she replied. "Let us leave this place … this asylum." Then she smiled at Benny and squeezed his hand. "Please just show me the way."

Benny started to escort Trudy out of the room but stopped at Denning's body and retrieved the key Paul had collected from Aldred's bedchamber. He held out a lantern while he instinctively wished the others in the great hall to extinguish as they progressed toward the doorway to the staircase. *Wouldn't want to start a fire now, would we?* He pulled his hand away from hers momentarily and placed it at her eyes as they passed the dead sergeant's head at the bottom of the staircase. Paul's eyes glared at Benny. *Sorry, Sarge,* he thought.

Finding he did not need the key, Benny left it at home in the door lock at the top of the stairwell after closing the door and engaging the lock. Once the two made their way down the winding steps, Benny found the mirror at the landing reflected more than their images, just as Trudy's mirror had done. Through their translucent reflections, he could see the universe. He was glad the small anteroom with the skeletons and coffin, not to mention all the tools used in the phantom's slaughters, was located at the opposite end of the dungeon. He preferred Trudy not be exposed to seeing the remains of her apparent other self. She had enough to condense already in that pretty little mind of hers.

He set down the lantern on a table to one side of the mirror next to another unlit lantern. He smiled at Trudy, holding her hand, and turned back toward the asylum one last time before stepping through the surface of the mirror. He raised his left hand in a middle-finger salute to bid adieu to the evil place. "Good F'ing bye, cruel world."

Dressed in black slacks and socks under her white cloak, Trudy held Benny's left hand tightly, enthusiastically accepting his invitation to leave the asylum, as she followed him through the surface of the mirror. She wore a broad smile.

The instant Benny stepped through the mirror's surface, everything around him went black. He experienced no sensation of floating in space at high speed, as he had when he had passed into the asylum with Sergeant Denning. Beforehand, he had thought about asking Trudy to leave the white-hooded cloak behind, but as an afterthought, he figured one innocent souvenir wouldn't harm anything. It might not even make it through to the other world . . . the real world or just turn to dust out there in outer space, as Lord Lawrence had done. But if it did survive and make it through, maybe it could be their secret, their little reminder of what really did happen to them . . . together, down there in Benny's asylum.

F

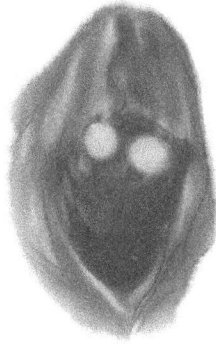

CHAPTER TWELVE

When Benny came out of his slumber, he found himself at his kitchen table. He was sitting there in his mostly vacant house with his forehead resting in the pocket of his bent left arm. He could not really call it a home; it had never felt like one, even before the marriage decomposed. He could hear the remains of his kitchen appliances humming, the refrigerator compressor. His laptop computer sat open in front of him, but the screen was black. He tapped at the space bar by manipulating his right forefinger close enough, but the screen did not respond. He supposed he had turned it off. He twisted his head toward the kitchen window, and though the blinds were closed, light peeped through over and around him. It was daylight, either early in the day or later afternoon. He rationalized it was probably sometime in the morning. It had been early evening when the whole escapade had begun out there in the F'ing universe and the damn castle or whatever it had been. *Benny's asylum, my ass,* he thought.

His second thought moved to wondering how the heck he got back home. He had no recall, no recollection of ever getting back home, back to Trudy's apartment, or even back to Timbuktu. When he had stepped through the mirror, everything went black.

Then he had a third thought. And it dawned on him both Susan Baker and Paul Denning had been left behind, dead and butchered. Both victims were of the madman Lord Lawrence. Any recollection they had was also dead, done and gone, forever lost with them in the timeless realm of the asylum. They would sit there and rot unless someone crazy enough went back to retrieve their bodies … if doing so was even possible now considering the apparent demise of the phantom. *Just where the F did he go?* asked thought number four.

Did he need an alibi? Benny was certain somebody from the police department would be coming around asking questions and looking for some good answers. They were brothers-in-arms, so the interrogation would be relentless. "Where were you last night, Mr. Johnson? When did you last see Lieutenant Baker? Telephone records show she had placed a phone call to Sergeant Denning Friday evening. Why did she call him at his home after hours? When did you last see Mr. Denning? He left his home about seven p.m. apparently to meet with his superior officer and perhaps discuss your case? Your case, Mr. Johnson. And what about our Lieutenant Baker, Mr. Johnson? Her husband indicated she was to meet with someone at, let's see, Rita's Pub? She was to discuss your case? Could this someone be a certain Mr. Benjamin F Johnson to discuss your case? We understand you had made an appearance at Rita's Pub, apparently with an attractive female acquaintance fitting Lieutenant Baker's description. Where did you and this acquaintance go from there in such an apparent rush, Mr. Johnson?"

My case, he thought. Then he thought, *They'll think I'm F'ing crazy. They'll think I F'ing killed them and stuffed their bodies in a cardboard box somewhere.*

310

"Oh, *F*," he whispered as he raised his head. "What about their families?"

Benny tried to collect his thoughts as he squeezed his eyes, raised his head, and then brushed his hair back with the fingertips of both hands. All his muscles ached, and he was thirsty. He slammed the computer closed and swept away the four empty beer cans resting behind it onto the floor. Benny leaned back in his swivel chair and stretched his arms back as far as he could without tipping the chair over backward. He thought about sticking his head under the kitchen faucet and then sucking a long cool drink direct from its nozzle, and then he thought about how good a fresh cold beer would feel sliding down the old throat.

Damn, I'm thinking again, he thought. *I have to stop doing that all the time.* He decided to skip the water, so he chugged a beer, chucked it on the floor with its brothers, and then headed straight for the shower. He did not bother to shave or use any soap; he just stood under the hot water, trying to figure out where the hell the memories went from the time he stepped through the mirror, down in the dungeon with Trudy, until the time he woke up. There were no answers knocking on his door.

Benny pulled some clothes out of a lonely hamper. It remained waiting for soap and wash cycles plus a spin dry from a washer and dryer his ex had pilfered along with the rest of his life.

F it, he thought, *I need to head into the office.* So he decided not to change dirty clothes with dirty clothes, then he grabbed his car keys off the kitchen counter and headed for the garage. On another second thought, he stepped back to the kitchen, grabbed another beer, and picked up the phone to ring Trudy's extension. As usual, the F'ing system sent him to the depths of voice mail. *Damn.* He chugged the beer, slam-dunked it to the floor, and stomped into the garage. His car was ready and waiting, but he could not recall how the car got back from Trudy's place all by itself. There were a few things missing from the prior night. Thank goodness, he had not been drinking. Heck, two beers this morning were barely enough to straighten out his nerves.

The ride to the office was uneventful, and although he had never thought to check the time, he figured it had to be Saturday morning, somewhat early, as the traffic had not yet exploded with shoppers. The mostly empty parking lot at Corporate Drive told him indeed it was Saturday, probably not Sunday. Most of the overtime occurred on Saturday morning and early afternoon, unless BestEver was in the midst of another catastrophe claim. He thought not. Then he thought, *F, I have to get in touch with Frank and Warren and Betty and check up on the glass plant loss status.*

Dishevelled and grubby looking, Benny charged through the swinging doorway and headed straight past the elevator doors, two-stepping his way up the stairwell to the third floor and then ran directly into the office door at his end of purgatory. He plugged his computer into the docking station and fired it up. He thought about making his way out the hall to take a leak but figured the water fountain and johns were probably still off limits while the investigation of Helen's demise was continuing, and the places were being cleaned up of broken glass and bloodstains. He had not even bothered glancing down the hallway toward the johns when he had made his entrance. His mind was racing too much. He would need to head out the same door he came in and back down to the second floor to do his duty. *Again, F it.* But he really had to go and deposit the remains of those two beers. Or was it three?

Before he made a move to get up and tread his way out to the hallway, he glanced at the computer screen. It called for his password, so he complied and waited for the damn computer to load up. Once it sprang to life, Benny opened his email, and its inbox glared at him. BestEver Insurance provided him with a link for his voice-mail service direct into his electronic mail so he could listen to messages on his computer and screen them easier than with the phone before returning calls left by his clients, consultants, and associates. He saw five messages had come in since he left the office Friday evening, and the clock and date at the bottom corner of the computer told him it was 9:32 a.m. on Saturday.

He had lost only one night but knew he had lost a lot more than time in that hellhole. Susan and Paul were gone. Part of his life was gone, and a chunk of his memory was out there floating around someplace in the universe just like the damn phantom somewhere between here and the asylum. Benny wasn't sure how much more of the morning he could handle, but he tried to focus.

There was a little background noise from the small delegation of adjusters who were in for either a half day to catch up on paperwork or those chosen to log in overtime for the outstanding catastrophe claim suddenly slipping back to memory. *I don't get involved with most of those anyway,* he thought. *Those are mostly for Property people, storm damage from hurricanes, floods, wind, lightning. We might get something in Boiler, like from a power surge maybe causing some kind of electrical equipment damage, but not enough to call people in on weekends.* But even with the people on storm duty, handling catastrophe work, it was relatively quiet. Benny liked it that way. Nice and quiet. His dedication to the job amazed him. *I should be getting really F'ing drunk.*

He scanned through the emails the telephone service displayed, focusing on each of the individual caller's phone number. The first was from Frank, the electrical engineer. With his nerves still rattling from the cacophony of stimuli rushing through his brain, Benny clicked on the message. He had enough to contend with, let alone having to deal with a bunch of claims. *Two people were F'ing dead already!*

But he took a deep breath and listened to the message. Frank explained work was continuing to install the miles of electrical cable and the rental generators to get power back to the production areas. Electricians were focusing on maintaining power to the glass float tank and so far, the emergency generators installed for the production area were keeping the furnace hot enough to prevent a total collapse of the refractory. The used electrical switches were located, procured, and were being refurbished. But the insured would also be upgrading their system and was ordering new switchgear to be installed at a later date. Fair enough. BestEver could apply what they owed to the cost of the project, meaning the cost of replacing with like kind and quality, not necessarily new generation switchgear. At the end of his message, Frank indicated he was sorry Benny did not make it out to the plant the other day and would look forward to seeing him when Benny was back in action.

"Didn't make it to the plant?" Benny said aloud. "When I get back in action?" He scratched his head. "What is Frank talking about?" He thought, *I'll have to call him and find out what he's up to now. What a jokester.*

The next message was from Harry up at the home office. It had also come in after Benny left on Friday evening, about an hour or so after he had last spoken to him. Harry said he had just heard about the robbery. He was sorry and would talk to Benny bright and early Monday morning. *What robbery?* thought Benny. He kept listening. Harry explained he was surprised those three new losses were still on his roster, and he could not find any electronic notes. It was two days and counting. Benny had missed the required twenty-four-hour contact. "Not like you, Benny," said Harry. By the way, he added, "I had to put a couple of losses on your roster tonight. We had an avalanche of them come in right at the end of the day. On Friday, at quitting time of all things. Go figure. One of them is a 2,000-ton hydraulic press cylinder failure down in Indiana at an aluminum extrusion plant. Better plan to get down there on Monday. Try to have a good weekend, Benny."

I missed the contacts? I spent two or three hours on phone calls and putting in file notes. "What the hell is happening here?" he whispered. *I have to do those three all over again, and now I get two more? I'll be sitting here for the next eight or nine hours to catch up on all this stuff. It might as well be doomsday. And now I have to go to F'ing Indiana? On F'ing Monday F'ing morning?*

Shaking his head and gritting his teeth, Benny reluctantly clicked on a message from Warren. *Sorry you didn't make it, Benny,* he thought sarcastically. "Bring it on, Warren," he whispered. However, Warren apologized for not making it to Kentucky with the team because of a family emergency, and he hoped Benny had been able to get another photographer out to the scene to document all the fire and electrical damages. *What?* he thought, *Now I don't have any pictures? This is a gazillion-dollar loss for F sakes!*

"Holy moly," he whispered. "Man, am I ever in trouble. What the hell could possibly happen? Did my house with no furniture in it burn down in the past half hour?"

The next call was from the property adjuster at All American Insurance. Betty Bleau advised Benny he might want to get out to the plant himself and take a look at the electrical damage; there didn't seem to be much of any fire or smoke. *What the F? I was already out there with you, you dumb bitch,* he thought. *What do you mean no fire or smoke? It was nothing but fire and smoke. Ah, crap! I don't have any F'ing pictures! Now what do I do?*

So far, the day was not panning out so well for Benny and friends. Benny felt as though he had just run into a truckload of bowling balls dumped out in front of him on the Ohio turnpike while he was test driving a brand-new convertible. He was having trouble registering the influx of information. *They're all F'ing nuts,* he thought.

The fifth message came from a number Benny recognized right away. It was one he had made frequent calls to and one from which disturbing calls were frequently placed to him. It was the cell phone number for none other than Frances F Murphy. *Who in the world would be using her cell phone to call me? What the F?*

Benny clicked on the message. The voice was loud and clear, and it was unmistakably Frances F Murphy. But this was not the crabby lady curmudgeon Benny knew. This particular Frances F Murphy was polite and sounded casually . . . kind. The message had come in late Friday evening at 10:31 p.m., probably about the time the restaurant would be in cleanup mode, if it had not been shut down since her sadistically horrifying murder several days ago. *Jeez,* he thought, *hung through the back of the neck into her brain by a double-ended meat hook?*

He figured by ten-thirty at night, he would have been somewhere down in the asylum with Lieutenant Baker and Sergeant Denning, maybe about the time they stumbled into Trudy, or maybe after they, too, had already joined Helen and Mrs. Murphy in the twilight zone. *Mrs. Murphy, right?*

He grabbed his forehead with the tip of his right thumb and middle finger and shook it back and forth, staring down at the desk, trying to collect the rambling thoughts spinning around in his head. The dead people and all the new claim files he had to set up—five new setups—those could take him ten hours alone. And then the trip he had to book for somewhere in Indiana, a destination he had not even confirmed yet. A plane? A car? A plane and a car? The trip he had already made, but nobody could remember him being there? The dead cops' families? Trudy? Where was Trudy? He reached for a big gulp from his normally full sixteen-ounce cup of ice, water, and orange juice mix. Of course, the F'ing thing was empty.

He tried to refocus back to the restaurant and Mrs. Murphy. Ms. Murphy? He could not remember. But Benny felt the police tape at the restaurant likely still had the johns staked off. And there was all the blood splatter to clean up. No, the restaurant could not have been operating. The emailed voice mail must be wrong. Clearly Frances F Murphy—he remembered as much—was already dead and halfway underground by the time this message got posted to his email. It must have been delayed somehow. *I don't know how this F'ing voice-mail stuff works,* he thought. Ms. or Mrs. Murphy continued on to explain she was gathering the material he had requested and looked forward to seeing him again. She even went out of her way to tell Benny a complimentary dinner for two could be provided, if it was allowed by BestEver practices. Maybe he could bring the cute girl in the office. *You know, Benny,* she added, *Ms. Perkins, like the pancakes? Tee hee.* She had giggled.

Look forward to seeing ME, he thought. *Bring the pancake girl along?* The last comment was too bizarre for Benny to understand, to comprehend. *How could she possibly have known Trudy? Why was she acting so . . . F'ing nice?*

The last message he found on his email inbox was left earlier in the morning, Saturday. It was not a phone call. It was an email sent by tcperkins@besteverinsurance, and it arrived only a few minutes before he woke up at his kitchen table. It read, "Hi there, sleepyhead. Pull an all-nighter? Wish you would pull one with me." There was a PS message indicated several lines below the short message. It read, "R U Cuming?" And he figured it was no reference to any mysterious or anonymous author writing novellas under a fictitious pen name.

Wow, thought Benny, *that's a little bold, even for Trudy.* Then he looked at her address again. He had never really thought about it, and he had never really asked her about it. T.C. Perkins. Just what is the middle name of that young lady, Ms. Trudy Perkins. You know, like the pancakes? *Could it be Cathy? Christine? Candace?* He thought Kaitlin was spelled with a K. *But Catelin? No. Never. It would be Charles before it would be anything close to that name.*

Just then, he heard a *tap, tap, tap* at the fabric of his cubicle divider. He turned and found Trudy looking in at him from the aisle, hugging the divider with her folded left arm. Her chin was resting against the side of it. "Hi there, Benny," she began. "It's Charlie checking in to see how you're doing."

Charlie? The greeting smacked simultaneously at both his temples. Trudy was looking unusually gorgeous, and she was also looking unusually provocative. As she stepped clear of the divider, he saw she wore tight black denim slacks and a button-up, short-sleeve deep purple blouse. The top three buttons remained unfastened, revealing the tight black brief brassiere she was sporting. It pushed her modest breasts up and out. Her long sleek black hair was loose and pulled over the front of her left shoulder; it had been draping over the divider. The solid gold necklace she wore drooped down over the curvature of her breasts and was lost in their cleavage. Her tongue licked the left side of her upper lip gently, slowly.

Benny hesitated and then clicked out of the email glaring at him. He swiveled the chair around to face her. "Trudy," he began, "I can't remember how I got here this morning. I mean, I can't remember how I got home last night. I don't remember very much at all. All I can see in my head is us walking through the mirror, and then the next thing I know, I'm sitting at the kitchen dining table just like you were a second ago leaning over the divider, hugging the pit of my left arm."

"Walking through mirrors?" she replied. "That's a new one. I mean, sword fighting or getting me off the railroad tracks just in time is a bit of a run-of-the-mill kind of thing, but walking through mirrors? That's one I haven't heard before, Benny."

"You mean, you don't remember?" he asked.

"You must be working too hard, Benny," she said. "All that stress? Let me help you relax a little bit."

Then she slowly advanced toward him. Her sway was unusually seductive. She was never this forward with Benny.

Trudy bent over slightly and leaned into Benny while grasping the arms of the swivel chair around him, trapping him in the chair. She lifted her right leg and pushed her knee between his legs, then she lifted it slightly in and out, up and down, slowly massaging him in a manner for which he was unprepared.

"You get my message this morning, Benny?" she whispered. "You get *the* message?" She continued to massage with her knee.

Benny was beginning to sweat; he tried not to think about what was happening down below and up above. He could imagine she was awfully glad he had pulled her out of that asylum, but this was way more than he could expect . . . way more than he had ever fantasized. Then he asked her point blank, "What is your middle name, Trudy?"

"Come now, Benny," she said. She pulled away and began to backpedal to the edge of his cubicle. "Don't be silly. You know who I am."

"Of course, I do, but I was just wondering about your middle name, that's all." He could not understand why he was so nervous, but it happened every time those electrical or magnetic fields he and she wore around their auras converged. His nerves would rattle; he would shake.

She avoided the question. "So tell me, Benny. Are you . . . coming?" The way she had pronounced the last word, it could have been spelled with an *O* or with a *U*.

"Coming where, when?" he asked.

"I want you to come over to my place tonight, Benny." She began to play with the gold chain around her neck. She lifted it up and down slowly, feeling the slight tickle against her bare skin.

"To your place?" he asked, surprised.

"Of course, silly. I know you know where it's at. You were there last night. Remember, Benji?"

She toyed with the necklace again. And this time, she pulled it out from the embrace in that tight sexy bra ever so briefly. From a golden ring was suspended the pendant she had picked up off the floor of the asylum. She dropped it back down her blouse before Benny could size it up. His mind was already in overload.

If Benny had looked at the jewel, he might have recognized it looked exactly like the jewel the phantom had been wearing around his neck. It was the one he had sliced loose from the phantom's neck, if it had one at all. He would have been astonished, but he was too busy trying to overcome the turn-on Trudy had just displayed. His heart was in a sprint, racing against his breathing.

"Come over tonight, Benny. After we fuck, maybe we can go exploring. Come see what Trudy can do. There are a lot of mirrors out there. There must be millions and millions of mirrors we can discover."

"Trudy! Quiet! Somebody is going to hear you, and we're going to get our butts in trouble with HR. What's going on?"

"Wake up, Benny. Wake up from your fantasies. You don't need them anymore, Benny. Come and look into my eyes. Come see what a whore can do." Then she pulled the pendant out and swung it back and forth, as if she was the hypnotist.

Benny was slowly backpedaling himself in the chair. He could not believe what he was seeing; he could not believe what he was hearing. His mouth dropped open, his heart raced even faster, and his mind was spinning again. Then he heard a familiar voice in the background and turned toward it instinctively, but of course, he found only his computer screen. Trudy's email was open again, and her PS message had been magnified, taking up half the screen. R u CUMING?

Trudy turned, and raising her voice, she replied to the brief interruption. "One minute," she said. "I'll be right with you—" Then she turned to face Benny, smiling. "Helen."

Trudy lifted her eyebrows, watching Benny's response as his mouth dropped open, even further to a gaping pose. "Don't look so surprised," she told him. "You know who I am. Do you believe that mindless Lord Lawrence was any match against me? He thought he could claim my soul."

She stepped back in toward him. "Well, I let him have it, Benny. It didn't mean much to me anyway, not after what he had done to me and

Aldred. I let him borrow it. I let him think he could get away with it. But I found a way to get back at him, Benny. I learned a few things from Lord Lawrence, such as how to get into people's minds. It is amazing what you can do with people once you get inside their heads, Benny."

Benny was staring at her. His mouth was still held open, frostbitten. He could not believe what she was telling him. "You mean, you're trying to tell me you are somebody else, not Trudy? It's not possible. No. You're playing with me. You're playing a trick or something. This is too weird, Trudy, especially after what we went through together last night. You're starting to scare me a little. You must have taken something when you got back from the damn castle. Did they give you some more sedatives the other day when Lieutenant Baker was interviewing you? You remember her, right? Did the phantom guy give you some kind of drug?"

"Of course I'm not playing, at least not the way you are thinking. You have nothing to fear, Benny, nothing to be afraid of . . . not after the way you handled Lawrence down in that creepy old asylum of his. I can be anything or anyone you want me to be, Benny. You see, I am the one in control now. Trudy's mind was a little weak, don't you think? She was really easy to get inside of and take over, control her mind. But you know something? I just love her body. She could use a little bit more exercise down below though. You know where I mean? Think you can help me out there, Benny? I am, oh, so glad I found her. She really helped me take down Lawrence. I have so many things I want to do now since I have escaped from Lawrence's world."

"No, it's not possible. Nobody can get inside somebody's mind and just take control of them. That's not possible." His startled gaze dropped from her serene blue eyes to the freshly vacuumed carpet.

"I know how you think about me, Benny," she continued. "You can still think of me as Trudy. But me, I can get inside people's minds, even yours, Benny, deep into those places even you are not aware of what you are thinking."

She raised her eyebrows. "Bad Benny. You have some great fantasies. And now you can make them come true. But you don't even need them anymore. Now that Lawrence is gone, I have my dark soul back. He wanted a soul darker than his own, and I gave it to him. Well, I took it back, and now he is nothing, just a speck of dust. Fucking claim denied, Benny. I have been sitting there in his pathetic useless mind for centuries. He taught me a lot of things while I hid there waiting for the opportunity, when the time was ripe. But now I am the one in control."

She stepped closer, bending toward him again. "It was you all along who helped make this come true. You showed me the path. You and your world of fantasies. I've been inside your head for ages, Benny. You did the same old thing over and over when you were just a kid. Time to grow up, Benny. Make your fantasies come true, just like you did with me. Lawrence wanted a dark soul. Well, he found one too F'ing dark for him to handle."

"Trudy," Benny began, astounded. "What's going on? You can't be talking like that in here. Are you high or something? You must have taken some kind of drug when you got home. You did get home last night, right? I mean, I did or at least I woke up at home, but I can't remember getting back after we left the damn dungeon."

"Oh, Benny," she replied. "Poor little Benny. You were there, Benny, but most of it never happened. It was all in your mind, Benny. Remember Helen? It was you, Benny. You were Helen. I took you on a beautiful ride, Benny. And the restaurant? Never happened, Benny. Most of it anyway."

"What do you mean it never happened? Down in the castle? That dungeon?"

"Oh, you were there all right, Benny. But just long enough for you to pull me back through. I figured it out. Lord Lawrence was too damn stupid. I needed someone to bring me through. I needed an invitation. Remember what you said? Come with me, Trudy? Come see what Benny can do?" She tilted her head back and forth, prodding for acceptance. "How about let Benny take you home? Hmm?"

"I can't believe what I'm hearing," Benny said, looking up at her in wonder.

"I can place myself into your mind. Yours has been a wonderful place to explore, Benny. It was so much fun to manipulate your fantasies so you could experience them. Wasn't it fun to see the cops die? And Paul's head? It looked so much like, what do you call it? Ah, yes . . . a bowling ball? Forgive me . . . I am still adjusting to this world of yours. It takes time, you know? And believe me when I tell you I have plenty of time, Benny."

"This is all just too crazy. It all happened. I know it happened."

Trudy, or at least the person inside of Trudy, continued. "And I learned to place other people's minds into yours, Benny. Oh god, I had so much fun with you. And now that you brought me across, we can share it together. I can show you how, Benny. I can show you the way, just as your world of fantasy has shown me. Come with me, Benny. Come and look into my eyes. We have a world of mirrors at our fingertips. The world is ours to claim."

Trudy stepped closer to him again, almost nose to nose. Her devilish smile was piercing his wide-open frightened eyes. Her tongue pressed its way through her lips and washed them, left to right. She placed an image of it swirling around in his mouth smack-dab in the middle of his frightful thoughts of her in the white-hooded cloak. "Come with me, Benny," she whispered, again licking her upper lip. "Come see what a whore can do."

Then Trudy stepped away, back to address Helen's question. Sondra, the witch, stepped back and closed her office door between them. Something in her head told her to tread lightly when Trudy Catelin Perkins walked the aisles.

Benny popped his head out of the cubicle to follow Trudy as she paced away. He was shivering; his mouth was still held open in amazement, trying to shake the thought and taste of her French kiss. He was unable to believe what he was hearing, feeling. She turned back to acknowledge him, and then suddenly, she appeared in her white cloak; her right hand was caressing the pendant tucked safely between her right fingers. She smiled and blew him a kiss.

But Trudy was no longer walking. She was floating . . . backward, very slowly, not taking her eyes off his. And then she raised her left arm, snapping its fingers, the sharp pop reverberated throughout the office room, and its background noise fell silent.

And now the cloak was black. The hood was back over her head. Deep inside, her blue eyes had turned deep scarlet red. "My favorite colors, Benny," she whispered.

Something stirred inside Benny and prompted him to involuntarily begin walking toward her as she slowly floated backward toward the cubicles at his left where her workstation was situated directly across from Helen's little abode. As he walked, Benny looked side to side, observing the two rows of cubicles. Most of them were empty, but the occupied cubicles were also silent and still. The adjusters seated and those standing, holding phone receivers to their ears … they were just as void of voice and motion. Some of them had their mouths open in midsentence, midword.

Trudy slipped into her cubicle and glided to her seat, disappearing from Benny's view. When he reached the opening to their shared space, he found Helen seated. But she was reclining backward in her chair. She was stiffer than a statue and apparently in the midst of uproarious laughter. But the look on her face was maniacal. And the expression was exactly the same as the one Helen had witnessed, as she had been stranded deep into the universe. Although Benny had pictured Helen seeing him in the fantastical sequence of images, Benny was witnessing what he thought she had seen, but it was now with Helen's face. The only thing moving in the entire office beside the woman claiming she was no longer Trudy was the writhing puffy worms somehow supplanting Helen's hair from her skull.

He looked back toward Trudy. She was sitting, leaning back in her chair. Her legs were crossed under her black cloak. "I've relocated, Benny," she said. "Welcome to my asylum." She played with the pendant in her right-hand fingers and then snapped the fingers of her left hand once more.

The office chatter and hum of computers instantly filled Benny's ears. Helen was laughing at his right. "Man, do I ever have a joke for you, Benny," she said. "And it's about a guy named Benny, which makes it even funnier, but I guess you could use any guy's name. But this guy comes home from work early one day and finds his ol' lady with this stockbroker, both naked as bumblebees. He sees the guy is humping his ol' lady over on the living room couch. Benny walks in, looks down at them, and asks her what the heck she thinks she was doing. So his ol' lady looks up and tells the guy screwing her, 'See, I told you he was stupid!'"

Trudy was back in her black slacks and purple blouse, but all buttons were fastened in accordance with the company dress code for casual Friday and weekend day wear, with only the top collar button open. She was smiling, patting at the crystal snug as a bug between her breasts, and shaking her head side to side. "Poor Benny," she mouthed.

Benny looked from the cubicle, as he heard the entire office erupt in laughter. He stepped out into the aisle and found all of them were pointing at him, laughing and shouting teases. "Haha!" "Benny got himself a good screwing!" "Hey, Benny! I hear you just got F'd!" They were all standing there ridiculing him and shouting insults, degrading him. Laughing. Pointing. Laughing.

Benny could not speak. He backed away from the onslaught of derogatory behavior. His coworkers, his friends, and professional associates with their demeaning glares and pathetic indignations; they all pointed and laughed.

The look of terror in his eyes wrapped over his face. Benny made a vain attempt to wipe it away. He turned and looked back at Trudy for defense, for recognition, but she just shrugged her shoulders and mimed poor Benny one more time. He looked back at Helen but could not believe his eyes. There she was in living color. Living. She had rolled back in her chair again and was pointing at him through uncontrollable laughter. The bloodsucking worms had deserted her scalp; the devil's look had abandoned her face. He backed into the aisle again and began walking backward toward his own space, but his balance failed him. He began stumbling in circles, mumbling unintelligibly under his breath.

"No, no," he stuttered, "this can't be happening. It's impossible. This is not real!" His voice began to elevate. "She's dead, I tell you! Helen is dead! They're all dead! And she's a phantom, I tell you! Trudy is a phantom! The cops. The cops are dead too! Stay out of the johns! The phantom is going to get you! You're all going to die in there! Stay away from the asylum, I tell you. Stay away! It's in the mirror, I tell you. It's in the mirror. He is in the mirror. She is in the mirror. Something is in the mirror. It's the phantom, I tell you! The phantom!"

The heretofore quiet office was alarmed at this sudden disturbance. Other adjusters either occupied on their phones or their computers began stepping to the gateways of their cubicles. They were all wearing a look of dismay, puzzlement. *What is happening?*

Helen pushed her swivel chair back while removing her telephone headset after completing a conversation with the frequent flyer of the Mysterious Disappearance Club. Benny's sudden outburst had alarmed her. Concerned, she turned back and shared worried looks with Trudy. Her mouth was open but unable to find proper words. She was aware the word had previously spread across the floor of the office about Benny having been dumped by his wife, and all had been concerned for the B&M claim guy. His wife had eloped or had actually just split town with some rich Italian dude and left Benny divorce papers she had stuffed into the refrigerator. *Poor Benny. Now what is wrong with him?* They all thought. Defensively, the coworkers all stepped back but poked their nosy beaks out into the aisle, as they cautiously observed what was unfolding in front of them. One of them thought, *My god, I hope he doesn't have a gun.*

Backing away from them, nearly stumbling over, he reached into his right pocket. There nestled with his car keys was the lantern wick that had magically appeared in the castle. The dungeon? The asylum? He retrieved it and began waving it back and forth. "Look at this! It's the wick from the lantern, I tell you! It's the wick from the dungeon! They are down there, I tell you! The cops! The phantom! They're all real, I tell you! Just like this wick!"

Benny, twisting and spinning, seemingly lost and confused, turned at the break between the cubicles now at his left. He was teetering but making his way to the mid-office exit door, toward the hallway, and the restrooms.

The office staff stood motionless, looking to others in the room for solace, consolation. Under their worried looks, they could still hear him ranting through the door as he stumbled around in the hallway.

"Stay away! I'm warning you! They'll get you! Turn on the lights! Don't look at the mirrors! The dungeon! The wick! Stay away from the asylum!"

Nonchalantly blocking out the minor disturbance, Trudy answered her telephone's ring. "Good morning. This is Trudy C. Perkins, BestEver Insurance Property Claims. How may I assist you in having a BestEver day?"

F

EPILOGUE

The call came into the Lakeview Police Department from the BestEver Insurance company at 10:07 a.m. A local cruiser was deployed to the scene. The officer in charge arrived shortly thereafter with a personal aide. They joined the ambulance, a fire truck, and a second squad car. Someone had activated the fire alarm system, and the building had been vacated. Some of the building occupants went straight home after the incident, but the third-floor BestEver employees were asked to wait behind until they were screened and interviewed for firsthand observations.

It seemed a man had been heard screaming from within one of the restrooms. No one could get near him. No one even tried; the scene was too frightening. A BestEver employee had secured himself in one of the bathroom stalls and was screaming nonsense. Witnesses stated they heard him yelling about some kind of phantom people and an asylum and, possibly, a torture chamber. He was screaming about two cops going down there with him, and they were killed, murdered savagely. He said he could take us down there, as in you people, and he would show everybody the bodies.

The man had climbed up onto a toilet and apparently slipped, jamming his left foot in the trap area of the toilet and breaking his left ankle. Once the hospital attendants managed to pry open the stall door, they found the man had pulled out half the hair from his skull and was bleeding profusely from his scalp down over his face. It took the two medics and one of the police officers to subdue the man and administer a tranquilizer to calm him down.

The officers in charge of the investigation were Lieutenant Susan Baker and her aide, Sergeant Paul Denning. They had been conducting interviews out near the fountain in front of the building while the hospital attendants were busy on the third floor attempting to hold down the frantic man and suit him up with a straitjacket. After the disturbed man was wheeled out of the building, the officers then escorted several BestEver employees back upstairs to their office breakroom for further discussion to piece together the chain of events.

The two officers had recognized the man, although his appearance had changed dramatically, given the self-inflicted damage he had undertaken. A daytime robbery had been reported at his home several days earlier. But it was later discovered his wife had abandoned him with a wealthy stock futures broker and cleaned out the entire house, with the exception of his clothing, some kitchen appliances, a couple of twelve packs of light beer, and a set of divorce papers. Lieutenant Baker surmised the untimely breakup might have been a factor contributing to setting the man off on a tangent.

She had spoken with his boss who had been contacted at his Connecticut home. Benjamin Johnson, or Benny as he was known among coworkers, was known to be a workaholic and one of the better performers in his department. Harry Gordon had tried on numerous occasions to convince Benny to take some of his banked vacation, but he never relinquished. "Too many hot potatoes in the pot, Har. We need to butter 'em up and milk 'em down before they get cold."

Lieutenant Baker sat across from Mrs. Helen Jones and Ms. Trudy C. Perkins. They were apparently two of the employees to have possibly been the last to engage in conversation with Mr. Benjamin Johnson sometime that morning before he "flipped out," as one witness had observed.

"It kind of came from nowhere, Officer," said Helen. "Trudy and I were discussing a case about water damage, and then I was wrapping up a call from one of my claimants. About then, all of a sudden, Benny is walking down the aisle and yelling crazy things, like I was dead or something. He was mumbling things about mirrors and phantoms and dungeons. Crazy stuff. When I came in this morning, I saw Benny at his desk, but it looked like he was taking a nap or something. I said hi, but I didn't really get a response. I never saw him sleeping or whatever before. He was always working, doing three things at once."

"And, Ms. Perkins, do you have anything else to add to your previous statement?" asked Lieutenant Baker. "You seem to have had a bit closer relationship with Mr. Johnson. Is that true?"

"I guess you could say so. We would fool around a little. I mean, like friends, not really doing anything wrong. I mean, he was married at least until a few days ago. But he didn't seem to care a whole lot about her walking out, I think. Things were not going so well between him and his wife. Benny had a lot of dreams, a lot of fantasies he kind of ... shared with me." Trudy C. Perkins preferred not to elaborate on how Mr. Johnson had shared those fantasies, but the personal aide pressed on to get a response.

"For example?" asked the sergeant. "Please. We would like to understand his frame of mind." He looked for approval from Lieutenant Baker. She smiled.

"Well, Benny said one time, he got just as much enjoyment hearing the sounds of the F-word as he did picturing a couple of beautiful ponytailed young women wearing ball caps and tight bikinis holding hands to balance each other while rollerblading their way through a crowded boardwalk at a sunny beach. I guess Benny had a funny way of explaining things."

"Wow," said Susan Baker. "And you remembered all that?"

"I think we could read each other's minds a little bit. Some of the things he said and did kind of stuck inside me, I guess. I was even kind of hoping, with his divorce, we might, you know . . . maybe explore some possibilities together. I guess with everything going on inside his mind, it was maybe a bit too much for Benny. Poor Benny."

"One second, please," said Baker. She reached for her cell phone, which had beeped. A text message told her there was an active fire at 333 Elm Street. She looked toward Sergeant Denning. "Look familiar to you, Paul?"

"I'll be darned," he replied. "That's the place, all right." Baker looked back toward the two women to close the interview. "More bad news, I'm afraid, ladies."

"What is it?" asked Helen.

"Don't tell me his house is on fire," added Trudy. A nod with a facial expression of surprise by Lieutenant Baker told them it was precisely the case.

"Wow," said Lieutenant Baker, "That is what I call some kind of intuition. You two must have had some kind of connection."

After their brief but unspectacular interview, Helen Jones and Trudy C. Perkins huddled near their cars in the parking lot before leaving for home.

"Poor Benny," repeated Helen. "He is such a nice guy. I can't believe he cracked up. He is the last guy on the planet you could have guessed to spaz out right out of nowhere. At least he didn't start going after somebody with a machete knife or something."

Trudy replied, "And I thought maybe we had something going, you know, like after the news about his wife splitting with the rich Italian guy and all. Benny really thought he married a bitch. I mean, he really thought it. Poor Benny. I guess you never know what goes on inside somebody's mind, unless you are some kind of magician who can get right there inside of it and peep around. Maybe I was just dreaming."

"I guess we'll never know," surmised Helen. "But I hope it wasn't like the dream I had a few nights ago. And Benny was in it. He scared the hell out of me. I thought I was going to die. But then it ended really cool, and that's the part I remember most about it, just floating around the universe with all these stars floating by me. It was totally awesome."

I just couldn't resist, thought Trudy.

"Well, I should be getting home now and spend some time this afternoon with the kids," said Helen. "What are you up to? Any plans, Trudy Charles? I never knew what the *C* stood for until you gave that police officer your full name. How in the world did you ever get a middle name like that anyway?"

"Oh, that. My parents were getting up there in years when they had me. My dad had already broken sixty-two by the time I popped into the picture. He always wanted to have a boy. He called me Charlie until the day he died. My mom always called me Cat, sneaky," she said. She felt for the pendant inside her blouse. "I never thought I was sneaky, just curious, you know, like a cat. Me, I'm not sure what I feel like doing tonight. Who knows?"

"What about that sweetheart of a little niece of yours, Alicia?"

"Well," said Trudy. She gazed up at the sky, anticipating how the universe would look when the sun finally set for the day and the dark shroud covered it. "She has her mother." Trudy C. then shifted her gaze from the sky to the two cops who had been interviewing them, walking side by side back to their squad car.

"But you never stop talking about her," said Helen, surprised. "And you spend so much time with her. I thought you might want to get together with her."

Trudy had sounded indifferent, distant, not the everyday self who Helen was accustomed to these past couple of years. *Maybe it was the thing with Benny,* thought Helen.

As Baker walked next to Denning, she reached over with her right hand, pinching him on the left side of his butt. "What say you, big boy? Are you game for inaugurating the new SWAT vehicle? The ol' man is out of town."

"It's really big, I hear," he replied. "The wife is out with her mom today. We could pull out a gurney, but there's probably plenty of room on the floor, I guess."

"Okay," she agreed, "but I get the top. Don't want you squashing me, big boy."

"Whatever you say, Susie-Q. You're the boss."

The cops then picked up their pace into a hurried canter, splitting apart for opposite sides of the squad car doors.

Trudy C. smiled at her accomplishment. "I need to start thinking about me for a while, Helen. I can't just go around living in a fantasy world like Benny. I need to get out and go exploring, start doing new things. Who knows, maybe there is another Benny somewhere."

"Well, if he's out there, I sure hope you find him, Trudy. There are a lot of guys in the world." Helen smiled back optimistically at Trudy's broad smile.

And there are a lot of mirrors out there, Helen, Catelin thought. I'm going to explore them. "Yes, there are lots of opportunities out there."

"Yeah," Helen agreed, "opportunities for improvement!"

✦

Some five years later, young twelve-year-old Johnny woke from a nasty dream. He had seen himself restrained; manacles wrapped around his wrists and ankles. There he was back again in the familiar dark dungeon. He yawned and then felt the cool sensation from his wet underwear. He got up and out of bed, leaving the room dark so he would not wake his little brother. He stepped into the bathroom to remove his underpants and dry his crotch, leaving the room dark, just as he always did deep into the night. As he reached for the faucet to splash water over his face, the pretty woman stood there . . . in the mirror . . . smiling under the white hood partially covering her face and those beautiful haunting scarlet eyes.

+

The attendant peeked through the wire-reinforced, triple-paned window on the steel padlocked door. The man had been locked in confinement for the past five years, as he was too unstable to mingle with other patients at the asylum. He had never exhibited any violent characteristics, but his behavior was erratic. He was prone to random outbursts causing panic throughout the recreation room where patients gathered to mingle, play with games or toys, make craft items for relatives and friends, watch television, listen to music, or just sit and stare out in space through their blank faces. Other patients feared him because of his constant ramblings about a phantom lurking in the dark waiting to pull them through their mirrors into his asylum.

Not long after Benjamin Johnson had been committed, his ex-wife paid the facility a visit. With a farthing of the $250,000 cash settlement for the replacement cost coverage of the house totally destroyed by the fire, she felt obligated to fly from her villa in the Caribbean to pay homage to her beloved generous benefactor. As her name remained on the title to the property, she was the sole beneficiary, given Benny's current and diagnosed permanent mental state.

He'd had only one other visitor since he had been committed. She was a highly regarded citizen in the community of Lakeview. She had signed into the facility as Mrs. Frances F Murphy, even though it was common knowledge she was not married and carried no middle name. She had purchased a medieval-age framed mirror at an auction. She had no recollection of where the idea had come from; it had been spontaneous. She had also picked up an antique rocking chair. She was delighted the facility doctors and management decided that because the man was harmless and did not exhibit suicidal tendencies, the gifts might provide Mr. Johnson with some small measure of comfort.

The man usually slept through most of the day, waking to consume his evening meal about the time the sun set for the evening. Once awake, he settled into his rocking chair situated in front of the mirror bolted to a wall of the padded room. Eventually, he was served one more meal near daybreak when breakfast was being prepared for the balance of patients in the ward. The tray was set beside the rocker, and he never paid the attendants any attention. He just sat there, rocking slowly back and forth, staring at the mirror, and every now and then carrying a curious smile on his face. But he never spoke.

Attendants would later return and lift the sleeping man out of his rocker and place him on the single thin mattress bed set at the opposite wall. He would sleep all day until the routine was again repeated near sunset. And all night long, Benny would rock, look, and listen . . . deep within the rapture . . . the silence and solitude of his asylum.

F

ACKNOWLEDGMENTS

Without a clue of what story would follow the title, I made a promise when I left the world of insurance to write *Claim Denied*. There are far too many friends and associates to name, such as my Boiler Sis, King David, Bill & Larry, Tom, Ed & Warren (last names omitted to protect the guilty), and the list would be far too boring for most readers. However, the names and faces are planted in my mind.

You all know who you are, and I trust you all remember Jerry, a little bit on the crazy side, but not generally known to cross the line as far as our dear friend Benny in this book.

Some of you will recognize fictional characters I present in this book with names or perhaps personalities that are oh, so familiar, but not quite exact. But I promise you every one of them was purely and factually intentional. I only wish I could have mentioned all of you.

I have kept you all in my slightly demented mind, and thank you for the great experience and some of the best years of my life. Yes, we are insurance people, and we live just like normal people. We breathe just like normal people, and in some respect . . . we are just a little bit better.

OTHER TITLES

After his first book release, *Tom and Lovey: Under the Moon into the Wood*, a showdown with the devil's creations taking us from the Old West to modern times, G. R. turns to this psychological thriller, *Claim Denied*. Soon to be released is the *Tom and Lovey* sequel, *Pursuit of the Thunderbird*. Projects also planned for release include his voluminous epic tale of Sir Fredrik, Ruchelle the Beauty, and the young witty one—a tale of fantasy and horror twenty plus years in its inception, *Gairfield … as in the Air*.

You might also be interested in *Tom and Lovey: Under the Moon into the Wood*. Read the first two chapters and see reviews at my website.

www.grjerrybooks.com

CPSIA information can be obtained
at www.ICGtesting.com
Printed in the USA
BVHW040259261022
650240BV00013B/75

9 781643 769486